CANDY CANE MURDER

There was a figure spread-eagled on the snow at the base of the berm. It was Wayne Bergstrom and he'd obviously been pushed.

"Hannah?" Michelle sounded worried. "Are you okay?"

"I'm okay." Hannah choked out the words and took another deep breath. Andrea was right. The air did smell like Christmas trees. The stars and the moon seemed bigger too, illuminating the figure at the bottom of the far side of the snow bank in an intensely cold blue light. Everyone said you couldn't see color at night, but Hannah's mind filled in the colors. He was wearing red velvet and white fur, and there were candy canes scattered all over around him.

"Hannah?" Andrea asked again, and Hannah knew she had to say more. She didn't want her sisters to be so worried about her they'd try to climb the berm and see what she was seeing.

"Santa's dead," she said, seemingly capable of only two-word responses.

"You mean Wayne?" Andrea asked.

"Right." Hannah brushed the snowflakes, no two alike, from her sleeve. And that seemed to do the trick because the dam broke and the words rushed out. "Go back to the inn and get Bill and Lonnie. I'll stay until they get here."

Books by Joanne Fluke

CHOCOLATE CHIP COOKIE MURDER * STRAWBERRY SHORTCAKE MURDER * BLUEBERRY MUFFIN MURDER * LEMON MERINGUE PIE MURDER * FUDGE CUPCAKE MURDER * SUGAR COOKIE MURDER * PEACH COBBLER MURDER * CHERRY CHEESECAKE MURDER * KEY LIME PIE MURDER * CANDY CANE MURDER * CARROT CAKE MURDER * CREAM PUFF MURDER * PLUM PUDDING MURDER * APPLE TURNOVER MURDER * GINGERBREAD COOKIE MURDER * DEVIL'S FOOD CAKE MURDER * CINNAMON ROLL MURDER

Books by Laura Levine

THIS PEN FOR HIRE * LAST WRITES * KILLER BLONDE * SHOES TO DIE FOR * THE PMS MURDER * DEATH BY PANTYHOSE * CANDY CANE MURDER * KILLING BRIDEZILLA * KILLER CRUISE * DEATH OF A TROPHY WIFE * GINGERBREAD COOKIE MURDER * PAMPERED TO DEATH

Books by Leslie Meier

MISTLETOE MURDER * TIPPY TOE MURDER * TRICK OR TREAT MURDER * BACK TO SCHOOL MURDER * VALENTINE MURDER * CHRISTMAS COOKIE MURDER * TURKEY DAY MURDER * WEDDING DAY MURDER * BIRTHDAY PARTY MURDER * FATHER'S DAY MURDER * STAR SPANGLED MURDER * NEW YEAR'S EVE MURDER * BAKE SALE MURDER * CANDY CANE MURDER * ST. PATRICK'S DAY MURDER * MOTHER'S DAY MURDER * ENGLISH TEA MURDER * GINGERBREAD COOKIE MURDER * CHOCOLATE COVERED MURDER

Published by Kensington Publishing Corporation

CANDY CANE MURDER

JOANNE FLUKE
LAURA LEVINE
LESLIE MEIER

KENSINGTON BOOKS
http://www.kensingtonbooks.com

KENSINGTON BOOKS are published by

Kensington Publishing Corp.
119 West 40th Street
New York, NY 10018

ISBN-13: 978-0-7582-7462-5
ISBN-10: 0-7582-7462-9

First Kensington Books Mass-Market Paperback Printing: October 2007

10   9   8

Printed in the United States of America

Contents

These are how many pages are in each Book

168
Pages

130
Pages

124
Page

These are how
many pages are in
each Book

CANDY CANE MURDER

JOANNE FLUKE

Thanks to everyone at the Mysterious Galaxy Bookstore in San Diego for testing the Candy Cane Bar Cookies for me.

Big hugs to the two "crafty" sisters, Donna Williams and Dorene Higgons.

Chapter One

It was a dream, one of those bizarre fantasies she'd laugh about when she woke up. But not even in her worst nightmare had Hannah Swensen ever imagined she'd be transformed into an elf.

"Are you ready, Aunt Hannah?"

It wasn't a dream. That was Tracey's voice. Hannah mouthed a word she hoped wasn't in her six-year-old niece's vocabulary and then she answered the question. "I'll be out in a couple of minutes, honey."

The holiday season calls for a generosity of spirit, Hannah reminded herself as she pulled on bright green tights and struggled into the matching tunic top. The bottom hem of the tunic had long points of cloth attached like screaming red pennants hanging down around her waist. Each one was tipped with a jingle bell, so if by some miracle someone failed to notice her, the bells would announce her presence.

Her footwear was next. Hannah pulled on slippers with rollup toes in a shade of red so bright it hurt her eyes. She topped it all off with a pointed cap with more jingle bells in the same brilliant red, and avoided the mirror with the same dedication Transylvanian villagers had used to ward off vampires.

"Aunt Hannah?"

"I'm almost ready, Tracey."

"What's the matter? You sound funny."

"Elves are supposed to sound funny, aren't they?" Hannah tugged down the bright red points on her tunic. Perhaps it would stretch out and fit a little better.

"I guess. Better hurry, Aunt Hannah. It's six-five-six and Santa's supposed to be here at seven-oh-oh."

"Right." Hannah gave a fleeting thought to how much she missed the big hands and little hands on analog watches and risked a glance in the mirror. Her image hadn't changed for the better. The red of her hair was engaged in a full-scale war with the red of her cap, women who were more than two pounds overweight should avoid form-fitting tunics with bells that called attention to their figure faults, and with the possible exception of those who had fitness club memberships and actually used them, women over thirty should be wary about skipping in public. It was Santa who was supposed to jiggle like a bowlful of jelly, not her!

"Aunt Hannah?"

"Coming." Hannah tore her eyes away from the wreck-age of her self-esteem. If a dozen determined designers had gotten together for the sole purpose of creating an outfit that would be most unflattering for her, they couldn't have done a better job. She took a deep breath, grabbed the basket of miniature candy canes she would strew like rose petals in Santa's wake, and opened the dressing room door.

All thoughts of how dreadful she looked were erased as she caught sight of Tracey's beaming face. Playing Santa's elf for an hour wouldn't kill her. And since the large silver basket she was carrying had to contain at least a thousand miniature candy canes, there was an upside to the evening. She'd have plenty of candy left over to make Chocolate Candy Cane Cookies at The Cookie Jar, her bakery and coffee shop, tomorrow.

"You're perfect, Aunt Hannah!" Tracey said, taking her aunt's hand. "All the kids are going to love you."

And with that vote of supreme confidence, Hannah and her niece headed for the temporary stage that had been erected in the dining room of the Lake Eden Inn to wait for Santa to arrive.

"I see Mom!" Tracey said, peeking through the crack in the curtain. "And Aunt Michelle's there, too. They're getting the kids lined up."

Hannah walked over to take a look. She spotted her two younger sisters waiting in line with the children from the Winnetka County Children's Home. They had been bussed out for an early dinner and a gift from Wayne Bergstrom, who was playing Santa tonight. The children would go back to the Home right after their visit with Santa and then the adult Christmas party would begin.

Tracey glanced at her watch. "It's seven-one-three and Santa Wayne isn't here yet. I wonder why he's late."

"I don't know," Hannah answered, "but make sure you don't call him Santa Wayne in front of the kids. You know that Wayne is one of Santa's temporary helpers at Christmas time, but the other kids don't."

"Don't worry, Aunt Hannah. I won't tell."

Hannah took another peek through the slit in the curtains. The children in line were beginning to fidget. If Wayne didn't get here soon, Michelle and Andrea would have an insurrection on their hands.

And then it happened. Both Hannah and Tracey began to smile as they heard sleigh bells in the distance. From previous Christmas parties at the Lake Eden Inn, Hannah knew that Wayne carried a half-dozen sleigh bells attached to a red leather strap. They usually resided in one of the big patch pockets of his Santa costume, but he took them out when he came in the kitchen door and jingled them to build anticipation for his arrival, and as a signal for his elf to join him in the kitchen.

Hannah took one last look at the line of children. All talking, coughing, and wiggling had ceased. Instead there was silence, perfect stillness of voice and body, large and small. And every face wore an expectant smile. Santa was coming and even the teenagers who had seemed so jaded and blasé only moments before were now caught in the grips of heady expectancy.

"Better take your place, Tracey," Hannah whispered, giving her niece a little push toward the thronelike chair where Wayne would sit. Since some of the little ones had been afraid of the big, red-suited man with the white fur and the booming voice in years past, Sally had asked Tracey to stand next to Santa and reassure them.

When Tracey had taken up her position, looking like an angel with her shining blond hair and white velvet dress, Hannah gave a little wave and headed off to the kitchen. Her least favorite part of the evening was about to begin, the part where she skipped behind Santa and scattered cellophane-wrapped candy canes as he wound his way through the crowded dining room and up the steps to the stage. When Santa reached the top step, the curtains would open to reveal Tracey, Santa's throne, and the huge decorated Christmas tree. And once Wayne was seated and his elf had navigated the steps and taken her place by the Christmas tree, Michelle and Andrea would bring the children up, one by one, to greet Santa and receive their presents.

When she pushed open the swinging kitchen door, Hannah spotted Santa Wayne at the counter, perched on a tall stool and drinking something in a cup. Sally stood next to him, frowning.

"Something's wrong?" Hannah asked her, and it came out more statement than question. Of course something was wrong. Sally wouldn't be frowning if everything were perfectly all right.

"Wayne's got laryngitis and my hot peppermint tea isn't working. We're afraid he'll scare the kids when he talks to them."

Hannah realized that was possible, especially if Santa sounded gruff. "I could make an announcement."

"What kind of announcement?" Santa Wayne asked in a rasping voice that left no question about his ability to speak in normal tones.

"I could tell the kids that you ran into some thick fog over Greenland and you had to sing 'Jingle Bells' really loud so your voice would bounce off the ice caps and Donner and Blitzen wouldn't fly into them."

"That's the dumbest thing I ever heard!" Santa Wayne rasped.

Hannah shrugged. "I know, but I think it'll work. Do you want me to do it?"

Santa Wayne and Sally exchanged glances. "I guess it's better than nothing," he said, settling the question.

Smile. Scatter left, scatter right, Hannah told herself, trying not to pant as she skipped. She'd only covered about half the distance and she was already out of breath, puffing faster than the caterpillar smoking a hookah in Tracey's volume of *Alice in Wonderland.*

Uh-oh! There was Mike, her sometime boyfriend! Hannah put on the best smile she could muster and tried to pretend she was having the time of her life. The fact that those portions of her anatomy she often wished were smaller and firmer were bouncing up and down and sideways like a loose bar of soap in a shower stall didn't help. No one who saw her could possibly call her graceful. The best she could hope for was that they might consider her a good sport.

Only a few more yards to go. Hannah concentrated on skipping forward and peppering her audience with candy canes. At least she'd finally figured out why the green leggings she wore were called tights. It was because they were tight. Extremely tight. So very tight that she felt like a sausage about to split open on a blazing hot barbecue grill.

The ordeal was almost over and Hannah stopped to toss another few candy canes as Wayne climbed the steps to the stage. Then the curtains opened and the audience applauded as he gave Tracey a smile and sat down in his chair. He patted his knee, and Tracey climbed on to whisper in his ear. It was a sweet and heartwarming scene, and Hannah was grateful that everyone in the audience was watching Santa with Tracey as she climbed the steps to the stage and took her place to do what her Grandma Ingrid had always called *speak her piece.*

"Santa almost didn't make it tonight," Hannah spoke the words she'd been rehearsing in her head, "so let's give him a big round of applause to show how glad we are he made it here to the Lake Eden Inn."

The audience broke into loud applause and once it had diminished in volume, Hannah continued with her story. "Did you know that there was an awful storm at the North Pole when Santa started his Christmas journey?"

"No!" several children shouted, and Hannah gave them a smile. "There was, believe me. Santa didn't think he was going to make it, but do you know what he did?"

"No!" This time the response was louder and Hannah went into her story about the polar ice caps and the fog as heavy as green pea soup. "So Santa had to sing all the way to the coast of Newfoundland to keep his reindeer from crashing into the ice caps. And he sang so loudly and so long, he strained his voice."

The younger children in line were nodding gravely.

They'd believed her, just as she'd known they would. "Would you like to hear how funny Santa sounds?" she asked.

There was a clamor of yeses and not all of them came from the children. Some of the adults were getting into the spirit of the evening, too.

"Would you please say *Ho Ho Ho* for us, Santa?" she requested, turning toward him.

"Ho, Ho, Ho!" Santa Wayne exclaimed hoarsely, and some of the children giggled. That drew a good-natured laugh from the adults and Hannah figured she'd done her part. There was only one more thing to mention. "So you won't be afraid of Santa's scratchy voice, will you?"

"No!" several children shouted and almost all of them shook their heads. Her mission was accomplished and Hannah skipped over to take her place next to the mound of color-coded presents. The Santa, Tracey, and Elf Show was about to begin.

Hannah and Tracey knew the drill. They'd even rehearsed it with Sally. Hannah would hand Tracey the appropriate present, Tracey would carry it to Santa, and Santa would give it to the child on his lap. Norman Rhodes, Hannah's other boyfriend, would snap a picture for posterity. Then Michelle would escort the child to the rear of the line as Andrea brought the next child forward.

The smallest children were at the front of the line and Hannah studied the mound of presents. They were arranged by age group. All she had to do was work from left to right and everyone would get an age-appropriate present. The packages were also color coded. If they were wrapped with gold and green paper, they were for the girls. The boys got presents wrapped with silver and red paper.

The next few minutes were busy. Hannah chose the

gifts, Tracey gave them to Santa, and Santa presented them. The children were delighted and Hannah was really getting into the spirit of the season by the time she picked up the last present. It was over. And she hadn't died of mortification. Perhaps the mirror in Sally's dressing room had waved the wrong way and caused her to look larger than she actually was. And perhaps all that skipping had jumbled her brain and affected her ability to separate reality from wishful thinking.

There was standing applause as the children, all of them clutching their presents, were led out the door to their waiting bus. And then the curtains closed and Hannah fanned herself with her tasseled cap. Except for a few dropped candy canes and one toddler who would absolutely not sit on Santa's lap and screamed bloody murder despite Tracey's, Hannah's, Andrea's, Michelle's, and Santa's best efforts, all had gone smoothly.

Sally was waiting for them in the wings and she handed Santa Wayne another cup of hot tea. "That was even better than last year! Sip some tea, Wayne. Your throat must hurt from talking to the kids."

"Thanks. Hurts." His voice was as scratchy as sandpaper and he gave a rattling cough.

"I don't like the sound of that," Sally told him. And then she turned to Hannah and Tracey. "You were wonderful, Tracey. And Hannah . . . your speech about Santa's sore throat was just the thing."

"Whatever," Hannah said, waving off the compliment even though she thought it had been pretty good herself.

"Here's your receipt for the presents, Wayne." Sally passed him a folded sheet of paper. "Mayor Bascomb did it through the Lake Eden Boosters this year."

"My receipt?"

"You know, the one you need for your corporate

taxes. Mayor Bascomb said to tell your accounting department that the Boosters got their nonprofit status in June last year. He'll fax you a copy of the paperwork for your files."

"Right." He shoved the receipt in his pocket and turned to Hannah. "I'll need the rest of that candy. I'm playing Santa at the store tomorrow."

What a cheapskate! Hannah thought. And being a cheapskate was probably how rich people got rich in the first place. Wayne Bergstrom owned Bergstrom's Department Store, the busiest and most profitable retailer at the Tri-County Mall. He had displays of miniature candy canes at every checkout counter, the tubs stacked one on top of the other like red and white striped pyramids. There was no reason he needed to take what Hannah had come to think of as *her* leftovers.

"Here," Hannah said, handing over the basket.

"It's her basket," he said, gesturing to Sally. "Dump the candy in my pocket." Then he held open one of the massive pockets on the jacket of his Santa suit, and waited for Hannah to dump them in.

"I'll drop off the elf costume at the store tomorrow unless you want it now," Hannah told him. "It'll only take me a couple of minutes to change."

"Keep it. We couldn't sell it anyway now that you stretched it out. You can use it again next year."

"No flying pigs around here," Hannah muttered just under her breath, and she was rewarded by a startled chortle from Sally. When Sally had asked her if she would be Wayne's regular elf for future Christmas parties at the Lake Eden Inn, Hannah had responded with, *Sure, when pigs fly!*

With Sally struggling to maintain her composure, Hannah was just searching around for a topic of polite conversation when Sally's husband, Dick, walked up.

"Good job, Wayne." Dick clapped him on the back. "The kids loved you. Go change out of your suit and I'll mix you a Peppermint Martini."

"Tempting, but not tonight," he answered in his husky voice. "Got to rest my throat."

"Hot water, honey, and lemon," Hannah advised him. "It's like making hot lemonade. Then pour in a little brandy and top it off with grated nutmeg."

"Does the brandy help?" he asked her, clearing his throat with obvious difficulty.

"Not really. Your throat still hurts just as much, but after three or four cups, you don't care anymore."

PEPPERMINT MARTINI

Hannah's 1ˢᵗ Note: These recipes are from Richella and Priscilla, Dick Laughlin's bartenders at the Lake Eden Inn. Dick says if you don't have martini glasses, you should run right out and buy them. Both Dick and Sally swear that these martinis taste a hundred percent better in martini glasses.

5 ounces good grade vodka
2 ounces white crème d'menthe
½ ounce peppermint schnapps

Combine in a shaker and shake with ice. Strain into two martini glasses and garnish with miniature candy canes hooked over the rims of the glasses.

PEPPER MINT MARTINI

Hannah's 2ⁿᵈ Note: Here's the second recipe. You may notice that "pepper" and "mint" are separated in the title. The reason will become obvious when you read the recipe.

6 ounces pepper vodka
2 ounces white crème d'menthe
one fresh sprig of mint

Crush the mint with the back of a spoon. Combine with the other ingredients in a shaker and shake with ice. Strain into two martini glasses and garnish with miniature candy canes hooked over the rims of the glasses.

Chapter Two

Hannah gave one more glance in the mirror and this time she smiled. Claire Rodgers, her business neighbor on Main Street, had chosen Hannah's party outfit from her selection at Beau Monde Fashions. Claire and Hannah had worked out a barter system in the two years they'd been neighbors. Hannah dropped in with cookies for Claire, and Claire sold Hannah fashionable clothing at her cost. Tonight's outfit was a color Hannah had always wanted to wear, one she thought of as "lavender blue," the title of one of her grandmother's favorite folk songs. She'd always assumed it would clash with her hair, but Claire had urged her to try it on and it worked perfectly. The romantic lines of the long, draped jacket hid two of her figure faults, and the black silk pants emphasized her height and made her look thinner.

One last smoothing pat to the curls she'd given up trying to tame while she was still in grade school, and Hannah was ready for the party. She turned to look at the elf costume still hanging on a hook. Wayne had told her she could have it, but she knew she'd never wear it again unless someone had a gun to her head. And even then, she might take several moments to think it over. If she left it there behind the door, perhaps someone would take it before the night was over. Someone who'd enjoy it. Someone who didn't have bright red hair and ten extra pounds around the middle.

"How're you doing, Hannah?" a voice greeted her as she stepped out of the dressing room and Hannah turned to see Cory Reynolds, Wayne Bergstrom's brother-in-law, leaning up against the wall. Since there was no other reason he'd be in this particular hallway, he was obviously waiting for her.

"Fine, Cory. How about you?" Hannah put on a smile. Cory was a nice enough guy, and it wasn't his fault that his sister had married a rich tightwad like Wayne.

"Things are good. I just wanted to tell you that the story you told about how Wayne lost his voice was great."

"Thanks. I was hoping it would work. Wayne sounded awful."

"I know. He's even worse now. I ran into him outside the back door and he said he was going straight home to have some of that hot lemonade and brandy you told him about."

"Good. It should make him feel better."

"I really didn't think he'd be able to do Santa tonight. I even offered to take over, but he wouldn't have it."

Too bad you didn't, said the voice in Hannah's head, *because maybe you would have given me the rest of those candy canes!* But that was meanspirited and this was the Christmas season. She could afford to be a little charitable. "Has Wayne been hoarse all day?" she asked.

Cory shook his head. "He was fine at noon. We had a manager's meeting at the store during lunch."

"You mean you had to give up your lunch break?"

"Yeah, but at least it was on a weekday. Sometimes we have managers' meetings on Saturdays. Or Sundays. Wayne says that anyone who's not willing to come in twenty-four/seven will never be a manager at Bergstrom's."

"I'll bet that makes him really popular," Hannah muttered. But she must have said it a little louder than she thought, because Cory gave a startled bark of laughter.

"It doesn't put him in the top ten for the Best Boss of the Year award. But it's like he always says . . . it's his money and it's his store. He can run it any way he wants to."

"What department do you manage?" Hannah continued to make polite conversation.

"Wonderful Weddings. I moved there last year from Men's Clothing. We book weddings and provide everything the wedding party needs."

"Sounds nice," Hannah said, wondering why Cory had chosen to talk to her. Perhaps he was just lonely, now that Wayne had left?

"So tell me about Wayne's laryngitis," she prompted. "Sally said he could barely talk when he came in the kitchen door."

"That figures. He called me around five-thirty on my cell phone and he was already pretty hoarse. I had to ask him to repeat himself a couple of times and it didn't exactly make him happy. That's when I asked him if he wanted me to take over for him at the party."

Hannah heard Sally's voice over the loudspeaker, inviting everyone to come to the buffet tables. Cory heard it too, and he extended his arm. "Shall we, Hannah?"

"Absolutely. Thank you, Cory." Hannah took his arm and hoped he hadn't heard her stomach growl as they headed off to join the line for the buffet.

Sally's dessert buffet was splendiferous. Hannah eyed a piece of Italian Apple Tort and was about to succumb to temptation when she remembered how tight the tights on her elf costume had been.

"Trying to decide?" Mike asked, causing her to jump.

"Trying to resist," Hannah corrected him. "How do you do that anyway?"

"Do what?"

"Sneak up on people."

"We learn it in cop school." Mike flashed her a grin that made her stomach do a little flip-flop. If someone conducted a poll of the single, divorced, and widowed women in Lake Eden, Minnesota, Mike Kingston, Chief Detective at the Winnetka County Sheriff's Department, would be a shoo-in for most desirable husband. "Too bad you took off your costume. I thought you looked cute in it."

Hannah stared at him for a minute in utter disbelief and then she said, "I think the county pays for that."

"Pays for *what?*"

"Eye surgery. I understand they're doing wonders with lasers now."

Mike laughed so loudly several guests at the buffet turned to look at him. "Very funny, Hannah. But I really did think you looked cute. If you're not going to have a slice of that apple thing, do you want to dance?"

Did she want to dance? Hannah ranked that question right up there with *Do you want to breathe?* Did she want Mike to put his arms around her and hold her close? Did she want to look up at him and realize that their lips were only inches apart? Did he even have to *ask?!*

"Hannah?" Mike prompted, and Hannah came out of her musings to realize that he was holding out his arm.

"Thanks, Mike. I'd love to dance," she said quickly, accepting his arm and walking with him to the dance floor.

Dancing with Mike must have broken the ice, because once the last notes of music had faded away, Norman appeared to claim her for the next dance. After that, Andrea's husband, Sheriff Bill Todd, piloted her around the floor. Then there was a series of local men, one right after the other, including Cory Reynolds, Mayor Bascomb, Doc Knight, Reverend Knudson, her host Dick Laughlin, and the town druggist, Jon Walker.

"I'm not moving for at least ten minutes," she declared, sinking into a chair at the table she was sharing with her sisters. She slipped off her shoes and wiggled her feet, hoping that the feeling would eventually return to her toes.

"Feet hurt from all that dancing?" Andrea asked her.

"Sure do. And skipping in those pointy toed elf shoes didn't help either." She glanced around and didn't spot Bill. Lonnie Murphy, one of Bill's deputies and Michelle's date for the evening, was nowhere in sight either. "Where are Bill and Lonnie?"

"Lonnie's dancing with his mother. His dad's outside fixing a car," Michelle explained.

"And Bill's dancing with Barbara Donnelly," Andrea named the head secretary at the sheriff's station. "I'm so glad she's not married!"

Michelle and Hannah exchanged a *Did-you-understand-that?* glance, immediately followed by a *Not-me!* shrug.

"Okay, I'll bite." Hannah caved in and turned to Andrea. "Why are you glad Barbara's not married?"

"Because then her husband would ask me to dance, and I'd have to do it to be polite. And I'm too tired to dance. I made four batches of Whippersnappers this afternoon."

Hannah stared at her sister in utter amazement. When most women talked about "batches," they were referring to cookies, brownies, muffins, or some type of baked goods. Surely Andrea had another explanation. As far as Hannah knew, her sister didn't even know how to turn on her oven, much less mix up a batch of anything and bake it.

"Tracey has her dance class Christmas party tomorrow and I promised Danielle I'd make enough for everybody. Most of the other mothers are bringing refreshments, too."

There was total silence while Hannah and Michelle digested that information. Refreshments meant food, and both of them knew that Andrea's only culinary skill was heating water in the microwave for instant coffee or Jell-O.

"What's the matter?" Andrea asked, realizing at last that her sisters were perfectly silent.

"We're wondering what . . . uh . . . Whippersnappers are," Michelle explained.

"They're cookies."

"You baked *cookies?!*" both Michelle and Hannah exclaimed in unison.

"Yes, I did. And they were so easy! Carli Spurr e-mailed me with the recipe. You remember Carli, don't you? She coached the cheerleading squad."

"I remember," Hannah said, her mind flying through dire possibilities. Perhaps, through some miracle, Andrea had managed to mix up and bake several batches of cookies, but they couldn't possibly be good. Of course she couldn't say that without hurting her sister's feelings, and Andrea looked very proud of her accomplishment. It would be kinder to pretend that everything was fine, at least until she found out more.

"I've never heard of Whippersnappers before," she commented, fishing for information. "What kind of cookie are they?"

"I made lemon. Carli said you could make any flavor, and Tracey really likes lemon."

"Lemon's good." Hannah gave a quick smile, but she felt more like groaning. Lemon cookies usually called for lemon zest and she was almost positive Andrea had never heard of it.

"Did you have to go out and buy a zester?"

Michelle asked the question, and Hannah turned to give her a quick nod. She was willing to bet that they were on the same page.

"What's a zester?"

That answered *that* question! Hannah gave a little groan before she responded. "A zester is like a grater for lemon peel," she explained.

"Why would I need that? There's no lemon peel in Carli's recipe."

"No lemon zest, either?" Hannah quizzed her, trying to cover all the bases.

"No. What does lemon zest do?"

"It makes things taste really lemony," Michelle answered her.

"Well, I didn't need any zest, because my Whippersnappers taste nice and lemony without it. Is that a word?"

"Yes. Zest is the yellow part of the lemon peel," Hannah told her.

"Not *that*. I was talking about *lemony*. Is lemony a word?"

"If it's not, it should be," Hannah settled that query and moved on toward her objective. "If Michelle and I drop in at Tracey's party, can we taste your cookies?"

"Sure, but you don't have to wait until then. Just give me a ride home and we'll have some. Bethie caught a little cold and I want to check in on her."

"Good idea," Hannah said, giving her sister an approving nod. Andrea had been a nervous first-time mom with Tracey, reading every baby care book she could get her hands on, and trying to follow everyone's advice. Of course that was impossible, but Andrea still felt like a failure as a mother whenever Tracey cried. Finally, in desperation, she'd gone back to work as a real estate agent and hired the best nanny in Lake Eden, "Grandma" McCann, to take care of Tracey.

"Won't Bill mind if you leave?" Michelle asked her.

"No. He's already danced with me twice, and that's all the time he has for me tonight. He's got fifteen ladies to go."

"Fifteen ladies?" Hannah asked, glancing at Michelle, who looked every bit as puzzled as she felt.

"I asked Sally for an advance copy of the guest list and Bill and I made up our game plan last night. A sheriff has certain obligations, you know, especially if he wants to serve more than one term. Bill has to play politics and dance with all the important women here."

"Are you talking about women who are married to important men?" Michelle asked, frowning a bit.

"Not necessarily. Rose McDermott is on Bill's list. You might not think she's important, but a lot of local people go into the café. If Rose likes Bill and thinks he's doing a good job, she'll mention it and that can influence a lot of people when they go to the polls."

"You're right." Michelle looked thoughtful.

"And then there's Bertie Straub. She's not shy about telling her customers down at the Cut 'n Curl who they should vote for."

Hannah was amused. The next election for county sheriff was over three years away. "So you're already launching Bill's campaign?"

"It's never too early to play politics." Andrea glanced around the room and spotted her husband, deep in conversation with Mayor Bascomb. "Just let me tell Bill I'm leaving and we can go."

"Can I go with you?" Michelle asked, when Andrea had left.

"Sure. But I thought Lonnie was bringing you back to my place."

"He was. But he's pulling a late shift and it'll save him a trip."

"If you go with us, you're going to have to taste Andrea's cookies," Hannah warned.

"I know. But my nose is all stuffed up and I won't be able to taste much. I'll just chew and swallow. And then I'll tell her how delicious they are."

Hannah wished that she had a similar ailment, hoping she'd be able to lie convincingly. Praising Andrea's cookies would constitute a lot more than a little white lie, but it would make her sister very happy.

"It smells like Christmas trees out here!" Andrea said, taking a deep breath and expelling it in a cloud of white vapor.

"That's because we're walking past a whole grove of blue spruce," Hannah told her.

They walked in silence for a moment, and then Andrea held out her gloved hand. "It's snowing again. I just love knowing that every snowflake is different. We learned it in school. They called it one of nature's miracles because no two are alike."

"That's what they thought back then," Hannah said. "But then Jon Nelson, a cloud physicist from Kyoto, Japan, found that it's probably not true for the smaller crystals, the ones that barely develop beyond the prism stage."

There was another long silence. Hannah was about to tell them more about the physicist from Japan when Michelle almost stumbled over a drift of snow on the walkway.

"Careful," Hannah warned, and Michelle stopped walking.

"Let's just stand here for a minute and look at the stars. It feels like you can reach out and touch them, they're so huge tonight! They weren't like this last night when Mother had us over for dinner."

"That's because it's darker out here," Hannah explained. "Lake Eden has streetlights on every corner, and there are lights in all the houses. If you combine the lumens from the old-fashioned globe streetlights Dick and Sally put in on this walkway and add the lights they have at the inn, it doesn't add up to a fraction of the output of a single arc light in the parking lot at Jordan High."

Both Michelle and Andrea turned to look at her and Hannah immediately realized her mistake. She was offering science textbooks when what they wanted was poetry.

"Of course maybe it's not true," she said, trying to ameliorate the damage.

"Maybe *what's* not true?" Andrea asked, and Hannah could tell she was still upset about the snowflakes.

"All of it. But let's take the snow crystals first. That same cloud scientist compared the number of possible snowflake shapes with the number of atoms in the universe. It would be impossible for scientists to examine them all."

"So he really doesn't know." Andrea looked very relieved. "It's just a theory, right?"

"That's right."

"How about the stars?" Michelle asked.

Hannah stuffed her gloved hands in her pockets. "They could be bigger tonight," she said, crossing her fingers. "It's not an absolute certainty. I like to think the stars and the moon react to us when we watch them. That makes the night magical."

This drew smiles from both of her sisters and Hannah relaxed a bit. She had to remember to curb her impulse to be realistic and practical when her sisters wanted whimsy and romance.

"Uh-oh!" Michelle stumbled again. "I just stepped on something slippery," she said.

"What?" Hannah asked.

"I don't know."

"Hold on a second." Hannah drew a tiny flashlight from her pocket. "Norman gave this to me the last time I dropped my keys in the snow." She switched on the light and trained the beam on the walkway. "You were right here and you slipped on . . . this!"

"What is it?" Michelle asked.

"A miniature candy cane wrapped in plastic." Hannah held it up so both of them could see it. "It's one of Wayne Bergstrom's and he must have dropped it on his way to the parking lot."

"You seem pretty happy about finding it," Michelle commented, reacting to the smile on her older sister's face.

"I am. I know it's mean of me, but I'm glad he lost it. I wanted to keep the leftover candy canes to try out a new cookie recipe, but he told me he wanted them all back for his next Santa appearance."

Andrea just shook her head. "Wayne's such a tight-wad. It's not like he doesn't have more. And they probably cost him practically nothing. What were you going to use them for?"

"Chocolate Candy Cane Cookies. And now I can't make them until I buy some candy canes."

Both Andrea and Michelle gave little groans of dismay and Hannah was gratified. "If Wayne dropped one, he probably dropped more, especially if he's got a hole in his pocket. Let's keep looking. I don't think it's snowed enough to completely cover them."

"Are you going to use them for the cookies?" Michelle wanted to know.

"No, I'll buy my own. I just think it would be really funny if we collected them all and gave them back to Wayne at the store tomorrow."

"Here's one!" Michelle called out, spotting another

cellophane-wrapped candy at the side of the pathway. "It looks like he's dropping one every ten feet or so."

"This is fun," Andrea commented, rushing ahead to pick up a candy cane. "It's like in Hansel and Gretel, except there aren't any birds or breadcrumbs."

The walk to the parking lot had turned into a game, each sister trying to find the next candy cane. They had about a dozen when the trail of candy canes abruptly stopped.

"What happened?" Andrea, the current holder of Hannah's miniature flashlight, spread the light around in a circle. "We haven't found anything for over ten yards."

"How do you know it's over ten yards?" Michelle asked.

"Believe me, I know how far you have to go for a first down. Bill used to play football, remember?"

Neither Hannah nor Michelle voiced any argument to that. Not only had Bill been the best quarterback in the whole county, Andrea had been the head cheerleader at Jordan High.

"Do you think Wayne ran out of candy canes?" Michelle asked Hannah.

"I don't think so. The basket was big and it was over half full when Wayne told me to stuff the candy canes in his Santa suit pocket."

"The hole in his pocket didn't mend itself," Andrea pointed out.

"Right. Wayne must have left the walkway for some reason. Let's check the sides of the path. If we can find the point where Wayne veered off, we'll start finding candy canes again."

Michelle led them back to the point where she'd found the last candy cane. "This is the place," she said, pointing down to the snowy walkway. "Where do we look now?"

"You and Andrea check your side of the path. If you don't find anything, come back and give me the flashlight so I can check my side. If Wayne is still leaking candy canes, we'll find them."

"Why wouldn't he be leaking candy canes?" Andrea wanted to know.

"I could be wrong about how many are left. Or maybe he noticed that they were falling out and he put them in another pocket."

Hannah waited while Andrea and Michelle checked their side of the walkway and came back.

"Your turn," Andrea said, handing her the flashlight. "We'll wait right here while you check."

Hannah moved forward with the flashlight, sweeping the beam over the snow. She was about to give up and admit defeat when she spotted four candy canes near the edge of the path.

"I've got some," she called out and her sisters hurried over.

"Why are there so many here?" Michelle asked, bending down to pick them up. "It looks like they all fell out at once."

"Maybe he slipped," Hannah theorized.

"Or maybe he got tired of holding his hand over the hole and decided it wasn't worth it," Andrea added her take on it. "I don't think he'd do that, though."

"Why not?" Michelle asked her.

"Because he's too cheap. Every time he dropped one, he'd be adding up how much it cost him. Mother used to say that Wayne had the first nickel he ever made."

"I remember that," Michelle said with a laugh. "She told me Wayne pinched it so hard, the buffalo squealed and ran away."

"Look at this." Hannah pointed to another candy cane a foot or so away. "The trail picks up again here and keeps going."

The three sisters followed the candy cane trail to a bank of hard-packed snow the plow had left when Dick had cleared the inn's parking lot after the last snowfall. Behind it and a few feet back was another bank of snow and ice, rising even higher than the first. By the end of a snowy winter there could be several banks lining the perimeter of the lot. When one berm got too high for the snowplow blade to reach and dump, Dick started another snow bank in front of it.

"I see candy canes going all the way up that snow bank," Michelle said, illuminating them with Hannah's flashlight. "I wonder why Wayne climbed way up there."

"There's only one way to find out," Hannah told her.

"Not me." Andrea pointed down at her high-heeled boots. "That's hard-packed snow and these boots were expensive. I could break off a heel."

"I can go with you," Michelle offered.

"No way. Mother just bought you those suede boots and they're going to get ruined."

"It's okay. I really don't mind."

"No, but Mother will. And if Mother minds, I'll never hear the end of it. Just stay here with Andrea and I'll take a quick peek."

Hannah dug in with her heels and her hands, and started to climb up the bank of snow. It was a good eight feet tall with fairly steep and slick sides, and the ascent wasn't easy. She slipped a couple of times, but she kept going until she'd pulled herself up on the top. She opened her mouth to make a joke about being King of the Hill, a reference to the children's game they'd played in the winter every recess in grade school, but then she saw what was on the other side and the joke died a quick death on her lips. There was a figure spread-eagled on the snow at the base of the berm. It was Wayne Bergstrom and he'd obviously been pushed. Making snow angels wasn't in his repertoire.

"Anything there?"

Michelle's voice floated up to her, and Hannah swallowed with difficulty. She took a deep breath, expelled it in a cloud of white, and croaked out one shaky word. "Yes."

"You sound really funny," Andrea commented. "Are you all out of breath?"

Hannah knew *she* wasn't the one who was out of breath. Wayne Bergstrom was, but she couldn't quite manage to say anything that sarcastic.

"Hannah?" Michelle sounded worried. "Are you okay?"

"I'm okay," Hannah choked out the words and took another deep breath. Andrea was right. The air did smell like Christmas trees. The stars and the moon seemed bigger too, illuminating the figure at the bottom of the far side of the snow bank in an intensely cold blue light. Everyone said you couldn't see color at night, but Hannah's mind filled in the colors. He was wearing red velvet and white fur, and there were candy canes scattered all over around him.

"Hannah?" Andrea asked again, and Hannah knew she had to say more. She didn't want her sisters to be so worried about her they'd try to climb the berm and see what she was seeing.

"Santa's dead," she said, seemingly capable of only two-word responses.

"You mean Wayne?" Andrea asked.

"Right." Hannah brushed the snowflakes, no two alike, from her sleeve. And that seemed to do the trick because the dam broke and the words rushed out. "Go back to the inn and get Bill and Lonnie. I'll stay and guard the crime scene until they get here."

Chapter Three

"He is just the sweetest kitty in the world!" Andrea crooned, scratching Moishe under the chin. The moment they'd entered Hannah's living room, the twentysomething-pound, orange-and-white cat that Hannah had found shivering on her doorstep over two years ago, had made a beeline for Andrea and climbed up in her lap.

Hannah just smiled, deciding not to burst her sister's bubble and mention the fact that she was holding a canister of salmon-flavored treats that Moishe adored, and doling them out to him every time he nudged her with his head.

By tacit agreement, they hadn't discussed Wayne Bergstrom's death. It didn't seem to be an appropriate topic of conversation when they stopped by to check on Bethie and Tracey, and pick up the plate of cookies Andrea wanted them to try. Hannah had pulled Grandma McCann aside to fill her in, but the three sisters hadn't mentioned Wayne's name on the trip to Hannah's condo complex, either. Perhaps it was simply an attempt at avoidance. If they didn't mention it, it might go away. Or perhaps it was a delaying tactic and all three of them wanted to enjoy their time together for a little while longer before discussing such a gruesome topic. Hannah figured they'd have coffee first, a little fortification with a mug of Swedish Plasma was in order while they tasted Andrea's cookies, and then they'd talk about Wayne Bergstrom and the distressing sight she'd seen from the top of the snow bank.

"The coffee should be ready soon," Hannah said, craning her neck to see if the carafe was full. It wasn't, and she glanced at the plate of cookies that Andrea had baked. The cookies were pretty, a nice rich yellow with powdered sugar on the tops. They *looked* good, but looks didn't count for everything when it came to baked goods.

"I hope Bill isn't late," Andrea said, frowning slightly. "He told me he thought they'd be here by midnight to take our statements, but something could happen to delay him."

"If he's really late, you can catch a nap on the couch," Hannah told her.

"Or share the guest room with me," Michelle offered. "It's a king-size bed."

Andrea shook her head. "I don't think I could sleep, not after what I saw tonight!"

"What *who* saw?" Hannah begged to differ. "You didn't see anything."

"No, but you told me about it. And I have a very active imagination. There's something really awful about Santa being dead."

"*Wayne* being dead," Michelle corrected her. "Don't think of him as Santa and it won't seem so bad. Think of him as that old skinflint department store owner who wouldn't approve you for a Bergstrom's credit card so you could charge that luggage you wanted for your honeymoon."

Andrea blinked. "You're right. And that *does* help. Not that he deserved to die, but I really didn't like Wayne at all." She turned to Hannah. "Do you think that's really bad of me?"

"Not really. As far as I know, there's no rule of etiquette that says you have to like somebody just because they're dead. If you didn't like them alive, you probably won't like them after they're dead, either." She paused to crane her neck again and gave a sigh of satisfaction. "The coffee's ready. I'll go get it and then let's taste your cookies."

"Oh!" Andrea looked very nervous. "I really hope you like them. They're the first cookies I've ever made by myself."

Hannah made quick work of gathering what they needed in the kitchen. The topic of Wayne's death had come up earlier than she'd expected. When she came back with a tray containing three mugs of coffee and cream and sugar for Andrea, she set it down in the center of the table and reached for one of Andrea's cookies before she could take the coward's way out and claim that she was too full from Sally's Christmas party buffet.

Family love knows no bounds, she said to herself, but the words that came out of her mouth were different. "These look wonderful," she said, taking a leap of faith and biting into one of her sister's cookies.

Hannah was well aware that both Andrea and Michelle were watching her like hawks as she chewed. And swallowed. And smiled.

"Good!" she said, doing her best not to sound too surprised. "I like these, Andrea!"

"Really?"

"Yes," Hannah said and took another bite. "How about you, Michelle?"

Michelle gave her the same look Hannah imagined a prisoner being led to the gallows would wear. But she managed to smile as she obediently took a cookie and bit into it. There was a moment of silence and then an expression of total surprise crossed her face. "These are *good*, Andrea!"

"Well, don't look so shocked." Andrea gave a little giggle. "Carli told me that everybody in her family liked them."

"They're wonderful," Hannah said, finishing her first cookie and reaching for another. "And you actually made them all by yourself?"

"Well . . ." Andrea faltered a bit and then she shook her head. "Not exactly."

"What does *that* mean?" Michelle wanted to know.

"I didn't do it entirely by myself. Grandma McCann showed me how to preheat the oven and put them on the cookie sheets. But that was only for the first couple of times. After that, I did it by myself."

Even though they weren't an overly affectionate family, Hannah couldn't help it. She reached out to give her sister a hug. "Good for you! Are you going to give me the recipe, or is it a big secret?"

"It's not a secret, and it's really easy. They take only four ingredients."

"You're kidding!" Hannah was amazed. The cookies had a light but complex lemon flavor. They were soft and a bit chewy inside, and the outside was almost crunchy.

Andrea went on. "I think that's why Carli sent me the recipe. She remembers the bake sales the cheerleaders used to have to raise money for uniforms."

Hannah remembered them too. When she discovered that Andrea and her friend, Janie Burkholtz, were buying Twinkies at the Lake Eden Red Owl to sell at the fund-raising bake sales, she started baking homemade cookies for them.

"What are the four ingredients?" Michelle asked.

"A package of lemon cake mix, two cups of Cool Whip, an egg, and powdered sugar."

Lemon cake mix! Of course! Hannah felt like rapping the side of her head with her knuckles for being so dense. Andrea had told them she hadn't used zest or lemon juice, but the cookies were still lemony. The flavor had to come from somewhere and making cookies from lemon cake mix should have occurred to her.

"That's all there is," Andrea continued. "Just the four ingredients. Any more and I probably couldn't have done it."

"Well, you did it very well," Hannah told her, pouring them all more coffee.

"Thanks. I'm going to try chocolate next. Maybe I could even mix in a few of those tiny chocolate chips. That might be good."

Hannah just stared at her sister. This was a whole new side of Andrea she'd never seen before.

"And then I was thinking of doing white cake mix with some kind of cut-up fruit like cherries or apricots. Why are you staring at me like that?"

"Because that's how great recipes are developed. You start with something basic and branch out. Sometimes it can be as simple as running out of one ingredient and substituting something else." Hannah passed the plate of cookies to Michelle. "We've got three left, one for each of us. And then we'd better get down to business."

"You're going to figure out who killed Wayne?" Andrea asked, taking her cookie and making short work of it.

"I don't even know if anyone did . . . yet," Hannah reminded her. "It was night, he was at the bottom of the berm, and I was at least eight feet above him. I guess it's possible he slipped and broke his neck."

"But why was he up there in the first place?" Michelle asked.

"He could have climbed up to enjoy the view," Andrea suggested. "What was it like up there?"

"It wasn't what I'd call a scenic vista. The only thing I

could see from the top was the snow bank behind it and the cars in the parking lot."

"Okay." Michelle gave a quick nod. "Then maybe he had to . . . you know. And he didn't want to walk all the way back to the inn."

"So he climbed up a slippery eight-foot snow bank instead of just ducking behind a handy tree?" Hannah asked her.

"Never mind. It was a dumb idea," Michelle admitted.

"Wait a second," Andrea looked thoughtful. "Maybe he didn't climb up there. Maybe somebody dragged him up there and pushed him down the other side to kill him."

"Why go to all that trouble when you could just shoot him, or stab him, or club him to death right there on the path?" Hannah asked the pertinent question.

"Because the killer was afraid somebody might come along and catch him? Or . . . oh, I don't know. Let me find out if it was an accident. Bill should know by now."

"You're going to call Bill?" Michelle asked as Andrea took her cell phone out of her purse.

"No, I'm calling Sally."

"Sally at the inn?" Michelle followed up with another question.

"That's right. She can tell me if Vonnie Blair's still there at the party."

"Doc Knight's secretary," Hannah said, beginning to get an inkling of what her sister was doing. "And if Vonnie's still there, it's probably not murder. Is that right?"

"You got it."

As Andrea punched in the number, Michelle turned to Hannah. "Maybe you got it, but I didn't get it."

"It's simple. If Doc Knight thinks it's murder, Bill will ask him to rush the autopsy. Doc knows how important it is and he'll do it right away. And since Doc has such awful handwriting, he'll call Vonnie on her cell phone and ask her to come out to the hospital to type up the transcript of the autopsy tonight."

Michelle's puzzled expression smoothed out and she looked very impressed. "Wow. Andrea's devious."

"She gets it from Mother," Hannah explained. "Mother can think of the most roundabout ways to get the latest gossip."

"Thanks, Sally," Andrea said, and snapped her cell phone shut. And then she looked over at them. "It's murder. Vonnie left with the paramedics who transported Wayne to the hospital. Doc Knight must have been able to tell right away."

As usual, Andrea was the scribe. Not only did she have good organizational skills, she also had the neatest handwriting of the three sisters. Michelle's had deteriorated when she'd gone off to college. After two years at Macalister, her notes were cryptic, filled with abbreviations that only she could decipher. Hannah, on the other hand, tended to print whenever she wrote something she hoped to read later.

"Here you go. A brand new steno notebook." Hannah handed her sister one from the stash of notebooks she kept in every room. "Do you need a pen?"

"I have one." Andrea reached in her purse and pulled out what Hannah termed a "dress pen," since the barrel was gold and studded with sparkling white stones.

"Pretty fancy," Michelle commented, leaning closer to gaze at the pen. "Are those rhinestones, or diamonds?"

"I'm pretty sure they're rhinestones. It was a present from a client and the house he bought was a fixer-upper." Andrea flipped to the first blank page and wrote Wayne Bergstrom's name at the top. "We don't know the time of death, or the method. What do you want me to write down?"

"We could list the time I found him," Hannah suggested, "but I didn't look at my watch."

"I did." Michelle said. "When you said Santa's dead, I pressed the button to light the time and it said ten twenty-two."

Andrea started to write it down, but Michelle grabbed her hand. "Put down ten-seventeen," she said.

"Wait a second," Hannah was confused. "I thought you said you looked at your watch and it was ten twenty-two."

"That's right. But I always set my watch five minutes ahead. It keeps me from being late to class."

"How does it keep you from being late if you *know* your watch is five minutes ahead?" Hannah asked her.

"It's simple. If I start counting on that extra five minutes, I set my watch ten minutes ahead and psych myself out."

All was silent as Hannah digested that. It seemed her youngest sibling hadn't inherited the logic gene.

"Okay. Ten-seventeen." Andrea jotted it down. "Do we know what time Wayne left for the parking lot?"

"Ten after eight," Hannah responded.

"Are you sure your watch isn't five or ten minutes fast?" Andrea teased her.

"I didn't look at my watch. I glanced at the clock in Sally's kitchen as Wayne went out the back door. We can check it to make sure it's accurate."

Andrea flipped to another page and started a list of things they had to do. "Got it. We'll run out to the inn and check Sally's kitchen clock tomorrow."

"That means Wayne was killed between eight-ten and ten-seventeen," Michelle pointed out. "That's a window of just a little over two hours."

"When we go out tomorrow, let's see how long it

takes to walk from Sally's kitchen to that berm," Hannah suggested. "Even if you're poking along taking your time, it can't be more than five minutes."

Andrea made another note. "Got it," she said. "If you're right, it means that Wayne was probably killed around eight-fifteen, or eight-twenty."

"Unless he stopped to talk to someone on the path," Michelle argued. "You know how people are when they meet each other at a party. They stop and talk for a while. He could have met up with his killer after he talked to somebody."

"Good point," Hannah said.

"We should get a guest list from Sally and check to see if anyone at the party met Wayne on the walkway." Merrily winking rhinestones, or diamonds, or whatever they were, Andrea's pen flew across the page. "It's a couple of degrees above freezing tonight. If you were dressed for the weather, you could stand there and talk for five or ten minutes without getting cold."

Michelle nodded. "But Wayne wasn't dressed for the weather. Hannah said he was wearing his Santa suit." She turned to Hannah. "Do you think it was as heavy as a parka?"

"I don't know. It looked heavy, especially with all that fur, but I didn't actually feel the material."

"They sell the same Santa suit at Bergstrom's," Michelle told them. "I saw a whole rack of them when I was shopping for boots with Mother."

"We'll go out there and check." Andrea added another line to her *To Do* page, and then she let Moishe capture her pen and bat it around for a moment.

"Mother!" Hannah exclaimed.

"What about Mother?" her sisters chorused in perfect unison.

"When she calls to read me the riot act for finding another body, I'll ask her to go shopping at Bergstrom's and check out the Santa suits. It's her favorite store at the mall."

"And she'll be so pleased she's helping us solve Wayne's murder, she'll forget all about criticizing you?" Michelle guessed.

"That's the general idea."

"It could work," Andrea offered her opinion. "Mother's hard to distract, but a trip to Bergstrom's right before Christmas could do it."

LEMON WHIPPERSNAPPERS

Preheat oven to 350 degrees F.,
rack in the middle position.

1 package *(approximately 18 ounces)* lemon
cake mix, the size you can bake in a 9-inch
by 13-inch cake pan *(Andrea used Betty
Crocker)*

2 cups Cool Whip *(measure this—Andrea
said her tub of Cool Whip contained a little over 3 cups.)*

1 large beaten egg *(it's okay to just whip it
up in a glass with a fork)*

½ cup powdered *(confectioner's)* sugar in a
separate small bowl *(you don't have to sift
it unless it's got big lumps)*

Combine dry cake mix, Cool Whip, and beaten
egg in a large bowl. Stir until it's well mixed.

Drop by teaspoon into the bowl of powdered
sugar and roll to coat the cookie dough.

Place the coated cookie drops on a greased *(Andrea used Pam, but any nonstick cooking spray is
fine)* cookie sheet, 12 cookies to each sheet.

Bake the cookies at 350 degrees F., for 10 minutes. Let them cool on the cookie sheets for 2 min-

utes or so, and then move them to a wire rack to cool completely.

Yield: approximately 4 dozen light and lovely cookies.

Hannah's Note: Andrea showed me the recipe. Carli wrote that this is an old church recipe and that you can use any flavor cake mix in these cookies. She especially likes Lemon Whippersnappers in the summer because they're simple to make and very refreshing.

Chapter Four

"No!" Hannah groaned, categorically refusing to open her eyes. She reached for the snooze button on her alarm clock to shut off its infernal electronic beeping before it could fully wake her, but there was something wrong with her arm. It wouldn't move! She could wiggle it slightly, but that was all. Had she suffered some type of debilitating injury while she slept? Or was she only dreaming that her arm was partially paralyzed?

There was only one way to find out and that was to open her eyes. Hannah groaned again and forced her eyelids up and open. In the dim wattage cast by the nightlight she'd bought the last time she'd climbed out of bed in the dark and stubbed her toe, she could see her arm, under the blanket, stretched out on the bed and perfectly immobile. But there was something different about it. Some time during the night it had swelled up to at least three times its normal size. That didn't bode well!

Hannah wiggled her fingers, feeling the tingles that accompanied a cut-off blood supply. It was clear her arm had gone to sleep. But why was it swollen? Had she suffered some kind of neurological damage without even waking up?

As Hannah stared at the limb that had betrayed her while she slept, she saw two small peaks rise up from the vicinity of her armpit. The peaks were attached to a round fuzzy orb and for a moment Hannah was puzzled. Then she gave a startled laugh as she realized what had happened. The peaks and the fuzzy orb belonged to Moishe. The temperature must have dropped below freezing in the middle of the night, because he'd left his usual place at the bottom of her bed to seek warmer climes above. No wonder her arm had gone to sleep! It was buried beneath over twenty pounds of dozing cat.

"Come on, Moishe . . . get off my arm!" Hannah rolled over with difficulty and reached across her own body to give him a push. This elicited a protesting yowl, but he climbed off, and Hannah's arm was freed from its furry burden.

The first thing Hannah did with her newly restored hand was shut off the alarm. She was awake now, and the urge to slumber for another five minutes was a wee bit easier to resist, especially when she reminded herself that today would be a busy day. Not only did she have cookie and dessert baking to do for her bakery and coffee shop, she'd agreed to cater luncheon at her mother's regency romance club Christmas meeting.

Michelle had gone home with Andrea last night and they planned to head out early this morning to take care of several items on the *To Do* list. They'd start off by driving to the Lake Eden Inn to check the clock in Sally's kitchen, pick up a copy of the guest list for last night's party, and time their walk from the kitchen door that Wayne Bergstrom had used to the base of the snow bank where Hannah had found his body. During the afternoon, they'd do a little reconnoitering with their male counterparts. Andrea would pump Bill for information about the investigation, and Michelle would find out what Lonnie knew. The three sisters would compare notes that evening when they met at Andrea's house for dinner.

"Coffee," Hannah breathed and it was more of a prayer than a statement. She needed caffeine and she needed it now, before Newton's First Law of Motion, the one about inertia, came into play. A body at rest tended to stay at rest. And applying this principle of physics to her own life meant that if she didn't get up soon, she might fall under the First Law and just sit on the edge of her bed, staring at the wall all day.

"Coffee. Coffee now!" It was as close to a cheer as she could come up with in the cold predawn of a December morning, but it served to whet her appetite for the hot, aromatic brew her great grandmother Elsa had called Swedish Plasma.

Before she had time to think, which would only have served to confuse her, Hannah was on her feet. And then her feet were moving, heading down the hallway toward the kitchen. The coffeepot that had activated automatically five minutes before her alarm clock had sounded was now sitting on the counter with a full carafe of the world's most popular life-sustaining potion, just waiting for her to imbibe.

"You, here. Me, there," she said to the cat who followed her into the kitchen, batting at the ends of the belt she'd forgotten to tie on her robe. Moishe appeared to understand his mistress's pidgin English because he backed off immediately and took up a position of hope by his empty food bowl.

Hannah had her priorities straight. It took every corner of her partially alert mind to do it, but she opened the combination padlock on the broom closet, pulled out the forty-pound sack of kitty kibble that Moishe loved, and dumped a full measure into his bowl. She replaced the kibble, replaced the padlock, and *then* she poured her first cup of coffee.

"Uff-dah!" she groaned, audibly revealing her Minnesota roots as she sank down on one of the chairs that had come with her Formica-topped breakfast table. She glanced over to see if Moishe was eating and was about to pick up her mug of coffee for that first bracing sip, when she saw something red out of the corner of her eye.

It was a red scarf tied around the handle of her refrigerator. For several moments Hannah was genuinely puzzled, but then she caught sight of the mixing bowl and utensils washed and stacked on the counter, and everything became clear. When everyone had left last night, at shortly before two in the morning, Hannah had intended to go straight to bed. Unfortunately her mind was still racing and there was no way she could sleep. Instead of wasting valuable time tossing and turning, she'd flicked on the lights in the kitchen and mixed up a batch of cookies. They were experimental, something she'd been planning to try for several months, and the dough was chilling in the refrigerator. That was the reason she'd tied her scarf around the handle of the refrigerator. It was to remind her to take the dough with her when she left for work, so that she could bake it at The Cookie Jar. If the cookies were as good as she expected them to be, she'd serve them at her mother's club luncheon.

First things first, Hannah told herself, raising the mug of coffee to her lips. She breathed in deeply, inhaling the antioxidants in the steam that some researcher claimed would save coffee kiosk employees from lung cancer. Hannah thought that would be lovely, but she didn't believe it for a second. On the other hand, what could it hurt? She'd been inhaling the steam from coffee for years simply because she loved the aroma.

Another deep coffee-flavored sniff and it was time to enjoy the brew. Hannah was just about to take that first scalding sip when the telephone rang.

"Mother!" she exclaimed, in the same voice she would have used if she'd skidded off the road and into a ditch. She swallowed fast, taking a sip while she could, and glanced over at her Mother-barometer. Sure enough, Moishe's fur was bristling and he'd puffed up like a Halloween cat. He'd also begun to make the growling sound, deep in his throat, that meant, *Maybe you're bigger than I am, but I'm gonna shred those pantyhose you're wearing.* It wasn't a guarantee that Delores Swensen was on the other end of the line, but Hannah's feline roommate was right a whole lot more than he was wrong.

Hannah took another sip of her coffee and then she stood up to reach for the wall phone. She sat right back down again, knowing that no previous conversation with her mother had ever lasted less than fifteen minutes, and answered. "Hello, Mother."

"I wish you wouldn't do that, Hannah!" Delores gave a deep sigh that was so forceful, it almost tickled Hannah's ear. "What if I wasn't me?"

"Then you'd need to see a psychiatrist, because you'd have an identity crisis."

"Hannah!"

"Sorry, Mother."

Delores gave an exasperated sigh that was almost as loud as her previous sigh. "You always say that, and you still answer the phone that way. But I didn't call to argue with you."

"I'm glad to hear that," Hannah said, winking at her cat, who was still puffed up several times his size, preparing to take on any predator.

"I'm not going to argue, but I *do* have a bone to pick with you, Hannah."

Hannah took another sip of coffee, wisely saying

nothing. Her mother was only mildly upset. If she'd been extremely upset, she would have called Hannah by her first and middle names.

"Bill called me this morning to ask me about Melinda."

"Melinda who?" Hannah asked, wondering what in the world her mother was talking about.

"Melinda Bergstrom, Wayne's wife. Surely you remember Wayne Bergstrom. You found his *body* last night. And you found it practically in front of your sisters!" Delores delivered another sigh that made the phone give an odd little sound that probably meant it had exceeded its decibel level. "You have *got* to stop doing this, Hannah Louise!"

Uh-oh! Hannah's mind shouted out a warning. Delores only used her middle name when she was what her father had called, "loaded for bear."

"I'd love to stop doing it! It's not like I enjoy finding murder victims, or anything like that. I only climbed up on that snow bank because we were curious and I didn't want them to do it."

There was silence for a moment. Delores was thinking it over. "Well . . ." she said finally, "that's good. It's good that you were sparing your sisters' sensibilities. That's an admirable quality."

Hannah came very close to gasping out loud in surprise. She'd never gotten off so easily before. It was best to change the subject now, while she was still ahead of the game.

"Thank you, Mother. Now about the luncheon today, I need some sort of a timeline."

"What do you mean?"

"We're having quiche and it's best if it's warm. How many awards will you be presenting before you want me to serve lunch?"

"Let me see . . . three of our members are getting their five-year manor houses. They're darling little miniatures of English Manor Homes. I found them in a catalogue and ordered them from London."

"Will there be speeches after you present them?"

"No, dear. They're limited to thirty seconds to thank us. But there will be three more presentations. Carrie's getting her ten-year curricle with a matched pair."

Hannah knew her mother was talking about a carriage pulled by two horses. "To put in front of her manor house?" she guessed.

"Exactly. Since she's the oldest living member, I told her she could have one minute to speak."

"Okay," Hannah said, hoping her mother wouldn't use that particular phrase. Carrie Rhodes, her mother's friend and partner in the antique business, wouldn't appreciate being called the oldest living member. And come to think of it, did that imply that the Lake Eden Regency Romance Club also had members who were dead?

"Did you hear me, Hannah?"

Her mother's voice pulled her back from contemplating whether one had to be alive to be a member of an organization, and Hannah was quick to apologize. "Sorry, Mother. I didn't quite catch that."

"I asked you if you'd have enough quiche so that Norman could eat with us. He's coming to take pictures of the award ceremony on his lunch hour."

"Of course. I always have extra. You know that, Mother."

"And you did remember that I asked for a vegetarian alternative?"

"I did. We're having two kinds of quiche, one vegetarian and the other with meat."

"How about dessert? Did you manage to come up with something authentic to the time period?"

"I think so. I call them Regency Seed Cakes. They had oranges back then, didn't they? I seem to remember someone talking about a greenhouse-type room with fruit trees."

"That would have been an *orangery*, dear. It was like a solarium with exotic plants and trees. Most of the expensive mansions had them."

"Good. Well, these are a little like lemon poppy seed cake, except that they're cookies made with oranges and poppy seeds."

"They sound wonderful, dear!"

I hope so, Hannah thought, but she didn't want to worry her mother by telling her the Regency Seed Cakes were last night's invention and she hadn't had time to test them yet. It was much safer to say nothing and change the subject. "What time do you want me to serve the quiche, Mother? If you can give me an estimate of the time, I'll make sure they're still warm."

"Let me think, dear." There was silence for a moment and then Delores spoke again. "We're starting at noon and the awards are first. I think we should be through in ten minutes. Although . . . we do have a special award for Jenny Perkins, of course."

"Jenny who?" Hannah asked. She was almost certain she'd never met a Jenny Perkins at any of her mother's club meetings.

"You knew her as Jenny Bergstrom, but now she's Jenny Perkins again. She took back her maiden name after the divorce."

Hannah hadn't known that Wayne's ex-wife was in town!

"I'll call her this morning to make sure she's coming. I hope so. Poor Jenny will need the support of friends at this sad time in her life."

"What sad time? Haven't Wayne and Jenny been divorced for at least five years?"

"Six, to be exact. But Jenny married Wayne right out of high school and she was utterly devastated when he filed for divorce. He was her first love, and a woman never gets over her first love. Wayne's death is bound to open old wounds for Jenny."

"Just as long as Jenny didn't open *new* wounds in Wayne," Hannah muttered just under her breath.

"What was that?"

"Nothing, Mother. Just thinking out loud. You said you'd call Jenny this morning. Is she staying with friends?"

"No, she didn't want to put any of us out. We all offered our guest rooms, but she booked a room at the inn."

Hannah decided not to plumb for any more information. If Delores suspected that Jenny had just moved to the top of her eldest daughter's suspect list, she'd go right back to being angry again.

"Will you call me at the shop as soon as you know if Jenny's coming?" Hannah asked.

"Of course. But why?"

So that I can watch her like a hawk and maybe even interrogate her while I'm serving the quiche, Hannah thought. But of course she didn't say that to her mother. Instead she settled for, "I'll pack up some chocolate cookies and send them back to the inn with her."

"That's a good idea, dear. Chocolate always helps in times of stress. I was thinking of picking up some chocolate truffles at Fanny Farmer's."

The lightbulb went on in Hannah's mind and grew into a powerful halogen. Fanny Farmer's was in the Tri-County Mall, and so was Bergstrom's Department Store. Now was the perfect time to ask her mother to find out about the Santa costumes they sold at Bergstrom's. "Chocolate truffles would be great, Mother. And since you're going to the mall anyway, could you do one little thing for me?"

"You want me to buy you that absolutely darling purse I told you about?" Delores guessed.

Her mother sounded so hopeful, Hannah almost caved in. It was true that her huge shoulder bag purse was showing some serious wear. But the purse Delores had wanted to buy for her was one-fourth the size of her current bag. What would she do with all of the absolutely essential items she now carried?

"That's very sweet of you, Mother," Hannah hedged. "Thank you for offering, but that's not it. What I really want is for you to do a little sleuthing."

"Sleuthing? Does that mean you're going to work with Mike on the case?"

"Not exactly. Mike's going to work on the case. And I'm going to work on the case. But we're not necessarily going to work together. He was here last night to take our statements and he warned me to stay out of it."

Delores gave a laugh. "Oh, he always warns you to stay out of it! And we've never listened to him before. He gets his nose out of joint every time we come up with a good lead, but he knows how much he needs our help. He just can't admit it, that's all."

Hannah grinned. Her mother was using the plural personal pronoun and that meant she was ready to join in the hunt for Wayne's killer. "You're probably right, Mother."

"I know I'm right. On the other hand, there's no sense in antagonizing him. He *is* the law, after all. We'll just have to be very hush-hush about what we're doing. Now what sleuthing can I do for you at the mall, dear?"

"Could you go into Bergstrom's and pick up one of those big tubs of miniature candy canes for me? I'll pay you back later."

"Of course I can. But what does that have to do with Wayne's murder?"

"Absolutely nothing. But while you're there, I'd like you to take a look at the Santa suits they sell. I need to know how warm they'd be if you wore one of them outside in the winter."

"Oh, my! I had no idea!"

Hannah was confused. "No idea of *what?*"

"That poor Wayne was wearing his Santa suit when he was murdered! Just wait until I tell the girls! Of course I have to be careful not to say anything in front of Jenny. I wouldn't upset her for the world."

Hannah just shook her head. Delores had one foot on the end of the dock and the other in the rowboat. It would be interesting to see which foot won out. Would it be friendship? Or juicy gossip?

"I have to hang up now, dear. I need to call Carrie and fill her in. I'll take her out to Bergstrom's with me. Her niece works in Fine Jewelry and we can pump her for information."

There was a click and the line went dead. Hannah shrugged, hung up the phone, and turned to glance at her kitchen clock. Her mother's call had lasted less than five minutes. That was a new world's record.

"It's okay. She's gone now," she said to the cat who was staring at the phone with deadly intent. He had taken an instant dislike to Delores and not even the shrimp she occasionally brought him had sweetened his opinion of her. "Come on, Moishe. Let's get you some more breakfast."

Under normal circumstances the word breakfast would have resulted in an immediate dash to the food bowl. But this time the culinary magic of kitty crunchies didn't work. Moishe continued to stare at the phone with his fur bristling and his tail swishing back and forth like a scythe.

"Uh-oh," Hannah breathed, wondering what she should do. She had to take a shower and get ready for work, but there was no way she could leave Moishe alone with the phone without risking a cord peppered with puncture wounds.

"Okay. I'm calling in the big guns." Hannah picked

up the phone and dialed. A moment later she had Lisa on the phone.

"Did I wake you?" she asked.

"No, we were just sitting down to breakfast. I heard about Wayne Bergstrom on KCOW."

Hannah sighed. She should have known that Jake and Kelly, the wacky radio hosts of *News at O'Dark-Thirty,* would have the latest scoop. "Did they say anything about me?"

"Oh, yes." Hannah's young partner gave a little chuckle. "They said you discovered Wayne's body. And then they joked around about how Lake Eden's Cookie Lady had murder on the menu again."

"We're going to be packed today," Hannah said with a groan. "And I've got the Regency club luncheon."

"That's okay. I can handle the shop by myself."

"I know you can handle it on a normal day, but everybody and their cousin's going to stop in to ask questions."

"And you won't be there to answer them," Lisa pointed out. "So I guess they'll just have to sit there and buy more cookies and coffee while they wait for you to come back."

"Okay, but I'm still going to call around and see if I can get some help for you."

"It's all taken care of. I talked to Marge and Dad and they're going to help out."

"Great!" Hannah glanced down at her feline and remembered the reason she'd called Lisa in the first place. "Do you have time to do a quick favor for me?"

"What is it?"

"I'm going to hold the phone out and I want you to say hi to Moishe. Otherwise he's going to hop up on the table and kill it while I'm taking my shower."

There was silence for a moment and then Lisa laughed. "Your mother called?"

"That's right. Just let him hear your voice and he'll calm right down." Hannah lowered the phone toward her feline and held it out. "Listen to this, Moishe. It's Lisa."

"Hi, Moishe." Hannah could hear Lisa's voice faintly as she held the phone at arm's length. It sounded tinny and very small, the same sort of voice a mouse might use if mice could speak.

Moishe pulled back, away from the sound at first. But then he seemed to realize that the voice was talking to him and he moved closer again.

"How are you this morning?" Lisa continued the conversation and Hannah began to smile. Moishe had moved another step closer and he'd started to rub his cheek against the phone.

"You're such a good boy, Moishe," Lisa said, and Hannah's cat began to purr. "Did Mommy give you your breakfast yet?"

Moishe turned and made a beeline for his food bowl. That surprised Hannah so much, she almost forgot to reclaim the receiver.

"Are you still there, Moishe?" Lisa asked.

"It's me," Hannah said with a grin. It was the first time she'd ever been mistaken for her cat! "Thanks for talking to him, Lisa."

"You're welcome. Did he know it was me?"

"Absolutely. When he recognized your voice, he started to nuzzle the phone and purr. And then you mentioned breakfast and he went straight to his bowl. I think he's forgotten all about . . ."

"Don't say it and remind him!" Lisa cautioned, before Hannah could utter her mother's name.

"Right. I'll see you at the shop in an hour."

Once she'd hung up the phone, Hannah poured herself another cup of coffee and carried it into the bathroom. It was the old carrot and the stick routine.

Her mug of hot coffee would sit on the counter by the sink while she took her shower. If she hurried, it would still be hot and tasty when she emerged. If she took too long, it would be tepid. As she stepped in under the steaming spray, she thought about incentives and how well they worked. Money was a powerful incentive and it could act as a motive for murder. If she could find out the details of Wayne's will and who would inherit his considerable estate, it could lead them to his killer.

REGENCY SEED CAKES

DO NOT preheat oven—this
dough needs to chill.

1 cup *(2 sticks, ½ pound)* butter
2 eggs
2½ cups white *(granulated)* sugar
6 Tablespoons poppy seeds
1 teaspoon baking powder
1 teaspoon baking soda
1 teaspoon salt
1 teaspoon orange extract
½ teaspoon orange zest *(optional)*
5 cups flour *(don't sift it)*
¾ cup orange juice *(I used three-quarters cup
  Minute Maid)*

You will also need: ½ cup white *(granulated)*
sugar in a small bowl for later, when you bake the
cookies.

**Hannah's 1st Note: You can mix up these cookies
by hand, but it's a lot easier with an electric mixer.**

Melt the butter in a pan on the stove, or in the
microwave in a small bowl or measuring cup for 1
minute 15 seconds on HIGH. Let it cool while you
mix up the following ingredients:

In a large bowl combine the eggs with the white
sugar. Beat them until they're well blended.

Add the poppy seeds, baking powder, baking soda, and salt. Mix them in thoroughly.

Add the orange extract and then the orange zest, if you decided to use it. *(Orange zest is finely grated orange peel—just the orange part and not the white. The white is bitter and leaves a bad aftertaste.)* If you can't find orange extract in your store, you can use vanilla instead. Mix well.

Cup your hands around the bowl with the melted butter. If it's not too warm to hold comfortably, start your mixer and pour it slowly into your mixing bowl. *(That's so it doesn't slosh over the sides!)* If it's still too hot to add and you think it might cook the eggs in your bowl, let it cool a little longer before mixing it in.

Add two cups of the flour now. Mix it in.

Add the orange juice to your bowl. Mix it in and then add the rest of the flour. *(You should have three cups left to add.)* Mix thoroughly. This dough will be quite stiff.

Give the bowl a final stir by hand and cover it with plastic wrap. Stash it in the refrigerator for at least 2 hours. Overnight is fine too!

65

When you're ready to bake, preheat your oven to 375 degrees F., rack in the middle position.

Prepare your baking sheets by lining them with parchment paper and spraying the paper with Pam, or another nonstick cooking spray.

Hannah's 2nd Note: If it's snowing outside and you're all out of parchment paper and your car won't start for the trip to the store to get more, don't worry about it. Just spray your cookie sheets with Pam or whichever nonstick cooking spray you have on hand. If you do this, you'll have to let the cookies cool on the sheets for at least 5 minutes before you transfer them to wire racks, but that's okay. It's a lot better than trudging a mile through the snow to get to the store when you don't have to.

Take the chilled dough out of the refrigerator and make dough balls, about an inch in diameter, with your hands. Drop them in the small bowl with the sugar and roll them around to coat them. Then place them on the cookie sheets, 12 to a standard-size sheet. Press them down slightly when you place them on the sheets so they won't roll off on the way to the oven.

Bake the cookies at 375 degrees F. for 7 to 10 minutes. *(Mine took about 9 minutes.)* Let them cool on the pan for a minute and then pull off the parchment paper and transfer the paper and cookies to a wire rack.

Hannah's 3rd Note: If you didn't use parchment paper, follow the cooling directions in my 2nd note.

If the dough begins to get sticky and you start to have trouble rolling it with your hands, return it to the refrigerator while the cookies are baking and take it out again when you need to make more dough balls.

Yield: approximately 8 dozen tasty cookies.

Chapter Five

Hannah had just finished packing up everything she needed for the luncheon when Lisa came in through the swinging restaurant-style door carrying a tub of miniature candy canes, and a large shopping bag with Bergstrom's logo emblazoned on the front. "Your mother was just here and she dropped these off for you," she said.

"I know about the candy canes. I asked her to pick them up for me. I'm almost afraid to ask, but . . . what's in the shopping bag?"

"Two things. The first is a Santa suit."

"But I wanted her to look at it, not buy it!"

Lisa laughed. "That's exactly what she said you'd say. She bought it for Bill so that he could play Santa at the sheriff's department Christmas party. She says she'll give it to him later, after you take a good look at it."

"Okay. What's the second thing in the bag?"

"A new purse. She says she just wants you to see it. You don't have to keep it if you don't want to."

Hannah groaned. "So you think she'll be insulted if I don't keep it?"

"She's your mother. Of course she'll be insulted. You'll have to use it at least once, Hannah."

Hannah wanted to object, but Lisa was right. It was

inevitable. Delores was determined to give her the purse and it might just be time to clean out her old one, although she hated to admit it. "Later," she said, deciding to tackle that problem once she'd solved Wayne's murder.

"You'd better get going if you want to preheat those ovens down at the community center."

"I'm just going to crush some of those candy canes for the batch of Chocolate Candy Cane Cookies I've got in the cooler."

"I'll do that while you're gone. Do you need help loading your truck? Marge and Dad are out front taking care of the customers so I can carry stuff out for you."

"Not a problem. I've got it covered." Hannah glanced at her partner. Lisa was wearing the frilly dress apron they used in the coffee shop and her light brown hair was pulled back in a ponytail. She looked like what Hannah's grandmother would have called "a slip of a girl," but Grandma Ingrid would have been wrong to dismiss Lisa Herman Beeseman so lightly. Not only did Lisa work full time at The Cookie Jar, she also kept what Hannah's grandmother would have termed a "preacher-ready house," cooked nutritious meals for her new husband every night, and visited her father, who had Alzheimer's, at least five times a week. Lisa was on the go every second, and Hannah often wished she had that kind of energy. She told herself it was because a twenty-year-old possessed double the energy of women who'd passed the thirty-year milestone, but that probably wasn't true.

"Did you use the invisible waitress trick?" Hannah asked her, referring to the strange phenomenon she'd discovered the first day she opened her coffee shop. If two customers were having a private conversation, they kept right on talking about confidential matters while Hannah or Lisa refilled their coffee mugs, or delivered their cookie orders. It was as though the moment Hannah or Lisa picked up a coffee carafe, or a tray of cookies, they became incapable of overhearing anything that was said. Armed with the invisible cloak of a frilly serving apron, they ceased to exist as living, breathing human beings and turned into part of the woodwork.

"You bet I used it," Lisa replied with a grin. "When you first told me about it, I thought you were crazy, but it works every time I do it. I didn't hear anything though, not unless you want to count Cyril Murphy's crazy theory about what happened to Wayne."

"What's Cyril's theory?"

"The part I heard had to do with alien abductions gone bad."

"I didn't know Cyril believed in aliens!"

Lisa shrugged. "It doesn't surprise me. It's a lot like believing in the Little People. Cyril tells everybody he believes in them."

"He's Irish. He has to say he believes in leprechauns even if he doesn't. It goes with the territory along with the pot of gold at the end of the rainbow, kissing the Blarney Stone, and drinking green beer on St. Patrick's Day. What did you hear Cyril say?"

"I have to tell you what happened first."

"Okay." Hannah motioned to a stool at the stainless steel work counter and Lisa sat down. "Go ahead."

"Cyril came in with Brigit and they sat at a table with Rick and Jessica," Lisa named Cyril's wife, oldest son, and daughter-in-law. "Jessica was talking about how nice Sally's party was and how much fun they were having until Mike came over and put Rick to work interviewing everybody."

"Go on."

"Then Brigit asked Rick for more particulars about how Wayne died, and Rick told her he wasn't supposed to give out any information. And Brigit wanted to know why not since Jake and Kelly had announced on KCOW that it was a massive blow to the back of the head that had caved in Wayne's skull and caused his death."

Hannah made a mental note to try to get her hands on the crime scene photos. If she remembered correctly, Wayne had been wearing his Santa hat when she found him. The hat was made of thick, furry red material and it had a wide cuff of white fur all the way around it. The blow must have been delivered with considerable force to cave in Wayne's skull right through his padded hat.

"Then they started to talk about who could have killed Wayne. Rick didn't say much and I figured he was a little uncomfortable about maybe leaking some information without meaning to do it, but Jessica and Brigit were talking about all the people Wayne had overcharged at the store. And then Cyril spoke up and said he knew exactly how Wayne had died, and the killer was going to get away with it."

"That's when the subject of alien abduction came up?" Hannah guessed.

"That's right. But first Cyril asked them if they'd noticed how bright the moon was last night. And they all said they'd noticed."

"Cyril's right about that. I noticed it, and so did Andrea and Michelle. We even commented on it when we were walking to the parking lot."

"Well, Cyril said the reason it was that bright was because the aliens were refracting the moon's energy with the hull of their giant space ship. And what they'd thought was the moon was really the hull of the ship."

Hannah snorted. She couldn't help it. "Oh, boy!"

"That's not all. Cyril claimed that the aliens practiced thought control on Wayne, drawing him off the path and making him climb up the side of that steep snow bank."

"Why would they do that?"

"That's what Jessica asked him. And Cyril said the reason they wanted Wayne to climb up to the top was so they could take a better look at him."

"They were too nearsighted to see him on the ground?" Hannah's grin grew wider.

"I guess so. Or maybe they just didn't refract enough of the moon's energy to light him up." Lisa gave a little giggle. "Anyway, that was when Brigit had to leave the table. She pretended to have a bad cough, but I could tell she was laughing."

"Can't blame Brigit for that."

"I know. I almost lost it, too. But Cyril kept right on talking. He said that when the aliens caught sight of the white fur on Wayne's Santa costume, they assumed he was an animal instead of a human. And since they had already abducted enough animals, they pushed him back down the snow bank."

"Killing him in the process?"

"That's what Cyril said. Is he crazy, or what?"

Hannah was about to agree that the master mechanic who fixed her cookie truck had slipped several cogs. But before she could say that, she remembered a small notice she'd read in the *Lake Eden Journal*. The Wolf Pack Lodge would be holding their annual Whopper Contest next week. If she remembered correctly, Cyril had won last year with his story about how the porcupine got its quills. "He's not crazy," she said.

"He's *not?*"

"No, he's just practicing for the Whopper Contest."

Lisa rolled her eyes. "I don't think it's very nice to joke about murder. Of course Cyril isn't exactly mourning Wayne Bergstrom, either."

"What do you mean?"

"Herb said they got into a really big fight a couple of days ago at the garage. Herb was picking up his squad car and there they were really going at it. Cyril was accusing Wayne of trying to put him out of business, and they were yelling, and shaking their fists, and . . . oh, gosh!" Lisa stopped speaking and her mouth dropped open. When she recovered enough to speak again, she raised shocked eyes to Hannah. "You don't think that . . . ?"

"Anything's possible," Hannah told her. "One thing's for sure. I'm going to call Herb the minute I get those ovens turned on and find out all about it."

Edna Ferguson, the head cook at Jordan High and Hannah's helper for the luncheon, came into the kitchen at the community center and sniffed appreciatively. "They're going to love your quiches," she said.

"I hope so." Hannah stared down at the lineup she'd just taken from the oven. "What's our E. T. L.?"

Edna looked puzzled for a moment and then she laughed so hard, her tightly wound gray curls bounced. "Estimated Time of Luncheon?" she asked.

"That's right."

"I'd say twenty minutes. The last club member just came in and your mother's getting ready to present the awards."

Hannah was confused. Delores had called her at the shop to say that Jenny Perkins had canceled, and so had one other award recipient. "I talked to Mother this morning and she thought the awards would take only ten minutes."

"It always takes longer than they think it will. I've been coming to these things for years now, and everybody always wants to thank somebody. It's their time in the limelight, you know? I call it the Oscars at Lake Eden."

"You're right," Hannah said. But unlike the Academy Awards, she couldn't crank up the music to get the winners to stop talking. There was one thing she could do though, and she turned to Edna with a question. "Do you know if there's a fan around here?"

"You mean an exhaust fan?"

"No, a window fan. It doesn't have to be very big."

Edna turned on her heel and headed for the big walk-in pantry. In just a moment, she was back with a small round fan that looked ancient. "How's this?"

"Perfect, if it still works."

"It does. I used it last summer. Where do you want me to set it up?"

"Behind the row of quiches. Then I want you to open the shutters to the pass-through window an inch or two, and turn on the fan."

Edna looked puzzled as she hooked up the fan and opened the shutters. "What are you doing, Hannah?" she asked.

"Aroma therapy."

"Aroma ther . . . oh!" Edna gave a very girlish-sounding giggle for someone who'd passed the age of consent more than thirty years previously. "You're a clever one, Hannah! And it ought to work. Once they get a whiff of your quiches, the only person they'll want to thank is the cook!"

COUPLE OF QUICK QUICHES

Preheat the oven to 350 degrees F.,
rack in the middle position

Hannah's Tips on Quiche: Quiche is easy. Really. Yes, the title is French, but really it's just egg pie. It's a custard, a rich savory one, (that means it's not sweet like a caramel custard or a traditional custard pie,) and it's filled with meat and cheese, and other good stuff to eat. Quiche is not just a ladies' luncheon entrée, served in slim slices on fine china and accompanied by an impertinent little Chardonnay. It's real food that guys enjoy. Even if your husband drives a truck, swears like a trooper, rolls up his T-shirt sleeves to hold his cigarette pack, and can shovel the driveway with one hand tied behind his back even after a night on the town, he'll still love a hearty, meaty quiche. (Hint from Hannah: Try Quiche Lorraine first, and call it "Bacon & Egg Pie".)

One quiche will serve from three to six people. *(Six if you have other things to eat on the side, three if you're going to serve just a salad and quiche.)* Decide how many people you want to serve and plan accordingly. I always make at least 2 quiches. It gives my guests a choice for the second piece and the leftovers are great for breakfast the next morning.

QUICHE LORRAINE

Preheat the oven to 350 degrees F.,
rack in the middle position.

The Quiche Lorraine Pie Shell:

You can mix up your favorite piecrust recipe and line a 10-inch pie plate. Or . . . you can buy frozen shells at the grocery store. *(If you decide to go the grocery store frozen pie shell route, buy 9-inch deep-dish pie shells.)*

Hannah's 1st Note: There's no need to feel guilty if you choose to use the frozen pie shells. They're good and it's a real time saver. I happen to know that Edna Ferguson, the head cook at Jordan High, has been known to remove frozen pie shells from their telltale disposable pans and put them in her own pie tins to bake! *(Sorry Edna—I just had to tell them.)* **Stack your pie shells in the refrigerator, or leave them in the freezer until two hours before you're ready to use them.**

Prepare your piecrust by separating one egg. Throw away the white and whip up the yolk with a fork. Brush the bottom and inside of your piecrust. Prick it all over with a fork and bake it in a 350 F. degree oven for 5 minutes. Take it out and let it cool on a wire rack or a cold stovetop while you mix up the custard. If "bubbles" have formed in the crust,

76

immediately prick them with a fork to let out the steam.

The Quiche Lorraine Custard:

5 eggs
1½ cups heavy whipping cream ***

***If you and your guests are on a diet, you can substitute Half 'n Half for the heavy cream, but it won't be as good!*

Hannah's 2nd Note: You can do this by hand with a whisk, or use an electric mixer, your choice.

Combine the eggs with the cream and whisk them *(or beat them with an electric mixer)* until they're a uniform color. When they're thoroughly mixed, pour them into a pitcher and set it in the refrigerator until you're ready to assemble the rest of your quiche. You may notice that you're not adding any salt, pepper, or other seasoning at this point. You'll do that when you assemble the quiche.

Hannah's 3rd Note: You can mix up the custard ahead of time and store it in the refrigerator for up to 24 hours. When you're ready to assemble your quiches, all you have to do is whisk it smooth and pour it out from the pitcher.

The Quiche Lorraine Filling:

2 cups grated Gruyere cheese *(approximately 7 ounces)****
1 cup diced, well-cooked and drained bacon
½ teaspoon salt
½ teaspoon freshly ground black pepper
¼ teaspoon ground cayenne pepper
    (optional—use if you like it a bit spicy)
¼ teaspoon ground nutmeg *(freshly grated is best, of course)*

***If you can't find Gruyere, use really sharp white cheddar and that'll be fine. And if you can't find white cheddar, use really sharp yellow cheddar.

Sprinkle the grated cheese in the bottom of your cooled pie shell.

Spread the cup of diced bacon on top of the cheese.

Sprinkle on the salt, and grind the pepper over the top of the bacon.

Sprinkle on the cayenne pepper *(if you decided to use it).*

Grate the nutmeg over the top.

Put a drip pan under your pie plate. *(I line a jellyroll pan with foil and use that.)* This will catch any spills that might occur when you fill your quiche with the custard mixture.

Take your custard mixture out of the refrigerator and give it a good whisk. Then pour it over the top of your Quiche Lorraine, filling it about half way.

Open your oven, pull out the rack, and set your pie plate and drip pan on it. Pour in more custard mixture, stopping a quarter-inch short of the rim. Carefully push in the rack, and shut the oven door.

Bake your Quiche Lorraine at 350 degrees F., for 60 minutes, or until the top is nicely browned and a knife inserted one-inch from the center comes out clean.

Let your quiche cool for 15 to 30 minutes on a cold stovetop or a wire rack, and then cut and serve to rave reviews.

This quiche is good warm, but it's also good at room temperature. (I've even eaten it straight out of the refrigerator for breakfast!)

HOLIDAY QUICHE

Preheat the oven to 350 degrees
F., rack in the middle position.

The Holiday Quiche Pie Shell:

You can mix up your favorite piecrust recipe and line a 10-inch pie plate. Or . . . you can buy frozen shells at the grocery store. *(If you decide to go the grocery store frozen pie shell route, buy 9-inch deep-dish pie shells.)*

Hannah's 1st Note: There's no need to feel guilty if you choose to use the frozen pie shells. They're good and it's a real time saver. Stack your pie shells in the refrigerator, or leave them in the freezer until two hours before you're ready to use them.

Prepare your piecrust by separating one egg. Throw the white away and whip up the yolk with a fork. Brush the bottom and inside of your piecrust. Prick it all over with a fork and bake it in a 350 F. degree oven for 5 minutes. Take it out and let it cool on a wire rack or a cold stovetop while you mix up the custard. If "bubbles" have formed in the oven, immediately prick them with a fork to let out the steam.

80

The Holiday Quiche Custard:

5 eggs
1½ cups heavy whipping cream ***

***If you and your guests are on a diet, you can substitute Half 'n Half for the heavy cream, but it won't be as good!*

Hannah's 2nd Note: You can do this by hand with a whisk, or use an electric mixer, your choice.

Combine the eggs with the cream and whisk them *(or beat them with an electric mixer)* until they're a uniform color. When they're thoroughly mixed, pour them into a pitcher and set it in the refrigerator until you're ready to assemble the rest of your quiche. You may notice that you're not adding any salt, pepper, or other seasoning at this point. You'll do that when you assemble the quiche.

Hannah's 3rd Note: You can mix up the custard ahead of time and store it in the refrigerator for up to 24 hours. When you're ready to assemble your quiches, all you have to do is whisk it smooth and pour it out from the pitcher.

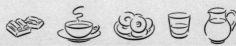

81

The Holiday Quiche Filling:

1 red bell pepper, washed, seeded and diced
   into bite-sized pieces
1 green bell pepper, washed, seeded and
   diced into bite-sized pieces
1 cup herb-seasoned stuffing mix ***
1 cup grated Swiss cheese *(I used Jarlsberg)*
1 cup grated Monterey Jack cheese
$\frac{1}{2}$ teaspoon onion powder
$\frac{1}{2}$ teaspoon salt
$\frac{1}{4}$ teaspoon black pepper *(freshly ground is
   best)*

****If you use the kind of stuffing mix that's made
of croutons, crush them a bit before you measure
out one cup. The stuffing mix is necessary because it
soaks up the liquid given off by the bell peppers as
they bake.*

**Hannah's 4th Note: This is the vegetarian quiche
I served at Mother's Regency Romance Club Christmas luncheon. If you'd rather have it with meat, just
sprinkle a cup of cubed ham, chicken, or turkey over
the bell peppers when you assemble it. Norman
wants me to try it with anchovies. Norman LOVES
anchovies.**

Spread the red and green pepper pieces out in the bottom of your pastry-lined pie pan.

Sprinkle the cup of herb-seasoned stuffing mix over the top of the peppers.

Spread the grated Swiss cheese and the grated Monterey Jack cheese on top of the stuffing mix.

(Put the meat in here if you want to use it, or the anchovies.)

Sprinkle on the onion powder and the salt.

Grind the pepper on top.

Put a drip pan under your pie plate. *(I line a jelly-roll pan with foil and use that.)* This will catch any spills that might occur when you fill your quiche with the custard mixture.

Give your custard mixture a good whisk. Then pour it over the top of your quiche, filling it about half way.

Open the oven, pull out the rack and set your pie plate and drip pan on it. Pour in more custard mixture, stopping a quarter-inch short of the rim. Carefully push in the rack, and shut the oven door.

Bake your Holiday Quiche at 350 degrees F., for 50 to 60 minutes, or until the top is nicely browned and a knife inserted one-inch from the center comes out clean.

Let it cool for 15 to 30 minutes on a cold stovetop or a wire rack, and then cut and serve.

I think this quiche is better when it's warm, but Lisa says Herb likes it cold.

Chapter
Six

"This is really sweet of you, Norman," Hannah said, opening the back door of his car and placing the bags of cookies she'd prepared on the seat. Once she'd stashed the goodies, she got into the front seat and smiled. It was warm inside Norman's car. And warmth was a luxury in the winter in Minnesota. Even though Mike had fixed the heater on her cookie truck, it was still drafty and the cavernous space in the back was always cold in the winter months.

"I enjoy going places with you, Hannah." Norman backed out of the parking spot and headed down the alley that ran in back of Hannah's shop. "You know I like helping you investigate, and Doc Bennett's filling in for me for the rest of the day at the clinic."

Hannah glanced at Norman's profile as he drove down the alley and turned onto Third. He wasn't what any woman would call a heartthrob, but he *was* nice looking. It was his personality that catapulted him straight to the top of the handsome category. Her great grandmother Elsa used to say, *Handsome is as handsome does*, and it was true. Norman was kind, intelligent, sweet, and caring. They were qualities that Hannah held dear, right along with Norman's sense of humor, his kindness, and his willingness to indulge her chocolate-loving soul.

The afternoon sun sparkling on the snow that had fallen the previous night was so bright that Hannah almost wished she'd worn sunglasses. And then, before she could do more than think it, Norman had opened the glove compartment and was handing her a pair.

"Here," he said. "It's really bright out today."

Hannah slipped on the sunglasses. "So how long have you been doing it?"

"Doing *what?*"

"Reading my mind."

Norman waggled his eyebrows at her. "As kindred souls we share our thoughts in a way that others can only envy."

"Very poetic!"

"I know. It must be a reaction to all that flowery language at the Regency luncheon."

"That could be. But you *did* read my mind."

"Not really. I just noticed that you were squinting, that's all."

Norman clicked on his turn signal and they made a left turn at the bright green shamrock-shaped sign that spoke of Cyril's heritage. Hannah's truck hadn't required Cyril's services for several months and she hadn't had occasion to visit the garage. During this time, a new building had been erected between the huge corrugated shed that housed the used cars Cyril sold, and the garage itself. The garage was a fairly large structure containing four work bays in the rear and gas pumps out in front. The new building was attached to the side of the garage and there was a bright green sign just under the roof that read, SHAMROCK LIMOS. The building had a door that was presently rolled up and Hannah could see three sparkling white limousines parked inside.

"Looks like Cyril is branching out," Norman said,

pulling past the pumps and parking at the side of the new building. "The last time I was out here, he had just one limo."

"Business must be good," Hannah said, reaching in back to select one of the bags while Norman got out and walked around the car to open her door. They had arrived at an unspoken arrangement over two years ago. Norman knew that Hannah could open her own car door, but he liked to do it for her. And although Hannah bristled slightly, sitting there and waiting for him to do something she could perfectly well do for herself, she let him do it because it pleased him.

Norman took her arm and Hannah let him. This time it wasn't an unspoken arrangement; it was necessity on both of their parts. It was icy and their chances of falling were greatly diminished if they hung on to one another. Slipping and sliding, they made it around the side of the building and through the door to the garage.

Cyril was sitting behind the counter, talking to one of his mechanics. Hannah knew he was a mechanic because everyone who worked at Murphy's Garage wore shamrock-green coveralls. Cyril gave them a wave to acknowledge them, said something about rotors, tolerances, and millimeters, and the mechanic hurried back into the first work bay.

"Hannah. Norman." Cyril gave them a smile that made his eyes crinkle. He was what Hannah's dad would have called "black Irish." His hair was curly black and his eyes, under dark expressive brows, were such a deep blue color, the pupils were just barely distinguishable from the irises. "Something wrong with the cookie truck?"

"Not a thing," Hannah answered, handing him the bag of cookies. "These are for you. They're Christmas Date Cookies."

Cyril looked pleased as he accepted the bag. "Thanks,

Hannah. They're my favorites. What did I do to deserve cookies?"

"It's not what you did. It's what you're going to do."

"Uh-oh." Cyril gave a long sigh. "This must be about Wayne Bergstrom. I figured you'd hear about that fight we had sooner or later, and it looks like it's sooner. Who told you?"

"Two people," Hannah said and left it at that. It was a slight exaggeration, but it all depended on how you counted. Lisa had told her about the fight, but Herb had been the one to tell Lisa.

"So you think I killed Wayne?"

"Of course not!" Hannah shook her head. "You couldn't have done it. You're Irish."

"What does *that* have to do with it?"

"Your heritage is part of your personality. My dad was part Irish and he explained it to me. If an Irishman's mad enough to kill somebody, he doesn't lie in wait like some coward and attack when nobody's looking. He takes his enemy on fair and square in front of everybody in town."

Cyril threw back his head and laughed. "Your dad was part Irish, all right! He told you a whopper and you bought it."

"I guess I did," Hannah said with a laugh, glad that the story she'd made up on the spur of the moment had worked to relax Cyril. "But you didn't lay in wait and kill Wayne last night, did you?"

"No. I was mad enough to do it, but I had another sort of revenge in mind."

"What was that?" Norman asked.

"I was going to undercut him and sabotage his limo business. It probably would have bankrupted me before it was over, but it would have been worth it."

It took a few minutes and some cogent questions for the story to come out, but at last they had the facts. The reason Cyril had bought two more white limousines was that Wayne had promised to use his limo service for the weddings he booked through the new Wonderful Weddings department at the store.

"I thought it was all set. Wayne promised to use Shamrock Limos, and I promised I'd get two more cars."

"But Wayne reneged on his promise?" Hannah guessed.

"That's right!" Cyril's eyes glittered and both Hannah and Norman could tell that he was still steaming about it. "Wayne decided to start his *own* limo service. And since we didn't have a signed contract, I couldn't prove he'd agreed to use Shamrock Limos."

"That would have burned me up, too!" Norman said, and then he turned to Hannah. "Can we take Cyril off the suspect list?"

"Just as soon as he tells us his alibi." Hannah pulled out her steno pad and flipped to the suspect page. "Did you watch Wayne play Santa last night?" she asked Cyril.

"Sure did. And right after that, I went out to take a look at Florence Evans's van. She said it was cutting in and out, and she didn't want to get stuck on the way home."

"And that was in the parking lot?"

"No, she parked in front in the loading zone. She told me she figured she was entitled since she was carrying all the Christmas stockings the Women's Club stuffed for the kids at the Home."

"Works for me," Hannah said. "As far as we know, Wayne left by the back door and went around the side of the building to the path that leads to the parking lot. Did you see him?"

Cyril shook his head. "I must've been busy working on Florence's car. I fixed the problem, it was a loose spark plug, and then we went back inside."

"And you were with Florence the whole time?"

"Most of it. She went back in a couple of times to bring me coffee, but she wasn't gone more than five minutes. When we got back inside, Sally was telling everybody the buffet was open and we got in line with Brigit."

Hannah and Norman said their good-byes and left the warmth of the garage. A light snow had started to fall and as they walked to Norman's car, Hannah was thoughtful. Cyril had an alibi, but it wasn't exactly a get-out-of-jail-free card. Even if Florence substantiated his story, it was possible that Cyril had seized his opportunity and killed Wayne in the few minutes that Florence was inside getting coffee for him.

"Where to?" Norman asked, once he'd settled Hannah in the passenger seat and climbed in behind the wheel.

"The mall?" Hannah phrased her answer in the form of a question, something that had always driven her a little bit crazy when she watched *Jeopardy*. "I'd like to check with Wayne's brother-in-law Cory if he's in today. He's head of the Wonderful Weddings department."

"Fine with me. I need to pick up something for Mother anyway. So far, all I've got is a book and that's not enough for Christmas. Maybe you can help me choose something."

Hannah was about to make a sarcastic crack about the blind leading the blind when she remembered something Delores had told her. "I think you should buy her a silk wreath."

"You mean . . . a Christmas wreath?"

"No, a flower wreath. Delores just bought one made from dried pink roses for her guest bath and Carrie thought it was beautiful. She said she might look for one for herself, but she wanted hers to be blue hydrangeas."

"I'm not really big on flower names. Are hydrangeas the velvety looking blue flowers clumped together on a stalk?"

"Good description! But hydrangeas aren't just blue.

They can also be pink, depending on the pH value of the soil."

"That's interesting," Norman said, and Hannah knew he was one of the few guys who would think so.

"Grandma Ingrid liked the pink ones," Hannah went on. "She used to take me outside to garden with her and I remember helping her dig around the hydrangea bushes so she could sprinkle in some chemical."

"It was probably lime. She would have used aluminum sulfate or sulfur if she'd wanted the blue. Maybe I should plant some hydrangeas. They're like nature's litmus strips."

"Red cabbage."

"What?"

"Red cabbage really *is* nature's litmus strip. I noticed it when I tested Minnie Holtzmeier's recipe for Scandinavian Red Cabbage for the Lake Eden cookbook."

"Now why doesn't this surprise me?" Norman glanced at her, gave her a quick smile, and then quickly returned his attention to the road. He'd been in Minnesota long enough to know that it was dangerous to get distracted when you were driving in the winter. "What, exactly, did you notice?" he asked her.

"I shredded some red cabbage in the food processor and kept it in some cold tap water in the cooler until I was ready to use it. By that time it was bluish purple instead of red. Tap water is slightly alkaline, isn't it?"

"Usually. I'm almost sure it is here in Lake Eden."

"That's what I thought. When I'd finished gathering the other ingredients, I drained the red cabbage. The water was fairly blue by that time. Then I added the dry red wine the recipe called for and the cabbage turned red again."

"The red wine was acidic." Norman gave her another quick glance. "You would have made a good scientist, Hannah. You're very observant."

"And you're not," Hannah smiled to take the sting out of her words.

"What makes you think I'm not observant?"

"Because we just passed the last entrance to the mall and now you have to look for a place to turn around and drive back."

CHRISTMAS DATE COOKIES

Do not preheat oven quite yet.
This dough must chill before
baking.

2 cups chopped pitted dates *(You can buy chopped dates, or sprinkle whole pitted dates with a quarter-cup flour and then chop them in a food processor. I couldn't find chopped dates, and a 10-ounce by weight container of whole pitted dates ended up being exactly 2 cups when I chopped them in my food processor.)*

$\frac{3}{4}$ cup boiling water

1 cup melted butter *(2 sticks, $\frac{1}{2}$ pound)*

2 cups white *(granulated)* sugar

2 teaspoons baking soda

$\frac{1}{2}$ teaspoon salt

4 beaten eggs *(just beat them up in a glass with a fork)*

2 cups semi-sweet chocolate chips *(that's a 12-ounce package)*

$5\frac{1}{2}$ cups flour *(don't sift—pack it down in the cup when you measure it)*

$\frac{1}{2}$ cup white *(granulated)* sugar in a small bowl for later

93

Pour the boiling water over the chopped dates, give them a stir with a fork, and set them aside on the counter to cool.

Melt the butter in a microwave-safe bowl *(I used a pint Pyrex measuring cup)* for 90 seconds on HIGH. Set the melted butter on the counter to cool.

In the bowl of an electric mixer, combine the white sugar, baking soda, salt and eggs. Beat well. *(If you don't have an electric mixer, don't worry. You can do this by hand, but it'll take a bit of effort.)*

Feel the bowl with the date mixture. If you can hold it comfortably in your hands, add it now and mix thoroughly. If it's too hot, let it cool another couple of minutes.

Once the dates are mixed in, add the chocolate chips to your bowl and mix. Then add the melted butter and mix thoroughly.

Add the flour in half-cup increments *(that'll be 11 half-cups)* beating after each addition. Take the bowl from the mixer, give it a final stir by hand, cover it with plastic wrap, and place it in the refrigerator for at least 2 hours to chill. *(Overnight is fine, too.)*

When you're ready to bake, preheat the oven to 325 degrees F., rack in the middle position. *(Yes, that's 325 degrees F.—most of my cookies bake at 350 degrees F., but these are best if they bake slowly at a lower heat.)*

Roll the dough into walnut-sized balls with your hands. This dough may be sticky, so roll only enough for the cookies you plan to bake immediately and then return the bowl to the refrigerator.

Roll the dough balls in the bowl of white sugar and place them on a greased *(or sprayed with nonstick cooking spray)* cookie sheet, 12 to a standard sheet. Flatten them slightly with your hand so they won't fall off on the way to the oven.

Bake at 325 degrees F. for 10 minutes. Cool on the cookie sheet for a minute or two and then remove the cookies to a wire rack to finish cooling.

Yield: 8 to 10 dozen great cookies. You can freeze any extras for up to 3 months in freezer bags.

Hannah's Note: All the Murphy men are crazy about Christmas Date Cookies. Michelle said she baked a whole batch one day when Lonnie was visit-

ing her at Macalister. They ate about a dozen and then they ran out of milk. Michelle dashed to the corner grocery to buy some and when she got back, every single cookie was gone!

Chapter Seven

The shadows of the pine trees were beginning to lengthen and cant toward the east as Hannah and Norman turned in at the Tri-County Mall. It was two-thirty on a Saturday afternoon and it seemed that everyone who lived in the Tri-County area was out at the mall shopping.

"I've never seen it this crowded before," Hannah said, eyeing the rows of cars in the parking structure.

"Only fifteen shopping days before Christmas."

Hannah turned to him in surprise. "I didn't know you counted things like that."

"I don't. There was a big sign at the entrance."

"I didn't notice."

"I know. So *now* who's the observant one?"

"Neither one of us. Or maybe both of us. Whatever." Hannah grinned and shrugged it off. "I think we're going to have to park in the back forty and walk in."

"The back forty?"

"It dates back to the days when there were large family farms. The back forty was the section of land farthest away from the farmhouse."

"Oh. Like the toolies."

"Right."

Norman turned down another row and braked to a

stop when he encountered a driver parked in the middle of the garage, effectively blocking traffic from both directions.

"There's one in every parking lot," Hannah commented. "She's waiting for that couple to load all their packages in the trunk and she's determined to get their space."

"And she's going to make everyone behind her wait until she does," Norman added.

"Makes you wish for an accordion car."

It took Norman a moment, but then he nodded. "One with collapsible sides?"

"You got it. Then we could skin right past her, idle in front of her and snag that parking spot before she could get it. But they don't make accordion cars, so we're stuck. Do you want a cookie while we wait?"

"Sure. Do you have anything in chocolate?"

Hannah laughed. "I've got four different kinds and three are chocolate. Do you want Angel Pillows, Devil's Food Cookies, or Chocolate Candy Cane Cookies?"

"Hold on. I've never had a Chocolate Candy Cane Cookie. What are those?"

"They're rich dark chocolate cookies with a sugary candy cane topping."

"Sounds great! I'd like to try one of those."

Hannah turned around and reached into the backseat for the correct bag. "I brought another dozen of these in one of my signature bags for Cory." She pulled out two cookies and handed one to Norman. "Here you go."

The cookies were exactly as she'd described them, and the contrast of the sweet, dark chocolate with the tongue-tingling peppermint coating was deliciously startling.

"These are your best cookies," Norman said, finishing his first cookie and dipping in the bag for a second.

"I thought the Old Fashioned Sugar Cookies were your favorites."

"They were until I tasted these."

"Fickle," Hannah teased him.

"If I am, it's understandable. My favorite cookie is the cookie I'm eating at the moment." Norman stepped on the gas as the driver ahead of them finally pulled into her parking spot and ceased being a roadblock. "I feel lucky. Let's try that first row again."

Norman's lucky feeling turned out to be a premonition of good things to come. As they turned down the first row, a van parked right next to the entrance backed out. Norman quickly nabbed the spot and before you could say *Jolly Old Saint Nicholas*, Hannah and Norman were stepping through the double entrance doors and into the mall.

"Whoa," Hannah said, stopping in her tracks.

"This way, Hannah." Norman pulled her out of the mainstream of traffic and over to the side. "What's wrong?"

It was a rare occasion for Hannah. She was completely at a loss for words. Strains of loud Christmas carols were assaulting her ears, the combined scents of popcorn and potpourri were overpowering, and the voices of hundreds of holiday shoppers created a roaring buzz in her head.

"Are you okay?" Noman asked her.

"I will be. It's just too much to take in all at once." Hannah eyed the milling crowds of people, the flashing colored lights, and the Christmas decorations. Combined as a class that she called *holiday madness*, they seemed to be occupying every available foot of wall and floor space. "All these people. All these flashing lights and decorations. All this noise. Christmas is breaking out all over!"

Norman laughed. "You don't do much Christmas

shopping at the mall, do you?" he said, and it was more a statement than a question.

"Not if I can avoid it. If Claire doesn't have what I need at her dress shop, and I can't get it from the drugstore, I pick up the phone and order it from a catalogue. Maybe we should just forget it, Norman. I'm not sure if Cory's here today anyway. I can always call him at home tonight."

"No way. We drove all the way out here and at least we can check to see if he's there." Norman reached out to take her arm. "Just hang on to me and I'll get you to Bergstrom's."

"But really, Norman . . . maybe we should just . . ." Hannah's protests died a quick death as Norman pulled her forward and out into the Christmas mêlée.

It was exactly as advertised; shopping was better in Bergstrom's. It had nothing to do with the quality of the merchandise or the availability of helpful, well-informed salesclerks. The interior of the posh department store was quiet, almost hushed compared to the hubbub outside in the mall. There were considerably less people in Bergstrom's and Hannah thought she knew why. The exclusive department store was expensive and the words "clearance," "blowout sale," and "rock bottom price" had never passed the lips of the staff. Bergstrom's was not the place to shop if you were looking for a Christmas bargain. Everyone including Hannah knew that.

"Better?" Norman asked, leading Hannah toward the escalator in the central part of the store.

"Much better. We'd better find a clerk and ask where the wedding department is."

"I know where it is. It's on the third floor, right across from the travel agency."

"You've been there?" Hannah was so surprised she almost stumbled as she stepped onto the escalator.

"No, but I've used the travel agency. They booked my flight to the dental convention in Seattle last year. There was a wall with a sign on it that said, MORE PROGRESS AT BERGSTROM'S. PLEASE EXCUSE OUR DUST. When I asked one of the workers what they were building, he said they were putting in a wedding department."

Hannah felt vaguely disappointed as they rode up to the third floor. She wasn't sure why. She was glad that Norman hadn't made plans for a wedding when he'd asked her to marry him, plans that he would have had to cancel when she'd decided not to marry anyone quite yet. At the same time, it would have shown his commitment and proven to her that his proposal hadn't been just a gut reaction to the fact that Mike had proposed first. Telling herself she had no right to want such a commitment when she was unwilling to reciprocate, she stepped off the escalator, turned toward the wedding department, and came face to face with a pair of giant gold wedding bells tied together with a giant gold ribbon that said, WONDERFUL WEDDINGS.

"This is it," Norman said, quite unnecessarily.

Hannah eyed the huge bells that adorned the tall gold archway leading into the department. "Pretty fancy!"

"Shall we?" Norman held out his arm.

Oh boy! Hannah muttered under her breath as she took it. If anyone they knew saw them walking into the wedding department arm in arm, tongues would wag all over Lake Eden.

"Hannah!"

Hannah turned to see Cory Reynolds coming toward them. "Hi, Cory. I'm so sorry about your brother-in-law."

"So am I," Cory said. "Wayne was a wonderful man. Melinda can't seem to stop crying. She tried to come in today, to say a few words to the staff, but I made her stay home."

"Very wise," Norman said.

"Thank you. But please let's not mar this happy occasion with sad tidings. How may I help you two today?"

Hannah was stunned for a moment, but then she recovered her voice. "Actually . . . it's not quite like that. Norman and I aren't here for a wedding. We came because we really need to ask you some questions about Wayne. Is there somewhere we can talk in private?"

"Yes. Of course." Cory turned and led the way down a hallway to several rooms. He chose one, opened the door, and motioned them inside. "Will this do?"

"It's perfect," Hannah said, admiring the comfortable look the decorator had achieved. The room resembled a living room with comfortable furniture, some tasteful flower prints on the walls, and a tray containing bottled water and an ice bucket.

"Water?" Cory asked them.

"No thanks," Hannah answered for both of them.

"I hear you're looking into Wayne's death," Cory opened the conversation as he took a bottle of water for himself.

"Yes, unofficially," Hannah made that clear. "It's just that I saw Wayne only minutes before he died and then I found him like that."

Cory shivered slightly. "I know. All night I kept thinking that if I'd walked out to the parking lot with him, I might have prevented it."

"Or you might have been killed right along with your brother-in-law," Norman pointed out.

Cory was silent for moment. He was clearly thinking it over. "You're right. *What ifs* don't do any good. I didn't go out to the parking lot with Wayne, so I'll never know what would have happened if I had."

"We need to ask you about Cyril Murphy," Hannah

said, taking charge. "Did you know that Wayne promised Cyril he'd use Shamrock Limo Service for weddings booked through your department, and he reneged on his promise?"

"Wayne said it was all a giant misunderstanding, and I know he talked to Larry about it."

"Larry?" Hannah asked.

"Larry Helms. He's been Wayne's lawyer for years."

Hannah filed the name of the lawyer away for future reference. "It sounds like more than a misunderstanding to me. I heard they were yelling at each other."

"I *know* they were yelling at each other."

Hannah stared at him in surprise. "How do you know that?"

"I gave Wayne a ride to the garage and I was sitting in the car waiting for him. I saw the whole thing. They were yelling at each other and waving their fists. I thought I was going to have to break up a fight, but then Wayne stalked away and came back to the car."

"Do you think there was bad blood between Cyril and Wayne?" Hannah asked.

"You mean . . . do I think Cyril Murphy might have killed Wayne over that limo thing?"

"Yes. That's exactly what I mean."

Cory propped his elbows on the table and covered his eyes with his hands. It was a contemplative pose and he thought about it for a long moment. Then he lowered his hands. "It could have happened that way."

"Okay. That's exactly what I wanted to know." Hannah stood up and Norman followed suit.

"So . . . no wedding?" Cory asked, giving a small smile.

"Not yet," Norman answered. "But we'll let you know when. And where."

Hannah shot him a quick look and decided to let it go. This wasn't the time to discuss the risk of assuming too much.

"These are for you," she said, producing the bag of cookies she'd earmarked for Cory. "I thought you might be able to use a little chocolate. The endorphins will make you feel better."

Cory gave her a smile that wavered slightly. "Thanks, Hannah. That was really sweet of you. I'll give some to Melinda."

"That's okay. We've got some for her, too." Norman spoke up quickly. "Do you think we could drop them off? We wouldn't stay, of course. We know how devastating this whole thing must be for her."

Hannah shot a quick glance at Norman. He didn't take the lead in an interrogation often, but when he did, he was usually right.

"Yes," she said, quickly adopting Norman's vernacular. "We thought Melinda might appreciate a tangible expression of friendship and comfort."

Cory hesitated for a long moment. "Well . . . I think that would be very kind of you, provided you didn't stay too long. She's exhausted, you know. Poor Melinda is still suffering from the shock of losing her husband."

"Of course, the poor dear!" Hannah said, pouring it on with both pitchers. The flowery language was difficult to master and she wished she'd taken lessons from Digger Gibson, Lake Eden's mortician and funeral director. "Not to worry. We'll just drop the cookies off and leave."

"That's fine. Thank you for being so understanding. I'll give Melinda a call and tell her to expect you."

CHOCOLATE CANDY CANE COOKIES

Preheat your oven to 350 degrees F.,
rack in the middle position.

Cookie Dough:

4 squares unsweetened baking chocolate
   (4 ounces)
$1\frac{1}{4}$ cups *($2\frac{1}{2}$ sticks, 10-ounces)* chilled butter
2 cups white *(granulated)* sugar
2 beaten eggs *(just whip them up in a glass
   with a fork)*
2 teaspoons baking soda
$\frac{1}{2}$ teaspoon salt
$\frac{1}{3}$ cup corn syrup
2 Tablespoons water
1 Tablespoon *(3 teaspoons)* vanilla
4 cups flour *(pack it down in the cup when
   you measure it)*

Topping:

$\frac{1}{4}$ cup sugar
$\frac{1}{4}$ cup finely crushed mint candy canes *(about
   12 mini candy canes)*

Melt the butter and the chocolate squares together, mix them thoroughly, and set them on the
counter to cool. You can do this in a microwave-safe
bowl for 3 minutes on HIGH, or in a pan over low

heat on the stovetop. *(I do it by microwave in a Pyrex one-quart measuring cup.)*

Hannah's 1st Note: If you like a strong peppermint flavor, use 2 teaspoons of vanilla and one teaspoon of peppermint extract instead of the Tablespoon (3 teaspoons) of vanilla extract that's called for in the recipe.

In a large bowl, combine the white sugar and the eggs. Beat the mixture until it's a uniform pale yellow color.

Add the baking soda and salt. Mix them in well.

Mix in the corn syrup, water, and the vanilla.

Hannah's 2nd Note: Whenever I measure something sticky like corn syrup, maple syrup, or honey, I spray my measuring cup with Pam or another nonstick cooking spray first. Then the sticky stuff slides right out and it's easy to wash the cup.

Cup your hands around the bowl with the butter and chocolate. If it's cool enough to hold comfortably, add it to your bowl now and mix it in. If it's not, let it cool a bit more and then add it.

Add half of the flour to your bowl. *(That's 2 cups.)* Mix it in. Then add the remaining flour *(that's 2 cups)* and mix thoroughly.

Give the bowl a final stir by hand, cover it with plastic wrap, and let it rest on the counter while you spray your cookie sheets with Pam or another non-stick cooking spray and crush your candy canes.

While your oven is preheating, crush your candy canes.

Hannah's 3rd Note: I unwrap my candy canes, stick them in a heavy plastic bag, and hit them with a little rubber mallet I got from Dad's hardware store before we sold it. Lisa says she does hers almost the same way, except she puts a board over the bag and bangs on the board with a hammer. Any way you want to crush them is fine—just be really careful with hammers and mallets if you have ceramic tile counters. You can also break them in pieces with your hands and then pulverize them in a food processor with the steel blade. (Read your instruction manual to make sure the food processor you have will handle a task like this.)

I probably shouldn't tell you this, but last summer when Andrea, Michelle, and I were staying out at Mother's lake cottage, we couldn't find a hammer, so I put the candy canes in a triple layer of plastic bags and Michelle backed over them several times with the car. (It worked.)

Measure out a quarter cup of finely crushed candy canes and place them in a small bowl. Add a quarter cup white granulated sugar and mix it all up with a fork. *(The goal is to get an equal amount of sugar and crushed candy cane on each of the dough balls that you'll make.)*

Roll the dough into one-inch diameter balls with your hands. This dough may be sticky, so roll only enough for the cookies you plan to bake immediately and then return the bowl to the refrigerator.

Roll the dough balls in the bowl of topping and place them on the greased cookie sheets, 12 balls to a standard sheet. Flatten them slightly with a metal spatula or the heel of your impeccably clean hand.

Bake the cookies at 350 degrees F. for 8 to 10 minutes. Cool them on the cookie sheet for a minute and then remove the cookies to a wire rack to complete cooling. *(If you leave them on the cookie sheet for more than a minute, they may stick. It's not the sugar—it's the crushed candy canes. They melt and then stick to your baking sheets.)*

Yield: approximately 8 dozen yummy cookies

Chapter Eight

The special elevator that carried them up to the penthouse over Bergstrom's department store had been opulent with gold-tone mirrors and a pink velvet bench that ran around its perimeter. Hannah had never seen an elevator with seating before, and she was even more impressed when it rose to the fifth floor in one smooth motion and the doors whispered open to reveal even more luxury.

The foyer they stepped into could have graced any one of several five-star hotels. Two walls were covered with a silvery silken material that matched the pillows on the pink and light green silk couches. Wing chairs in light blue silk were grouped around oval-shaped gold tables with mirrored tops, their beveled edges trimmed in gold. The other two walls were made entirely of glass, affording a spectacular view of the pine-dotted snowscape outside.

"Holy Hannah!" Hannah breathed, taking her own name in vain. "This is even better than Teensy's Penthouse!"

"Better than *what?*"

"Teensy's Penthouse. Tracey put it on her Christmas wish list. It's the hot item this year and all the stores I called are sold out. There was one that had it, but they wanted a hundred and twenty dollars. And that was without Teensy!"

"And Teensy is a doll?"

"She's not *just* a doll," Hannah corrected him. "Teensy is a fully articulated reproduction of a female child in miniature. She has her own series of children's books and DVDs, and there's a Saturday morning cartoon. She's a little rich girl with a fabulous wardrobe and all sorts of places they call *environments* like ski chalets, thoroughbred horse farms, and ocean cottages. Teensy lives in the lap of luxury."

Norman smiled. "Correction. Teensy's *manufacturer* lives in the lap of luxury."

"Sir? Madam?" The same maid who'd answered the door and taken their coats addressed them from the doorway. "Mrs. Bergstrom will see you now. Please follow me."

Hannah and Norman were led past priceless artwork and more ornate furniture as they traversed the wide carpeted hallway to an arched doorway near the rear of the penthouse.

"Through here, please," the maid said, opening the arched door and stepping aside. "Mrs. Bergstrom wishes to meet with you in the indoor garden. She designed it shortly after her marriage and it's her favorite spot to entertain. Just follow the path to the seating area by the fountain."

As Hannah and Norman entered the warm, humid space, they gave nearly simultaneous gasps of surprise. It was a tropical paradise filled with exotic plants, ferns, and even trees. Flowers in riotous colors were blooming everywhere, enough to keep a florist in business for the whole winter season.

"Wow!" Hannah said, turning to Norman. "The only other time I get to see this much green in the winter is on St. Patrick's Day. This is just like Mother's *orangery*."

"Your mother's what?"

"*Orangery*. Mansions in England had them during the Regency period. It was a solarium, an indoor green-house, with all sorts of exotic plants, fruit trees, and flowers."

"I think this probably qualifies," Norman said, gazing around him. "It's like a jungle in here. Or maybe a rain forest. I'm not that well acquainted with the difference."

"It's paradise," Hannah said, "especially in the dead of winter." It was true. Melinda's solarium was a paradise requiring only constant temperature and humidity monitoring, and expert gardening. To add to the sensory delights, the indoor garden had two walls and a ceiling made of glass. The frigid winter scene outside was a startling juxtaposition to the lush tropical illusion inside.

"This way," Norman indicated a path made of smooth round stones. "She said there was a fountain and I can hear falling water."

Hannah looked down at the stones on the walkway as she followed Norman. She figured they were probably fabricated. As far as she knew, stones were like snow-flakes. If you made it your life's work, you might find two that were exactly the same, but you certainly wouldn't be lucky enough to find the thousands of identical pebbles it had taken to line Melinda Bergstrom's solarium walkway.

Hannah hadn't seen Melinda recently, but the former-model-turned-wife hadn't changed one iota. She was seated in a rattan peacock chair by the fountain and she was just as svelte and impeccably groomed as she'd been when she'd strolled down the runway. She was wearing what Hannah assumed was a designer pantsuit made of black velvet that set off her light ash-blond hair and her peaches-and-cream complexion. Her feet were encased in black sandals with stiletto heels, something that gave

Hannah pause. Would a grieving widow wear stiletto heels? Perhaps, if she happened to be a former model. But wouldn't a grieving widow who'd been crying all night and day have swollen eyelids and blotchy cheeks? She'd have to ask Andrea if there was a way to hide prolonged tears with makeup.

"Mrs. Bergstrom." Norman stepped forward to take Melinda's outstretched hand. "We're so sorry for your loss."

Hannah took her cue from Norman. "This must be a very difficult time for you."

"Oh, it is. I can't seem to stop blaming myself. I should have gone with Wayne instead of keeping my appointment with Pierre."

"Pierre from *Le Petit Salon*?" Hannah asked, naming the exclusive beauty shop downstairs in the mall.

"That's right. Pierre came up to style my hair at seventhirty, right after they closed the salon. He was still here when the deputies came to tell me that Wayne was . . . was . . ." Melinda gave a quavering sigh and her voice trailed off.

"I'm glad you had someone with you," Hannah said, filing away the information she'd been given for later. "Cory probably told you, but Norman and I came up to bring you some of my Devil's Food Cookies. We thought maybe the chocolate might help to make you feel better."

"How sweet of you!" Melinda accepted the bag Hannah handed her and peeked inside. "They smell so good."

"They're very popular down at The Cookie Jar. Have one and tell me if you like them."

"I really shouldn't. So many calories. You make them with real butter?"

"Yes." Of course she made them with real butter.

Minnesota was a dairy state and no scientist had yet found a perfect substitute for butter.

"Maybe I'll have one tonight after dinner." Melinda folded the bag closed and set it on the rattan table in front of her chair. "Do sit down. Would you care for coffee? Or tea?"

Hannah shook her head. "No, thank you. I'd like to use your powder room, though, if that's all right."

Norman shot her a startled look. He knew she'd gone off to the ladies' room shortly before they'd caught the elevator to the Bergstrom penthouse.

"Certainly. I'll ring for Emily. She can show you the way."

"There's no need to call your maid." Hannah stood up. "Just give me directions and I'll find it."

"Turn left when you leave here, and then turn to the right when you get to the next hallway. There's a guest bath three doors down on your left."

As Hannah walked away, she heard Norman begin to praise Melinda's design for the solarium. Norman might not know exactly what she was up to, but Hannah knew he'd keep Melinda busy talking until she got back.

Instead of following Melinda's instructions, Hannah turned in the opposite direction. She passed a huge master suite and noticed a large piece of mahogany furniture against one wall. It was a valet stand, the sort of standing rack that held a man's hat, suit, and shoes. This piece of furniture was a quadruple valet stand with an upholstered bench in the center. Each side was flanked by two valet stands, one raised as high as the mirror in back of the bench, and the one at normal height. The massive piece of furniture was decorated with carvings of stag, and deer, and moose. It was the most magnificent piece of furniture Hannah had ever seen.

Hannah paused, letting her eyes roam the room. This master bedroom was larger than her whole condo. There were walk-in closets on either side of the room and the doors were open. Hannah spotted men's clothing in one closet, and absolutely nothing in the other. Had Melinda moved out of the master bedroom, unable to bear the loneliness of the suite she'd shared with her husband?

Afraid she might be caught staring for too long, Hannah moved on down the hallway. She turned the corner and passed another bedroom with an open door. This one was obviously Cory's. There was a shirt hanging just inside the door. It was in a see-through dry cleaner's bag and she recognized the distinctive gold and silver shirt that Cory had worn the previous evening.

Hannah walked on to the next room. The door was ajar and she made it even more so. This was a woman's bedroom. There were fresh flowers on the ornate dresser, and another set of see-through dry cleaner bags containing party dresses and women's suits. Hannah was about to go on to greener pastures when something she spied turned this room into a shade of emerald she couldn't resist.

It was a photo album, sitting on a table by the window. Photos could be revealing, and Hannah wanted to take a quick peek. If a guest was staying here with Melinda and Cory, she might have information about why Wayne was murdered. There was only one way to tell who that guest was. Hannah had to get a look at the photo album before Melinda's maid came in search of the wayward visitor who had missed the guest bathroom and was in some other part of the penthouse.

Hannah glanced up and down the hallway. No one was in the immediate vicinity. She knew she was taking a chance, but she ducked in the open door and hurried to the table with the album.

The photo album had initials on the front in fancy gold script. The letters were so stylized that they were difficult to read, but Hannah was almost positive that they were M. A. A.

In the space of no more than a heartbeat, she opened the album and looked inside. It was a family album. There was a wedding with people Hannah didn't recognize. And then there was a baby in a baptismal gown. The father holding her looked proud and happy and the mother, who was standing at his side, looked a lot like Melinda Reynolds Bergstrom!

She was taking a chance standing here snooping, but there was no way she could squelch her curiosity. Hannah flipped through the pages, gazing at pictures of a small girl being steadied by her dad on a hobbyhorse, a preschooler riding a tricycle, and a little girl getting on a school bus, waving at whoever was holding the camera. There were pictures of family vacations with mom, dad, and daughter. One was taken at the Wisconsin Dells. Hannah recognized Storybook Gardens. There was another series of snapshots of Crystal Cave in Wisconsin. These were obviously Melinda's parents, and as Melinda grew older, Hannah recognized her. But where was Melinda's brother, Cory? He wasn't in any of these early family photos.

Hannah made a lightning quick search of the album. Christmas in grade school, no Cory. A family trip to Itasca to see the origin of the Mississippi River, no Cory. The family at Melinda's high school graduation, no Cory. There wasn't one single picture of Melinda's brother, and that was unusual to say the least!

Now for the room. Was it Melinda's? Hannah thought that it must be. There were several framed magazine covers that Melinda had posed for, hanging on the walls.

When had she moved here, next to Cory, instead of sharing the master suite with her husband? Hannah made a quick survey of the bedroom, gathering information. There was an archive-size stack of modeling magazines in the white wrought-iron bookcase against the far wall, and every inch of the closet was filled with clothing. There were personal items in the dresser. Hannah pulled out a few drawers to check the contents, and she noticed gardening books on another table, their pages marked by colored tabs. One gold-colored slipper peeked out from beneath the bed, and a silk dressing gown was tossed on a chair in the corner. It was an assumption, but Hannah made it without quibbling. This was Melinda's room and she'd been using it for quite a while.

Hannah's head snapped up as she heard footsteps. Someone was coming! She glanced around quickly, and headed straight for the bathroom. She shut the door just a heartbeat before she heard someone enter the bedroom.

"Miss Swensen?" It was a voice Hannah recognized. Emily the maid was looking for her. "Are you in here, Miss Swensen?"

"I'm in the bathroom," Hannah answered, flushing the toilet to add credence to her words. She was busted, caught red-handed, snooping in Melinda's bedroom. But why was Melinda sleeping in this bedroom when the master bedroom was right down the hall?

There was no time to think about that now. She was going to have to do some fast talking and hope that Emily would buy it. Hannah took a deep breath, opened the door, and gave the maid her brightest smile.

"I hope I found the right bathroom," she said. "I forgot whether Melinda said to go left, or right."

The maid looked suspicious for a brief moment and then she smiled. "You didn't, but that's all right. I'll escort you back to the garden. Mrs. Bergstrom paged me. She was afraid you were lost."

"I guess I was!" Hannah said. "But I'm glad you're here, Emily. I'd like to know if this is Melinda's bedroom."

"Oh! Well . . . yes. Yes, it is. But that's Mrs. Bergstrom's private business. I can't say anything more."

"Of course you can," Hannah interrupted her. "Your employer's dead, murdered in cold blood, and his widow doesn't seem to be grieving very much. Do you think she cares?"

"Not that one!" Emily said, shaking her head. "There's no love lost there and there wasn't on his side, either." She moved closer and continued in a whisper. "I'm almost sure Mr. Bergstrom was going to divorce her, not that he said anything to me, of course. But it wasn't a real marriage, if you know what I mean. And now . . . I'd better take you back before she comes after both of us."

Once back inside the tropical paradise, Hannah ignored Norman's curious glance, and sat down next to Melinda. They made polite conversation for a moment or two, and then Melinda took them on a tour of the most unusual and exotic flora that she had imported. Hannah admired brightly colored blooms that looked more artificial that real to her, smelled scents so heady they came close to making her sneeze, and pretended overwhelming interest in natural fertilizers and climate control. Then, mercifully, it was time to render their polite good-byes, repeat their condolences, and leave.

"Well?" Norman asked when they had boarded the elevator and were safely on their way down to the store.

"Well, what?"

"Well, why were you gone so long? And what did you discover?"

"No Cory," Hannah said, summing up her findings in two words.

"What?"

"I found Melinda's family photo album. There were lots of pictures of Melinda and her parents, but not one single picture of Cory. Maybe Cory had a big fight with his parents and they took all his pictures out of the photo album. Or maybe Melinda did, and she removed them. Or . . . maybe there was something wrong with Cory that he didn't get fixed until he left home."

"Like what?"

"Like a birthmark he had removed. Or maybe Cory was really Melinda's sister Corrine before she had the sex change."

Hannah started to laugh, but she quickly sobered as she thought of another possibility. "Or . . . maybe Cory isn't Melinda's brother and that's why he isn't in the family album."

"That's interesting," Norman commented. "Don't you want to know what I found out while you were gone?"

"Absolutely."

"I found out everything I really didn't need to know about exotic plants, flowers, and berries."

"Lucky you." Hannah stepped off the elevator and spotted the decorator dried wreath department, right where Delores had said it would be. "Let's go buy a peony wreath for your mother, and then go straight back to The Cookie Jar. I want to see if Lisa's hit pay dirt with her invisible waitress trick."

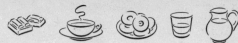

DEVIL'S FOOD COOKIES

Do not preheat oven—this dough
needs to chill.

2 cups flour
1¾ cups white *(granulated)* sugar
½ cup cocoa powder ***
½ teaspoon salt
1 teaspoon baking soda
½ cup melted butter *(1 stick, 1/4 pound)*
1 beaten egg *(just whip it up in a glass with a fork)*
½ cup extra strong coffee *(I brewed French Roast double strength)*

½ cup white sugar in a small bowl *(for later)*

*** *A Word of Warning about COCOA*
When cocoa is used in any of my recipes, make sure to use plain old American cocoa (I usually use Hershey's unsweetened cocoa.) There are many designer cocoas on the market. They're wonderful in their own right, but they won't work in my recipes. Make sure you don't buy cocoa mix, which has powdered milk and a sweetener added. Stay away from Dutch process cocoa—it has alkaline added. Also beware of cocoas that are mixed with ground chocolate or other flavorings. They won't work either. Things were simpler in my grandmother's day (and this Devil's Food Cookie is one of her recipes.)

If you're in doubt, check the ingredients that are listed on the container of cocoa. It should say "cocoa" and nothing else.

In a large bowl, mix the flour, sugar, cocoa powder, salt, and baking soda. Once these dry ingredients are combined, add the melted butter and mix thoroughly.

Add the beaten egg and mix thoroughly.

Add the strong coffee and mix thoroughly.

Chill the dough in the refrigerator for at least one hour. *(Overnight is fine, too.)*

When you're ready to bake, preheat the oven to 350 degrees F., rack in the middle position.

Roll the dough into one-inch diameter balls with your hands. This dough may be sticky, so roll only enough for the cookies you plan to bake immediately and then return the bowl to the refrigerator. Roll the dough balls in the bowl of white sugar and place them on a greased cookie sheet, 12 balls to a standard sheet. Flatten them slightly with the heel of your impeccably clean hand so they won't roll off on their way to the oven.

Bake at 350 degrees F. for 8 to 10 minutes. Cool on the cookie sheet for a minute or two and then remove the cookies to a wire rack to finish cooling. *(If you leave them on the cookie sheet for too long, they'll stick.)*

Hannah's Note: When Lisa wants to make these fancy for a cookie catering job, she drizzles them with fine horizontal lines of white powdered sugar icing. Then she mixes up chocolate powdered sugar icing and drizzles them with fine vertical lines. Here are the frostings she uses:

White Powdered Sugar Icing:

1 cup powdered *(confectioner's)* sugar
½ teaspoon vanilla
¼ teaspoon salt
2 to 4 Tablespoons light cream

Lisa's 1st Note: There's no need to sift the powdered sugar unless it has big lumps.

Line up your cookies, shoulder to shoulder, on a sheet of waxed paper.

Mix the powdered sugar with the vanilla and the salt. Add the light cream gradually until the frosting is the consistency you want.

Put the frosting into a plastic food storage bag. Twist the top closed and cut off one of the bottom corners to let out the frosting. Squeeze it out and drizzle it in fine lines over your cookies.

Chocolate Powdered Sugar Icing:

1 cup powdered *(confectioner's)* sugar
$\frac{1}{4}$ cup cocoa
$\frac{1}{2}$ teaspoon vanilla
$\frac{1}{4}$ teaspoon salt
3 to 6 Tablespoons light cream

Turn the paper with the partially frosted cookies 90 degrees so that the thin lines of chocolate frosting will crisscross the white frosting.

Mix the powdered sugar with the cocoa. Blend it in until the resulting mixture is a uniform color. Add the vanilla and the salt. Add the light cream gradually until the chocolate frosting is the consistency you want.

Put the chocolate frosting into a plastic food storage bag. Twist the top closed and cut off one of the bottom corners to let out the frosting. Squeeze it out and drizzle it in fine lines over your cookies.

Let the frosting dry thoroughly and then pack the cookies in single layers in a box lined with wax paper.

Lisa's 2nd Note: If you want to be really fancy, you can make powdered sugar icing with food coloring and use other extracts besides vanilla.

Chapter Nine

"It was all speculation," Lisa answered Hannah's query when they got back to The Cookie Jar, "but there was *one* interesting thing."

"And that was?" Hannah prompted.

"Carrie thinks Jenny Bergstrom was in the family way when she left Lake Eden."

Norman raised his eyebrows. "My mother actually said, *in the family way?*"

"Yes." Lisa turned to Hannah. "And your mother said, *No way, Jose. Dream on.*"

Norman gave a huge sigh, but Hannah noticed that his eyes were twinkling. "I always suspected it, but now I know it's true."

"What's true?" Hannah asked.

"Your mother is cooler than my mother."

Lisa cracked up, and both Hannah and Norman turned to look at her.

"Sorry," she said, still giggling. "It's not *cooler* anymore. Now it's *rad*, or *phat*, or something like that. It changes every month, or so. The only way you can keep up is to watch the sitcoms on television."

Hannah turned to Norman and gave him a little pat on the arm. "It's okay. I knew exactly what you meant."

"Vernacular aside, do you think my mother knew what she was talking about?" Norman asked Lisa.

"She seemed pretty sure of herself." Lisa turned to Hannah. "And she managed to convince your mother."

"If she convinced Mother, it's probably true."

"Jenny left town before she started to gain weight, or anything. And she never said anything about it in her letters to her friends in Lake Eden."

"Okay." Hannah got up to pour more coffee for all of them. Marge and Jack were still manning the shop and they had a little time to talk. "What else did Carrie say?"

"She said she almost came right out and asked Jenny, but then she heard about the divorce and she thought she must be wrong."

"Why?" Hannah was curious.

"Because Wayne always wanted children and he would have forgotten all about marrying the *bimbo,*" Lisa glanced at Norman, "your mother's word, not mine, and gone straight back to Jenny if she'd told him that she was pregnant."

"Oh, boy!" Norman gave a little groan. "The one thing I always loved about Lake Eden was that it could never be featured on a reality show. But now . . . I'm not so sure."

Hannah laughed. "Don't worry about it. Gossip in a small town isn't that interesting unless you live there, and *Dancing with the Bovines* won't make it. Unless they decide to hold the summer Olympics on Winnie Henderson's farm, Lake Eden doesn't have a prayer of being on national television."

"Hey, Hannah."

Mike strode in shortly after Norman had left and Hannah's heart began to beat like a trip hammer. Why did he have this effect on her? She wished she could control it, but that sudden breathlessness and leap in blood pressure seemed to be eons beyond the control of biofeedback.

"Mike," Hannah replied, pouring two mugs of coffee from the kitchen pot while her hand was still steady. "Would you like a couple of Linda's Shortbread Pecan Cookies?"

"Who's Linda?"

"Lisa's cousin. She sent us the recipe."

"Sure, I'll try a couple. I promise I'll never refuse *anything* you offer me. You can count on that."

Mike gave her a devilish grin and Hannah almost didn't make it to the work island with the mugs of coffee intact. He was implying a lot more than he should, but she didn't really dare to react. If she accused him of a suggestive comment, he'd act all innocent and tell her it was all in her head.

"Hold on and I'll get a plate of cookies," she said, setting the coffee down on the work island and never quite meeting his eyes.

It didn't take long to fill a plate with cookies and put them down in front of Mike. Hannah waited until he'd eaten two and washed them down with a whole mug of coffee. Then she got up to pour them more. "So how did you like them?" she asked, sitting down across from him once more.

"Great! Cover them with a napkin or something, will you, Hannah? Otherwise I'm going to eat them all."

"You're going back out to the sheriff's department, aren't you?"

"Right after I leave here."

"Mother picked up something for Bill and she doesn't want him to hang it in his closet at home. She's afraid Tracey will see it and stop believing in Santa Claus."

"I take it it's a Santa costume?"

"Bingo. She bought it this morning at Bergstrom's."

"No problem. I'll take it out there and hang it in Bill's closet."

Hannah waited, but Mike didn't say anything else. The man was a genius when it came to holding his tongue. They sat there in silence for the space of a half-cup of coffee and then Hannah caved in.

"How's the investigation going?" she asked.

"It's going. How about you?"

"What do you mean?" Hannah assumed the most innocent expression she could muster.

"I know you're asking questions. And I know people talk to you. Do you have anything I should know about?"

Hannah took a brief second to consider what she should give Mike so that he could give her something in return. "One thing," she said.

"What's that?"

"I know the name of Wayne's lawyer if you want to ask about his will."

"That was next on my list, but you can save me some time. Who is it?"

"Larry Helms. He's with Helms, Jackson, and Connors out at the mall."

Mike reached in his pocket for his notebook and pen, and wrote it down. "Thanks, Hannah."

"You're welcome. Did you happen to examine the Santa suit that Wayne was wearing?"

"Not personally. The crime lab has it. What did you want to know about it?"

"I was just wondering if there were any candy canes left in Wayne's pocket."

"Why do you want to know that?"

"Just curious. Wayne was such a tightwad about those candy canes. I asked him if I could have the ones that were left, and he told me he needed them for the next time he played Santa, and he told me to pour them in his pocket. I guess they all fell out the hole."

"*What* hole?"

"The one in Wayne's pocket. There must have been a hole. And the candy canes dropped out of the hole and onto the path. That's how we found him. We followed the trail of candy canes."

"Right. Do you want me to find out about the hole and the candy canes?"

"Sure, if you've got a spare minute. But I'm just satisfying my curiosity. I figured Wayne was being cheap when he said he needed to use the rest of the candy canes."

"I've heard that before!"

"Heard what?" Hannah asked, wondering how many other people had asked about Wayne's candy canes.

"What a cheapskate Wayne was. Even his ex-wife implied that. She thought it might relate to his murder. But I came away with the impression she still had a lot of affection for him."

"You talked to Jenny?"

Mike flipped open his notebook. "Jennifer Perkins Bergstrom. That's right."

"What did you think of her?"

"I told you already. She's the only one I've talked to so far who seemed really sorry her ex-husband was dead."

"I hope she's okay. I have to go out to the inn to see her tonight."

"To ask her questions?"

"No, to deliver cookies. Mother wants me to take a dozen of something chocolate to Jenny. She thought it might help."

"Good idea. It doesn't happen often, especially when I'm working a murder investigation, but I couldn't help feeling sorry for her. *She* was the grieving widow. The current wife didn't seem all that upset."

"I agree," Hannah said, before she could think better of it.

"You saw Melinda Bergstrom today?"

"Actually . . . I brought her some cookies. Chocolate."

"Your mother's idea again?"

"No, it was Cory's. Norman and I drove out to the mall to get a Christmas gift for his mother. We ran into Cory and he mentioned that Melinda had been crying all night. I had some cookies with me, and we took her some."

"Hmm." Mike gave her a long, level glance. "What did you think of Melinda?"

To give, or not to give. That was the question. Hannah decided that it couldn't hurt to have the law on her side. "Melinda didn't seem to be mourning Wayne's death very much, but you already know that. I found it particularly interesting that she didn't share the master suite with her husband. Her bedroom's down the hall right next to her brother's."

"She *told* you that?"

"No. I just . . ." Hannah searched for a phrase to explain that she'd fibbed and snooped, but she couldn't come up with one that was socially acceptable. "I just found out, that's all."

Mike gave her another long, level glance, and Hannah was sure it was the same glance he used in the interrogation room. "What else did you just find out?" he asked.

"Well . . . nothing really. Except that she knows a lot about plants. Her maid is named Emily, if that helps."

"Right." Mike stood up to go. "Let me know if you hear anything you think I should know. And remember to leave the investigating . . ."

". . . up to the professionals," Hannah finished the sentence in tandem with him. "Hold on a second and I'll wrap up these cookies. You can take them out to the station with you."

LINDA'S PECAN SHORTBREAD COOKIES

Preheat oven to 350 degrees F.,
rack in the middle position.

1 cup white *(granulated)* sugar
1 cup brown sugar***
1 cup *(2 sticks, ½ pound)* salted butter
1 cup vegetable oil *(Canola is NOT a vegetable—the oil's from a weed!)*
1 beaten egg
2 teaspoons vanilla
1 teaspoon baking soda
1 teaspoon salt
1 teaspoon cream of tartar *(critical!)*
1 cup uncooked oatmeal *(I used Quaker's Quick)*
1 cup Rice Krispies
4 cups flour
2 cups chopped pecans *(measure after chopping)*

*** *Brown sugar is nothing more than white sugar with added molasses. All you have to do to make 1 cup brown sugar is to measure out a cup of white sugar and drizzle in 2 teaspoons of molasses, and then mix well. You can mix it with a fork and a little muscle, or with an electric mixer and a little electricity. It's your choice. Knowing this little trick eliminates the necessity of keeping brown*

131

sugar, the kind that develops hard lumps, on hand in your pantry.

Put one cup of white sugar and one cup of brown sugar in the bowl of your mixer. Zoop them up together to make really light brown sugar.

You have two choices with the butter. You can let it come up to room temperature on its own, or you can soften it in the microwave. If you're in a hurry and you don't want to wait for nature to take its course, do this:

Unwrap a stick of refrigerated butter. Put it on a paper plate. Nuke it for 5 seconds on HIGH in your microwave. Roll it forward so the topside is now on the side. Nuke it for another 5 seconds on HIGH. Roll it forward again and nuke it for another 5 seconds on HIGH. Repeat rolling forward again and nuking for 5 seconds once again. You're done. Take the plate out of the microwave and dump the butter into your mixing bowl.

Repeat the whole thing for the second stick of butter.

Once you've added the butter to your mixing bowl, mix it until it's smooth.

132

Pour in one cup of vegetable oil and add one egg. Mix it all up together at slow speed.

Add the vanilla, baking soda, salt, and cream of tartar. Mix it all up together.

Add the cup of oatmeal and the Rice Krispies. Mix thoroughly.

Add 4 cups of flour to your bowl in half-cup increments, mixing after each addition.

Take the bowl from the mixer, give it another stir with a spoon, and mix in 2 cups of chopped pecans by hand.

With your hands, roll dough balls approximately 1-inch in diameter and place them on the cookie sheet, 12 to a standard-sized sheet.

Bake at 350 degrees F. for 12 to 15 minutes or until golden brown around the edges. *(Mine took exactly 12 minutes.)*

Let cool on the cookie sheet for 2 minutes and then transfer to a wire rack to complete cooling.

Yield: 9 to 11 dozen yummy shortbread-type cookies

133

Chapter Ten

Hannah removed another leftover quiche from Andrea's seldom-used oven and set it out to cool on a rack. Their dinner plans had gone awry. Michelle had begged off. She was having dinner with Delores and Carrie, and then the three of them were going to call everybody who'd been at Sally's Christmas party. Even though the deputies had already interviewed everyone who'd been there, Delores had decided it was worth a try. They'd already divided the guest list into three parts. There were the people Carrie knew best, the people Delores knew best, and the younger crowd that Michelle knew best. When Hannah had talked to her sister earlier, Michelle had been certain that the three of them could get more candid information from a friendly phone call than the sheriff's deputies had gotten at the party last night.

Another few minutes and the quiche would be cool enough to cut and then it would be time for the second shift to eat. She'd fed Tracey and Grandma McCann while Andrea had spoon-fed baby Bethany, who had recently graduated from purees to small chunks. Then the kids and "Grandma" had gone off to the den to watch a new Christmas movie with animated penguins who'd lost their Christmas presents and had to find them before Christmas Eve. Andrea had gone upstairs to change. They were going to go out to the inn to talk to Wayne's ex-wife right after they'd eaten their dinner.

"Is it cool enough to eat?" Andrea asked when she came into the kitchen again.

"I hope so. I'm hungry." Hannah sliced the quiche while Andrea dished up salads. They sat down across from each other, picked up their forks, and for long moments there was silence broken only by the sounds of chewing.

"This quiche is absolutely delicious," Andrea finally said, finishing the last of her slice and looking longingly at the three slices still left on the serving plate.

Hannah smiled her thanks. "I'm glad you liked it. Have another piece."

"I'm thinking about it. It's made with cream, right?"

"Yes."

"Uh-oh. And there's butter in the crust?" Andrea waited until Hannah nodded and then she asked her next question. "How about cheese?"

"There are a couple of kinds of cheese."

"A couple? Uh-oh. How much cheese?"

Hannah thought about dissembling, but it wasn't nice to mess with somebody else's diet. "Quite a bit of cheese," she admitted, "probably the equivalent of two ounces per slice."

Andrea gave a little whimper. "I don't suppose you used low-fat cheese."

"Nope."

"Uh-oh. Tell me about the bacon pieces."

Hannah thought about that for a moment. "They're well drained," she said.

"Oh good!" Andrea gave a relieved smile. "Then I guess I'll have another piece!"

* * *

The parking lot at the Lake Eden Inn was full, but Hannah "found" a space by parking at an angle with the rear end of her cookie truck partially elevated on the rim of hard-packed ice that had been left by the snow-plow around the perimeter.

"Okay," she said, opening her door. "You're wearing boots, aren't you?"

"Of course. They're the ugly silver moon boots Bill gave me when I got pregnant with Tracey and he was afraid I'd slip on the ice."

"I thought you hated those."

"I do, but they keep me from slipping on the ice. And besides, nobody's going to see me until I get inside and then I'll change to my shoes."

Hannah glanced down at her old moose-hide boots. She'd left her shoes at The Cookie Jar. Unless she wanted to leave her boots in the cloakroom and pad up to see Jenny in her stocking feet, she'd better look for the pair of ballet-type pull-on slippers she usually carried in the back of her truck.

"You *do* have shoes, don't you?" Andrea asked, glancing down at Hannah's boots.

"I do." Hannah did her best to exude confidence as she opened the back of her truck and rummaged around for her slippers. Luck was with her and she found them. "Here they are," she announced, holding them up for Andrea to see.

"Great. Let's go then. It's freezing out here."

The air was crisp, the night inky black with the moon shining blue and cold against the snow. When Hannah looked up at the night sky, the stars appeared jagged, as if they were made of shattered ice crystals. There was a beauty in the frosty night that made her wonder what it would have been like to live in an ice cave. If anyone *could* live in an ice cave. She really wasn't sure.

"Brrrr! It's must be close to zero!" Andrea moved a

little closer to Hannah. "I'm worried about the crab apple tree Bill and Tracey planted in the backyard. I hear it's supposed to drop down to minus fifteen tonight."

Her sister's comment brought Hannah back from thoughts of wooly mammoths and glaciers. "Where did you hear that?"

"I saw the weather report on KCOW," Andrea named the local television station.

"Then don't worry. They're always wrong."

"Are you sure?"

"Positive. Remember last August when they said we were going to have a whole week of rain? They called it the storm of the century and said it would bring us at least six inches before it cleared up. And then it was sunny and warm every day?"

"I remember. I stood in line to buy a new umbrella and I never used it."

"Hold on," Hannah said, grabbing Andrea's arm. "Stand right here and look over at the inn."

"But why should . . ." Andrea swallowed the rest of her own question as realization dawned. "Never mind. I get it. This is where you left the path last night. And you found Wayne's body just a few feet from here."

"Exactly. That's why I want you to look at the inn. How many windows can you see from here."

There was a moment of silence while Andrea peered into the night. "I can't see the first floor at all," she said. "The trees are too tall. But I can see the last four rooms on the second floor. And if I can see them, they can see us."

"Exactly. The moon was bright last night and if someone in one of those rooms happened to be looking out toward the parking lot . . ."

"They could have seen Wayne's killer!" Andrea interrupted her. "Do you want to check with Sally to see who had those rooms last night?"

"Absolutely. Chances are, all Sally's guests were at the party and those rooms were empty at the time Wayne was murdered. But it can't hurt to ask."

The rest of the walk was accomplished in silence. Both sisters were chilled from the winter cold and didn't feel like speaking until they were sitting on a bench in the cloakroom changing from boots to shoes.

"Do you want to see Jenny first?" Andrea asked.

"No. We'll get the names from Sally and then we'll go up to visit Jenny."

"Fine with me. Just let me comb my hair and fix my makeup."

Hannah thumped the side of her head with her hand. "Makeup. I knew I was forgetting something. If a woman cries all night and all morning, is there anything she can do with cosmetics in thirty minutes or so to make herself look as if she hasn't been crying?"

"No."

"No?"

"Not in thirty minutes or so. Cosmetics are really good, but they can't perform miracles."

"So if somebody cried that long, it would show?" Andrea nodded and Hannah asked her next question. "*How* would it show?"

"Well . . . there's the obvious. Her eyes would be swollen and the skin on her face would be puffy. It would be blotchy too, but she might be able to cover that up with makeup. Are we talking about Melinda Bergstrom here?"

"Yes. Norman and I saw her this afternoon and she looked just as beautiful as she did when she was modeling."

"Then she was lying if she said she'd been crying all night and most of the morning."

"She didn't say it. Her brother Cory did."

"Then Cory was lying. There are things you can do to

reduce the swelling, but they all take time. Melinda wouldn't have looked beautiful unless . . . what was the lighting like?"

"It was daylight. We met her in a solarium filled with plants and it had a glass ceiling. The sun was shining."

"That cinches it!"

"What?"

"Sunlight. Even if she used the best makeup and applied it like an artist, there's no way she could hide it in strong sunlight."

"That's what I thought, but I wanted to check to make sure."

Andrea slipped on a pair of forest green shoes that went perfectly with her stylish pantsuit. "It's pretty clear Melinda didn't love Wayne since she didn't shed any tears for him. Do you think the maid was right and Wayne was planning to divorce her?"

"I don't know."

"Maybe Wayne told her he wanted a divorce and she killed him."

"Impossible."

"Why not? It happens all the time on television. The rich older husband says he wants a divorce, the gorgeous trophy wife sees all that money flying out the window, and she kills him before he can file the papers."

"That makes perfect sense except for one thing."

"What thing is that?"

"Melinda's got an air-tight alibi. Pierre from *Le Petit Salon* was with her from seven-thirty on. I stopped there to check before Norman and I left the mall. He did Melinda's hair at the penthouse and they were having a glass of wine in the solarium when Mike and Bill knocked on the door to notify her that Wayne was dead."

"Drats!"

"I know. It would have tied everything up in a neat little bow."

* * *

Getting the list from Sally was easy. Resisting the dessert buffet they were serving in the dining room was difficult. Hannah was still thinking sinful thoughts about Sally's newest chocolate creation as they walked down the hallway and pushed the button for the elevator. "Mike told me about his interview with Jenny. He said she seemed to be grieving for Wayne a lot more than Melinda was."

"Really?"

"That's what he thought. It's up to us to see if we agree with him. When we get up to Jenny's room, make sure you sit right next to her so you can check her makeup. I want to know if she's been crying."

Andrea looked a bit shocked. "But we know Jenny! She's a friend of Mother's!"

"I know that, but this is a murder case. Everyone's a suspect until they're eliminated."

The elevator doors slid shut and it shuddered slightly. Then there was a series of whooshes and faint faraway machinery sounds that boomed and banged as they were lifted to the second floor. The doors slid open to reveal a coral pink wall with a gilt-edged mirror hanging over a granite-topped table that Hannah was willing to bet had come from the quarries at Cold Spring, Minnesota. There was a bouquet of fresh flowers on the top of the table, but it was clear that the bouquet had other origins. Since it was winter in the Midwest, Hannah was willing to bet that the flowers came from warmer and sunnier places.

"Sorry," Andrea said as they stepped out of the elevator and started down the thickly carpeted hallway. "It's just that I remember Jenny, and I let my emotions get in the way. I'll check her makeup for you."

"Thanks. I remember her too, and I liked her. Mike said she was in her room alone at the time of Wayne's murder, and that means she doesn't have an alibi. Let's just hope that she'll tell us something that'll clear her."

The room Jenny occupied was at the end of the corridor and it had a perfect view of the path leading to the parking lot. It was a beautifully decorated mini-suite with a sitting room containing a couch by the window, a television set, and two chairs on either side of a coffee table. The sleeping area was hidden behind two decorative folding doors that could be closed or left open. Jenny had them open and Hannah could see a queen-size bed with a flowered coverlet, a tall dresser with ample drawers for any guest, a walk-in closet with mirrored doors, and an archway that Hannah assumed would lead to the bathroom.

Jenny was just as Hannah had remembered her, a pleasant-looking woman in her late forties with brown hair, stylishly cut, that was streaked with gray. She was dressed in black slacks and a black sweater that was embroidered with Hannah's favorite flower, lilacs.

"Hello, Jenny." Hannah stepped in first and handed her the cookies. "These are called Angel Pillows."

"Some of your famous cookies. Thank you, Hannah."

"We wanted to bring you something, because we're so sorry for your loss."

The moment that the words were out of her mouth, Hannah wished that she could call them back. They were exactly the same words that Norman had spoken to Melinda. But in this case, they seemed more appropriate. One look at Jenny's swollen face, and Hannah was willing to bet that Mike was right and she'd been crying all night and all day over her ex-husband's death.

Andrea gave Jenny a big hug. "This is so awful for you. I can tell you've been crying your eyes out for hours and hours. You still loved him, didn't you?"

Hannah tried not to look as shocked as she felt. Andrea had jumped in with both feet. She waited until her sister and Jenny had seated themselves on the couch next to the window and then she took a chair directly across from them and waited for Jenny's response.

"It's true," Jenny said with a sigh, "even though Wayne could be a real pain at times. And both of you know how cheap he could be. It used to make me angry when he'd give me something I really needed for birthdays and Christmases, like a set of tires for my car, or a new steam iron, or a toaster. He just hated to spend money on anything he thought was frivolous. I think it was probably a reaction to his background."

"Really?" Andrea prompted.

"Wayne's father owned a small general store in South Dakota. Wayne told me it was thriving when he started first grade, but then his father made some bad investments and he lost everything. They had to move to Wayne's grandparents' farm and they barely made both ends meet. I'm no psychiatrist, but I think Wayne was afraid he'd lose it all, the way his father did, and he'd have to go back to a life like that. And that's why he hated to spend any of the money he earned."

"You're probably right," Andrea responded. "That would be enough to turn anyone into a careful spender."

"Careful spender?" Jenny gave a little laugh. "That's a polite way to put it. Wayne was a tightwad. There's no two ways about it. But he was *my* tightwad and I loved him. That's one of the reasons I left town. I was devastated when he filed for divorce so he could marry that . . ." Jenny stopped and swallowed hard, " . . . that *model* of his. And he spent so much money on her. Every time he gave her a gift, my friends would call to tell me about her new piece of jewelry, or her new car, or whatever."

Andrea looked very sympathetic. "That must have

been difficult to hear, especially when he'd been so cheap with you."

"Oh it was, believe me! But I really thought he'd come to his senses and admit he'd made a big mistake."

"And he'd come crawling back to you?"

"That's right. But he didn't. And after the divorce was final and they set a wedding date, I had to leave."

"But he gave you enough money to get along, didn't he?"

"Yes. I didn't get rich, but I got a decent settlement."

"Do you mind if I use your bathroom, Jenny?" Hannah broke into what had been basically a two-person conversation.

"Of course I don't mind. Just go through the bedroom and to the left."

Hannah was glad when Andrea started talking, claiming Jenny's attention once again. She got up and headed out of the room, wondering just how long she could be gone. The bathroom excuse had worked really well at Melinda's penthouse and it was worth trying here in Jenny's mini-suite. Hannah was almost positive that Jenny had loved Wayne, but that didn't mean she hadn't killed him.

Since the folding doors were open and Jenny could be watching, Hannah headed straight for the bathroom. Once inside she was hidden from view, and Hannah leaned against the doorjamb, letting her eyes do a search of the room.

Everything was perfectly ordinary, from the three nice suits hanging in the closet to the array of cosmetics on the dresser table. Hannah was actually considering crawling across the floor to search under the bed when she spotted something unusual in the corner.

It was a large pink box with purple stars scattered across its surface. Because she'd tried to buy it for Tracey,

Hannah knew that Teensy's environments came in bright pink boxes with purple stars. But what was a divorced woman on a tight budget doing with an expensive children's toy? Could Carrie be right? Had Jenny been pregnant when she'd left Lake Eden? There was only one way to find out and Hannah got straight to it.

"I see you've got a Teensy environment," Hannah addressed Jenny as she came out into the living room again.

"Oh, yes. Yes, I do. I picked it up at the airport in Minneapolis right after I landed."

"Is it for your daughter?"

Jenny clasped her hands together tightly as she nodded. "Yes, it's for Anna. She's five now. But I never told anyone here in Lake Eden. How did you know?"

"Carrie thought you were pregnant when you left, but she wasn't sure. Is Wayne her father?"

"Yes."

"Did he know?"

Jenny's face turned pale. "I was going to tell him this morning. He . . . He's the reason I came back here."

The story came out in bits and pieces, interspersed with fresh tears, but Hannah managed to put it all together. Wayne had called Jenny in Florida and asked her to come back to Lake Eden. He told her that he'd made a terrible mistake when he'd left her for Melinda and he begged for her forgiveness.

"He said he wanted to get back together." Jenny stopped to dab at her eyes with a handkerchief that had been drier at the start of their conversation. "And he said he'd already told Melinda. We were supposed to meet this morning for breakfast and work out the details."

"And that's when you were going to tell him about Anna?" Andrea asked her.

"Yes. I didn't want to do it on the phone. I wanted to

see his face, judge his reaction, make sure he really wanted his daughter."

She wanted Wayne alive, not dead, Hannah thought. But the lack of discernable motive didn't completely clear her.

"I didn't tell the police everything I did," Jenny admitted, looking more than a little embarrassed. "I guess I was afraid that handsome detective would think I was acting like a teenager with her first crush."

"Why? What did you do?" Hannah asked, giving her an encouraging smile.

"Wayne and I had a signal when we were in high school. He lived on the next block and when he walked by my window and I was home, I used to open it and coo like a mourning dove. It was my way of saying, '*I love you.*' He'd whistle back like a whippoorwill and that was his way of saying, '*I love you, too.*'"

"That's sweet," Andrea said.

Sweet, but silly, Hannah thought, but of course she didn't say it. Instead, she asked, "Did you coo at Wayne when he walked past your window?"

"No. I was all ready to do it, but he never walked past."

"Is it possible you missed him?" Andrea asked her.

"No. I sat right there waiting. I was really excited to see him again, even if it was just through a window. I kept looking for Wayne right up until I saw all the flashing lights when the deputies drove up in front."

ANGEL PILLOWS

Preheat oven to 275 degrees F.,
rack in the middle position.
*(Not a misprint—that's two hun-
dred seventy-five degrees F.)*

**Hannah's 1st Note: Don't even THINK about
making these if it's raining. Meringue does best on
very dry days.**

3 egg whites *(save the yolks to add to scrambled eggs)*
¼ teaspoon cream of tartar
½ teaspoon vanilla
¼ teaspoon salt
1 cup white *(granulated)* sugar
2 Tablespoons flour *(that's ⅛ cup)*
1 cup chocolate chips *(6-ounce package—I
used Ghirardelli's)*
½ cup chopped nuts *(I used pecans)*

Separate the egg whites and let them come up to
room temperature. This will give you more volume
when you beat them.

Prepare your baking sheets by lining them with
parchment paper *(works best)* or brown parcel-
wrapping paper. Spray the paper with Pam or an-

other nonstick cooking spray and dust it lightly with flour.

Hannah's 2nd Note: You can do this by hand, but it's a lot easier with an electric mixer.

Beat the egg whites with the cream of tartar, vanilla, and salt until they are stiff enough to hold a soft peak. Add the cup of sugar gradually, sprinkling it in by quarter cups and beating hard for ten seconds or so after each sprinkling. Sprinkle in the flour and mix it in at low speed, or fold it in with an angel food cake whisk.

Gently fold in the chocolate chips and the chopped nuts with a rubber spatula.

Drop little mounds of dough on your paper-lined cookie sheet. If you place four mounds in a row and you have five rows, you'll end up with 20 cookies per sheet.

Bake at 275 degrees F. for approximately 40 (forty) minutes, or until the meringue part of the cookie is hard to the touch.

Cool on the paper-lined cookie sheet by setting it on a wire rack. When the cookies are completely

147

cool, peel them carefully from the paper and store them in an airtight container in a dry place.

Hannah's 3rd Note: The refrigerator is NOT a dry place!

Yield: 3 to 4 dozen melt-in-your-mouth cookies.

Chapter Eleven

"Sorry I'm so late tonight, Moishe," Hannah apologized to her furry roommate as she spooned some vanilla yogurt into one of the antique cut glass dessert dishes that Delores had given her several Christmases ago. It had been seven-thirty by the time she'd dropped Andrea off at her house and driven home. Of course she'd fed Moishe right away, and now it was time for a little dessert.

"Go ahead and eat," Hannah told him carrying the dish out to the coffee table and setting it down. "I'll have mine later. I need to make a few notes while the conversation with Jenny is still fresh in my mind."

While her cat licked rather daintily at the yogurt, oblivious to the fact that Hannah's mother would have suffered a coronary event if she'd seen how her expensive gift was being used, Hannah paged through what she thought of as her murder book and jotted down the new facts she'd learned from Wayne's ex-wife.

"Wayne had to walk around the side of the building," she said, causing Moishe to look at up her in midlick. "There's no other way to get to the parking lot. But Jenny swears he didn't and that's substantiated by Cyril Murphy, who also swears he didn't see Wayne."

Chin in hand, unaware that she was a modern, female, clothed version of Rodin's *The Thinker*, Hannah went through the possibilities. "There's only one conclusion to reach. Even though I saw him go out that way, Wayne didn't walk from the back door to the parking lot."

Moishe looked up at her and purred, and Hannah interpreted that as approval for her logic. "Thanks. I know my conclusion is logical, but it doesn't make sense. I followed the trail of candy canes that fell out of the hole in Wayne's pocket and his body was only a few feet from the path. The way it stands now, I said goodbye to Wayne and he went out the back door in his Santa suit. He disappeared before he went around the side of the building and down the path to the parking lot, but he reappeared behind the snow bank, dead. That's impossible. Or if it's *not* impossible, I can't think of any scenario that could account for it."

The phone rang, and Hannah almost cheered. It temporarily interrupted her frustration and she was smiling as she reached out to answer it. It was Norman and her smile grew wider.

"Hi, Norman. What's new with you?"

"A lot. I just finished doing a little research. One of the plants Melinda showed us this afternoon has small pink blossoms that contain deadly poisonous stamens in the center."

"Which plant was that?"

"Fresindodendrun Rhochlepeous, the giant variety. The dwarf is perfectly benign."

"I don't remember it."

"No reason you should. It was just a plant with green leaves and small pink blossoms. The only reason I looked it up was that you said it was pretty, and Melinda gave kind of a funny smile."

"But she must have shown us a hundred different plants. How did you remember the name?"

"I didn't. I took along my pocket recorder and ... hold on. Cuddles is climbing the bookcase again and she's stuck on *The Republic*."

Hannah waited while Norman rescued Cuddles, the cat he'd recently adopted, and he was back on the line. "I didn't know you read Plato."

"One of my friends in Seattle gave me his complete works. She thought it would expand my mind."

Hannah gripped the phone a little tighter, wondering if the "friend" had been Beverly Thorndike, Norman's former fiancée who was now a dentist in Seattle. But before she could even think about asking, which she wouldn't have done in any case, Norman went on talking.

"The plant's common name is Flower of the Shroud, and the symptoms of poisoning are virtually undetectable unless you already suspect it and know what to look for."

"And you know what to look for?"

"I do now. It causes renal failure over a period of several weeks. The symptoms are swelling and a slight yellowing of the skin. She did it, Hannah. And when the poison didn't work fast enough, she hit him over the head."

"For the money?"

"Yes. It's a powerful motive, Hannah."

"But Melinda couldn't have done it. You know that. You were with me when we talked to Pierre. He swears he was with her the whole time. And for proof, he said to just look at her roots and see if we could find any brown."

"Huh?"

"Never mind. It's a blonde-thing. Andrea explained it to me. Did you think he was lying?"

"No. I just wish I could ignore the facts and go with my gut instinct. I *know* Melinda had something to do with Wayne's death. Everything about her is such a fake."

Hannah couldn't help but smile. That was exactly the way she felt about Melinda.

"Okay, so maybe Melinda's in the clear," Norman went on. "How about Cory? He seems devoted to her. I think Melinda could have talked him into killing Wayne."

"Maybe she could have, but he didn't do it, either. Cory was with me when Wayne was killed."

There was a long silence while Norman thought that over. And then he gave a long sigh. "Pretty handy, if you ask me! They've both got motives and they've both got alibis."

"I know. Hold on a minute and let me write down what you said about the poison."

Hannah's pen flew across the paper as she jotted notes. She only hoped that she could read them later. It was possible that Melinda had been poisoning Wayne with stamens from the plant that Norman had mentioned when his life had been ended, much more abruptly, by a blow to the head. If that were the case and Doc Knight collaborated that Wayne's liver was enlarged, Melinda could be charged with attempted murder.

"Hannah?"

"I'm here. I'm just wondering if I can get Doc Knight on the phone tonight and find out if Wayne's liver was enlarged."

"I'll do it, and I'll call you as soon as I know. Are you going out tonight?"

"I might run out to the mall. I want to question Cory again."

"Why? You said he couldn't have done it."

"I need to find out the name of Melinda's gardener."

"Okay. I'll get back to you as soon as I can. Take your new cell phone with you and don't forget to turn it on. Doc Knight will probably have to get back to me, and I'll let you know as soon as I know."

"Thanks, Norman," Hannah said, hanging up the

phone and turning to the cat, who couldn't be less interested. "I have to know if Melinda or Cory requested that particular plant, or if either of them knew it was poisonous. I'll think of some excuse to ask Cory for the gardener's name."

Moishe looked up at his mistress and gave a yowl that was midway between, *Figure something out, lady with no fur,* and, *If you're leaving, don't forget to give me more food.* Hannah recognized the look, and gave him more food. She was about to go out the door when the phone rang again.

"So soon?" she said, assuming it was Norman with Doc Knight's answer.

"So soon what?"

It was Mike's voice. Hannah did an abrupt turn-around and apologized as she did so. "Sorry, Mike. I thought you were someone else."

"I was me the last time I checked."

"Of course you were. So what's up?"

"There isn't any."

"There isn't any what?"

"Hole. There's no hole, Hannah. I called the crime lab and they checked it for me. No hole."

It all came back in the rush. She'd asked Mike to check the Santa suit Wayne was wearing for the hole in the pocket. But there wasn't a hole. And that meant that Andrea had been right about her Hansel and Gretel analogy. The miniature candy canes had been dropped deliberately. Had Wayne known that he was in danger and dropped candy canes to lead someone to the scene of his murder?

Hannah reined in her imagination. No, that was simply too far-fetched. But what if the killer had murdered Wayne and then dropped the candy canes deliberately so that the body would be found?

"Are you okay, Hannah?"

"I'm fine," Hannah pulled herself together enough to answer normally.

"Anything new on your end?"

"Not really. It's all speculation."

"Okay, then. Let me know if you get anything."

"I will."

Hannah felt a bit guilty as she hung up the phone, but she told herself that there was no reason to tell Mike about the poisonous plant that Norman had discovered growing in Melinda's *orangery*. She'd tell him if Doc Knight confirmed that Wayne's liver was enlarged, but not before. In the meantime, she had to hurry if she wanted to get out to the mall before it closed for the night.

Chapter Twelve

The mall was closing. Hannah could tell by the long string of cars coming toward her as she approached the entrance. One frustrated Christmas shopper was beeping his horn, as if the sound might make the dozens of cars in front of him go faster.

Hannah turned in at the outside entrance to Bergstrom's Department Store. There was no one behind her and the parking lot that flanked the Christmas tree lot at the side of the store was deserted. Hannah pulled right up in the loading zone next to the lot and jumped out of her truck to rush toward the door. She ran past a sign saying that they were expecting a fresh shipment of Douglas fir trees tonight, past another that listed the prices per foot, and around the corner of the building to the entrance. The bright lights were off and there was only dim lighting inside the store, but she hoped she could catch an employee leaving late who would call Cory and ask him to come down from the penthouse and talk with her.

The door was locked, but she could see someone moving inside. Hannah hammered on the door with gloved fists until she got his attention and he moved toward her. The lights were dim, but as he drew closer she realized that he was in a Santa suit.

"I'm Hannah Swensen and I need to see Cory," she shouted, hoping he could hear her through the heavy glass door. "It's really important."

"Hold on," the man dressed as Santa shouted back. Then he unlocked the door and ushered her in.

"Is Cory still here?" Hannah asked him.

"He's here."

The Santa gave a chuckle and pulled off his hat, white wig, and beard. It was Cory! Hannah was so startled, her mouth dropped open.

"I didn't recognize you in that costume," she said, feeling a bit embarrassed. "I guess you must have been playing Santa tonight."

"That's right. The guy I hired to replace Wayne called in sick."

"Well, you make a great Santa," Hannah complimented him, and then she got down to business. "I came out here to ask you a couple of questions."

"Ask away." Cory said.

"The first thing I need is the name of Melinda's gardener."

"Why do you need that?"

Hannah was all ready with her excuse. She'd devised it on her drive out to the mall. "I told Mother about Melinda's beautiful solarium and one of her friends wants to hire her gardener to do something similar on a smaller scale for her."

"Okay. It's Curtis something-or-other. I can't think of his last name right now, but he comes tomorrow and I'll get his card for you."

"There's one more thing."

"What's that?"

"I'm having trouble with the timeline on the night that Wayne was killed. I saw him leave the inn the back way, wearing his Santa suit. And that's the last time I saw him alive. I found his body later in the evening."

"Right. What's troubling about that?"

"Cyril Murphy was out in front of the inn, working on Florence Evans's car. He didn't see Wayne walk past and Wayne had to walk past him to get to the path where I found him."

"That's easy to explain. Come with me for a second. I need to turn off more lights." Hannah walked into the interior of the store with Cory as he continued to talk. "Wayne wouldn't have said anything to Cyril. For one thing, they were on the outs because of the limousine thing. And for another thing, Wayne had laryngitis. If Cyril didn't see him, Wayne probably hurried on by and figured that was a good thing."

"That's exactly what I thought, at first. But when I went out to the inn tonight, I talked to one of Sally's guests and her room has a perfect view of the side of the building and the path to the parking lot. She was in her room when Wayne left the stage. She heard the applause he got. That's when she started watching for him to pass by her window. But he never did."

"She must have looked away for a minute or two and missed him. I watched him walk around the corner and then I dashed back in. It was cold out there! And I know he didn't come back inside for any reason. I was standing right there waiting for you, and I would have seen him down at the end of the hall."

"I'm sure you would have." Hannah gave a quick nod. "It's not like he could blend with the party crowd. That Santa suit would stick out like a sore thumb."

"You're absolutely right. Do you mind if I take this off, Hannah? These things are really heavy."

"Go ahead."

Hannah watched while Cory took off the top part of his Santa suit. He was wearing a regular shirt under it and that gave her an idea. "Think about this, Cory," she said. "What if Wayne was wearing regular clothes under his Santa suit? Then he could have taken off the suit, hidden it somewhere, and slipped back inside. Would you have seen him if he'd done that?"

Cory began to frown. "I'm not sure. Maybe not."

"Was Wayne in the habit of wearing regular clothes under his Santa suit?"

Cory's frown deepened. "I don't know. Let me call Melinda and I'll find out."

As Cory disappeared around the corner, Hannah came close to laughing. He looked ridiculous in big red Santa pants with white fur cuffs, topped by a regular shirt. It reminded her a bit of a centaur, the top half of a man rising from the back half of a horse. If he'd greeted her that way at the door, she would have recognized him immediately. But it was almost impossible to tell who was inside a Santa suit. Unless you recognized the voice, of course.

It was one of those frightening moments of clarity when the pieces of the puzzle flew together from every direction. They locked into place with a series of lightning fast clicks, sounding like a million tiny firecrackers that illuminated the dim and confused picture in her mind. Cory killed Wayne. He'd rolled Wayne's body behind the snow bank, planted the candy canes so someone would discover him, and then, while everyone was waiting for Wayne to appear as Santa, he'd put on another Santa suit, perhaps even the one he was wearing tonight, and appeared in Sally's kitchen as Santa Wayne with laryngitis. It was the reason he'd seemed a bit confused when Sally had handed him the receipt from Mayor Bascomb. Santa Wayne would have known what it was, but Santa Cory didn't.

Immediately after the party, Santa Cory had stepped outside the back door, ditched his Santa suit, and stepped back in, dressed for the party.

He used me as his alibi and I fell for it! Hannah thought, gritting her teeth. *Norman's gut is right. Cory is probably in it with Melinda.* And at almost the same time she had another thought that had her moving at top speed toward the door. *He knows I know and he's going to kill me!*

A third thought, one in bright neon capital letters for emphasis, flashed across the screen in her mind. RUN, it said. RUN FAST!

Hannah ran faster than she'd ever run in her life, and she arrived at the heavy glass door, breathless. Locked. It was locked and Cory had the keys. There had to be another way out!

Another thought flashed through Hannah's mind. *They expect another shipment of trees and I parked in the loading zone.* The moment it occurred to her, Hannah rushed toward the annex.

The annex was a large enclosure with three cinderblock walls. The fourth wall was the back wall of the store. In the summer, this area was used as a garden center and shade cloth was attached to form a temporary roof. In December, a sliding roof was attached. It was capable of being opened when the weather permitted, and closed at night when the store was locked. Right now it was locked and a single rope of white twinkle lights were strung across the ceiling to provide a bit of light. Tall space heaters, the type used in patio restaurants, sat every few feet to provide warmth. Now they were cold and dead, the way Hannah would be if she didn't get out the delivery door and into her truck before Cory caught her.

Dozens of frozen trees were stacked by the far wall, far away from the nearest space heater. They were still in their protective netting and they looked like coneshaped green carrots. Employees would take them into the thawing and flocking tent, a large area draped with heavy construction plastic that held in the heat from several space heaters. The trees would thaw and their branches would loosen so that prospective buyers could see their real shapes.

The delivery door was right in front of her. Hannah grabbed the handle to jerk it open, but the corrugated metal door didn't budge. It was locked. The stacked trees she'd seen must have been the Douglas firs and they'd been delivered already.

Hannah eyed the wall. It was at least twelve feet high. Even if she could somehow manage to climb it, the sliding roof was closed. There was no escape there. Her only chance of surviving was to hide and hope that Cory hadn't seen her dash into the annex. He couldn't search the whole store. It would be impossible. She might be able to elude him until time for the store to open in the morning.

Attempting to think positive thoughts was difficult. It was cold in the annex and although she was dressed for winter, a parka wouldn't protect her all night. If Rayne Phillips on KCOW television was right, and Andrea had reported it accurately, it was going to be a bitterly cold night.

The warmest place in the annex would be the thawing and flocking tent. Hannah lifted the flap, dashed into the tent, and gave a huge sigh of relief. The large area was filled with thawed trees and their branches would hide her from view. And it was at least twenty degrees warmer than it had been in the main part of the annex.

Hannah chose a spot in the very center of the group of trees waiting to be flocked because those had the fullest branches. The tree in front of her bore a tag saying that it had been purchased by Doug Greerson for the lobby of the Lake Eden First Mercantile Bank. The word *"white"* was written under Doug's name and Hannah knew that he always ordered a tree flocked in white, and Lydia Gradin, his head teller, trimmed it with blue lights and decorations.

At least there was no snow on the ground. Hannah shifted from foot to foot, trying to stay warm. She judged it to be several degrees above freezing in the warming tent, but the frozen ground beneath her feet seemed to send up cold waves through the soles of her boots, and she shivered. It would help if she could move closer to the space heater, but the trees surrounding it were just starting to thaw and their branches weren't full enough to hide her.

Hannah glanced at the tree on her left. It was for Bertie Sraub, the owner of Lake Eden's beauty parlor, the *Cut 'n Curl*. Naturally Bertie's tree would be pink. Two cans of pink flocking sat on the ground under her tree, caps already loosened, all ready to be used in the morning. The former owner of the *Cut 'n Curl* had decorated the shop with pink flamingoes. While Bertie wasn't as wild about the huge birds as the former owner had been, she did like pink and she'd left the walls and the shades that color.

Hannah's heart leapt into her throat as she heard heels clicking against tile. Someone was coming! The door to the annex opened, letting in a bright burst of light, and Cory stood there in silhouette.

"I know you're here, Hannah. I saw you run in the door."

Hannah's heart raced, thumping so loudly she was almost afraid he'd hear it. Cory knew she was here! But perhaps he was just faking, hoping that she'd panic and give away her position.

"Guess the cat's got your tongue, but that's fine. We can do this the hard way. I haven't played Hide 'n Seek since I was a kid. You can change hiding places if you like. I'll be right back."

The door closed, cutting off the bright light. Hannah wasn't sure whether Cory had left, or not. It didn't really matter. She had chosen the optimal spot and she wasn't going to move unless she had to.

A weapon. Hannah glanced around in the dim light and cursed neat employees. There was nothing useful on the ground, no carelessly dropped screwdrivers, hammers, or metal Christmas tree stands. Except for the two cans of pink flocking under Bertie's tree, the area was as spotless as an army barracks right before an inspection.

Hannah moved quickly, flipping off the caps and shaking the cans of flocking. She didn't have much in her arsenal, but she planned to use what she had. If she could hide here until Cory lifted the flap and came into the tent, she could hit him in the face with . . .

There was an explosion of lights and sound that made Hannah's senses reel. Cory had turned on the bright lights and music. Santa's Winter Wonderland tree lot was in full swing. Through Hannah's slightly blurred perspective behind the plastic sheeting, the red and green Christmas train chugged its way around the perimeter of the area, the colored lights on the huge Christmas trees in the corners flashed on and off, and the loudspeakers blared the strains of "We Wish You a Merry Christmas" sung by a chorus of penguins with red and green stocking caps next to the cash register.

For one long moment, Hannah just stood there, too shocked to do more than blink. And then she saw Cory coming straight toward the thawing and flocking tent with an ax in his hand, and her survival instinct kicked in. *When in doubt, attack.* It was one of her father's favorite phrases. She'd always thought it was original with him until she'd heard it in an old movie. But it seemed appropriate now, and Hannah wasted no time thinking about it. She just waited until Cory lifted the flap and stepped inside, and then she hurtled forward and blazed away with double-barreled spray cans, covering his face with pink flocking before he could even raise his arms.

Cory screamed as the spray hit his eyes. He clawed at her but a blind, pink-flocked adversary was not that difficult to elude. Hannah stepped to the side, sprayed him again, and he dropped the ax. Hannah grabbed it and tossed it into the stand of trees behind her.

He was trying to wipe his eyes and Hannah knew it would be only a matter of time before he recovered enough to strike out at her. She had to render him immobile while he was still reeling from pain and shock.

The netting machine. The moment that Hannah remembered the machine she'd seen right outside the entrance to the tent, she grabbed his arm and pushed him through the opening. Another spray in the eyes and another shove with her hand, and he fell onto the chute where trees were placed for netting so that they could be carried home on the roofs of cars. Two more sprays for good measure and she turned on the machine. With a grinding of gears caused by a burden that was twice as heavy as usual, Cory was carried forward to be wrapped with several layers of netting that rendered him immobile and covered him with bright yellow plastic mesh from head to toe.

There was a phone on a pole decorated like a candy cane with red and white stripes. Hannah dialed nine, the usual code to get an outside line, and was rewarded by a dial tone. Nine-one-one seemed unnecessary. Cory was trussed up like a mummy, and there was no way he could get free. Instead of dialing the police, Hannah called Norman.

"Hi, Hannah!" Norman sounded glad to hear from her. "I tried calling you a couple of minutes ago, but your cell phone was off."

"It's recharging," Hannah said, crossing her fingers

at the little white lie she'd just told, and hoping he wouldn't be too upset with her if he ever discovered that she had it in her purse, but it was turned off and she'd forgotten it was there. "Did you hear from Doc Knight?"

"He called me back about five minutes ago. I was way off base, Hannah. He checked and Wayne's liver was fine."

"That's okay. I'm sure Melinda would have tried to poison him if she'd known that her plant was poisonous. But it doesn't matter now. I've got the killer. It's Cory."

"Cory?! But I thought he was with you when Wayne was murdered."

"That's what he wanted us to think. Will you call Mike for me? I've got Cory netted up here at Bergstrom's Christmas tree annex, and I need him taken into custody before someone hangs lights and tinsel on him and props him up in the living room."

Chapter Thirteen

Hannah was on top of the world. Not only had she caught Wayne's killer, Jenny had insisted on giving her Teensy's Penthouse so that Tracey would have it for Christmas. It was currently sitting under Andrea's Christmas tree, wrapped in gold paper and tied with a huge red bow. It was the night after Cory had been taken into custody and they were all gathered at Andrea's house for coffee and dessert.

"This is just wonderful, Andrea," she said, even though she was seated on the couch between Norman and Mike. It was a small couch and she couldn't help but feel like the filling in a Norman and Mike Oreo.

"It's a gorgeous tree," Michelle said, admiring the huge Norway pine that sat in front of the picture window.

"Thanks. Bill picked it out at Bergstrom's. I love to get trees there. They're so careful with the netting." Andrea stopped and made a face. "Sorry, Hannah. I forgot for a second."

"That's okay. I'm just glad their netting machine could take a few extra pounds!"

"That reminds me . . ." Norman leaned forward to talk to Mike. "How'd you get that netting off Cory?"

"We rolled him on his back and used scissors."

Norman shook his head. "It's a good thing I'm not a cop."

"Why's that?" Bill asked him.

"Because I might have been temped to hit him with a stun gun for what he almost did to Hannah."

Hannah turned to smile at Norman. He looked perfectly serious.

"What makes you think I didn't?"

Hannah turned to look at Mike. He looked perfectly serious, too.

"Time for coffee," Andrea announced, getting up to take the tray from Grandma McCann, who'd just come in from the kitchen. "I hope you left room for dessert. Hannah brought her Candy Cane Bar Cookies."

"Because Cory's behind bars?" Norman asked.

"Of course." Hannah turned to Bill. "I just wish we could have gotten Melinda for something or other. I know she didn't poison Wayne, but I wish she wouldn't inherit all that money."

"She won't. Want to tell her, Mike?"

Mike turned to Hannah. "I did a little checking after we talked. I kept thinking about how his former wife was the one who was grieving. And she was getting nothing. And Melinda, who didn't seem to care about Wayne at all, was inheriting everything. So I ran her."

"Jenny?"

"No, Melinda."

"And you came up with something?" Hannah crossed her fingers, a leftover habit from childhood.

"It turns out she's Melinda Ann *Ames* Reynolds Bergstrom."

"Melinda Ann *Ames*?" Hannah asked, remembering the photo album with the initials M.A.A. on the cover.

"Ames was Melinda's maiden name. Reynolds was the name of her first husband. And she never bothered to get a divorce from Cornell Reynolds."

"Cory?"

"One and the same. They had a good thing going, living in luxury at Wayne's expense. They had it made until Wayne told Melinda that he was divorcing her so he could remarry his ex-wife."

"Then they had to do something quick if they wanted the good life to continue," Bill picked up the story. "So Cory killed Wayne right before he was ready to leave for his Santa appearance, put his body in the trunk of his car, and drove out to the Lake Eden Inn. When he got there, everyone was already inside, so he dumped Wayne's body behind the snow bank, left the trail of candy canes that you found in the road, and went inside to play Wayne as a Santa with laryngitis."

"And I bought it," Hannah muttered. "I was standing right next to him and I didn't know he wasn't Wayne."

Norman patted her on the shoulder. "Don't feel bad. He had us all fooled."

"Can you charge Melinda for conspiring with Cory to murder Wayne?" Michelle asked.

Mike shook his head. "I wish we could, but the D.A. says there's not enough evidence. Cory won't talk and Melinda's being very careful not to implicate herself."

"So she's going to get off with no charges at all?" Andrea looked highly disappointed.

"That's right," Bill answered her, "but she'll also get off with no money. Cory and Melinda were still married when Melinda tied the knot with Wayne. According to Stan Levine, that's bigamy and it makes any claim she has on Wayne's estate invalid. Thanks to you and Hannah, we know about Wayne's daughter. She's his closest living relative and she'll inherit."

"That's perfect!" Hannah was pleased. "Maybe now Jenny will move back here with her friends."

Grandma McCann appeared in the doorway, carrying baby Bethany. Tracey walked beside her, bearing the tray that Hannah had brought with Candy Cane Bar Cookies.

"Sorry," Tracey said, setting the platter on the coffee table. "Bethany and I had two from the middle."

Hannah laughed. It was true. There were two bar cookies missing from the middle of the platter. "That's okay. How did you like them?"

"I'm not sure," Tracey said, reaching out for another. And then when Andrea gave her a censorious look, she pulled her hand back. "May I have another one, please?"

"Yes." Andrea struggled to keep a straight face.

"Chock-it!" Bethany said, reaching out toward the platter. And then, when everyone turned to look at her, she repeated, "Chock-it!"

"Did she just say *chocolate?*" Bill asked Andrea.

"I think so. I don't know what else it could be."

Bill started laughing. "But she hasn't even said *Daddy* yet!"

"That's my niece," Hannah said, grabbing a bar cookie and holding out her arms for another niece after her own heart.

CANDY CANE BAR COOKIES

Preheat oven to 350 degrees F.,
rack in the middle position.

1 cup butter *(2 sticks, 1/2 pound)*
1 cup white *(granulated)* sugar
1 egg *(just whip it up with a fork in a glass)*
1/4 teaspoon peppermint extract
1/2 teaspoon salt
2/3 cup finely crushed miniature candy canes
    (measure after crushing)
6 drops red food coloring
2 cups flour *(not sifted—pack it down when
    you measure it.)*
1 cup semi-sweet chocolate chips *(that's a 6-
    ounce bag)*

2 cups semi-sweet chocolate chips *(that's a
    12-ounce bag)*

Melt the butter in a microwave-safe bowl for 1
minute 30 seconds on HIGH. Set it on the counter
to cool.

Place the sugar in the bowl of an electric mixer
*(you can also do this by hand, but it'll take some
muscle,)* add the egg, and beat it until it's a uniform
color.

Add the peppermint extract, salt, and finely
crushed miniature candy canes. Mix it all up.

Add the 6 drops of red food coloring. Mix it in thoroughly.

Feel the bowl with the butter. If you can cup your hands around it comfortably, you can add it to your mixing bowl now. Mix it in slowly at low speed. *(You don't want it to slosh all over!)* If it's still too warm to add, wait until it's cooler and then do it.

Add the flour in half-cup increments, beating after each addition.

Take the bowl from the mixer and stir in one cup chocolate chips by hand.

Spread the batter evenly into a greased *(or Pammed)* 9-inch by 13-inch pan. Bake it at 350 degrees F. for 25 minutes or until it feels firm on the top.

Remove the pan from the oven and sprinkle it with the remaining two cups of chocolate chips. Immediately cover the pan with a piece of heavy-duty foil or a cookie sheet. *(That keeps the heat in.)* Let it sit for three minutes. Then take off the cookie sheet, or foil, and spread out the melted chips like frosting with a rubber spatula or frosting knife.

Cool completely and then cut into brownie-sized pieces.

Index of Recipes

Baking Conversion Chart

These conversions are approximate, but they'll work just fine for Hannah Swensen's recipes.

VOLUME:

U.S.	Metric
½ teaspoon	2 milliliters
1 teaspoon	5 milliliters
1 tablespoon	15 milliliters
¼ cup	50 milliliters
⅓ cup	75 milliliters
½ cup	125 milliliters
¾ cup	175 milliliters
1 cup	¼ liter

WEIGHT:

U.S.	Metric
1 ounce	28 grams
1 pound	454 grams

OVEN TEMPERATURE:

Degrees Fahrenheit	Degrees Centigrade	British (Regulo) Gas Mark
325 degrees F.	165 degrees C.	3
350 degrees F.	175 degrees C.	4
375 degrees F.	190 degrees C.	5

Note: Hannah's rectangular sheet cake pan, 9 inches by 13 inches, is approximately 23 centimeters by 32.5 centimeters.

THE DANGERS OF CANDY CANES

LAURA LEVINE

For my loyal theater companion and technical advisor,
Michele Serchuk

Chapter One

Ah, Christmas in Los Angeles. There's nothing quite like it. Chestnuts roasting on an open hibachi. Jack Frost nipping at your frappucino. Santa in cutoffs and flip-flops. It's hard to get in the holiday spirit when the closest you get to snow is the ice in your margarita, but I was trying.

On the day my story begins, I was attempting to take a picture of my cat Prozac for my holiday photo card. I thought it would be cute to get her to pose in a Santa hat. Prozac, however, was not so keen on the idea. And I still have the scars to prove it.

The only holiday Prozac gets excited about is Let's Claw A Pair of Pantyhose to Shreds Day. Not a national holiday, I know, but one celebrated quite often in my apartment.

I kept putting the Santa hat on her head, only to find it on the floor by the time I picked up my camera.

"Oh, Prozac!" I wailed after about the thirtieth try. "What's wrong with you? Why can't you wear a simple Santa hat?"

She glared at me as if to say, *I refuse to look like a fool for the amusement of your friends and relatives. I've got my dignity, you know.*

This from a cat who's been known to swan dive into the garbage for a Chicken McNugget.

I was beginning to think E. Scrooge may have had the right idea about Christmas when the phone rang. I recognized the voice of Seymour Fiedler of *Fiedler on the Roof Roofers*, one of the not-so-long list of clients who use my services as a freelance writer.

"Jaine, you've got to come over to the shop right away."

I wondered if he wanted me to punch up the Yellow Pages ad I'd just written for him. Although for the life of me I couldn't see how I could possibly top *Size Doesn't Matter. We Do Big Jobs and Small.*

But he wasn't calling about the Yellow Pages ad.

"I'm in big trouble," he said, his voice a hoarse whisper.

"What's wrong?"

"I'm being accused of murder!"

Mild-mannered Seymour Fiedler, a man I'd never once heard utter an angry word, accused of murder? Impossible!

"Hang on, Seymour. I'll be right over."

I grabbed my car keys and headed for the door, just in time to see Prozac celebrating a whole new holiday— Let's Poop on A Santa Hat Day.

Chapter Two

Seymour's shop was in the industrial section of Santa Monica, a no-frills box of a building whose only concession to whimsy was a huge plaster fiddle on the roof.

His wife, Maxine, who doubled as his bookkeeper, sat at her desk out front, weeping into a Kleenex.

"Oh, Judy!" she cried, looking up at me with red-rimmed eyes. "It's all too awful!"

Maxine was a fiftysomething woman with fried blond hair and a fondness for turquoise eye shadow, most of which had now rubbed off on her Kleenex. For as long as I'd been working for Seymour, she'd been calling me Judy. Every paycheck she'd ever written had been made out to Judy Austen, often in the wrong amount. Not exactly the sharpest blade in the Veg-O-Matic.

"Seymour's waiting for you," she said, gesturing to his office.

I found Seymour behind his desk, guzzling Maalox straight from the bottle. Normally a jovial butterball of a guy, Seymour showed no hint of joviality that day. His pudgy face was ashen, and sweat beaded on his balding scalp.

"Seymour," I said, "what on earth happened?"

He took a swig of Maalox and wiped his mouth with the back of his hand.

"One of my customers was putting up Christmas decorations on his roof last week and fell. He landed on the driveway. Cracked his skull and died instantly.

"And now," he groaned, "they're blaming me."

"But why?"

"I'd just finished re-roofing his house. And apparently some of the shingles were loose. They say that's why he fell. His wife is hitting me with a wrongful death lawsuit. I might even be arrested on criminal charges."

I shook my head in disbelief.

"The police are conducting an investigation," he said, "but they're just going through the motions. They're pretty much convinced it was my fault."

"Any chance one of your workmen screwed up?" I asked, wondering if maybe the cops were right.

"No way. I personally inspected the job when they were through.

"Oh, Jaine!" he said, mopping his scalp with an already-damp hankie, "I'm going to be ruined."

"Don't you have insurance for things like this?"

He let out a big sigh.

"That's just it. Maxine's been distracted lately. Our daughter's getting married, and she's been so busy planning the wedding, she forgot to mail in the last two premiums."

Holy Tarpaper. Poor Seymour was in deep doo doo.

"I swear, Jaine, when I left that roof, every shingle was nailed down tight as a drum. Something fishy's going on here and I want you to investigate."

"You think somebody was trying to kill your client?"

"That's exactly what I think. The only way those shingles could've gotten loose was if somebody went up there and loosened them."

Now those of you who picked up this book for Hannah Swensen's latest recipes are probably wondering: Why was Seymour Fiedler asking a freelance writer to investigate a murder? Shouldn't he be talking to a private eye?

Well, it just so happens I've solved a few murders in my time. It's a life-threatening hobby, I know, but it adds zest to my days and breaks up the monotony of writing about No-Leak Roof Warrantees.

"Of course, Seymour," I said. "I'll be happy to investigate."

"How can I ever thank you, Jaine?" His eyes shone with gratitude.

Money might be nice, I couldn't help thinking.

"Of course, I'll pay you your going rate," he said, as if reading my thoughts.

Now my eyes were the ones shining with gratitude. My job docket was a tad on the empty side, and I desperately needed the money for Christmas gifts.

"In fact," Seymour said, "let me pay you something right now."

He whipped out his checkbook and wrote out a check with a heartwarming number of zeroes.

I was sitting there thinking of the lavish gifts I could buy my parents and, not incidentally, a new cashmere sweater I'd been lusting after at Nordstrom, when Seymour broke into my reverie.

"I, um, wouldn't try to cash that check right away." He looked at me sheepishly. "I don't exactly have enough in my account to cover it. Between our daughter's wedding and my lawyer's retainer, I'm sort of strapped."

Bye-bye, cashmere. Hello, polyester.

"But I'm sure the check will clear some time in February," he added hopefully. "Or March. Maybe April."

I told him not to worry and scooted out of his office before he had me cashing the check in July.

I stopped at Maxine's desk on my way out to say good-bye.

"So long, Judy," she sniffled, her Kleenex by now pulverized in her palm.

"Try not to worry." I gave her a reassuring smile. "I'm sure everything will be okay."

I was sure of no such thing, but she looked so damn pathetic sitting there with mascara tracks down her cheeks, I had to say something.

"I hope so. I don't know what I'd do if they ever arrested Seymour."

My attention was momentarily diverted from Maxine's grief by the sight of an untouched cheeseburger at her side.

Gosh, it smelled good.

"Would you like my cheeseburger?" she asked, following my gaze.

"Oh, no, thanks," I said, eyeing the cheese oozing out from the sides.

"You sure? I'm so upset about what happened with those insurance premiums, I've totally lost my appetite."

One thing I've never lost is my appetite, and that burger smelled like heaven on a bun. But I couldn't possibly say yes, not if I expected to squeeze into a bathing suit by Christmas.

And squeezing into a bathing suit was definitely on my Holiday To Do List. That's because every year I spend Christmas with my parents in their retirement condo in Tampa Vistas, Florida—much of that time on display at the Tampa Vistas pool. True, I'm not rich or wildly successful like some of the other kids on display, but I'm all they've got, and my parents are determined to show me off.

It's a trip I dread every year. And not because I don't

love my parents. I do. If it were just the three of us, I'd be fine. But it's not just the three of us. Every year my parents invite my Aunt Clara and Uncle Ed and my cousin Joanie to join us, along with Joanie's husband Bradley and son Dexter. All of us bunking in a two-bedroom condo.

My mom calls it "cozy." I call it hell.

Joanie and her family get to sleep in the guest bedroom. Uncle Ed and Aunt Clara camp out in the den. And lucky me—I get to sleep on the living room sofa right next to the Christmas tree. You haven't lived till you wake up Christmas morning with pine needles up your nose.

And if all that weren't bad enough, I have to spend an entire week feeling like a blimp next to my cousin Joanie, a perfect size two—and that's *after* giving birth to Dexter.

Suffice it to say, the last time I wore a size two, I was in preschool.

All of which explains why I turned down that cheeseburger. I simply had to shed a few pounds before Florida.

True, I was feeling a bit hungry, but I made up my mind to stop off at the market and buy myself a nice healthy 100-calorie apple. That would tide me over till dinner. No burgers for me. No way. No how.

Okay, so I didn't stop off at the market for an apple. I stopped off at McDonald's for a quarter pounder. What can I say? I got in my car with the noblest of intentions, but the smell of Maxine's burger hounded me like a Hari Krishna at an airport, and I couldn't resist.

After licking the last of the ketchup from my fingers, I drove to the home of Garth Janken, Seymour's recently deceased customer. Janken lived in the megabucks north-of-Wilshire section of Westwood, a bucolic bit of suburbia, which—in the interests of protecting the innocent and staving off a lawsuit—I shall call Hysteria Lane.

The houses were straight out of a *Town & Country* spread, dotted with gracious elms and white picket fences running riot with rosebushes.

At this time of year, however, landscaping took a backseat to Christmas decorations. Clearly the people on Hysteria Lane took their decorating seriously. No mere Christmas-lights-and-a-tree-in-the-window on this block. Everywhere I looked, I saw animated Christmas figures. Santas waved, reindeers nodded, elves pranced. For a minute I thought I'd made a wrong turn and wound up at Disneyland. A far cry from my own modest neck of the woods, where the only animated figure I'd ever seen on a lawn was Mr. Hurlbut, the guy in the duplex across the street, after he'd had one eggnog too many.

The theme of Garth Janken's house was Christmas in Candyland. I could tell this was the theme by the gold-embossed CHRISTMAS IN CANDYLAND banner draped out front. Candy canes and sugarplums dotted the pathway to the front door, and perched on the roof on a carpet of pink flocking, amid a jungle of even more candy canes, was an elfin creature that I assumed was either the Sugarplum Fairy or Mrs. Claus after gastric bypass surgery.

As I climbed out of my car, I saw a mailman approaching. I decided to question him, hoping he'd seen something that would get Seymour off the hook.

"Excuse me." I flashed him my most winning smile. "Can you spare a few minutes?"

"I'm afraid I'm sort of busy right now," he said, sorting through some letters. "These weeks before Christmas are nuts."

He was an energetic guy, in a pith helmet and USPS shorts, tanned and well-muscled from toting all that mail in the sun. What a difference from my mail carrier, a somewhat less than motivated employee who manages to deliver my Christmas cards just in time for Valentine's Day.

"I promise it won't take long. I'm investigating Garth Janken's death."

"You a cop?"

"No," I demurred, "I'm a private investigator."

He looked me up and down, taking in my elastic waist jeans and unruly mop of curls lassoed into a scrunchy.

"You're kidding, right?"

I get that a lot. There's something about elastic waist jeans and scrunchies that tend to take away your credibility as a P.I.

"No, I'm not kidding. I'm representing Seymour Fiedler of *Fiedler on the Roof Roofers,* and I want to ask you a few questions about Mr. Janken's death."

"Man, what a mess," he said, shaking his head. "They'll never get the blood out of the driveway." He looked over at the Jankens's house and sighed. "Poor Mrs. Janken. Such a nice lady. I hope she'll be okay."

"Do you know if Mr. Janken had any enemies?"

He barked out a laugh.

"Ring a doorbell on this street, you'll find an enemy. Garth was an attorney. One of those sue-happy characters always threatening to haul somebody into court. Just about everybody disliked the guy."

"Anybody dislike him enough to want to see him dead?"

He blinked in surprise.

"You think what happened to Garth was murder?"

"Possibly."

His eyes took on a guarded look.

"Hey, I don't want to go accusing anybody of murder."

Rats. I hate it when people are discreet.

Then he took a deep breath and continued.

"But Mr. Cox sure looked like he wanted to kill him sometimes."

Yippee. He wasn't so discreet after all.

"Mr. Cox?"

He pointed across the street to a mock Tudor house with an elaborate display of animated reindeer out front.

"Willard Cox. He and Garth were always at each other's throats. Especially this time of year, over the Christmas decorations."

"They fought over Christmas decorations?"

"It's nuts, I know. But the neighborhood association gives out an award for the best decorations, and the competition gets pretty fierce. Folks around here will do anything to win. You know what Garth's dying words to his wife were? Not 'I love you' or 'Hold me close.' No, his dying words were, 'Call in a decorator and finish the roof!' Which is exactly what she did as soon as the police let her.

"Anyhow, Garth always won the contest and it drove Willard crazy. Before Garth and his wife moved here, Willard used to take home the prize every year. He was constantly accusing Garth of stealing his ideas and sabotaging his displays. Last year he claimed Garth beheaded his Santa Claus. Things really blew up a few months ago when Garth ran over Pumpkin."

"Pumpkin?"

"Willard's dog. Willard and his wife used to keep Pumpkin out in the front yard. She barked a lot and Garth was always complaining about her. One day Pumpkin got loose from the yard while Garth was backing out of his driveway, and he ran her over. He claimed it was an accident, but Willard was convinced he did it on purpose. That's when I thought he was gonna kill him."

Wow, this guy was a fount of information, Wolf Blitzer with a mailbag.

But the fount was about to run dry.

"Hey," he said, checking his watch, "I've really got to go now."

"Just one more question." I trotted after him as he started up the street. "You ever see anybody up on the roof in the days before Mr. Janken's death?"

"Nope. Nobody but the roofers."

Sad to say, it was an answer I was to hear over and over again in the days to come.

I thanked him for his time, and headed back to Candyland to speak with the bereaved widow.

Cathy Janken was a real-life version of the sugarplum fairy on her roof—a delicate blonde with porcelain cheeks and enormous blue eyes. She came to the door in a pastel pink sweat suit the same color as the flocking on her roof, her platinum hair caught up in a wispy ponytail.

I gazed at her enviously. Sure, her husband had just died. But on the plus side, the woman actually managed to look skinny in a pink sweat suit. If I dared to wrap my body in pink velour, I'd bear an unsettling resemblance to the Michelin man.

"Mrs. Janken?" I asked, trying to figure out if her ashen pallor was a result of grief or sunblock.

"Yes," she said, blinking out into the bright sunshine. "Can I help you?"

Something told me she might not want to talk to me if she knew I was a private eye, not when she was in the midst of suing my client for several million dollars. So I'd decided to try another tactic.

"I'd like to speak with you about your husband's unfortunate demise," I said in my most professional voice. "I'm an insurance investigator with Century National."

I flashed her my auto insurance card which I'd cleverly had laminated on my way to McDonald's. It's amazing how laminating things makes them look official.

"You representing Seymour Fiedler?" she asked.

"Yes, I am."

Doubt clouded her baby blues. "I don't know if I should be talking with you. What with the lawsuit and all."

"I'm afraid you have to, Mrs. Janken. California state law. Plaintiff in a wrongful death suit must give a deposition to the defendant's insurance representative."

A law I'd just made up on the spot. But she didn't know that. At least I hoped she didn't.

"Okay," she sighed. "C'mon in."

Bingo. She bought it!

She ushered me into her living room, a fussy space done in peachy silks and velvets.

Above the fireplace was a framed portrait of Cathy and a fleshy man with dark, slicked-back hair, a feral grin, and a predatory gleam in his eyes that even the artist couldn't quite camouflage. Presumably, the late Garth Janken. I could easily picture this barracuda fighting tooth and nail to win the Christmas decorating contest.

Cathy perched her wee bottom on a silk moiré sofa, and I took a seat across from her on a dollhouse-sized armchair. I teetered on it cautiously, hoping I wouldn't break the darn thing, whose arms were as fragile as twigs.

Resting on a coffee table between us was a cut glass bowl of candy canes.

I happen to have a particular fondness for candy canes, along with just about anything else containing the ingredient sugar, but no way was I going to have one, not after that burger I'd just scarfed down.

"Help yourself," Cathy said, gesturing to the bowl.

Somehow I managed to say no.

"Garth loved those things." At the mention of her husband's name, her eyes misted over with tears. "I always told him they'd ruin his teeth, but he couldn't resist. 'Just one,' he used to say. 'It's not going to kill me.'

"Oh, God," she moaned. "If only he hadn't gone up on that roof!"

Suddenly the mist in her eyes became a downpour, and she was crying her heart out.

Now I happen to be a world class cynic, but it was hard to believe the sobs racking her body were an act. For whatever reason, Cathy Janken seemed to have genuinely loved her husband.

"Can I get you something?" I asked. "Some water?"

"No, I'm okay." She took a hankie from the pocket of her sweatpants and blotted her tears. "I've been like a faucet ever since the accident.

"So," she said, forcing a smile, "how can I help you?"

I took a deep breath and began my spiel, choosing my words carefully. She seemed awfully fragile, and I didn't want to start her crying again.

"We at Century National are very sorry for your loss, Mrs. Janken, but we don't believe our client is responsible for your husband's death. Mr. Fiedler insists every shingle was firmly nailed down when he completed the job."

"They certainly weren't nailed down when Garth fell."

"Actually, there's a distinct possibility your husband's death was not an accident."

"What?" Her eyes widened in surprise.

"Can you think of anyone on the block who might've wanted to see him dead?"

"No, of course not. True, Garth had his differences with some of the neighbors. He could seem tough on the outside, but he was a pussycat underneath. You just had to know how to handle him."

Something told me "handling him" involved lots of fishnet stockings and peekaboo lingerie.

"But I can't believe anybody wanted him dead."

"Not even Mr. Cox? I was talking to your mailman just now, and he said there was quite a bit of animosity between the two of them."

"Willard Cox is certifiably insane!"

Her porcelain cheeks flushed pink with anger.

"Last year he accused my husband of beheading his Santa Claus! Did you ever hear of anything so ridiculous? The head probably fell off in the wind. The year before that, he said Garth stole the nose off his Rudolph. He was just jealous because Garth kept beating him in the decorating contest. He even accused Garth of bribing Prudence Bascomb."

"Prudence Bascomb?"

"President of the homeowners association. She judges the contest each year. Garth didn't have to bribe her. Garth won because his decorations were the best!"

I wasn't about to say so out loud, but I wasn't convinced Garth's decorations were the best on the block. I'd seen the prancing reindeer on Willard Cox's lawn and they looked pretty darn impressive. I wondered if Garth had indeed been bribing the judge. I could easily imagine the barracuda in the portrait with payola up his French cuffs.

"I'm telling you," Cathy said, as if sensing my doubts, "Willard Cox is crazy."

"I heard he accused your husband of purposely running over his dog."

"Can you believe it?" Once again, her cheeks were dotted with angry pink spots. "He ran around telling everybody that Garth was a dog killer! Garth threatened to sue him for defamation of character. That finally shut him up."

"So do you think it's possible that Mr. Cox might have wanted your husband dead?" I asked.

She chewed on her pinky, and gave it some thought.

"I hadn't really considered it before, but I suppose so."

"And are you certain nobody else on the block might have wanted him . . . um . . . gone?"

"No. Nobody on this street is as crazy as Willard. The man is nutty as a fruitcake."

She was wrong about that. It turned out that Willard Cox had some stiff competition in the nutty-as-a-fruitcake department. As I would, much to my regret, soon discover.

Chapter Three

"Feliz Navidad, honeybun!"

Kandi Tobolowski, my best friend and constant dinner companion, raised her margarita in a toast. We were seated across from each other in our favorite Mexican restaurant, Paco's Tacos, a colorful joint famous for their yummy margaritas and burritos the size of silo missiles.

I took an eager gulp of my margarita. I'd spent a fairly frustrating afternoon questioning the neighbors on Hysteria Lane about Garth Janken's death. Willard Cox, my leading suspect, hadn't been home when I'd rung his bell. The few neighbors who were home on a weekday afternoon were no help whatsoever. They all agreed that Garth had been an unpopular guy, but nobody had any idea who might have hated him enough to kill him, nor had they seen anyone up on the roof in the days before his death—except for Seymour's roofers in their distinctive red *Fiedler on the Roof* baseball caps.

So it felt good to be here at Paco's, mellowing out with my good buddies, Kandi and Jose Cuervo.

"You'll never guess where Dennis and Kate and I are going for Christmas this year," Kandi beamed excitedly.

Dennis and Kate were Kandi's parents, a pair of avant garde freethinkers who thought it "cool" to be on a first name basis with their only child. (My parents, on the other hand, would never dream of letting me call them by their first names. I was practically in college before I even knew their real names weren't "Mommy" and "Daddy.")

"We're going skiing!" Kandi gushed. "In Aspen."

"Do you even know how to ski?"

"Well, no," she admitted, "but it doesn't matter. I can fake it."

"Kandi, I don't think you can fake skiing."

"We'll take lessons. It'll be fun!"

She grinned at me over her margarita, and suddenly I was flooded with envy.

Kandi *would* have fun. I could just picture her sipping hot toddies by a roaring fire, flirting with a cute ski instructor, while I was sipping Metamucil at the Tampa Vistas clubhouse, listening to my father and Uncle Ed fight over who won at shuffleboard.

By now our basket of chips was empty (final score: Jaine, 17; Kandi, $1\frac{1}{2}$), and I was happy to see our waiter approaching with our main courses. I'd debated between the low-cal chicken tostada and a simple grilled mahi mahi. It was an interesting debate. But in the end I went with two deep-fried chimichangas smothered with sour cream.

Kandi, as always, ordered the chicken tostada. Which is why she's an enviable size six—on a fat day.

I speared a hunk of guacamole from the top of my chimichanga. Yum!

"So where are you off to for Christmas?" Kandi asked, ignoring her tostada, although how anyone can ignore their dinner—even something as boring as a tostada— is beyond me. "Florida again?"

I nodded wearily.

"What are you going to do with Prozac? You're not taking her with you, are you?"

Once again, I nodded.

"You've got to be crazy. Didn't the airline threaten some kind of lawsuit last year?"

"Yes, but they never went through with it."

There's no doubt about it. Flying with Prozac is as close as you can get to hell without actually dying. Last year, she yowled nonstop for thirty minutes until the flight attendant broke down and brought her a first class meal.

She invariably manages to escape from her carrier and makes a beeline down the aisle for the one person on board violently allergic to cats. Last Christmas, Prozac's victim was not only allergic, but terrified of cats, and ran headlong into an oncoming beverage cart, knocking a carafe of very bad coffee into the lap of a nearby passenger. Hence the threatened lawsuit.

"I still don't see why you can't leave her home and have someone come in and feed her," Kandi said.

"Last time I tried that, I came back to find kitty pee on every pillow in my apartment. I was lucky I still had an apartment."

"Can't you leave her in a kennel?"

"I'm still paying off the medical bills from the last place she stayed. How she managed to bite her way through that kennel attendant's work gloves, I'll never know. But the poor guy had to be rushed to the emergency room for stiches. Anyhow, I can never go back there again. I'd be violating the restraining order."

Kandi shook her head in disbelief.

"Someday I'm gonna see that cat on *America's Most Wanted*."

We plowed through our meals (well, I plowed; Kandi plucked), and as Kandi chattered about her nifty new ski togs and the chalet she and her parents had rented, I couldn't help but feel sorry for myself. For once I'd like to spend Christmas with my parents, just the three of us. A nice quiet Christmas, sleeping in the guest room, free from invidious comparisons to my bikini-clad cousin Joanie.

Oh, well. I couldn't let myself wallow in self pity. So I did what I always do when I'm feeling sorry for myself: I took a deep breath, squared my shoulders, and ordered dessert.

I woke up the next morning still in a funk about my trip to Florida.

As I lay in bed, I thought of Kandi enjoying an elegant candlelit dinner with her parents while I sat watching Uncle Ed pick Christmas turkey from his teeth with a matchstick.

But there was nothing I could do about it. Like it or not, I was stuck at Tampa Vistas for the holidays. Hauling myself out of bed, I shoved all thoughts of Florida to that dusty corner of my mind reserved for unpaid bills and tax estimates.

After a nutritious breakfast of Paco's leftovers, I hunkered down on the living room sofa with the morning paper.

A headline in the *Calendar* section caught my eye.

GIRLFRIENDS CHANGE LIVES

I read the article with interest. It was about a volunteer organization called L.A. Girlfriends, founded by a nun named Sister Mary Agnes, where women volunteered to become mentors to motherless girls. It was a touching story, filled with heartwarming tales of women like me who'd managed to make a difference in the life of a young girl.

And suddenly I felt ashamed. Big time. I bet Sister Mary Agnes wasn't sitting around feeling sorry for herself. No, Sister Mary Agnes was out there, doing good in the world. It was high time I forgot my petty discontents, and did something noble with my life.

"I'm so ashamed of myself," I said to Prozac, who was curled up next to me on the sofa.

You should be. You haven't scratched my back for a whole six minutes.

"But that's all going to change. I'm going to forget about my trivial cares, and do something worthwhile."

You mean like getting me my own TV?

"I'm going to make a difference in the world!"

I'd like flat screen, if possible.

Wasting no time, I called the offices of L.A. Girlfriends and made an appointment to see them that morning. I'd zip over there on my way to Hysteria Lane.

I hurried off to shower and dress, filled with a newfound sense of purpose. Not only would I get Seymour Fiedler off the hook for that pesky criminal charge, but I'd bring joy to the heart of a motherless child.

I wondered if Mother Teresa started like this.

I was hoping to meet Sister Mary Agnes when I showed up at the modest mid-Wilshire offices of L.A. Girlfriends, but the birdlike woman manning the reception desk explained that the good Sister was away on a fund-raising tour. I'd be meeting with one of her valued associates, she informed me, leading me down the hallway for my interview.

"Ms. Austen," she said, opening the door into a small but sunny office, "meet Tyler Girard."

I blinked in surprise. I hadn't been expecting to see a guy, and certainly not one this cute. He had the kind of boyish good looks I'm particularly fond of. Big brown eyes, sandy hair that flopped onto his forehead, and a smile—as I was about to discover—sweeter than a Hershey's Kiss.

"So nice to meet you, Ms. Austen," he said, flashing me his sweet smile.

Usually I'm wary when it comes to members of the sloppier sex. You'd be wary, too, if you'd been married to The Blob. That's what I call my ex-husband, a charming fellow who wore flip-flops to our wedding and clipped his toenails in the sink. But flying in the face of past experience, my heart was doing carefree little somersaults.

"Have a seat," he said, "and I'll tell you about L.A. Girlfriends."

As he talked about how Sister Mary Agnes started L.A. Girlfriends fifteen years ago in a church basement, I found myself staring at the laugh lines around his mouth and wondering if he liked old movies and Chinese food as much as I did.

This totally inappropriate reverie went on for some time until I came to my senses. I hadn't come here to meet a guy, I reminded myself. I was here to do good in the world. I quickly banished all romantic thoughts from my mind and forced myself to focus.

"So," Tyler said, after he'd finished giving me a rundown on the organization, "tell me a little about yourself."

I told him about my life as a jack-of-all-trades wordsmith—writing ads, brochures, resumes, and industrial films—and how lately I'd been wanting to do something more meaningful with my time, to contribute something to society, as it were, and that L.A. Girlfriends seemed like the perfect venue for my charitable impulses.

I chattered on in this noble vein for a while, carefully omitting any references to the Jaine Austen who has been known to watch *Oprah* in the middle of the afternoon with a cat and a pint of Chunky Monkey in her lap.

He nodded thoughtfully throughout my spiel.

"Have you ever worked with young people before?"

"I used to babysit when I was a teenager. But I don't know if that counts. Most of the time," I admitted, "the kids were asleep."

For what seemed like an eternity but was probably only seconds, he looked into my eyes, saying nothing. I could see he was trying to get a reading on me. Oh, dear Lord, I prayed. Please don't let him see my shallow, selfish side, the side that filches ketchup packets from McDonald's and tears the *Do Not Remove Under Penalty Of Law* tags off pillows.

Finally he broke his silence with a smile.

"I have good vibes about you, Ms. Austen."

He had good vibes about me! I was going to be an L.A. Girlfriend!

"Why don't you fill out our application? We'll do a background check on you, and get back to you in a few days."

Phooey. It looked like I wasn't a shoo-in, after all.

"Don't worry," he said, seeing the disappointment in my eyes. "I don't anticipate any problems. I'm sure you'll check out just fine."

He flashed me another achingly sweet smile and I left his office on a high, ready to start my new altruistic life, thinking of how I'd soon be bringing joy to a motherless young girl.

Okay, so I was thinking about that smile of his, too. Heck, I'm only human.

Chapter Four

This time, the Coxes were home when I rang their bell. Willard's wife, Ethel, came to the door, a short, rosy cheeked woman in an old-fashioned housedress and apron, her hair a cap of tightly permed gray curls.

"Can I help you?" she asked, wiping her hands on her apron.

I flashed her my trusty Century National card and told her I was an insurance investigator looking into Garth's death. It had worked so well with Cathy Janken, I figured I'd try it again.

"Oh, my," she said, shaking her curls in disbelief. "I still can't believe that poor man is dead."

"You didn't happen to see anybody on the roof in the days before he died, did you?"

"Only those roofers," she said. "The ones with the red baseball caps."

"Do you mind if I talk to your husband? Maybe he saw something."

She hesitated a beat, trying to decide whether I was a burglar posing as an insurance investigator.

I guess I passed inspection.

"Come in, won't you, Ms.—what did you say your name was? I didn't get a very good look at your card."

"Austen. Jaine Austen."

"Such an interesting name!" she said, her eyes lighting up. "Are you any relation to the real Jane Austen?"

"Afraid not." I smiled weakly, having answered that question about 8,976 times in my life.

"Willard's out back," she said, waving me inside. "Come with me."

I followed her past a living room that clearly hadn't been decorated since Nixon was president, and into her homey kitchen.

"I was just fixing lunch," she said as my eyes zeroed in on a bowl of egg salad on her kitchen counter, thick with mayo and studded with chunks of hard boiled eggs.

Yikes, it looked good. I hadn't had lunch, and I was starving.

"He's in the yard."

"Who?" I asked, lost in thoughts of egg salad.

"Willard. My husband."

"Oh, right."

"He's putting CDs in the orange trees."

"CDs in the orange trees?"

"It's supposed to scare away the squirrels. Personally, I think it's a lot of nonsense, but Willard insists it works.

"Willard, dear," she called out the back door, "there's an insurance investigator who wants to talk to you."

I walked out into the yard, lush with bougainvillea and orange trees. Yes, I know it's not fair that we Californians get to pick oranges off our trees in December, but on the downside, we get to crawl along on the freeways at ten miles an hour for most of our commuting lives.

Willard Cox was standing on a ladder at one of the orange trees, stringing CDs from the branches, an athletic man in his seventies. The guy was obviously capable of climbing onto the Jankens's roof, I thought, as I watched him move with agile grace.

"Hello, Mr. Cox," I called up to him. "Mind if I have a word with you?"

"Just a minute," he barked, with clipped military diction. "I'll be right down."

Seconds later, he clambered down from the ladder, the CDs on his orange tree twinkling in the reflected light of the sun.

"Keeps the squirrels away," he said, pinging one of the CDs. "They don't like the glare. Bet my wife told you they don't work, but they do."

He snapped his ladder shut and propped it against the garage.

"So you're an insurance investigator." He looked me over with piercing gray eyes.

Uh-oh. It wasn't going to be easy to fool this guy.

"Yes. I'm representing Seymour Fiedler, the roofer who was working on Mr. Janken's house."

"Is that so? What company you with?"

"Century National," I said, praying he wouldn't ask me for identification. He'd never fall for my phony laminated card.

I breathed a sigh of relief when he didn't.

"So how can I help you?" he asked.

"We at Century National don't believe Mr. Janken's death was an accident. We believe someone tampered with the shingles on the roof."

"What are you saying? You think it was murder?"

"Yes, we do."

"It wouldn't surprise me. I hate to speak ill of the dead," he said, not hating it a bit, "but that man was a no good cheat and a liar."

"I heard he beat you a few times in the Christmas decorating contest," I prompted.

Blood rushed to his weathered face.

"He didn't win fair and square. He bribed the judge, that's why he won all the time. Not only that, he cheated.

Last year he beheaded my Santa Claus! He claimed it fell off in the wind, but it didn't just fall off. It was sawed off!

"Let me show you something."

He grabbed the ladder and I followed him as he brought it into his garage, a spotless haven complete with workbench and fancy built-in storage cabinets. A handyman's dream.

Propped up along one of the walls, in stark contrast to the white cabinets, were a chorus line of large red-and-white striped neon candy canes.

"Garth saw these being delivered to my house. And before I had a chance to put them up, he had candy canes up on his roof. He stole my idea!"

"Oh, Willard, honey. He didn't steal your idea. It was a coincidence."

We turned and saw Ethel standing in the doorway.

"Please, Ethel. He saw those candy canes being delivered, and beat me to the punch."

"Whatever you say, dear," she sighed. "I just came to tell you lunch is ready. You're welcome to join us if you like, Ms. Austen. I've made an extra sandwich."

"Oh, no," I said, thinking of all the mayo in the egg salad. Not after those chimichangas I had last night. I really had to exercise some self-restraint if I expected to cram myself into a bathing suit in Florida. "Thanks, but no."

Two minutes later I was sitting across from Willard and Ethel at their vinyl-topped kitchen table tucking into one of Ethel's heavenly egg salad sandwiches.

What can I say? I'm impossible.

When I finally came up for air, I resumed questioning the Coxes.

"Do you have any idea who might've wanted to see Garth dead?"

"Me, for starters," said Willard.

Ethel put down her sandwich, horrified. "Willard, how can you say such a thing?"

"He killed Pumpkin, didn't he?"

"It was an accident, Willard. A tragic accident. I simply can't believe Garth would run over a helpless little poodle on purpose."

"Well, I can."

At that moment, there was so much hate in his eyes, I thought he really might be the one who sabotaged the roof.

"I can't pretend I'm sorry he's dead," he said, as if reading my thoughts, "but I didn't do it."

"Anybody else on the block dislike him enough to want to see him dead?" I asked.

"There's Mrs. Garrison next door," Willard said. "She hated his guts ever since he reported her to the city for illegally removing a tree from the front of her house. She had to pay a big fine, and she was furious."

"You think she might've loosened those tiles on the roof?"

"I doubt it." Ethel smiled wryly. "She's eighty-six and uses a walker."

"How about Libby Brecker?" Willard suggested, beginning to enjoy this game of finger pointing. "She looks like a potential killer to me."

"What an awful thing to say, Willard!"

"I'm serious," Willard insisted. "There's something about that woman that's downright creepy. She's just a little too perfect, if you know what I mean. Like one of those Stepford Wives."

"Just because she takes pride in her house doesn't make her a Stepford Wife."

Ethel rolled her eyes, exasperated.

"I haven't felt right about Libby since the day she

moved in," Willard said, ignoring his wife's objections. "They say she's a widow. I'd like to know what happened to her husband."

"I'm sure he died of perfectly natural causes," Ethel said, taking a dainty bite of a gherkin pickle.

"That's the trouble with you, Ethel. You're too trusting. You believe any cock and bull story someone hands you."

"What was Libby Brecker's relationship like with Mr. Janken?" I asked, steering the conversation away from Ethel Cox's personality flaws and back to the murder.

"Hated him," said Willard.

"I'm afraid she did," Ethel conceded. "She accused Garth of poisoning her roses. Those roses of hers were her pride and joy."

"Why would Mr. Janken want to poison her roses?"

"Libby claims Garth was getting even with her for calling the police when one of his parties got too loud."

"Which house is Libby's?" I asked, eager to question this promising suspect.

"It's the two-story Spanish across the street," Willard said, "with the Swarovski Rudolph on the lawn out front."

"The Swarovski Rudolph?"

"Rudolph the Reindeer's nose is a Swarovski crystal," Ethel said. "Lord only knows how much it cost!"

"I tell you," Willard said, wagging his gherkin at me, "there's something strange about that woman."

I thanked the Coxes for their time and their egg salad and headed back outside, contemplating the nature of life on Hysteria Lane. Who would've thought there'd be so much hostility lurking beneath the surface of this picture-perfect block? It made the Middle East look like a picnic in the Amish country.

I was in the middle of a war zone, all right. Trouble was, I didn't know the good guys from the bad.

* * *

The nose on Libby Brecker's Rudolph was indeed a red crystal, in all probability a genuine Swarovski.

I found Libby on her lawn spritzing it with Windex. She was a plump woman with bright brown eyes and hair so glossy, I could practically see my face in it.

Once again posing as an insurance investigator, I flashed her my Century National card and explained that I was looking into Garth's death on Seymour's behalf.

"If it's all right with you, I'd like to ask you a few questions."

"Go ahead," she chirped. "Ask away."

By now she was down on her knees, buffing the runners on an elaborate wooden sleigh that was probably once owned by Currier & Ives.

I asked her if she'd seen anyone on the roof in the days before Garth's death and like everybody else I'd spoken with, she gave me the same disappointing answer.

"Just the roofers. Who, incidentally, seemed to be doing an excellent job. I was thinking of using them myself, but after what happened to Garth, *that's* not going to happen."

Poor Seymour. I was certain most people would react the way Libby had. If word of Garth's death got around, his business would be ruined.

"Of course, Garth was foolish to go up on the roof in the first place," she said. "You really need to hire a professional for that. I always do. But then I'm acrophobic. Dreadful fear of heights," she added, in case my vocabulary didn't extend beyond three-syllable words. "I get dizzy in high heels. Ha ha."

(Translation: *If you're hinting at foul play, sweetie, don't even think of trying to pin this on me.*)

"Are you sure you didn't see anyone else up on the roof, other than the roofers?

"Omigosh!" she cried, hitting her forehead with the palm of her hand. "I just remembered!"

At last! A lead!

"My cookies!" she said. "I've got cookies in the oven!"

So much for leads.

"C'mon inside, and we'll talk there."

I followed her into her house, past a border of newly planted rosebushes, little stubs with the nursery tags still on them. Probably replacements for the ones that had been poisoned.

"Take your shoes off," Libby instructed, kicking hers off. "I just waxed and buffed the floors, and I don't want to track in any mud."

We put our shoes on something Libby called her "mud rug," an area rug so pristine, it was hard to imagine it had ever been sullied by a speck of actual mud.

"I'll be right back," she trilled. "Make yourself comfortable in the living room."

She pointed to a room off the foyer and then scurried to the back of the house.

I made my way through an arched entranceway to the living room.

Yikes, I thought, looking around. The place was a real-life issue of *Martha Stewart Living*.

The furniture was upholstered in a palette of white and beige, accented by colorful throw pillows and strategically placed vases of fresh-cut flowers. Cinnamon spice potpourri scented the air. And framed in the window was a magnificent Christmas tree, studded with what looked like exquisite handmade ornaments—angels and snowflakes and fragrant pomander balls. What a masterpiece. It made the one at Rockefeller Center look like a blue light special at Kmart. I wondered if the resourceful Libby had grown the darn thing herself.

Padding around the room in my socks, hoping I wouldn't skid into a tailspin on the freshly waxed floors,

I came across a pine étagère filled with artfully arranged photos and mementos.

There was Libby on the beach with a sunburned pot-bellied man, both of them wearing leis, smiling into the camera. Her deceased husband, I presumed. There were several pictures of twin boys at various stages in their lives, from diaper days to high school graduation. But what caught my attention was a framed newspaper photo of Libby grinning at the camera, clutching a trophy. The headline above the photo read: *LIBBY BRECKER, 42, WINS ANNUAL ROSE COMPETITION FOR FIFTH CONSECUTIVE YEAR.* And indeed, proudly displayed and dramatically lit on a center shelf were five golden trophies from the West Los Angeles Gardening Club for *Most Beautiful Rose.*

Interesting, I noted, how the roses got better shelf space than her husband and kids.

Libby was crazy about her roses, all right. Crazy enough, I wondered, to have killed someone she thought poisoned them?

"I see you're looking at my family pictures."

I turned to see Libby sailing into the room with a tray of cookies and milk.

"The twins just went off to college this year," she said, putting the tray down on a gleaming pine coffee table. "Golly, I've missed them. Empty nest syndrome, you know."

Why did I get the feeling she was secretly relieved not to have to worry about the twins tracking mud onto her floors?

"I brought us some cookies."

She waved me over to the matching white sofas that fronted the fireplace and I sat across from her, sinking into a luxurious down cushion.

"Have one," she offered. "They're chocolate chip."

As if I didn't know. I can smell a chocolate chip cookie

baking in Pomona. And these looked particularly scrumptious, studded with chunks of chocolate and walnuts.

Of course, I couldn't possibly allow myself to have a cookie, not after the brownie I'd just had at Willard and Ethel's. (Okay, so I had a brownie at Willard and Ethel's. Okay, two brownies. Oh, don't go shaking your head like that. I'd like to see what *you're* eating right now.)

The last thing I needed was another calorie clinging to my thighs. But I couldn't say no, could I? Not after all the trouble she'd gone to put them on a tray and bring them out to me. No, under the circumstances, the only polite thing to do was eat a cookie. But just one, that was all.

"Thanks," I said, grabbing one. "They look scrumptious."

"They are," she said, with a confident nod.

I took a bite. I thought I'd died and gone to cookie heaven.

With great effort, I forced myself to resume my questioning.

"So do you know anyone on the block who might've wanted to see Garth dead?"

"Of course not!" Libby exclaimed, plucking an errant cookie crumb from her lap. "He wasn't a very popular man, but nobody actually wanted him dead."

"Nobody?" I asked, suppressing the urge to reach for another cookie. "Are you sure there wasn't anybody who had it in for Garth?"

"Well, maybe Willard Cox," she conceded. "He and Garth fought like cats and dogs. But I doubt Willard actually climbed up on Garth's roof and jimmied the shingles, if that's what you're getting at."

"Speaking of Mr. Cox," I said, grateful for the opening she'd just given me, "he happened to mention an altercation you had with Garth."

"Me?" A brief blip of annoyance flashed across her face.

"Yes, he said you accused Mr. Janken of poisoning your roses."

"Willard said that? How absurd!" She laughed a tinkly laugh about as genuine as Maxine Fiedler's hair color. "I never accused Garth of any such thing."

"I heard the same thing from a few other people," I lied, trying to rattle her.

But she was a cool customer.

"Golly, no," she smiled serenely. "Garth and I had a perfectly cordial relationship. I pride myself in bringing out the best in even the most difficult people."

"So you don't think he poisoned your roses?"

"Not at all," she cooed. "Roses get sick and die all the time. I'm sure Garth had nothing to do with mine dying, and if Willard Cox or anyone else said anything to the contrary, they're sadly mistaken.

"Gracious!" she said, jumping up from the sofa. "Look at the time!

"If I don't get started refinishing the twins' bedroom shutters, they'll never get done in time for Christmas break."

Her lips were smiling but her eyes had turned to steel. My audience with Libby had clearly come to a close.

I retrieved my shoes from her "mud rug" and as I did, I was gratified to see a defiant pink dustbunny clinging to the baseboard of her floor. Somehow the little devil had managed to escape annihilation during Libby's recent waxing and buffing fest.

More power to you, little dustbunny, I thought, as I put on my shoes.

I thanked Libby for her time and headed back out to my Corolla.

I wasn't buying her Little Miss Sunshine act, not for a minute. I'd bet my bottom Pop Tart her relations with Garth had been about as cordial as a Ku Klux Klan reception for Martin Luther King.

No, Libby Brecker had been lying through her perfectly whitened teeth. Now all I had to do was prove it.

Chapter Five

That night, after a Spartan dinner of tuna and a toasted English muffin (honest, that's all I ate!), I went out to the storage space behind my duplex and dug out my Christmas tree.

It was one of those wimpy tabletop models, with the ornaments already glued on—a sorry sight compared to the towering extravaganza at Libby's.

I used to have real trees with real ornaments, but Prozac, convinced the ornaments were evil spirits from hell, was constantly diving at them with the ferocity of a kamikaze pilot. The poor trees never stood a chance.

And so I was stuck with my pathetic tabletop model.

I plopped it down on an end table, and after dusting it off and draping it with tinsel, I turned to where Prozac was lounging on the sofa.

"How does it look, sweetie?"

She glared at it through slitted eyes and got to her feet. Tail erect and waving in anticipation of an ornament ambush, she cautiously approached it. Then she put her nose to one of the branches and took a sniff.

"So?" I asked. "What do you think?"

She sniffed under the tree, then turned to me.

What? No presents?

Then, having decided the tree was free of lurking enemies, she curled up and went to sleep.

Minutes later, I settled down next to her on the sofa with a cup of cocoa and a stack of Christmas cards. I'd long since conceded defeat to Prozac in the photo-card skirmish, and had picked up some cards with an old-fashioned drawing of Santa on the cover.

I got out my address book and began my task. I tried to think of heartfelt personalized messages in twenty-five words or less, but I couldn't concentrate. Ever since I'd left Libby's house that afternoon, I'd had the nagging feeling I'd seen something significant there. An elusive something I couldn't quite put my finger on.

Now I drummed my pen against my teeth, trying to remember exactly what it was. Images began flitting through my brain: The Swarovski Rudolph, the family photos, the newspaper clipping, the trophies, the handmade Christmas angels, the "mud rug," the defiant pink dustbunny—

And that's when it hit me. It wasn't a dustbunny I'd seen clinging to Libby's baseboard—it was a piece of flocking. *Pink* flocking. Just like the pink flocking I'd seen on Garth's Candyland roof!

True, Libby could have been working on a project of her own that involved pink flocking. The woman was probably working on more projects than the NASA space team. Nevertheless, I couldn't help wondering if she'd picked up that piece of pink fluff while jimmying the shingles on Garth Janken's roof.

Yes, folks. It's very possible that Libby Brecker's latest project had been Attempted Homicide.

Armed with my Dustbunny Discovery, I paid a visit to the cop in charge of the Janken case, Lt. Frank Di-Martelli.

DiMartelli worked out of the West Los Angeles precinct, a concrete bunker of a building in a none-too-glamorous part of town. I spent a good twenty minutes on a wooden bench exchanging pleasantries with a 6'4" transvestite named Cheyenne before the good lieutenant ushered me to his desk.

A laconic guy with droopy bloodhound eyes, DiMartelli nodded absently as I told him of my suspicions, all the while fiddling with a chocolate Santa on his desk. Occasionally he picked up a yellow legal pad and jotted down a note, but I had the sneaky suspicion he was working on his Christmas list.

"In other words," he said when I was through, "you're accusing Libby Brecker of murder because you saw a dustbunny on her baseboard."

"It wasn't a dustbunny. It was a piece of flocking."

"Are you *sure* it was flocking?"

"Of course, I'm sure."

He shot me a penetrating look from beneath his droopy lids.

"Pretty sure, anyway," I hedged.

"We'll check into it," he said. "When hell freezes over."

Okay, so he didn't say the part about hell freezing over, but I knew that's what he was thinking. Clearly he'd written me off as an interfering nutcase.

"Well, thanks for your time," I said, not feeling the least bit grateful. "And bon appetit," I added, with a nod to the chocolate Santa.

Then I got up and headed out the door.

I glanced back just in time to see him wad up the notes he'd just taken and toss them in the trash.

All in all, not a terribly satisfying meeting.

There was, however, some good news to report that week. I'd just come home from my fruitless visit to

Lt. DiMartelli, and was stretched out on my sofa, trying to dredge up the energy to tackle my Christmas cards. I'd abandoned my original plan to write heartfelt personal messages, settling for the slightly less imaginative "XOXOXO, Jaine." But now even X's and O's seemed like a lot of work, and I was lying there staring at the ceiling, when the phone rang.

After fishing it out from between two sofa cushions, I heard a soft male voice come on the line.

"Jaine? It's Tyler Girard."

Omigosh, the sweetie from L.A. Girlfriends!

I bolted up, suddenly rejuvenated.

"Congratulations, Jaine. You're now officially an L.A. Girlfriend."

"That's wonderful!" I squealed.

"I told you there wouldn't be any problems. We've already matched you with your Girlfriend."

"When do I meet her?"

"I'll fax you her background information and phone number, and you can set up a date."

"I can't wait!" I said, eager to start my life of selfless giving.

"I'll also send along a copy of our *Girlfriends Guidelines.* Some rules and regulations you need to follow. Nothing major. Suggested venues for your dates, stuff like that."

"How can I ever thank you for giving me this marvelous opportunity?"

"No need to thank us, Jaine. We're happy to have you on board. Oh, and while I've got you on the phone, there's something else I'd like to ask you."

No, I'm not married, and yes, I'd love to go out with you.

But he was not, alas, about to ask me out on a date.

"You mentioned at our meeting that you're a writer."

"Yes, I am."

"It so happens we've been looking for someone to write press releases for us. Have you ever done any PR?"

Okay, so it wasn't a date, but it was the next best thing. A potential job, always a welcome prospect at Casa Austen.

"Oh, yes," I assured him. "I've done lots of PR. Why, just last year I won an award for a promotional campaign I wrote."

"Really? Who was your client?"

Drat. I was hoping he wouldn't ask me this.

"Um. Toiletmasters Plumbers."

Not exactly the Fortune 500 image I was hoping to impart.

"And what were you promoting?"

Phooey. I was hoping to avoid this one, too.

"A new product of theirs. Called Big John."

"Big John?"

"A large-sized commode for large-sized people."

"Really? And you won an award for that?"

"Yes," I said, with as much dignity as I could muster. "The Golden Plunger Award from the Los Angeles Plumbers Association."

Miraculously, he did not burst out into gales of derisive laughter. On the contrary, much to my amazement, the next words out of his mouth were:

"Do you think you might be interested in doing some work for us?"

"Absolutely," I assured him.

"Great! I'll introduce you to Sister Mary Agnes at the Christmas party, and you can set up an interview with her."

"The Christmas party?"

"Yes, every year L.A. Girlfriends has a big Christmas bash."

"Sounds like fun."

"I'll look forward to seeing you there."

Was it my imagination, or was there a hint of romance in his voice? Was Tyler possibly angling for an L.A. Girlfriend of his own?

I hung up in a happy glow. I'd started out to do something charitable, and already I was being rewarded. Not only was there a possible job on my horizon, there might even be a date. With a really nice guy.

But the biggest reward, I reminded myself, would be the satisfaction I'd get from making a difference in the life of a motherless girl.

Yes, I, Jaine Austen, was about to leave the world of the Self-Involved and become one of life's Noble Givers.

Chapter Six

I had a date with an angel.

Really. That was my L.A. Girlfriend's name: Angel Cavanaugh, a twelve-year-old only child living with her dad, whose interests were listed on her profile as "outdoor activities" and "the arts."

When I phoned to set up the date, she was in the shower, and her father took the call.

"We're so grateful you're doing this," he said. "It means the world to us."

How wonderful to feel so appreciated. Why hadn't I discovered this volunteer stuff years ago?

I asked him what Angel wanted to do on our date, and he said anything I planned would be okay with her.

Then I hung up and went into a planning frenzy, making and discarding a dozen ideas. I finally decided that, since Angel liked outdoor activities, it might be fun to drive out to the Santa Monica Pier and toss a frisbee on the beach. One of the rules in the *Girlfriends Guidebook* was to stay away from expensive venues. The girls, they warned, mustn't see their mentors as a source of financial support. Which was lucky for me, since I was having trouble enough supporting myself.

The day of my "Girlfriends" date dawned clear and

bright, with a hint of winter chill in the air. A Los Angeles winter, that is—the temperature had dipped all the way down to the low seventies. A perfect day for a trip to the beach.

And so it was with an air of eager anticipation that I fed Prozac her Savory Salmon Entrails and nuked myself a bagel. I couldn't wait to get started on the first chapter of my new altruistic life. After a quick shower, I threw on a pair of jeans and a long-sleeved T-shirt, and grabbed a hoodie in case it got chilly out on the pier.

"Bye, Pro," I called out, when I was ready to leave on my great adventure. "Wish me luck."

She looked up from where she was napping on my keyboard.

I still don't see why you have to spend the day with some needy kid when you could stay home and scratch my back.

But she couldn't work a guilt trip on me. Not today. I headed out to my Corolla, brimming with good intentions, Mother Teresa in elastic-waist jeans.

I drove over to the address Angel's dad had given me, which turned out to be a low-rent apartment building a fender's throw from the 405 freeway. It was one of those two-story affairs with an outdoor stairway that looked like it had been a motel in a former life. As I climbed the metal steps to the Cavanaughs's apartment on the second floor, I could hear the dull roar of the freeway in the background.

Kevin Cavanaugh answered the door, a skinny guy in his late thirties. With hollow cheeks and dark circles under his eyes, he had the look of a guy in desperate need of a vacation. Or, barring that, a nap.

"So happy to meet you," he said, pumping my hand. "C'mon in." He ushered me into his living room, and once again I was reminded of a motel. All the essentials were there—sofa and TV and coffee table, but none of the frills. No sign of a woman's touch anywhere.

"Angel, honey." he called out. "Jaine is here."

We stood there smiling awkwardly at each other, waiting for Angel to come out. When some time had passed and there was still no sign of her, he shouted, "You ready, or what?"

"I'm commmmming!"

And then, to my amazement, a twelve-year-old hooker walked into the room.

Her skinny body was jammed into spandex capris and a midriff-exposing T-shirt, the words JAIL BAIT emblazoned in sequins across her flat chest. Completing the outfit were a pair of kitten-heel flip-flops and a faux leopard skin minipurse.

Good heavens. She looked like she was auditioning for a remake of Taxi Driver.

"For Pete's sake, Angel," her dad sighed. "You're not going to wear that, are you?"

"Yessss." She rolled her eyes. "I am."

"Well, come and say hello to Jaine," he said, shrugging helplessly.

Angel clomped over on her kitten heels and gave me the once-over.

Up close I could see that underneath her cloud of heavily teased dishwater blond hair, she was actually quite pretty. Clear gray eyes, nice little nose. Slightly protruding teeth, but all in all, a cute kid.

"She's my girlfriend?" she whined, eyeing my elastic-waist jeans and baggy T-shirt. "I told them I wanted someone who looked like Jennifer Aniston. Somebody who dresses nice."

Uh-oh. Maybe my new life of selflessness wasn't going to be so rewarding, after all.

"Angel, that's no way to talk," her dad chided. "Apologize this minute."

"Okaaaaay," she said, with another roll of her eyes. "I'm sorry."

"Kids," he said, shooting me an apologetic smile. "What're you gonna do?"

"A little discipline might help."

Of course, I didn't really say that. Lord only knew what it was like trying to rein in this kid.

"Don't worry about it," I said, with a confidence I didn't feel. "I'm sure we're going to get along just fine."

I shot her a hopeful smile. "Right, Angel?"

"Let's go already," was her cheerful reply.

"Do you have to go to the bathroom before you leave?" Kevin asked her.

"No, I don't have to go to the bathroom."

"Are you sure?"

"Yesss. I'm sure."

"What about a sweater? You're gonna need one in that top."

"Your father's right, Angel," I said. "We're going to the beach. It might get chilly out there."

"I don't need a sweater," she snapped. "Now are we going, or what?"

Kevin Cavanaugh shot me one last apologetic smile as we headed out the door. I was beginning to understand his hollow cheeks and baggy eyes.

"Good luck." With a feeble wave good-bye, he shut the door behind us. How I envied him being on the other side of that door.

Angel and I started down the metal steps, Angel clomping along in her rickety heels.

"Are you sure you're going to be okay in those shoes?"

"Yes," she hissed. "I'm going to be okay."

"Here's my car!" I said, trying to sound chirpy as I led her over to my Corolla.

"This is it?" She eyed my geriatric Corolla with unalloyed disdain. "Ugh. If I wanted to ride around in a crummy car, I could hang out with my dad. And even our car is nicer than this."

"Just get in," I said, resisting a sudden impulse to leap in and drive off without her.

She settled down on the passenger seat with a petulant plop.

"Buckle your seat belt," I instructed.

"I don't want to buckle my seat belt. It'll wrinkle my top."

"Buckle your belt!" I said through gritted teeth.

With an exasperated sigh, she buckled the belt and we took off.

"I don't want to go to the beach," she whined as I swung onto Santa Monica Boulevard and headed out to the ocean. "I want to go to the mall."

"We're not going to the mall."

"But I hate the beach. I want to go shopping."

"It said on your profile you liked outdoor activities."

"I do. I like shopping at outdoor malls."

"Forget it, Angel. We're not going shopping."

"But you're my Girlfriend. Aren't you supposed to buy me gifts?"

"No, I'm not supposed to buy you gifts. It specifically says so in the *Girlfriends Guidebook*."

"Oh, fudge." Only that's not the *F* word she used. "I woulda never signed up for this stupid Girlfriends thing if I knew there weren't gonna be any presents."

"You're not getting any gifts. And watch your language."

We rode the next few minutes in a tense silence, broken finally by Angel announcing:

"I gotta go to the bathroom."

"For crying out loud, Angel, your dad told you to go back in the apartment."

"Well, I didn't."

"It's too late now," I snarled. "Hold it in."

"Okay, okay. Don't have a snit fit."

By now my knuckles were white on the steering wheel. The enormity of my mistake was beginning to hit me.

I no longer felt the least bit like Mother Teresa. No, as I piloted our way those final blocks out to the pier, I felt like a lion tamer in a cage without a whip and a chair.

The Santa Monica Pier juts out into the Pacific, a rustic boardwalk dotted with restaurants and souvenir shops, right next to a small amusement park.

The minute I parked the car, Angel sprinted out to use the bathroom at one of the restaurants. I followed her inside and found myself in a tacky seafood joint with fishermen's netting draped on the walls and a giant stuffed swordfish hanging over the bar. As Angel hustled off to the ladies' room, I took a seat on a bar stool and eyed a bottle of Jose Cuervo. You'll be ashamed of me, I know, but I seriously contemplated ordering a margarita. At eleven in the morning. But sanity prevailed. Instead I asked for a glass of water, and gulped down a few Tylenol to quell the headache that was now throbbing in my skull.

I sat there for a while, waiting for the pills to take effect and ruing the day I ever saw that story in the paper about L.A. Girlfriends.

Then I checked my watch and realized that ten minutes had passed since Angel had gone down the corridor to the ladies' room. That's an awfully long time for a trip to the bathroom. And suddenly I panicked. Dire scenarios began flashing in my brain. What if she'd run away? What if she slipped out a back door? Or wriggled out a bathroom window? For all I knew, she was turning tricks in the men's room. Oh, Lord. Her father would never forgive me.

I jumped off the barstool and raced down the corridor to the ladies' room, or as it was known in this particular establishment, The Little Mermaids' Room.

"Angel?" I shouted, pounding on the door. "Are you in there?"

"Yeah, I'm here."

My knees buckled with relief.

"What's taking you so long?"

"I'm coming. I'm coming."

A few seconds later, she sauntered out with enough makeup on her face to stock a Cover Girl display.

"What on earth have you done to your face?"

"My dad doesn't like me to wear makeup, so I wait till I'm out of the apartment to put it on."

I considered making her take it right off again, but I knew it would be a battle royale and frankly, I didn't have the energy.

"Let's go." I took her by the hand and hustled her outside.

"So what're we supposed to do now?" she asked, squinting into the sun.

My first choice, going back inside for a round of margaritas, was clearly out of the question.

"How about a ride on the merry-go-round?" I suggested.

"Are you kidding?" she sneered. "That's for kids."

"What about the roller coaster?"

"Nah. I don't want to mess my hair."

"Then let's just walk around the pier."

"Okay, but if we run into any kids from my school, pretend you don't know me."

I ground my teeth in annoyance, wondering if anybody would notice if I tossed her over the pier.

And right away I felt ashamed. I really had to stop this negative thinking, and give the kid a chance. So Angel was a little difficult. That was all part of being a mentor. I bet Sister Mary Agnes dealt with lots of difficult kids over the years. I had to try to establish an emotional rapport, like they said in the *Girlfriends Guidebook*, and get her to open up to me.

"So tell me about yourself," I said. "What's your favorite subject in school?"

"Puh-leeese. I hate that place. It's like a prison. They won't even let you wear bustiers."

"You have any idea what you want to do when you grow up?"

"Marry a rich guy and move to Bel Air."

Why was I not surprised?

I asked her a few more questions, most of which were greeted with monosyllabic grunts. It was like talking to a fire hydrant.

"Look," she said, when I'd finally run out of steam. "There's a souvenir shop."

"Forget it, Angel. I'm not buying you a present."

"Well, you have to buy me lunch," she pouted. "I'm hungry."

For once, we were on the same page. I was a little peckish myself.

"How about a burger?" I said, pointing to a nearby burger stand.

"I don't want a burger," she whined. "I want nachos."

Needless to say, they didn't have nachos at the burger stand two feet away from us. So we trekked to every restaurant and snack shop on the pier till we finally found a place that sold them.

I got a burger and Angel got her precious nachos and we settled down on a bench to eat them.

"Mmm, this burger is good," I said, wolfing it down with impressive speed.

Angel took two bites of her nachos and yawned. Then, before I could stop her, she tossed them in the trash.

"What did you do that for?" I wailed. "We traipsed all over the pier for those stupid nachos."

"I wasn't hungry any more," she shrugged.

"Why'd you throw them away? I could've eaten them."

"I bet you could," she said, her voice ripe with innuendo.

"What's that supposed to mean?"

"Nothing." All wide-eyed innocence. "You said you could eat them, and I agreed."

"C'mon." I wadded my burger wrapper and slammed it into the trash. "Let's go play frisbee."

"Do we have to?"

"Yes, we have to."

"But I'll ruin my shoes."

"So take them off."

I took her by the hand and practically dragged her down to the beach.

"I'm cold," she whined, as we made our way toward the ocean.

"Your dad *told* you to take a sweater."

"Well, I didn't."

"Take mine."

I took off my hoodie and handed it to her. She looked at it like I'd just handed her a dead rat.

"Do you want it, or don't you?"

"Oh, all right," she said, putting it on. It hung on her tiny body like a bathrobe.

I reached in my purse and fished out the frisbee I'd brought along for our carefree day at the beach. Then I tossed it to her, only to have her gaze at it vacantly as it whizzed by.

"Do I have to go get it?" she moaned, staring at where it had landed. "It's so far away."

"Yes, Angel. You have to get it. That's how playing frisbee works. If you miss the frisbee, you have to go get it."

She took her sweet time and sauntered over to pick it up. At the rate she was going, I'd be on Medicare by the time she threw it back to me. At last she got it and tossed it back. A feeble toss that landed practically at her feet.

"Now it's your turn to get it," she smirked.

My jaw clenched in annoyance, I ran over to her and picked it up. I was standing so close to her when I tossed it back, she had no choice but to catch it.

"Okay," I grunted, "now throw it back."

I'd had gum surgery more fun than this.

Then, to my surprise, she flung her arm back and hurled the frisbee with decathlon force. I watched as it sailed into the ocean.

"Your turn to get it," she trilled.

For a minute I was tempted to let it float out to sea, but that's just what the little brat wanted.

So I took off my shoes, rolled up my jeans and waded out into the surf. The ocean was rough, and for a minute it looked like the frisbee was a goner, but then I saw it drifting back toward the shoreline.

I raced over and snatched it out of the water, holding it aloft in triumph.

So there, you little monster!

I stood at the shoreline, waving the frisbee at Angel and savoring my victory. Which was a major mistake. If I hadn't been standing there flapping that damn frisbee, I would've seen the wave that was about to break right behind me. And break it did, with a big wet thud against my fanny. The next thing I knew, I was sopping wet and dripping with seaweed.

I looked over at Angel. For the first time all day, she was smiling.

I checked my watch, and to my dismay, I saw that we'd been at the beach for little more than an hour.

Funny, it felt like decades. I'd planned on spending the whole afternoon with her, but I simply could not face five more minutes with this brat.

"C'mon," I said, yanking her by the elbow. "Time to go home."

"Fine with me," she snapped, and we trudged back together in icy silence to my car.

I dried myself off as best I could with a mildewy beach towel from the trunk of my car, then sped back to Angel's apartment with my foot on the accelerator, cursing every red light in our path.

At last, we pulled up in front of her building and got out of the car.

"So," she said, as we headed to the rickety metal staircase, "you taking me to the L.A. Girlfriends Christmas party?"

Was she crazy? Not if my life depended on it. I didn't care how nice Tyler was. Or what sort of job Sister Mary Agnes might offer me. Never in a million years was I seeing this spawn from hell again.

"Probably not. I think I'm going to be out of town on a business trip."

Was it my imagination, or did I see a flicker of disappointment in her eyes?

"Who cares?" she said, with an exaggerated shrug. "I didn't want to go anyway. I bet it's just a bunch of dorks standing around drinking punch."

And then, out of nowhere, she started gasping for air.

"Angel, what's wrong?"

She shook her head, unable to speak, and groped around in her purse. Finally she found what she was looking for. An inhaler. She clamped her lips around it and began pumping intently.

After a few terrifying seconds, she began breathing normally again. "Quit worrying," she said, seeing the fear in my eyes. "It's nothing. Just asthma. I've had it since I was a little kid." She tossed the inhaler back her purse. "Well, see ya round."

Then she started up the steps to her apartment, her bony shoulders stiff with pride.

As I watched her pathetic leopard skin purse flap against her hip, I was suddenly overcome with guilt. This poor kid was not only motherless, she had a debilitating illness. What sort of cold-hearted bitch was I to bail out on her after just one hellish date?

"Wait a minute," I called out.

She stopped in her tracks and turned to look at me.

"Yeah? What is it?"

"That business trip. I think I maybe be able to get out of it."

"Don't do me any favors. You just feel sorry for me because I've got asthma."

"That's not true," I lied. "I really think I can make it."

She shot me a skeptical look.

"Honest." By now I was begging. "I really want to go."

"Well, okay," she said, clomping back down the steps to my side. "And in case you decide to bring me a gift, here's what I want." She thrust an ad torn from a newspaper into my hand.

The kid never gave up, did she?

Then she tore up the steps to her apartment and began banging on the door with the relentless drive of a jackhammer.

"Pop!" she shrieked. "Open up!"

Kevin Cavanaugh opened the door, his face crumpling at the sight of her.

"Back so soon?" he called out to me over the roar of the freeway.

I pretended I didn't hear him and, with a merry wave, dashed off to the sanctuary of my Corolla.

Chapter Seven

I woke up the next morning, still recuperating from my encounter with Angel Cavanaugh (or, as I was now calling her, *Rosemary's Other Baby*).

I'd staggered home from our date, damp and shivering, and spent the next hour or so soaking in the tub, Prozac gazing down at me from her perch on the toilet tank.

I told you you should've stayed home and scratched my back.

I'd whiled away the rest of the day mindlessly watching sitcom reruns, getting up only to run out for some Chinese take-out. Okay, so I ran out for some Ben & Jerry's, too—to reward myself for surviving a whole hour and forty-six and a half minutes (but who's counting?) with Angel.

Now, after a restless night dreaming I was being chased down the Santa Monica Pier by a giant nacho, I lay in bed, gazing up at the ceiling. I thought about bailing out on L.A. Girlfriends and leaving Angel to another mentor, preferably one who'd spent some time as a prison warden.

But then I remembered how vulnerable she'd looked gasping at her inhaler, and I knew I had to give her another chance. Somehow, I vowed, prying myself out of bed, I had to make our relationship work.

I'd just sloshed some Hearty Halibut Guts into a bowl for Prozac and was standing at the kitchen counter, breakfasting on a cold egg roll, when the phone rang.

Seymour Fiedler came on the line, sounding light years more cheerful than the last time we'd spoken.

"Good news, Jaine. I just talked with my lawyer, and I may be off the hook for Garth Janken's death."

"That's great, Seymour."

"Now the cops think it was premeditated murder. In fact, they just brought somebody in for questioning. A guy named Willard Cox. Apparently they found some incriminating evidence linking him to Garth's death."

"What evidence?"

"I have no idea. All I know is they're questioning him."

"Do you want me to continue my investigation?"

"You may as well. Just in case they change their minds."

I hung up with an uneasy feeling in the pit of my stomach. Some of it was probably indigestion from that egg roll. But mainly, I was concerned about Willard. Something in my gut told me he was innocent.

I know he hated Garth, but there's a big difference between wishing somebody were no longer around to bother you, and actually trying to kill him. Besides, if Willard were really the killer, would he have been so openly vitriolic about Garth?

No, my gut was telling me that the cops had brought in the wrong suspect for questioning.

But what, I wondered, was the incriminating evidence they'd found?

I decided to pay a little visit to Ethel Cox and find out.

I made my way past the frolicking reindeer on the Coxes's front lawn and rang the bell.

Ethel came to the door, still in her nightgown. A far cry from the happy hausfrau I'd met the other day, her gray curls had lost their bounce and her once rosy cheeks were drained of color.

"Ethel," I asked, in what had to be one of the Top Ten World's Most Rhetorical Questions, "are you okay?"

"Willard's gone!" she cried, her eyes wide with fear. "The police took him away for questioning!"

"Try not to worry, Ethel. They'll probably release him in a few hours. Let me come in and make you some tea."

She nodded numbly and allowed me to lead her down the hallway to her kitchen.

Minutes later, we were seated across from each other with steaming cups of tea, laced with lemon and plenty of sugar. The warmth from the tea seemed to calm her a bit.

"Oh, Ms. Austen," she said, taking a grateful sip. "It's just awful. The police found a *Fiedler on the Roof* cap in Willard's toolbox out in the garage. They think he was the one who loosened those shingles on Garth's roof."

So that was the evidence Seymour had been talking about.

"I don't know how it could've gotten there," she said, bewildered.

Clearly this woman didn't have a suspicious bone in her body.

"Somebody may have put it there, Ethel. To frame Willard for Garth's murder."

"Oh, dear."

"Did any of the neighbors have access to the garage?"

"Actually, they all did. There's a little door on the side of the garage we never lock. In case the gardener wants to get in.

"To think," she said, the color rushing back to her

cheeks, "that some awful person would try to blame Garth's death on Willard. Who would do such a terrible thing?"

The first person who sprang to my mind was my lead suspect, Libby Brecker. Hadn't she said she'd been watching the roofers work? What if she'd seen one of them leave his cap behind? How easy to snatch it up, disguise herself as a roofer, and clamber up the roof to set Garth's deathtrap. And how easy to slip over when the Coxes were away and plant the cap in Willard's tool-box.

My musings were interrupted by the shrill ring of a phone.

"Oh, dear!" Ethel said, jumping up. "Maybe that's Willard!"

She hurried out of the room, her granny gown billowing behind her.

I sat there, stirring my tea, wondering whether Libby Brecker was indeed Garth's killer and/or whether Ethel had any brownies left over from the other day.

I know. I'm impossible, thinking about food at a time like this. I bet Sherlock Holmes never sat around wondering if Dr. Watson had any brownies in his kitchen.

I was in the midst of giving myself a stern lecture when Ethel came bursting through the door.

"Willard's in jail!" she cried.

"They arrested him?"

She nodded miserably. "He got into a fight with one of the police officers and threatened to 'punch his lights out.' Now they're holding him without bail."

She sank into a kitchen chair, dazed.

"Oh, Willard," she moaned, "what have you done now?"

Then she turn to me and said: "Do you know how to write a check, Jaine?"

I nodded, confused. Where the heck had that come from?

"Willard told me to pay the gas bill."

"And?"

"And I don't know how to write a check. Can you believe that? I'm seventy-two years old, and I don't know how to write a check."

She put her head on the table and burst out sobbing.

"Oh, God. What am I going to do without him?"

I jumped up and wrapped my arms around her.

"Don't worry, Ethel. They can't keep him there for long if he's innocent."

She looked up at me, her eyes wild with panic.

And in that moment I knew that, even worse than the fear of coping by herself, Ethel was afraid her husband might have really killed Garth Janken.

After teaching Ethel the fine art of check writing, I left her with a hug and a promise to keep in touch, and headed out into the bright sunshine, convinced that somebody had planted that roofer's cap in Willard's toolbox. I simply couldn't believe he'd be foolish enough to leave it there himself.

My money, as you know, was on Libby Brecker. But I had no proof she was the killer. I wasn't even certain that the flocking I saw on her rug came from Garth's roof, or that it was indeed flocking.

I had no idea where to turn next. My interviews with the residents of Hysteria Lane had been a bust, yielding no leads whatsoever. No juicy gossip about Decorating Wars or poisoned roses. Just some tepid complaints about Garth hosting loud parties, turning away trick or treaters at Halloween, and being—in the words of eighty-six-year-old Mrs. Garrison—"an old grouchpuss."

It was one of those moments when a lesser detective would have given up hope and drowned her frustrations in Ben & Jerry's. But not me. I wasn't about to waste valuable detecting time driving around in search of ice cream. No, sir. I drowned my frustrations in an Almond Joy I found buried at the bottom of my purse.

Actually, the rush of sugar was just what I needed. Standing there, inhaling my candy bar, I remembered that there was someone I still hadn't questioned—Prudence Bascomb, president of the local homeowners association. The lady Willard had accused of taking bribes from Garth.

Old Mrs. Garrison had pointed out her house to me, but so far I hadn't been able to catch her at home.

Licking chocolate from my fingers, I crossed over to Prudence's impressive white colonial.

Interesting, I noted, that her only Christmas decoration was a simple wreath on the door. Perhaps as judge of the decorating contest, she'd decided to put herself above the fray.

I rang her bell, but there was no answer. I was just turning back down the path when I saw the mailman coming up the street.

"Hey, there!" he waved, the sun glinting off the hair on his well-muscled forearms. I still couldn't get over the difference between this guy and my mail carrier, who bears an uncanny resemblance to Frankenstein's aide-de-camp, Igor.

I guess everything gets more attractive when you live north of Wilshire.

"How's your investigation coming along?"

"Slowly," I sighed. "This is where Prudence Bascomb lives, right?"

"Yep," he said, coming up the path with her mail. "But she's never home during the day. She's an attorney." He deposited the letters in her slot with brisk efficiency. "Has her own law office. In Century City, I think."

"Thanks. I'll try reaching her there."

"No problem," he said, hustling off on his rounds.

I whipped out my cell phone and got the phone number for Prudence Bascomb, Esquire, then called her office to set up an appointment.

"Her first available slot is two weeks from Monday," her secretary informed me curtly.

The Law Biz was clearly booming for Prudence.

"I was hoping for something a bit sooner. Like today."

"Are you kidding?" she said, as shocked as if I'd just asked her for a loan. "That's out of the question."

"Just tell Ms. Bascomb I want to talk to her about Garth Janken's death."

"Hold on," she commanded. For the next few seconds I was treated to the soothing strains of classical music, and then Ms. Congeniality came back on the line.

"Can you be here in twenty minutes?"

I could, and I was.

Chapter Eight

Prudence Bascomb got up to greet me, a tall, cool redhead in a designer suit that cost more than a Kia.

To call her fortieth floor corner office "impressive" would be like calling the Grand Canyon "large." Furnished with sleek modern furniture straight out of a decorator's showroom and carpeting so plush I could hardly see my Reeboks, it was an executive's dream come true.

But the most impressive feature was the view. Sweeping floor-to-ceiling windows revealed a breathtaking panorama of the city. On a clear day, which it was, you could see out to the ocean.

With an office practically in the clouds, one thing was certain: Prudence Bascomb was not afraid of heights.

I stood in the doorway, suitably awed.

"Come in," she said, waving me inside. "Have a seat."

She gestured to a sleek chrome and leather chair.

I sat down across from her, marveling at her sculpted cheekbones and startling green eyes.

"Can I have my secretary get you an Evian?"

"No, thanks."

When it comes to no-calorie water, I'm always able to Just Say No.

"Then let's get started, shall we? You wanted to talk about Garth Janken's death?"

"Yes, I'm afraid his fall from the roof may not have been an accident."

"Oh?" she said, her face an impassive Chanel mask.

"I think someone tampered with the shingles. Someone who wanted to kill Garth."

"Isn't that a little far-fetched?" she asked with a dismissive smile.

"Not really. In fact, the police think so, too. They just arrested Willard Cox this morning."

"Willard Cox?" Her brows lifted a fraction of an inch, her version of surprise. "I knew he and Garth had their differences, but murder? I find that hard to believe."

"I agree with you. I think somebody else is trying to frame him for Garth's death. The real killer."

"And who might that be?"

"I'm not sure. That's why I came to see you. Do you know anybody who might've wanted to see Garth Janken dead? Anybody he was at odds with?"

She smiled wryly.

"Garth Janken was 'at odds' with half the neighborhood. The man made enemies like Pringles makes potato chips. But I can't believe anybody on Hysteria Lane is a killer."

Same old, same old, I thought, stifling a sigh.

"Wait a minute," she said, tapping a perfectly manicured nail on her cheek in thought, "there *was* somebody else he was fighting with."

I sat up, interested.

"Who?"

"Peter Roberts. Garth's law partner. I heard through the grapevine that he and Garth were going through a particularly vicious split up."

How foolish of me. All along I'd been limiting my

suspects to people on Hysteria Lane. I should've known that a guy like Garth would make enemies wherever he went.

"Not that I'm saying Peter killed Garth, mind you," Prudence quickly added. "I'm not about to implicate anybody in a murder."

Spoken like a true attorney.

"Well," she said, her cool smile still lodged firmly in place, "if those are all your questions . . . ?"

"Just one more," I said, coming to the point of my visit. "What was *your* relationship with Garth like?"

"Mine?" She laughed a laugh singularly devoid of mirth. "I hardly knew him. Just to wave and say hello."

"You judged his house every year in the Christmas decorating contest, didn't you?"

For the first time since I walked in the door, a look of discomfort flitted across those gorgeous green eyes.

"Oh, yes. The contest. One of my chores as president of the homeowners association. I've really got to step down one of these days. It takes up way too much of my time."

"He won first prize five years in a row, didn't he?"

She reached for a crystal water glass at her elbow, and took a careful sip.

"Garth may not have been very popular, but he was amazing when it came to Christmas decorations. A true artist."

"Willard Cox says he was bribing you."

Bingo. I'd hit a nerve. Prudence's eyebrows shot up a whole half inch.

"That's absurd!" she said, an angry flush creeping up her cheeks. "Do I look like I need the money?"

I had to admit she didn't. But something about that contest had her worried. I'd bet my bottom Pop Tart on it.

"Garth Janken won first prize every year because he deserved to," she said, in a tone that brooked no further discussion. "Now if you'll excuse me, I've really got to get back to work."

And before I knew it, I was in an elevator, zipping down forty-plus floors to the Peon Level of the garage.

I headed to my car, filled with a much-welcome sense of accomplishment. My ten minutes with Prudence Bascomb had yielded two important facts.

Fact Number One: There was something decidedly fishy about the Hysteria Lane Christmas decorating contest.

And Fact Number Two: Garth Janken had a law partner who hated his guts.

But both of those facts paled in comparison to Fact Number Three, one I was about to discover as I made my way toward the exit—that parking in Prudence's Century City garage was a jaw-dropping fifteen bucks an hour.

I made a mental note to write a letter to the mayor about the exorbitant parking rates in Century City and headed back to my apartment for a bite of lunch.

In spite of the Almond Joy I'd wolfed down on Hysteria Lane, I was hungry. I had an untouched order of pork potstickers in my refrigerator which I intended to demolish the minute I got home.

Back in my apartment, I raced past the eternally napping Prozac and made a beeline for the kitchen. I grabbed the potstickers from the refrigerator and put them in the microwave, counting impatiently as the seconds ticked by. It's amazing how long thirty seconds can seem when you're starving.

Then, wouldn't you know, just when I'd snatched them out, the phone rang.

Argggh! Why does the phone always ring when you're about to shove a potsticker in your mouth?

"I'll be right back," I promised the little darlings, and raced to the living room to get the phone.

"Yes?" I growled, answering the dratted thing. Probably some stupid telemarketer.

"Am I speaking with Jaine Austen?"

"Yes, what is it?"

"It's Tyler Girard."

Oh, shoot. In my frenzy to get at those potstickers, I hadn't recognized his voice. Why had I been so grouchy? I wanted him to think I was sweet and upbeat, not a snarling harpy.

"Oh, hi, Tyler!" I gushed.

"It sounds like you were in the middle of something."

"Well, yes, actually. I was baking cookies for the homeless."

Huh? Where had *that* come from? Why on earth had I made up such an outrageous lie?

"For the Union Rescue Mission," I added in a fit of lunacy, referring to a local soup kitchen.

"Really? I didn't know they accepted homemade goods. I thought the stuff had to be packaged for security reasons."

"Oh, they know me down there. I've been doing it for years. In fact, they call me The Cookie Lady."

If I told one more lie, I'd be struck by lightning.

"So," he asked, "how was your date with Angel Cavanaugh?"

"Fine! Terrific. We definitely began to bond."

Would the whoppers never end?

"That's so gratifying to hear. It's always nice to know we've made a good match. I hope we'll see you at the Christmas party."

"We?"

I smelled a Significant Other lurking in the wings.

"Yes, I told Sister Mary Agnes all about you, and she can't wait to meet you."

I breathed a sigh of relief. The "she" in his "we" was Sister Mary Agnes.

"Well, you'd better get back to those cookies."

"Cookies?"

"For the homeless."

"Oh, right. My cookies."

I hung up, vowing to some day actually donate cookies to the homeless, and praying that Angel wouldn't spill the beans about our disastrous date. Then I hurried back to the kitchen for my potstickers, whose heavenly aroma had now drifted out into the living room.

What happened next was absolutely heartbreaking. Sensitive readers may want to get out their hankies.

I bounded into the kitchen, only to find Prozac curled up on the kitchen counter, belching softly, surrounded by what just five minutes ago had been my potstickers. Now they were mangled bits of dough, pathetic dim sum corpses.

Prozac, the little devil, had burrowed her way through the doughy wrappings and devoured every speck of pork inside.

"Prozac!" I wailed. "How could you? That was my lunch."

And quite delicious it was, too.

I picked up a limp piece of dough and stared at it balefully.

"How can one cat eat so much, so fast?"

Pretty impressive, huh?

For a desperate instant I considered eating the shards of dough, but don't have the vapors. I didn't.

Instead I had a nutritious lunch of English muffins and martini olives.

After which, I put in a call to Garth's law partner, Peter Roberts.

"Law offices of Janken and Roberts," a perky receptionist answered. "Oops, I mean law office of Peter Roberts."

Interesting, I noted, that Janken had top billing in the law practice.

"May I help you?" she asked in a friendly voice, about a zillion times more friendly than Prudence Bascomb's dragon lady secretary.

I asked if I could speak with Peter.

"Oh, I'm so sorry, he's in court all week. Would you like to leave a message?"

Once again, I posed as an insurance investigator looking into Garth Janken's death, and asked her to please have Mr. Roberts call me back as soon as possible.

"Of course," she promised. "I'll get the message to him right away."

Not two minutes after I hung up, the phone rang.

Wow, that *was* fast. Miss Perky really had gotten the message to him right away.

I answered it eagerly.

"Mr. Roberts?"

"No, this is not Mr. Roberts," a no-nonsense woman replied. "Am I speaking with Jaine Austen?"

"Yes."

"This is Elizabeth Drake from Century National Insurance Fraud Unit."

Gulp. I smelled trouble ahead.

"Ms. Austen, we received a call from a Mrs. Libby Brecker, inquiring about a Century National investigator named Jaine Austen."

Damn that Libby.

"The only Jaine Austen we have on our records is you, and you're a customer."

"A loyal customer, too," I hastened to assure her.

"Be that as it may, I must insist that you cease posing as a Century National representative or we shall be forced to terminate your policy."

After much groveling and promising to behave myself, I finally got off the phone.

Oh, well. It served me right for trying to pawn off my insurance card on Libby. I should've known that a woman who spent her days Windexing reindeer noses would turn out to be a sniveling tattletale.

Somewhat shaken from my brush with the formidable Ms. Drake, I settled down on my sofa to work on my Christmas cards while I waited for Peter Roberts to return my call.

By the time I'd XOXOXO'd my way through my address book at five P.M., I still hadn't heard from him.

It wasn't until later that night when Prozac and I were in bed watching *Roman Holiday* (Prozac has a thing for Gregory Peck), that he finally called.

I launched into my theory about Garth's roof being sabotaged and asked him if he had any idea who might have done it. I wasn't the least bit surprised to learn he had no idea, none whatsoever.

But then I got down to why I was really calling.

"By the way," I said, trying to sound casual, "I hear that you and Mr. Janken were on the verge of dissolving your partnership."

"As a matter of fact, we were. We'd been together fifteen years, and we decided it was time to call it a day. It was an amicable parting of the ways." Accent on the *amicable*. "Garth and I were very good friends."

He sounded about as believable as a congressman running for office.

"That's not what I heard. I heard your break-up was pretty ugly."

"Whoever told you that was wrong," he said, daggers in his voice. "Dead wrong."

And then he did a little casual questioning of his own.

"My secretary tells me you're an insurance investigator. Exactly who do you work for?"

"Oh, no," I said, eager to stay out of the clutches of the Century National Fraud Unit. "Your secretary must've misunderstood. I'm a private investigator."

"Is that so? Got a license?"

"Of course," I lied, and got off the phone before he could grill me any further.

That was no help at all. Peter Roberts would go to his grave, or possibly mine, insisting that he and Garth Janken were best buds. How the heck was I going to find out the truth behind their split up?

And then I remembered his perky secretary, and thought of an idea.

Chapter Nine

The next afternoon I got gussied up in a bizgal pant-suit I keep around for job interviews and IRS audits, and headed downtown to pay a little visit to Peter Roberts's secretary.

Peter's office was in a glass-and-steel high rise right off the freeway. A glance at the directory in the lobby told me the place was a veritable beehive of attorneys.

I took the elevator up to the twelfth floor and made my way down the hallway to The Law Offices of Janken and Roberts. I was happy to see that Peter hadn't gotten around to taking Garth's name down from the door. It would make it that much easier to bring it up in conversation.

I checked my watch. Ten of five. Right on schedule.

Launching Phase One of my plan, I took a deep breath and poked my head in the door. Peter's secretary, a pert Latina in her early twenties, sat at her computer, biting her lower lip in concentration as her fingers flew over the keyboard.

"Oh, hi!" she grinned, when she noticed me. I was relieved to see that she was as friendly in person as she had been over the phone. "I'm afraid Mr. Roberts isn't in right now. He's away in court all week."

Just what I'd been counting on.

"Actually, I wanted to talk to you."

"Me?"

"Yes, I just had a job interview down the hall and I'm wondering if you can tell me what it's like working here in the building. I'm trying to scope the place out before I make a decision."

"No problem," she said, waving me in. "Give me a sec and I'll be right with you. I was just finishing up for the day."

Exactly why I'd waited till late afternoon to drop by.

I sat down across from her, gazing enviously at her creamy olive skin and eyelashes thick as velvet. I really had to start moisturizing more often.

"Finito!" She closed out her program with a flourish and swiveled to face me.

"So which attorney did you interview with?"

"Allison Whittaker," I said, reeling off a name I'd seen on one of the offices down the hall. "Of Whitttaker and Wertz."

Her lush lashes blinked in surprise.

"Allison's secretary is leaving? Betty?"

"Yes, Betty," I nodded.

"I wonder why she didn't tell me. I guess her husband must've landed that job in Bakersfield.

"Hold on a sec," she said, reaching for the phone. "I'm gonna call Betty and congratulate her."

Acck. This was definitely not part of my plan.

"You can't do that!" I cried.

"Why?"

"Um. Because Betty just went home. I saw her get on the elevator."

"Oh, well," she shrugged. "I'll talk to her tomorrow."

Much to my relief, she put down the receiver and began filling me in on the doings at Whittaker and Wertz.

"You'll like working for Ms. Whittaker. Once in a while she'll ask you to pick up her dry cleaning, but that's about as bad as it gets. Watch out for Wertz, though. Their office is known around here as Whittaker and Flirts. The man comes on to all the secretaries. Which is pretty nauseating, considering he has a wife and three kids and a gut the size of the Goodyear Blimp. He made a pass at me my first day on the job. My boyfriend was furious when he found out. Correction. I should say, my fiancé. Hector and I just got engaged last month."

She thrust out her left hand, beaming with pride. A tiny diamond sparkled on her wedding finger.

"How lovely," I cooed.

"It's a whole half-carat. I told Hector I didn't need a real diamond. I said, Hector, cubic zirconia is good enough. But he insisted. Nothing but the best for my Sylvia, that's what he said. That's my name, incidentally. Sylvia Alvarez."

"I'm Charlotte," I lied, just in case she remembered my name from my earlier phone call. But her mind was miles away from office business.

"Hector and I are getting married in June!" she announced proudly.

"How wonderful. Congratulations."

"Hey, let me ask you something." She opened her desk drawer and pulled out a copy of *Modern Bride*.

"Which dress do you like better?" she asked, pointing first to a picture of an elegant Vera Wangish A-line and then to a frilly traditional nipped-at-the-waist model.

"They're both really nice."

"But if you had to choose."

"I guess I'd go with the A-line."

"Really?" Her brow furrowed in doubt. "I like the clean lines, but I've always dreamed of getting married in a Cinderella dress."

"With a figure like yours, you're bound to look great in either one."

A little shameless flattery couldn't hurt. And besides,

I wasn't lying. The fattest part of her body were her eye-lashes.

"You don't think I need to go on a diet?"

Why do the skinny ones always want to go on a diet?

"Absolutely not," I assured her. "You look amazing." And then I added, in what I must confess was a brilliant segue: "I guess you stay thin working for two attorneys. They must keep you hopping. What are they like, anyway?"

"Oh, I only work for Mr. Roberts. Mr. Janken is deceased." She lowered her voice to a confidential whisper. "A horrible accident. He fell off his roof putting up Christmas decorations! Did you ever hear of anything so gruesome? I told my father, 'Papi, don't you dare put Christmas lights on the roof this year. You could fall and hurt yourself. A tree in the window is good enough.'"

It looked like little Sylvia was a bit of a chatterbox. Now all I had to do was get her to chatter about Garth and Peter.

"What about Mr. Roberts? What's he like?"

And just like that, an invisible screen slammed down between us.

"Oh, he's a very nice gentleman," she said, stiffly.

Although perfectly willing to share the details of her wedding and her parents' Christmas decorations, she wasn't about to badmouth her boss, not yet, not until she knew me better. Clearly I'd have to win her trust.

Which was where Phase Two of my plan went into effect.

"So," I asked. "Is there a place to have lunch here in the building?"

"Oh, sure. There's a coffee shop downstairs. The food's pretty good."

"Any place to unwind after work?"

"There's The Legal Eagle, right next door. They have

a fantastic happy hour. People from the building go there all the time."

Just what I wanted to hear.

"I love their buffalo chicken wings. I've tried to make them at home, but I can never get the spices right. I think I'm adding too much cumin. Or maybe it's chili powder. I always get the 'c' spices confused."

"Hey," I said, as if I'd just thought of it on the spur of the moment. "Want to go there right now? I'm sort of wiped out from that interview and I could really use a margarita."

"I don't know," she hesitated. "I really should get home."

"My treat. For helping me out."

She flashed me another grin. "Okay, what the heck? Hector's working late tonight anyway."

She locked up the office and off we trotted to The Legal Eagle, Phase Two of my plan now in full swing. With any luck, I'd get Sylvia tootled enough to dish the dirt about Garth and Peter and their "amicable" split up.

Sylvia was right about those buffalo wings. They were scrumptious. Spicy, but not too spicy. I absolutely could not allow myself to eat more than two. Three, tops. Okay, five at the outside.

Happy Hour had just begun when we showed up and the place was doing a brisk business. It was one of those ersatz turn of the century pubs with a massive mahogany bar and mock gaslight sconces on the walls. We managed to snag two seats at the bar, in grabbing distance of the buffalo wings, and I quickly proceeded to order us two frosty margaritas.

I was thrilled to see Sylvia suck hers up like a Hoover.

This was going to be a piece of cake. She'd be tootled in no time, and dishing the dirt with a trowel!

Or so I thought.

She got tootled all right, but all she wanted to talk about was that dratted wedding of hers.

"So do you really like the A-line?" she asked, the minute we were seated.

It took me a minute to realize she was still talking about her wedding dress.

"Oh, yes," I assured her, "it's lovely."

"I'm afraid it's too plain."

"Then maybe you should go with the Cinderella dress."

"I know, but that might be too fussy."

I took a healthy slug of my margarita. Yes, this was definitely going to be tougher than I thought.

No matter how much I tried to deflect the conversation away from her wedding, she kept coming back to it like a well-trained homing pigeon. I learned every detail of her floral arrangements (violets, to match her bridesmaids' lilac gowns), her deejay (Hector's cousin Ricardo, aka "Little Ricky," who, in case you're interested, does a dynamite Elvis impersonation), and the cake (an agonizing fifteen minute dissertation on the merits of yellow cake with chocolate cream frosting versus white with strawberry preserves). I thought I'd died and gone to Wedding Planning Hell.

"The thing that's really got me worried," she said, starting in on her second margarita, "is Estella."

"Estella?"

"Hector's mother. What a witch. I can't tell you how awful she's been."

Oh, yes, she could. And she did. Another excruciating half hour dragged by as I heard each and every one of Estella's many character flaws.

By now I'd long passed my five-Buffalo-wing limit and was inhaling them faster than the speed of light.

"She's always criticizing me," Sylvia whined. "Nothing I ever do is good enough. The first time I cooked dinner for Hector and his parents, I made a roast chicken. Okay, so I was stupid and didn't know anything about cooking, and I forgot to take out the plastic bag with the liver and gizzards and stuff.

"Well, you'd think the world came to an end. That was three years ago, and to this day, Estella tells anybody she meets about the time I cooked the chicken with the plastic bag inside."

I tsk-tsked in sympathy, desperately trying to keep my eyelids propped open.

"I just know she's going to ruin my wedding. Somehow she'll think of a way to screw things up. I wouldn't be surprised if she interrupts the ceremony to tell that stupid chicken story."

"I'm sure she won't do that."

"Don't bet on it," she said, polishing off her second margarita and signaling the bartender for a third. "The woman is capable of anything. Did I ever tell you about the time I caught her going through my underwear drawer?"

"Yes, I believe you mentioned that about ten minutes ago."

"Let me tell you, it's been utter hell to live through."

And listen to, too.

"At least there's no stress at your office," I said, gamely trying to steer the conversation back to Garth and Peter. "Your boss sounds like a really nice guy."

"He's okay, I guess," she said, licking the last of the salt from the rim of her margarita glass. "Although he can be awfully fussy when it comes to his coffee. He swears he can tell the difference between Equal and

Sweet 'N Low. Heaven forbid I make a mistake and get him Sweet 'N Low—"

Enough, already! I had to be firm and nip this Artificial Sweetener Tangent in the bud.

"I guess you must really miss Mr. Janken."

"Are you crazy? He was one nasty S.O.B."

"Really?" I sat up straight, finally interested in what she had to say.

"Thank goodness I wasn't his secretary. He ran through them like water. Couldn't keep one to save his soul. So demanding. He made Estella look like a saint."

"How did he get along with Mr. Roberts?"

"He didn't. Peter put up with him for years, but finally he had enough. He wanted to dissolve the partnership. At first Garth didn't seem to care. But then when he learned that his biggest client was switching his account over to Peter, he hit the roof. Garth stormed into Peter's office, screaming at the top of his lungs."

At last—after packing away three margaritas and two $12 shrimp cocktails—she was finally on a roll!

"I was sitting at my desk, and I heard him clear as day: *If you think you're taking The Great Litigator with you,* he shouted, *you're crazy!*"

"The Great Litigator?"

"That's what Garth called his client, because the guy was constantly suing people. *You're not taking him or anybody else with you,* he told Peter. *I know what you did back in Ohio, and I've got evidence to prove it. I intend to report you to the bar association. And when I do, you're going to lose your license so fast your head will be spinning.*"

"Ohio? What did Peter do in Ohio?"

"I don't know," she said, shrugging. "Little Ricky called to talk about wedding music then and I got distracted."

Darn that Little Ricky.

Oh, well. I'd still gotten quite an earful. Garth had

been threatening Peter with disbarment. Which sounded like a viable motive for murder to me.

"Gosh, look at the time," I said, making a big show of checking my watch. "It's been fun chatting, but I really should be going."

"Thanks for the margaritas, Charlotte. And the shrimp cocktails. I can't believe I ordered two of them."

Neither could I. But I assured her it had been my pleasure and waved to the bartender for the check.

He brought it over with impressive speed, and just when I was stifling a gasp over the total, I heard someone say:

"Hey Sylvia, how's it going?"

I looked up and saw a tall well-dressed black woman heading toward us.

"Betty!" Sylvia blinked, confused. "What are you doing here? Charlotte said she saw you leaving hours ago."

Oh, crud. It was Betty, the secretary I was supposed to have met this afternoon.

"Do I know you?" she asked me, puzzled.

"Sure," Sylvia piped up. "You guys met when Charlotte interviewed for your job today."

"What are you talking about?" Betty said. "I'm not leaving my job. And I didn't go home hours ago."

Uh-oh. My cue to exit.

"Well, see ya round."

And without any further ado, I slapped fifty bucks on the bar, grabbed a chicken wing for the road, and got the heck out of there.

I drove home, filled with a sense of accomplishment— and enough Buffalo wings to stock a chicken farm.

Thanks to my successful, if costly, rendezvous with Sylvia, I now had a new suspect to add to my list.

Garth had been threatening to rat on Peter Roberts to the bar association. What incriminating evidence had Garth been holding over Peter's head? And more important, how the heck was I going to get my hands on it?

I'd bet my bottom Pop Tart it was stashed away somewhere in Garth's house.

Which meant I had no choice, really, but to tootle over to Hysteria Lane and break into the place.

Chapter
Ten

At seven A.M. the next morning, I was parked across the street from Cathy Janken's house on my first ever professional stakeout.

It had been hell hauling myself out of bed at six to get ready for this gig, but now that I was here I was starting to feel quite Private Eye-ish. I'd come fully prepared with breakfast, lunch, a thermos of coffee, and an audiotape of *Anna Karenina* I'd bought ages ago and never got around to listening to.

And, of course, a bottle to tinkle in.

Hey, I'd seen *Stakeout I* and *II*. I knew the ropes.

I was prepared to camp out in my car until I saw Cathy leave her house. At which point I'd scoot over and do a little Breaking and Entering.

I was keeping my fingers crossed, though, that none of my stakeout accessories would be necessary. I remembered the sweat suit Cathy had been wearing when we first met, and I was hoping she was one of those maddeningly noble people who start the day with a workout at the gym.

But no such luck.

Hour after hour dragged by with no sign of Cathy.

By eight A.M., I'd finished my breakfast. By nine A.M., I'd finished my lunch. I tried to get into *Anna Karenina*, but in spite of three cups of coffee zinging through my veins, I was bored to tears. By the time the last chapter rolled around, I was rooting for the train.

Five hours, four coffees, and two diet Cokes later, I was desperate to take a tinkle.

I took out the empty liter bottle of Sprite I'd brought along for this purpose and eyed it with dismay. How on earth was I ever going to do this? I could never get my aim straight in the ladies room at my gynecologist's office; no way was I going to do it in a Sprite bottle. Had I lost my mind, bringing along a bottle with such a tiny neck?

Now what the heck was I supposed to do?

I couldn't very well ring a neighbor's bell and ask to use their bathroom.

For a few agonizing minutes I tried to hold it in, but it was impossible. With an angry curse, I started the car and sped over to the nearest Jack in the Box where I availed myself of their facilities. Okay, so I picked up an order of fries while I was at it. It had been ages since I'd eaten my lunch at nine A.M., and I was hungry.

Grabbing my fries, I got in the Corolla and raced back to Hysteria Lane. Just my luck, Cathy had probably strolled out of the house the minute I'd gone.

But no. Lady Luck finally decided to give me a break.

Just as I was pulling back into my stakeout space, I saw Cathy come out of her house and drive off in her SUV.

The minute she was gone, I leapt out of the Corolla and grabbed a gift-wrapped box from the backseat. There was nothing actually inside the box. I'd brought it along in case one of the neighbors saw me snooping around. I'd just tell them I was bringing Cathy a Christmas gift. Clever of me, wasn't it?

A darn sight smarter than the Sprite bottle, anyway.

I reached back in the car for a final handful of fries,

then trotted across the street and rang Cathy's bell. I wanted to make sure nobody was home. Maybe there was a cleaning lady inside just waiting to pounce on me.

But nobody answered the door, and satisfied that the coast was clear, I crept around the side of the house, testing for open windows.

Everything was sealed tighter than a Beverly Hills facelift.

And suddenly I was overcome with doubts. What if none of the windows were open and I had to force open one of the doors? I'd brought along my professional Breaking and Entering Tool (a shish kebab skewer I'd grabbed at the last minute), but really, I had no idea how to force open a door. I had a hard enough time getting the wrapping off a CD. What made me think I'd be able to hack my way past a dead bolt? And even if I did, what if Cathy had an alarm system? True, there weren't any security signs out front, but what if she had one?

Just when I was about to slink back to the Corolla in defeat, I spotted a small window above a jasmine bush at the back of the house. The bush was camouflaging the window, but on closer inspection, I saw that it was open.

Thank heavens. I wouldn't have to force any doors and set off any alarms.

I scurried to the window and tossed my empty Christmas package under the jasmine bush. Then I hoisted myself up to the ledge, which was no easy feat with those prickly jasmine branches scratching my fanny.

Shoving my upper body in the room, I saw that it was a guest bathroom. What a lucky break that Cathy had left the window open.

And that's when my luck came to a screeching halt. The upper half of my body sailed through the window without incident, but sad to say, my lower half did not have such an easy time of it. Somewhere in the dreaded hip/tush zone, I'd come to a standstill. Yes, like 99 percent of all the bathing suits I've ever tried on in my life, the window frame was too small for me. My hips simply wouldn't squeeze through.

In defense of my hips, I should tell you that the window was pretty darn small. That's probably why Cathy had left it open in the first place. Clearly she wasn't expecting any anorexic cat burglars. I should've realized I might not have squeezed through, but I hadn't, and it was too late now. I'd just have to climb down and give up this stupid breaking and entering plan.

I started to push myself back out of the window. But, to my horror, I couldn't budge.

Oh, crud. I was stuck.

What a nightmare. Eventually one of the neighbors was bound to notice a tush hanging out of Cathy Janken's house. Why the heck had I scarfed down all those chicken wings last night? Not to mention breakfast—and lunch—this morning. And that last handful of fries. What if those last few fries had wedged me in for good?

By now I was in an advanced state of panic. Any minute now the cops would come and arrest me! My name would be splashed all over the papers. I could see the headlines: FANNY BANDIT FOILED IN REAR ENTRY!

Just when I was cursing the day I ever heard of Seymour Fielder and *Fiedler on the Roof Roofers*, I noticed a jar of hand lotion on the bathroom counter. Could I possibly use that as a lubricant and grease my way loose? It was a long shot, but worth a try. I reached for the lotion, but it was just out of my grasp. Grinding my teeth in frustration, I tried once more.

And then a miracle happened. Somehow, in stretching my muscles, I must've loosened up that fraction of an inch I'd needed to set myself free. Because suddenly

I found myself popping through Cathy's window like a human champagne cork.

I slid onto her imported tile counter, gasping for air, and clinging to a towel rack for dear life.

Me and my hips had made it, after all.

Plucking jasmine blossoms off my rear, I set out in search of Garth's home office. After everything I'd just been through, I sure hoped he had one. I found what I was looking for at the front of the house, across from the living room: A masculine library cum office, with built-in bookcases, leather furniture and hunting prints galore. Very British Lord of the Manor. But what caught my eye was the cherrywood desk by the window, complete with laptop and hand-tooled leather desk accessories.

Wasting no time, I scooted over to it and began rifling through the drawers.

The top drawer contained the usual assortment of rubber bands and paperclips, as well as a bottle of Viagra and a lifetime membership card from The Hair Club For Men.

I now knew that the impressive mane of hair I'd seen in Garth's portrait wasn't his own, and that he'd needed a little help in the dipsy doodle department. All very interesting, but no help whatsoever in my search for incriminating evidence against Peter Roberts.

I hoped I'd have better luck with the two deep file drawers on either side of the desk. The first one contained nothing but some old computer manuals and a pair of gym socks. And the other was locked.

Oh, well. I'd just have to break out my trusty shish kebab skewer and bust the lock open.

But, as I was about to discover, shish kebab skewers are totally useless when it comes to breaking a lock.

After a frustrating ten-minute struggle, I gave up on the skewer and finally managed to pry the drawer open with Garth's Mark Cross letter opener.

Much to my relief, I saw that it was filled with files.

I quickly started rifling through them. First, under the P's for Peter. Then the R's for Roberts.

Nothing.

Then I remembered what Sylvia overheard Garth saying to Peter: *I know what you did back in Ohio.*

I looked under the O's. And sure enough, there it was: A file labeled OHIO.

Inside I found a single piece of paper: a reprint of a newspaper clipping from the *Cleveland Plain Dealer,* dating back twenty years, about the arrest of Peter Robert Simmons, 19, for grand theft auto.

You didn't have to be Sherlock Holmes to figure out that Peter Roberts and Peter Robert Simmons were one and the same. Young Peter had no doubt gone straight, dropped the *Simmons* from his name, and become a successful attorney. And he would've gone on suing people happily ever after if Garth hadn't dug up his criminal past and threatened to rat on him to the bar association.

All of which meant Peter Roberts had a perfect motive for murder.

That clipping had just catapulted him to the Number One spot on my suspect list. I debated about whether I should take it with me and hand deliver it to the cops, but I decided against it. Removing it from the house without a warrant would probably be tampering with state's evidence. I'd just have to leave it there, and tell the cops about it later.

I was putting it back in the drawer when I saw a familiar name on one of the files. In my earlier haste to find Peter's name, I hadn't noticed it. But now it popped out like a neon sign. Right behind PLUMBING EXPENSES, I saw a folder labeled PRUDENCE.

I reached for it eagerly, and pulled out an 8 x10 photo of a gorgeous redhead, posed against a velvet backdrop, wearing nothing but a smile and a G-string. Down at the bottom of the picture, it said: *Brandy Alexander, Stripper Extraordinaire.*

I'd never seen that naked body before, but the face was unmistakable. It was Prudence Bascomb. A lot younger and a lot trashier. But it was Prudence, all right.

Holy Moses. Garth hadn't been bribing Prudence to win the Christmas decorating contest. He'd been *blackmailing* her. For all I knew, he was putting the squeeze on her for money, too.

What a mother lode of evidence I'd just uncovered. Between digging up dirt on Peter and Prudence, Garth had been one busy little extortioner.

Thrilled with my discoveries, I returned Prudence's file to the drawer and headed back out to the foyer. I just hoped Cathy wouldn't notice the mangled lock on the desk.

I was about to slip out the front door, when I glanced into the living room and saw the bowl of candy canes that had been there the day I first visited Cathy.

Gosh, they looked good.

Oh, for crying out loud. What was I thinking? Hadn't I just gone through the humiliation of having my hips wedged in a bathroom window? I couldn't possibly allow myself to feed them one more empty calorie! Absolutely not. No way. No how.

As if.

Two seconds later I was sprinting into the living room, reaching for one of the little suckers.

Just as I was about to grab it, I heard the front door open.

"Come on in," I heard Cathy saying.

Damn it! Cathy was home, and she had someone with her.

I looked around for a place to hide. Not a closet or armoire in sight. So I made a mad dash for the sofa and crouched down behind it.

Please don't let them come into the living room, I prayed. *Let them go to the kitchen or the dining room. Anywhere but the living room.*

"Come on into the living room," Cathy said.

Argggh.

"I can't stay long, babe," I heard a man reply as they walked into the room. "I've got to get back to work."

Whoa, Nellie. There was a man in the house and he was calling Cathy "babe." Something told me this wasn't a condolence call.

"C'mon, Jimmy," Cathy cooed. "Work can wait. And besides, didn't you have a present you wanted to give me?"

"So I did, dollface. So I did."

Before I knew it, Cathy and this Jimmy guy were on the sofa, going at it like two crazed rabbits. Clothes started flying—lace bra, thong undies, a pair of boxer shorts. Finally, a man's blue denim shirt sailed over the back of the sofa and landed at my feet. And not just any blue denim shirt. I blinked in amazement when I saw a US Postal Service logo on the front.

Yikes. It looked like Cathy Janken was having an affair with the hunky neighborhood mailman!

I'll spare you the details of what happened next.

Let's just say I'm surprised they didn't set fire to the sofa cushions.

"Oh, Jimmy," Cathy sighed when it was over. "We're going to be so happy together. You'll never have to lift another mail pouch for as long as you live. I've got more than enough money for both of us. Garth left me a very wealthy woman."

"You know I don't care about money," Jimmy protested feebly.

Yeah, right. Just like I didn't care about pepperoni pizza.

"I really gotta get back to work now, babe," he sighed. "I still got mail to deliver."

Acck. The moment I'd been dreading. Any second now, he was going to reach behind the sofa to pick up his shirt and discover me cowering there.

I thought about making a run for the door, but was too terrified to move.

"Don't go," Cathy pleaded. "Not yet. How about a nice hot bath for two?"

Yes! Yes! Please take a bath! You both need one after the gymnastics you've just been through!

"Let's make it a quick shower. I got a million packages in my truck."

Okay, a shower's good, too. Just go!

And they did. Limp with relief, I heard them scampering up the stairs.

The minute the shower started running, I crawled out from behind my hiding space and raced into the foyer, past Jimmy's mail cart, and out the front door.

The last thing I heard as I made my break for freedom was Cathy singing "Besame Mucho" at the top of her lungs.

So much for the grieving widow.

My muscles had been through the wringer that afternoon, what with crouching behind a sofa for twenty minutes and being shot like a cannonball from a bathroom window.

So the minute I got home, I ran myself a steamy, muscle-relaxing bath, billowing with strawberry-scented bubbles. I sank down into it and sighed in ecstasy.

What a difference forty-eight hours makes.

Just two days ago, I had one measly suspect, and now I had them coming out of my ears.

For starters, there was Cathy Janken. I was still reeling over the tender love scene I'd just witnessed. Clearly her tears on my first visit had been an act. She probably disliked Garth as much as everybody else. Maybe even more. The question was, had she bumped him off to bankroll a happy new life with her macho mailman?

Next, there was Peter Roberts. Garth was threatening to expose his criminal past and get him disbarred. Had Peter sent him tumbling to his death before Garth could carry out his threat?

And what about Prudence Bascomb, aka Brandy Alexander, stripper extraordinaire? Did she scamper up Garth's roof to put an end to his pesky blackmail demands?

Last but not least, there was Libby Brecker. I hope you haven't forgotten that pink flocking stuck to her baseboard. I sure hadn't. No, she was still very much alive and well on my suspect list.

"So who did it?" I asked Prozac, who was sprawled on top of the toilet tank. "What do you think?"

I think it's time you got out of that tub and fixed me dinner.

She jumped down from the toilet and started waving her tail in her patented Feed Me wag.

"Forget it, Pro."

Minced Mackerel Guts would be nice.

"It's not going to happen."

With bacon bits on top.

"I am not budging from this tub. Not for at least a half hour. There's dry food in your bowl if you want some."

But I want Minced Mackerel Guts.

More tail waving, accompanied by a plaintive yowl.

"You'll get your Minced Mackerel Guts. In a half hour. Not a minute sooner."

Okay, be that way.

She shot me a dirty look and slunk out the door.

I really had to start disciplining that cat more often; the way she bossed me around was disgraceful. No wonder she ran riot on an airplane. She was spoiled rotten. I vowed that from then on, I was going to be a new sterner cat owner.

I was lying there, feeling quite proud of the new Disciplinary Me, when Prozac came sashaying back in the room with a brand new pair of pantyhose dangling from her mouth.

How that cat manages to open my lingerie drawer is beyond me, but she does it all the time. I'm surprised she hasn't figured out how to call for pizza.

I think I'll nibble on your pantyhose while I'm waiting for dinner.

Needless to say, thirty seconds later, I was in the kitchen, water puddling around my ankles, opening a can of Minced Mackerel Guts.

Prozac stood at my feet, gazing up at me with what I could swear was a smirk.

I thought you'd see it my way.

"Some day I swear I'm going to put you up for adoption."

Yeah, yeah. In the meanwhile, don't forget the bacon bits.

Chapter Eleven

You know how sometimes you go to sleep with a problem and you wake up the next morning and the answer to your problem is staring you right in the face?

Well, that may happen to you, but it sure didn't happen to me.

I got up the next morning, still clueless about which of my suspects had sabotaged Garth's roof.

Oh, well. I'd just have to let everything percolate in my brain and hope that the answer would come to me eventually. In the meanwhile, I needed to take time off from the case and go Christmas shopping.

Every year I vow to buy gifts early and avoid the last-minute crunch. But you know me. I make a lot of vows I don't keep. (See Discipline the Cat Vow.) In just a matter of days I'd be boarding a plane to Florida and so far, I hadn't bought a single gift. I couldn't afford to procrastinate one minute more.

So, fortified with a wholesome breakfast of peanut butter on a Pop Tart, I headed off to do battle at the mall.

I zipped over to Century City and pulled into a coveted parking space right near the escalators, congratulating myself for getting out of the apartment by ten A.M. and beating the crowds.

My game plan was simple.

This year, I would not stand in a daze agonizing over what to buy. I would be a kamikaze shopper, choosing my gifts quickly and decisively.

It didn't matter what I bought, anyway. Whatever the gift, my mom always says, "Oh, darling. I could've bought it for less on the shopping channel." Really, if you bought my mom a new house, she'd tell you she could get it for less on the shopping channel.

No, this year, I would march into Macy's and buy practical gifts that everybody could return for something they really wanted. No dithering, no shilly-shallying. If I stuck to my schedule I'd be out of there in an hour.

Hah!

Three hours later, I was still wandering around in a daze, wasting time looking at impractical, impossible-to-pack items like rotisserie cookers, musical flowerpots, and macrame hammocks (perfect for Cousin Joanie's Chicago condo).

By the time I finally managed to get my act together and pick out my unimaginative assortment of ties, scarves, pajamas and slippers, the stores were crowded and long lines were snaking at the registers. What would've taken minutes to buy hours ago, now took forever.

Finally, when the whole horrible ordeal was over and my credit card lay gasping in my wallet, begging for mercy, I headed over to the food court to reward myself with a corn dog and fries.

Which, I have to say, were pretty darn delicious.

I sat there, inhaling my food, grateful that I had a whole 364 days before I had to go through this nightmare again.

And then, just as I was polishing off my fries, I remembered Angel Cavanaugh, and her sledgehammer hints for a Christmas gift.

I'd checked out the L.A. Girlfriends guidebook, and sure enough, although normally frowned upon, "modest gifts" were permitted at Christmas.

I rummaged in my purse till I found the newspaper ad Angel had given me, for a pair of jeans from a store named Hot Stuff. Scrawled in the corner of the ad, in Day-Glo pink marker, were the words: "I wear a size 0."

I almost choked on my Coke when I saw what they cost: Eighty bucks!

No way was I spending $80 on that kid. Twenty dollars was "modest" enough for me and my MasterCard.

Then I remembered Angel sucking at that inhaler of hers, gasping for air, and a wave of sympathy washed over me. I thought of her crummy apartment and her overworked dad. Something told me she wasn't going to be getting a lot of gifts this Christmas. Or any other Christmas, for that matter.

Oh, what the heck? I was already in hock to Master-Card for decades to come. What was another $80?

With a weary sigh, I tossed my corn dog wrapper in the trash, and set out to buy a pair of Hot Stuff jeans.

Luckily, there happened to be a Hot Stuff store in the mall. But not-so-luckily, when I got there, I discovered they were sold out of jeans in Angel's miniscule size 0.

"Would you like me to see if I can find a pair in another store?" the bouncy teenage clerk asked.

Hot Stuff was one of those stores geared to the Clearasil Set, whose idea of a size Large was my idea of a handkerchief.

"That would be great."

She called around and minutes later got off the phone, grinning.

"Good news! They've got one pair left out in Glendale. I told them to hold it for you."

"Glendale?"

I gulped in dismay. Do you know what it's like getting from Century City to Glendale in L.A. Christmas traffic? Think the Donner Party, with palm trees.

No way was I going to trek all the way out there for Angel Cavanaugh.

Then once more the image of Angel sucking on that inhaler flashed before my eyes, and the next thing I knew I was crawling along on the freeway, watching my fingernails grow. I swear, I would've made better time on a walker.

It took me nearly two hours to get there, and another twenty minutes to circle around looking for a parking spot. Finally I found one at the far end of the lot and hiked over to the Hot Stuff store.

A vacant-eyed teenager sat at the checkout counter, chatting on the phone in what I could only assume was a personal call.

"She didn't! Really, Cheryl? She actually said that? Why, I'd never speak to her again if I was you, Cheryl. No, sir. I'd tell her exactly where she could put that pom-pom of hers!"

I stood there listening to this fascinating monologue for a few minutes, then finally managed to get her attention.

"Hey! You, with the phone glued to your ear. You've got a customer. Remember us? The people you're supposed to be helping?"

Okay, so what I really said was "Ahem," but she got the message.

"Hold on a sec," she said to Cheryl, then turned to me with an irritated sigh. "How may I help you?"

"You're supposed to be holding a pair of jeans for me at the register."

She stared at me blankly. "I don't have any jeans here."

"Sure, you do. They called a couple of hours ago from Century City."

"I dunno about any call. I just started my shift five minutes ago."

"Could you please just look behind the counter for a pair of jeans."

"Oh, all right."

With a grudging sigh, she poked behind the counter.

"Nope," she gloated. "No jeans here."

"Are you sure?"

"Look for yourself if you don't believe me."

I looked, and she was right. Nada. Zip. A jeans-free zone.

Grinding my teeth, I showed her the ad from the paper.

"You have any of these jeans?"

"Over there," she said, pointing vaguely to a rack in the back of the store.

I hurried over to the rack and checked out the jeans. Thank heavens, there was one pair left in a size 0. I was just about to reach for them when I felt someone tap me on my arm.

I turned to see a short roly-poly woman at my side.

"Would you mind helping me out?" she said, smiling sweetly. "I need one of those sweaters."

She pointed to some sweaters stacked on a shelf above the jeans.

"No problem," I said.

"Thank you so much! I need a pink one in a size small. It's for my niece. All the kids seem to love this place."

"Don't I know it," I said, reaching up to get the sweater.

I turned to hand it to her and I saw, to my consternation, that she'd taken my size 0 jeans from the rack.

"Excuse me. I was going to buy those."

"Oh?" she said, still smiling sweetly. "So was I."

"But I saw them first."

"Well, I've got them now."

For the first time I noticed a glint of steel behind that smile of hers.

"You don't understand. I called the store and told them to put these jeans on hold for me."

"What a pity they didn't."

"I drove out here all the way from Century City in rush-hour traffic."

"And all for nothing!" she tsk-tsked. "Well, thanks for helping me with the sweater."

She traipsed off with the jeans clutched to her ample bosom. And I went a tad ballistic. I charged after her, lunging for the jeans like a bull with anger management issues. But she wasn't about to let go of them. Not without a fight.

And that's exactly what happened.

I'm ashamed to say we had a most undignified tussle over those jeans.

I leapt into the fray with confidence. My roly-poly adversary was a good twenty years older than me. Surely I could take her down.

But she was a surprisingly tough fireplug of a lady. After much mutual pushing and clawing, she managed to land a powerful shove that left me flat on my fanny, the contents of my purse scattered on the floor around me.

"Bye, now!" she trilled, skipping off to the register. "And thanks again for the sweater."

Muttering a string of curses not fit for your delicate ears, I gathered my belongings and stormed over to the checkout counter, where the clerk was ringing up her sale.

"I just love the holiday season!" she chirped to the bored teenager. "It's such a happy time of year, don't you think?"

"Whatever," grunted the clerk.

"I hope you can live with yourself," I hissed in Ms. Fireplug's ear.

But she went on chatting, blithely ignoring my eyes boring holes in her back.

Finally the clerk finished her end of the transaction and asked Ms. Fireplug for her credit card.

"Of course, dear!"

She reached into her purse, and suddenly her good mood vanished.

"My wallet," she gasped. "I've lost my wallet!"

"Hah!" I crowed. "That's what you get for being such a lowdown sneak."

"If you're not gonna buy this stuff," the clerk sighed, "I gotta do a void."

"I'll take those jeans," I piped up.

Together the clerk and I managed to pry the jeans from Ms. Fireplug's fingers. And after the original sale was voided, I whipped out my credit card and paid for them.

Now it was Ms. Fireplug's turn to stand glaring at me.

"There you go, Ma'am," the clerk said, handing me the jeans in a gift box. "Have a nice day."

"Oh, I will. I most definitely will."

Then I reached into my pocket for a little something I'd found when I'd been crawling on the floor picking up the contents of my purse.

"I believe you dropped this in our scuffle," I said, tossing Ms. Fireplug her wallet.

And then I headed out into the mall, the sweet sounds of her curses following in my wake.

* * *

I had just started the Himalayan trek back to my car when I noticed a store that stopped me in my tracks. The place was called The Cap Shack, and a sign in the window said: PERSONALIZED BASEBALL CAPS FOR ALL OCCASIONS.

And there in the corner of the window was a bright red cap with the words *Fiddler on the Roof* embroidered across the front. Fiddler, not Fiedler. The play, not the roofers. It was the only theatrical title among the *Old Fart, I Love Grandma,* and *Kiss Me, I'm Irish* baseball caps on display. What, I wondered, was it doing there?

Suddenly the wheels in my brain, rusted from a day at the mall, started spinning. I had a hunch how the *Fiddler* cap got there and I marched inside to see if I was right.

A skinny kid with a bobbing Adam's apple sat behind the counter, a baseball cap on his head.

"Welcome to The Cap Shack," he intoned with all the enthusiasm of a funeral director.

"Hi, Francis." I knew his name was Francis because it said so on his hat. "I'm hoping you can help me out."

"You looking for work? Trust me. You don't wanna work here. It stinks."

"No, I'm not looking for work. I just want to know if you keep a record of your job orders."

"Sure. We keep 'em for six months."

"You think I could take a look at them?"

"Sorry," he said, with a lugubrious shake of his head, "I'm not allowed to divulge personal information about our customers."

Now before I write another syllable, you've got to promise that what happened next stays between us. Don't go ratting on me to Century National, okay?

In spite of the stern warning I'd received from Elizabeth Drake, I whipped out my Century National insurance card and gave one last performance as Jaine Austen, Insurance Investigator. (I swear, Elizabeth, if you're reading this, I'll never do it again!)

"You're really investigating a murder?" Francis asked, his eyes bugging with excitement.

"Yes," I nodded solemnly. "And I need to see those books."

Lucky for me, Francis was a gullible soul, and minutes later I was sitting behind the counter poring through a thick looseleaf binder of Cap Shack back orders.

It wasn't long before I came across what I'd been hoping to find—a work sheet for a red *Fiedler on the Roof* cap.

All along I assumed someone had stolen one of Seymour's caps to sabotage Garth's roof. But I was wrong. Someone had the cap specially made to order. Someone who later planned to take advantage of Willard Cox's very public feud with Garth and frame him for the murder.

Eagerly, I checked out the customer's name.

Claudia Jamison.

It had to be a pseudonym. Oh, well. What did I expect? That the killer would use her real name?

But at least now I knew it was a woman.

The question was—which woman? Cathy, the cheating wife? Prudence, the ex-stripper? Or Libby, the Stepford homemaker?

Unfortunately, "Claudia" had paid for the cap in cash, so there was no way to track her down through a credit card.

"Do you remember this woman?" I asked Francis, showing him the work order. "Claudia Jamison?"

I had a feeling this guy had trouble remembering his own name, but it was worth a shot.

"Are you kidding?" he said. "You know how many customers we get in here?"

Not many from the looks of it, but I wasn't about to contradict him.

"Wait a minute. Here's my supervisor. Maybe he'll remember."

I looked up to see Francis's "supervisor," a beanpole of a kid who couldn't have been more than eighteen.

"Hey, Denzel," Francis said to his boss. "This lady's an insurance investigator. She's investigating a murder."

"Cool." Denzel smiled, revealing a mouthful of braces.

"Do you remember this order, Denzel?" I asked, showing him the work sheet. "For a *Fiedler on the Roof* baseball cap?"

His eyes lit up with what looked like actual intelligence.

"As a matter of fact, I do. We made a mistake on it, and had to do it over again. The first time we wrote *Fiddler on the Roof.*

"Actually," he said, pointing to the red cap in the window, "that's our mistake over there."

I gave myself a mental pat on the back. That's what I'd thought had happened.

"Do you remember the lady who ordered it?"

"Yeah, I do."

"Really?" I felt like kissing him, braces and all. "What did she look like?"

"She was a tiny lady, wearing a pastel sweat suit."

Ta-da. Puzzle solved. At last I knew who'd climbed up Garth's roof.

Not tall, statuesque Prudence. Or plump, stumpy Libby. Neither one of them was remotely tiny. But Cathy, a delicate doll of a woman, fit the description to a "T." And she had a pastel sweat suit; she'd been wearing one the day I first came to visit.

What's more, her initials were C. J. As in Claudia Jamison.

Yes, folks. It looked like I'd just found myself a killer.

Chapter Twelve

It had been ages since I'd scarfed down that corn dog at lunch, and by the time I got home, I was starving.

And I wasn't the only one. Prozac looked up from her perch on top of the TV and greeted me with a hostile stare.

Where the heck have you been? I'm fainting with hunger.

"Oh, don't be such a drama queen," I said, dumping my Christmas gifts on the sofa. "There are cats in Asia who could live for a week on one of your snacks."

Just move it, okay?

After feeding Prozac a gourmet dinner of Luscious Liver Tidbits and grabbing a fistful of pretzels for myself, I put in a call to Lt. DiMartelli, eager to tell him about Claudia Jamison aka Cathy Janken. But he wasn't there, so I left a message, begging him to pretty please get back to me as soon as possible.

I figured I'd wait for his call soaking in the tub with a glass of wine and a pepperoni pizza. But when I checked my phone messages, all plans for a catered bath went flying out the window.

Hey, Jaine. Tyler Girard's voice came on the machine. *I'm calling to remind you tonight's the night of the L.A. Girlfriends Christmas party. Hope you haven't forgotten.*

Acck! I sure had.

The fun starts at seven. See you there!

Seven? Holy mackerel. It was already 6:45.

Kissing my bath good-bye, I showered and dressed with Indianapolis 500 speed.

Then I grabbed Angel's gift and headed for the door. "Bye, Pro!"

She didn't look up from where she was snoring on my computer keyboard. Now that she'd gotten what she wanted, she had no more use for me.

If I didn't know better, I'd swear she was my ex-husband.

I drove over to the party, humming an off-key version of "Frosty the Snowman," not the least bit tired from my eight grueling hours at the mall.

On the contrary, I was feeling quite perky at the thought of seeing Tyler. How nice of him to call and remind me about the party. I couldn't help thinking that he was interested in me. And not just as a volunteer.

I pulled into the parking lot of St. Philomena's, a beautiful old church out in Santa Monica where the party was taking place, and checked my hair in the rearview mirror. Not a pretty picture. There'd been no time to blow it straight, and now I was stuck with the ever-popular Finger in the Light Socket Look.

Oh, well, I thought, getting out of the car, there was nothing I could do about it. At least I'd managed to throw together a decent outfit: jeans, a red cashmere turtleneck, and a yummy pair of high-heeled suede boots I'd bought on sale at Nordstrom.

Pulling my sweater down over the dreaded hip/tush zone, I sucked in my gut and headed inside.

* * *

The unmistakable aroma of Swedish meatballs greeted me like an old friend when I walked in the door. The party was in full swing, L.A. Girlfriends milling about, filling their plates from a buffet table groaning with goodies.

A Christmas tree was set up in a corner of the room. And in an ecumenical nod to the minorities, a Hanukah menorah and Kwanzaa candleholder were both aglow with candles.

I was relieved to see that most of the Girlfriend Volunteers were pleasant, average-looking gals, much like Yours Truly, hovering in the non-threatening Middle to Upper Middle of the 1-10 scale.

When it came to Tyler Girard, I didn't need any competition, thank you very much.

"Hey, Jaine. I was afraid you weren't going to make it."

Speak of the darling devil, there he was at my side, smiling that endearing smile of his. I'd been so busy scoping the competition, I hadn't seen him come up behind me.

"I'm sorry I'm late," I said, thinking how nice he looked in his chinos and crew neck sweater.

"Oh, I understand. Traffic's a bear. Sister Mary Agnes just called. She's going to be late, too."

"How nice," I murmured.

Uh-oh. That hadn't been the right thing to say, had it? I'd been staring at Tyler's eyes, trying to decide if they were brown or hazel, and hadn't really been paying attention.

"I meant, how nice that I'll finally get a chance to meet her."

"She's really looking forward to meeting you, too." Then he glanced down at my Hot Stuff package. "I see you brought a present for Angel."

"Who?"

"Angel. Your Girlfriend."

Drat. I really had to stop staring at him and concentrate.

"Oh, right."

"It looks expensive. I hope you didn't go over the twenty dollar limit."

"Actually, I did. I know I shouldn't have, but it's something Angel had her heart set on."

"That's very kind of you."

"Well, Angel and I really bonded on our date."

At that moment I caught a glimpse of Angel at the buffet table, and the sight of her skinny arms reaching out to fill her plate brought on a fresh wave of sympathy for the kid. Maybe we hadn't bonded on our date. But I knew we would, eventually.

"I'm so glad it worked out," Tyler said. "I was afraid she might be a handful."

"Oh, no," I fibbed. "Not at all."

"Well, now that you're here, let's go get you some dinner. You hungry?"

"A little," I said, trying not to look like the kind of person who can pack away a dozen Swedish meatballs in a single seating.

"We'd better grab your chow before the festivities begin."

"Festivities?"

"Yes, after dinner, we open the presents and then Sister Mary Agnes gives a little speech. And then we wrap things up with dessert and coffee."

"Sounds like fun."

"Oh, it will be."

He beamed me another heart-melting smile which I beamed right back at him. And then, just as we were establishing meaningful eye contact, a willowy blonde came sashaying over to his side—one of the few 9's in the crowd—and grabbed him by the elbow.

"Tyler, honey," she cooed. "I'm going to steal you away."

I glared at her, fuming.

"Beat it, blondie."

Okay, I didn't really say that. I just stood there, faking a stiff smile, fighting my impulse to strangle her.

"C'mon, sweetheart," she said. "I want to introduce you to my husband!"

With that my smile turned genuine, and my homicidal urges subsided. This harmless woman was married.

Tyler shrugged helplessly.

"Catch you later," he called out to me as she pulled him away.

I stood there for a dreamy minute wondering what it would be like to be caught by Tyler, preferably in the Honeymoon Suite of the Four Seasons Hotel.

Then I headed over to the Christmas tree. This whole L.A. Girlfriends thing had worked out wonderfully well. True, my initial date with Angel was a bit of a disaster, some might say of *Titanic* proportions, but that was bound to change. Gradually she'd open up to me, and we'd form a bond that would no doubt last all our lives.

I put Angel's gift under the tree, lost in a reverie of Angel all grown up and graduating from Berkeley, valedictorian of her class, thanking the woman who changed her life, Jaine Austen Girard, when I heard someone calling my name.

I turned and saw Kevin Cavanaugh, in a frayed sport coat that hung loosely on his thin frame.

"I'm so happy to see you here," he said. "I thought maybe you'd given up on Angel, the way you raced off the other day."

"Oh, that. I had an emergency with my cat. A dental problem. Abscessed tooth. Had to be pulled. You don't know what it's like trying to find a cat dentist on a weekend."

What was wrong with me? Couldn't I just tell a fib without writing a novel about it?

"I'm just glad you're here. You don't know how much this means to Angel. I realize she can be difficult, but she's had a pretty rough time of things."

"Oh, I know," I nodded sympathetically. "What with her asthma and all."

"Asthma?" Kevin blinked, puzzled. "Angel doesn't have asthma."

"What?"

"Don't tell me that's what she told you."

"Well, actually—"

"No, I mean it. Don't tell me. If I hear that kid has told one more lie, I don't know what I'll do."

He shot me a pleading look, his pale eyes watery with despair. The guy was just a step away from jumping off a cliff into a mental breakdown. And I wasn't about to push him over the edge.

"Oh, no!" I assured him. "She never said that. I must've misunderstood. I'll go have a little talk with her now and straighten everything out."

I gave him a cheerful wave good-bye, hoping he couldn't see the vein in my neck that was throbbing with fury, and marched over to Angel, who was still at the buffet table.

I thought of all the trouble I'd been through to get those jeans, the hours stuck in traffic, the horrible battle with Ms. Fireplug. All because I felt sorry for the poor little asthmatic waif. I was so mad, I was surprised steam wasn't coming out of my ears.

I found Angel in front of the Swedish meatballs, poking another little girl in the chest.

"But I can't afford to pay you protection money," the other kid wailed.

Stepping between them, I took the other kid by the shoulders and knelt down so we were face to face.

"Don't pay Angel a dime, sweetheart," I told her. "If she threatens you again, call me. I'll take care of it."

I gave her one of my business cards, then got up and turned to Angel, breathing fire.

"Did you bring my present?" she had the nerve to ask.

"Yes," I snarled, "I brought your present."

"Good. I'm gonna get it right now and make tracks outta here. This party's nothing but a bunch of dorks."

"Not so fast, kiddo," I said, grabbing her by the elbow. "We need to talk. In private."

My hand a vise around her wrist, I dragged her to a small pantry behind the buffet. Inside was a table laden with the desserts that were to be served after the gift-opening ceremonies. I was glad to see that nobody else was there.

"Whaddaya want?" she whined, as I yanked her inside and shut the door behind us.

"The truth. I know you don't really have asthma."

She shot me a defiant stare.

"So?"

"So, you lied to me."

"And you fell for it."

And then she smirked. The little monster was actually proud of herself.

"What about that inhaler?"

"I found it in the garbage."

Still smirking.

"I'm really angry, Angel."

"Oh, wow. I'm shaking in my shoes."

"Do you have any idea how much I paid for those jeans?"

"Yeah. $79.99. Plus tax."

And then, with that smirk planted firmly on her face, she said one more word that pushed me over the edge:

"Sucker."

"That's what you think, kiddo," I hissed.

I turned and started for the door.

"Where are you going?"

"To get my gift back."

"You can't do that!" she wailed.

"Oh, yeah? Watch me."

I'd just made it to the door and was about to reach for the knob when I felt something soft and squishy hit me in the neck.

I scraped it off and looked down at the remains of a chocolate éclair on my fingers. And my cashmere sweater. And my beautiful suede boots. Which, needless to say, weren't so beautiful anymore.

Angel's smirk had now blossomed into a malicious grin.

I marched back to the dessert table, determined to wipe it off her face, and grabbed an éclair.

"You wouldn't dare hit a kid," Angel sneered, as I held it aloft.

I hated to admit it, but she had a point. I was a grown woman. I wasn't actually going to demean myself by getting into a food fight with a twelve-year-old, was I?

Apparently, yes.

Because the next thing I knew I was smushing that éclair in Angel's face. And loving every minute of it.

"Hah!" I cried.

Actually, I only got as far as "H—" Because just then, she lobbed me in the mouth with a double fudge brownie. (Which, I might add, was quite delicious.)

But for once I did not take time to savor my chocolate. I lobbed her right back with a wedge of pumpkin pie, and she zapped me with a fistful of mocha mousse.

I retaliated with a volley of Christmas trifle, and she let me have it with a hunk of marshmallow-studded Jell-O.

I don't know how long we continued in this disgraceful vein. All I know is she'd just dumped the entire contents of an eggnog bowl over my head when I heard:

"Jaine, what's going on here?"

Wiping eggnog from eyes, I looked up and saw Tyler in the doorway, staring at us, aghast.

"She attacked me!" Angel said, suddenly the wide-eyed innocent.

"She started it!" I cried.

"She squished an éclair in my face," Angel sniffled, summoning fat tears to her eyes.

Man, this kid deserved an Oscar.

"Did you actually hit her with an éclair?" Tyler asked me, radiating disbelief.

"Only because she hit me first!"

"And then she threw pumpkin pie at me. And trifle, too!" Angel moaned piteously, channeling Orphan Annie, Little Eva, and Tiny Tim all in one.

Tyler's disbelief had turned to disgust.

"How could you, Jaine? She just a little girl."

"Oh, no, Tyler. That's where you're wrong. She's not a little girl. She's the devil's spawn. Five minutes with this kid is like a year in Guantanamo. I drove two hours in freeway traffic to buy her a pair of $80 jeans and had to fight Ms. Fireplug all because I thought she had asthma which was a total lie, and I don't care if I did find Garth's killer at the mall, she got the inhaler from the garbage!"

Okay, so I was rambling a tad. I was upset.

"Killer? What killer?" Tyler asked. "And who's Garth?"

I never got to answer his questions because just then we were joined by another visitor.

"What on earth is happening in here?"

Tyler gulped. "Sister Mary Agnes!"

I looked over at the stumpy woman standing in the doorway, and blinked in disbelief.

Omigosh.

It was Ms. Fireplug!

Whatever happened to the good old days when nuns wore wimples and long black robes so you knew they were nuns and didn't wind up wrestling them to the floor for a pair of Hot Stuff jeans?

I mean, really, if I'd had any idea that Ms. Fireplug was a nun that afternoon, I would've handed over the jeans, wished her a Merry Christmas, and trotted off to the food court to drown my frustrations in a frozen yogurt.

"I knew she was trouble the minute I saw her," she now said to Tyler.

"Do you two know each other?" he asked.

"We've met," I managed lamely.

"She stole my wallet."

"That's not true!" I protested. "She dropped it and I was returning it to her."

Tyler stared at me, slack jawed, disillusionment oozing from every pore. Whatever spark I'd felt between us had been stomped to oblivion.

"It's no use trying to explain," I sighed. "I'll just go."

"Maybe you'd better," he said softly.

By now a gaggle of L.A. Girlfriends had gathered around the pantry door, whispering among themselves.

With as much dignity as I could muster under the circumstances, I plucked a piece of fudge brownie off my fanny and walked past the gauntlet of their disapproving glares.

Outside the church, I passed a statue of Philomena, the patron saint of lost causes. She seemed to be gazing down at me, pity in her eyes.

Sorry, kiddo, I could almost hear her saying. *Wish I*

could help, but you're too much of a lost cause, even for me. Try Bernadette over at Lourdes.

Then I trudged to my car and drove home in a cloud of humiliation and assorted desserts, leaving chocolate stains on the seat of my Corolla that I have to this day.

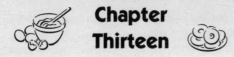

Chapter Thirteen

For two blissful seconds the next morning I had no memory of the Girlfriends debacle, but then it all came rushing back to me like an overflowing septic tank.

What was wrong with me, getting into a food fight with a twelve-year-old? I was a failure as a volunteer and a disgrace to freelance writer/private eyes everywhere.

What's more, I'd totally scotched things with Tyler, and had about as much chance of getting a writing gig from Sister Mary Agnes as I had of fitting into Angel's size 0 jeans. Which, incidentally, I never did take with me when I left. So the little brat would get to wear them, after all.

Oh, well. I had to keep reminding myself that if I hadn't been out in Glendale, I would never have discovered Garth's killer.

I made up my mind to forget about last night's fiasco and get back to Garth's murder, which, after what I'd just been through, was beginning to look like a ride in the wine country.

I put in another call to DiMartelli, but he wasn't in. The desk sergeant told me he was expected around noon, and I planned to be there the minute he walked in the door. Willard Cox would be convicted and serving a life sentence before the good lieutenant ever returned my call, and I was determined to tell him my story.

After a gourmet breakfast of Pop Tarts and Pancreas Entrails (the entrails were for Prozac), I got dressed and drove over to my dry cleaner. I figured I might as well get some errands done while I waited for DiMartelli to show up.

The clerk had a hearty chuckle when I asked him if he could get eggnog/éclair/brownie/chocolate mousse stains off my cashmere sweater and suede boots. Yes, indeed. Just about broke the meter on his giggle-o-meter.

I bid him a haughty good-bye and was heading back to my car with my ruined clothing when I realized I hadn't filled Ethel Cox in on what I'd discovered at the mall. She had no idea that, thanks to yours truly, her husband would soon be out of jail. So I decided to make a quick pit stop at Hysteria Lane and tell her the good news.

"Sweet little Cathy Janken?" Ethel blinked in surprise. "A killer?"

We were seated across from each other in her living room, where I'd just finished telling her about my adventures at The Cap Shack.

"Absolutely," I nodded. "She's having an affair with another man and wanted out of the marriage. So she sabotaged the roof, then later planted her specially ordered roofer's cap in Willard's toolbox to frame him for the murder."

"Oh, dear." Ethel shook her head in dismay. "That's just awful. To kill her own husband, and then to blame poor Willard."

Clearly she hadn't glommed onto the plus side of the story.

"Don't you see, Ethel? As soon as I tell the police how Cathy Janken aka Claudia Jamison ordered that roofer's cap, Willard will be off the hook."

"Do you really think the police will let him go?"

"I'm sure of it."

"Oh, Jaine! That's wonderful!" And for the first time since this mess began, I saw a smile on her face. "How can Willard and I ever thank you?"

Just seeing her smile was thanks enough. After my dismal failure as an L.A. Girlfriend, I was happy to finally bring joy to someone's life.

"I know!" she said. "Let's celebrate with some tea and homemade brownies."

You'd think after last night's flying dessert-a-thon I'd never be able to look at another brownie again, but you'd be wrong.

"Sure," I said, as always unable to resist the lure of chocolate.

"Make yourself comfy, sweetheart," she said, bustling off to the kitchen, "while I make the tea!"

Alone in the room, I got up to admire the Coxes' stately Christmas tree in the corner, heavily laden with elaborate reindeer ornaments. With any luck, Willard would soon be home to celebrate his reindeer-themed Christmas.

I wandered over to the fireplace, where a single stocking hung from the mantel, embroidered with the name "Pumpkin." Poor Pumpkin, I sighed. Clearly Ethel was having trouble letting go of her beloved pet.

I was just about to head back to the sofa when I noticed an airline ticket lying on the mantel. Snoop that I am, I picked it up and peeked at it. It was a round trip ticket to Bermuda, in Ethel's name, leaving Christmas day.

How odd. Why would Ethel be going to Bermuda at a time like this? Maybe she had relatives there and was going for emotional support. Still, it was strange she'd be leaving Willard alone in his time of crisis.

And then I saw something else on the mantel, something that sent a chill down my spine. It was a brochure for a quaint bed and breakfast. It wasn't the inn itself that jolted me. In fact, it looked like a very lovely place. No, what made the little hairs on my neck stand at attention was the name of the inn: The Claudia Jamison House.

Holy Moses. Could it be? Was Ethel Claudia Jamison?

At that moment I became aware of footsteps behind me. I whirled around to see Ethel coming at me—not with tea and brownies—but wielding one of Willard's huge neon candy canes.

The last thing I noticed before it came crashing down on my skull was what Ethel was wearing:

A pastel sweat suit.

Just like Claudia Jamison.

I came to on the floor near the Christmas tree, my wrists and ankles bound tightly with packing twine, my head throbbing like a bongo drum.

Ethel was kneeling over me, putting the finishing touches on the twine around my ankles.

How wrong I'd been about Ethel. All along, I thought she was a helpless housefrau. The woman was about as helpless as a Sherman tank.

I tried to lift my head and set off a thousand drumbeats of pain.

"Oh, dear!" Ethel looked around, startled. "I didn't realize you'd come to. You poor thing," she said, clucking in sympathy, "your head must be pounding. I'd give you an aspirin, but you'll be dead soon anyway. So why waste an aspirin?"

I gulped at this latest news bulletin, setting off a fresh

wave of bongo beats. If indeed I was headed for my final reward, I'd be darned if I was going to go without a fight.

"So you killed Garth," I said, stalling for time.

"Well, duh, as you young people say. Of course I did. Such fun pretending to be a roofer and loosening those shingles!"

"But why?"

"Because he killed Pumpkin. That was no accident. Garth ran over my poor baby on purpose. So naturally he had to die."

"But I don't understand. Why frame Willard for the murder?"

"Oh, Willard," she said, with a dismissive wave. "I'm so tired of that man, always bossing me around. Gave me his lunch order every day like I was a waitress at a restaurant. I swear, I never want to cook another meal for him as long as I live."

So Cathy Janken wasn't the only one who'd wanted to dump her husband. I'd been pinning my suspicions on the wrong desperate housewife.

"What a pill!" Ethel grumbled. "Forty-three years of marriage and we went on the same dratted vacation every summer. Fishing on Lake Arrowhead. I hung around the cabin all day, bored silly, while he caught fish. And then I had to clean the stinky things.

"I begged him to take me places. All my life I've wanted to lie on the sand in Bermuda, but no, he's so selfish. Everything's got to be his way or no way.

"So you see, dear, I had to get rid of him."

"Ever hear of a little thing called divorce?"

"Oh, no!" Ethel blinked, horrified. "I could never do that. It's a sin, you know."

Yikes. Murder and sending her husband to jail was okay, but divorce was a no-no. The woman had enough loose screws to open her own hardware store.

"I'd never kill Willard. I just wanted him out of the way. Besides, prison will be good for him. It's time he learned to take orders from somebody else for a change."

Our cozy chat was interrupted by the sound of my cell phone ringing in my purse.

"Don't get up, sweetheart," Ethel said. "I'll see who it is. Ha ha. That was a joke."

"I got it." And yet, I wasn't laughing.

Ethel scooted over to the sofa where I'd left my purse and checked out my caller ID.

"It's the police."

Great. *Now* they're getting back to me.

"I'm afraid you won't be returning this call," she said. "Or any other calls, for that matter."

She picked up a china tea cup from the coffee table and headed back to me.

"What a shame," she sighed. "If only you hadn't interfered. I didn't mind killing Garth, but you seem like such a nice girl. I hate to have to kill you, too."

"Then don't. I swear, I won't say a word to the cops. Honest. Garth was an awful man; he deserved to die. And as for Willard, hey, prison's not so bad."

"I wish I could believe you," she said, kneeling at my side, "but I'm afraid I don't."

"Now drink this, sweetheart. I brewed it while you were sleeping." She gently propped my head into a sipping position. "It's some lovely Constant Comment tea, with a tad of rat poison."

"Sounds tempting, but I'll pass."

"I really wish you'd drink it, dear. Otherwise I'll have to bludgeon you to death with my candy cane, and I really hate getting my carpet all bloody. But I will if I have to."

"Just what do you intend to do with my body?"

"Oh, I'll put it in the freezer till I get back from Bermuda. I'll figure out something then.

"Bottoms up," she said, holding the tea cup to my

lips. "Just remember. If you don't drink it, I'll bash your head in. And that won't be very pleasant, will it?"

No way was I going to open my mouth and drink this stuff. I had to do something to stop her.

"Okay," I lied, "I'll drink it. But can you grant me one last wish before I die?"

"That depends. What's the wish?"

"I'd really love one of your brownies. They were so darn delicious."

"How sweet of you to say so." She blushed with pleasure. "It's so nice to get a compliment for a change. I must've cooked 60,000 meals for Willard but did I ever get a thank you? No, I did not."

"So can I have one?"

"I'm afraid they're in the freezer."

"Can't you nuke one for me? And maybe heat up the tea? It looks sort of cold."

"Well, okay. But after the brownie, then you promise you'll die without a fuss?"

"Cross my heart."

Much to my relief, she got to her feet and started off for the kitchen.

"Don't even think of crying out for help while I'm gone," she warned. "Otherwise I'm going to have to gag you."

Damn. Plan A just went flying out the window.

As she skipped off to fix my Last Snack, my mind started racing. How the heck was I going to get out of this mess?

I craned my neck, looking for something sharp to cut the twine binding my wrists and ankles, but saw nothing.

Then I thought of another plan. It was a long shot, but it was the only shot I had. My head throbbing with every bump, I manage to roll myself behind the Christmas tree. Lucky for me, Ethel was not an expert in bondage. She'd bound me only at the wrists and ankles, which meant I could still bend my knees and elbows. And that gave me some degree of mobility. I had just managed to prop myself into a sitting position with my back up against the wall when Ethel returned with my brownie and poisoned tea.

"Oh, Jaine," she sighed. "Aren't you silly, trying to hide. I'm certain to find you."

She looked around the room and then spotted me behind the tree, as I was hoping she would.

"There you are, you foolish girl!"

She started toward the Christmas tree.

This was it, the moment of truth.

I raised my knees to my chest and sent up a last desperate prayer to the heavens.

Get me through this, and I swear I'll never have a food fight with a twelve-year-old or wrestle with a nun for as long as I live!

Then, with every ounce of strength in my body, I kicked the tree trunk.

For a terrifying fraction of a second, it looked like it wasn't going to fall, but then my prayers were answered. Ethel's eyes widened in shock as the tree toppled over, sending reindeer ornaments flying and pinning her underneath.

Now it was her turn to lie on the floor unconscious.

I scanned the wreckage for something sharp enough to cut twine. Not two feet away, I saw my instrument of escape. A shattered teacup, the one that had just a few seconds ago held my poisoned tea.

I maneuvered myself over to it, and managed to pick up a sharp shard of china. It wasn't easy with my wrists bound together, but eventually I sawed through the twine on my ankles. Then I sprang to my feet and raced over to Ethel's phone. Somehow I managed to punch 911 and scream for help.

Five minutes later, just as I was cutting through the twine on my wrists and the cops were banging at the door, Ethel regained consciousness.

She looked up at me, bewildered, from under the tree.

"That's the police," I told her.

She moaned softly.

"Don't get up, sweetheart," I said. "I'll let them in."

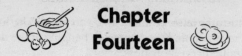

Chapter Fourteen

After checking out my story, the cops carted Ethel off to the prison wing of County General Hospital. When I finally limped home, I swallowed a fistful of Tylenol and spent the next heavenly hour or so soaking my aching muscles in a marathon bath. After which I collapsed into bed where I slept for twelve straight hours (near-death experiences tend to tucker me out) until Prozac lovingly clawed me awake for her breakfast.

In spite of a bump on my head the size of a potato puff, I felt fine. And starving. If you don't count those Tylenol, I hadn't had a thing to eat for nearly twenty-four hours. So I drove over to Junior's deli and treated myself to a hearty breakfast of bacon, eggs, hash browns, and an English muffin with strawberry preserves.

I'd come home and was working off my breakfast with a strenuous nap on the sofa, when somebody rang my doorbell.

You'll never guess who it was.

Angel Cavanaugh.

She stood on my doorstep in a *Hello Kitty* T-shirt and flip-flops, barely big enough to cast a shadow, a bouquet of flowers in her hand.

Her dad stood at her side, holding a shopping bag.

"Don't you have something to say to Jaine?" he said, nudging her with his elbow.

"I'm really sorry," Angel said, looking up at me with sheepish eyes. "For lying to you. And for getting you in trouble with Sister Mary Agnes."

Alert the media. She actually seemed to mean it.

"These are for you." She held out a bunch of supermarket daisies.

"Why, thank you!" I have to admit, my heart melted just a tad. "Won't you come in?"

I ushered them inside and hurried to the kitchen to put the daisies in water.

When I came back out, they were sitting on the sofa. Prozac, the shameless flirt, had wandered in from the bedroom and was shimmying in ecstasy against Kevin's ankles.

"Wow, you've got a cat!" Angel said. "I always wanted a cat."

"I'm not sure you want this one."

Prozac glared at me through slitted eyes. I swear, that cat understands English.

Don't listen to her, kid. I'm adorable.

With that, she leapt into Angel's lap and began purring like a buzzsaw.

"You have something else for Jaine, don't you?" Kevin said, once again nudging Angel with his elbow.

Reluctantly she plucked Prozac from her lap, and walked over to me with the shopping bag her dad had been carrying.

"Here are the jeans," she said, taking them out of the bag. "You shouldn't have spent so much money."

This time, I could tell her heart wasn't in it.

"That's okay," I said. "You keep them."

"Thanks!" She grabbed them back so fast, she almost got whiplash. "Can I go put them on?"

"Sure. You can change in my bedroom," I said, pointing down the hall.

"I can't tell you how much those jeans mean to her," Kevin said when she'd dashed off. "Angel doesn't get very many gifts. I'm all the family she's got. And, as you can imagine, she doesn't make friends very easily."

I could imagine, all right. In Technicolor and Dolby stereo.

"We've tried other mentoring programs, and you're the first person who ever stuck it out for more than an hour."

"You're kidding."

"I wish. That's why I'm so grateful to you. Anyhow, I called L.A. Girlfriends and explained how Angel lied to you about having asthma, and how she goaded you into the food fight. Which, incidentally, she loved. She said she hadn't had so much fun since the time she fingerpainted on our living room walls." He shuddered at the memory. "It took three coats of paint to cover that mess.

"Anyhow, Sister Mary Agnes has agreed to take you back. That is, if you want to see Angel again."

He looked at me like a puppy begging for a bone.

Acck. The thought of a date with Angel without intravenous Valium was daunting, to say the least.

But before I could fumpher an excuse, Angel came bouncing back into the room in her new jeans.

"They're great!" she beamed, a radiant smile lighting up her pinched face. "Thank you so much."

At the sight of that smile, my heart melted again.

"I was just telling Jaine the good news about L.A. Girlfriends."

"Yeah," Angel said. "They want you back. So how about it, Jaine?"

Angel smiled shyly. "Will you be my Girlfriend?"

By now my heart was the consistency of a pint of Chunky Monkey in the microwave.

"Of course," I said. "I'll be your Girlfriend."

"Great! They're having a sale at The Limited. Wanna go?"

"Forget it, Angel."

"Hey," she shrugged. "It was worth a shot."

Okay, so it wasn't going to be easy.

But like the kid said, it was worth a shot.

Epilogue

You'll be glad to know that Ethel Cox got her wish. She never has to cook another meal as long as she lives. The state is providing her with three meals a day at a prison for the criminally nutsy.

At first Willard visited her regularly, in spite of the fact that she refused to see him. After a while, though, he gave up. Last I heard, he was dating a woman he met in the Christmas decorations department of Home Depot.

Peter Roberts and Prudence Bascomb (aka Brandy Alexander) are still practicing law, and frankly I'm glad I never got around to telling the cops about what I'd discovered in Garth's file. So what if they've got dark secrets in their pasts? What attorney doesn't?

And remember Peter's secretary, Sylvia Alvarez? I saw her wedding picture in the paper not long ago. She and Hector finally tied the knot. I only hope the priest managed to get a word in edgewise during the ceremony.

Even more good news: Seymour Fiedler and his merry band of *Fiedlers* are back in business, plying their trade on the roofs of Los Angeles. In fact, they just finished Libby Brecker's place.

Speaking of Libby, I saw her the other day when I took a sentimental spin over to Hysteria Lane. She was out front, buffing her door knocker. She congratulated me for my work on bringing Ethel to justice (the police were kind enough to mention my name in their account of Ethel's arrest) and told me that Cathy Janken had sold her house and was living in an apartment in Van Nuys. Contrary to Cathy's expectations, Garth left her saddled with debt, which may have been the reason Jimmy the mailman dumped her for the UPS delivery gal he'd been seeing on the side.

Angel and I "dated" for a few months, until her dad got transferred to Sacramento. It was tough sledding at first (I wanted to throttle her when she threw her house keys into the La Brea Tar Pits to see if they'd sink), but gradually she stopped acting out, and I grew quite fond of her. We never bonded in the lovey-dovey way of my fantasies. But we definitely Scotch Taped.

Things were never the same between me and Tyler. Maybe because it's hard to have romantic feelings for a woman once you've seen her with chocolate mousse up her nose. But mainly because Tyler and Sister Mary Agnes (who, as the authorities discovered, wasn't really a nun) ran off to Acapulco with the proceeds from an L.A. Girlfriends fund-raiser. I should've known there was something fishy about a nun who'd go mano a mano for a pair of Hot Stuff jeans.

Finally, I'm happy to report I had a very merry Christmas that year.

Daddy and Uncle Ed got into a big fight over a Monopoly game, and when Daddy threw Uncle Ed's hotels—along with his toupee—in the Tampa Vistas pool, Uncle Ed got so mad, he checked his whole family into a Ramada Inn.

So Prozac and I had the guest room—and my parents—all to ourselves. How lovely to eat all the Christmas cookies I wanted, free from invidious comparisons to Cousin Joanie and her string bikinis.

And the flight to Florida wasn't nearly as bad as I thought it would be. Prozac didn't throw up on a single passenger.

Nope, this trip, she threw up on the captain.

But Homeland Security finally took her off their Most Wanted List, so we're free to travel again.

Catch you next time.

PS. If you're reading this during the holiday season, Prozac and I want to wish you a marvelous Christmas, a heavenly Hanukah and/or the coolest Kwanzaa ever.

Well, I do, anyway. Prozac just wants you to scratch her back.

CANDY CANES OF CHRISTMAS PAST

LESLIE MEIER

Prologue

A fire was crackling in the grate, Christmas carols were playing on the stereo and Lucy Stone was perched on a step ladder in the living room arranging strings of twinkling fairy lights on an eight-foot balsam fir her husband Bill had cut in the woods behind their old farmhouse on Red Top Road in Tinker's Cove, Maine.

"Watch out, Lucy," warned Bill, coming into the room with several battered brown cardboard boxes of ornaments. "You don't want to lose your balance and fall."

"I've just finished," said Lucy, slipping the last loop of wire over a branch and stepping down from the ladder.

Bill put the boxes on the coffee table and stood back, arms akimbo, admiring the tree. "It's the best we've ever had, I think. I've had my eye on that tree for a couple of years now."

"A special tree for a special Christmas," said Lucy, wrapping her arms around his waist. "It's Patrick's first."

"Not that he'll remember it," said Bill. "He's only nine months old."

"We'll remember. After all, it's our first Christmas as grandparents."

As if on cue, the dog's barking announced the arrival of Toby and Molly and the baby, who had come from their house on nearby Prudence Path. Feet could be heard clattering down the stairs as Zoe, at eleven the youngest of Lucy and Bill's children, ran to greet them. Behind her, moving more sedately but unable to resist the allure of their nephew, came her older sisters, Sara, who was a high school sophomore, and Elizabeth, home from Chamberlain College in Boston, where she was a senior.

"Look at how big he's gotten!" exclaimed Elizabeth, who hadn't seen the baby since Thanksgiving.

"Can I hold him?" asked Sara.

"No, let me!" demanded Zoe. "Let me hold him!"

"Careful there," cautioned Lucy, asserting her grandmotherly prerogative and scooping little Patrick up in a hug. Then she sat down on the couch with him in her lap and began unzipping his snowsuit, revealing a blond little tyke in a plaid shirt and blue jeans that matched his father's, and his grandfather's. She nuzzled his neck and Patrick crowed and bounced in her lap, delighted to be the center of attention.

"Elizabeth, you can get the cookies and eggnog, and everybody else can start trimming the tree. Patrick and I will watch. Right, Patrick?" But as soon as the boxes were opened and the first ornaments taken out, Patrick was no longer content to watch. He wanted to pull the paper out of the boxes and touch the ornaments, too. Deftly, Lucy distracted him with a cookie and took him over to the window, to look at the Christmas lights strung on the porch.

"It's starting to snow," she said. "It's going to be a white Christmas."

"Nothing unusual about that," said Bill, who was attaching a hook to a round red ball.

"We're only supposed to get a couple of inches," said Toby, pulling a plastic trumpet out of the box. "Hey, I remember this," he said, blowing on it and producing a little toot.

"Look at this one!" said Zoe. "It's baby Jesus in his manger, and if you shake it the snow falls on him!"

"Poor baby Jesus," said Molly, making herself shiver. "He must be cold."

"It snowed on me in my crib, when I was a baby, right in this house," said Toby. "Right, Mom?"

"He's making that up," declared Sara.

"And how could he remember, if he was a baby?" asked Elizabeth.

"That's silly," said Zoe. "It can't snow in the house!"

Lucy looked around the room, at the strong walls and the tight windows, the carpeted floor, and the brick fireplace where the fire crackled merrily, and then her eyes met Bill's. "We-e-ll," she said, "this house was in pretty bad shape when we first moved here."

"It was a nor'easter," said Bill, exaggerating. "The wind blew the snow through a crack. It was easy to fix, the window just needed some caulking."

"See, I was right," declared Toby.

"It was Christmas Eve," said Lucy. "Toby was two. I found him in his crib, with a little dusting of snow. But how did you remember?"

"I think you must've told me," said Toby. "To tell the truth, it just popped in my head this morning when Patrick woke up and I went into his room to get him."

Lucy smiled fondly at her grandson, who looked so much like his father at that age. Things had certainly changed since that awful winter of 1983. . . .

Chapter
One

December 1983

Only a week until Christmas. Not that it felt like Christmas. Lucy Stone was crouched awkwardly on the cracked linoleum kitchen floor in front of an elderly gas range, trying to reach all the way back inside the broiler despite her six-month pregnant belly to relight the oven pilot light that was always going out. No wonder, considering how drafty the old house was.

The flame finally caught and she sat back on her heels, gathering up the collection of wooden matches she'd used and groaning a bit as she hauled herself to her feet. She tossed the matches in the trash and washed her hands in cold water—it took a while for the balky hot water heater to produce anything remotely warm, much less hot—before returning to the cookie batter she was mixing. Spritz cookies, just like her mother always made. Except this year she had to make them because she wouldn't be seeing her mother, or her father, this Christmas. They were staying in New York City because Dad was making a poor recovery from heart surgery and was lingering in the hospital, needing all Mom's attention. That left Lucy, who could use some attention herself, out in the cold.

Literally out in the cold, she thought, switching on the mixer to cream the butter and sugar together. It didn't get much colder than coastal Maine and that's where she was, in the nowhere town of Tinker's Cove. It was certainly a far cry from the Upper West Side of New York City, where she and Bill and Toby, who was almost two, had lived in a tight three-and-a-half rooms overlooking Central Park. But what did space matter when you had the entire park with playgrounds and a zoo and even a carousel, and the American Museum of Natural History and the Metropolitan Museum of Art just steps away? When you could hop the subway to Battery Park for a breath of sea air and a walk along the water? Or a night out at a Broadway show? Or a quick trip to Bloomingdale's where they sprayed you with the newest fragrances and you could find the cutest little outfits for Toby?

Lucy switched off the mixer and set it on the kitchen table, then began adding the flour by hand. It was hard work but she was glad to have something to occupy her, something that would make it seem more like Christmas. Which was weird, she thought, because Tinker's Cove was one of those picture-perfect New England towns that looked as if it could be on a Christmas card. But even though the air smelled piney and the houses all had wreaths with red bows and the big fir tree in the center of town was decked with colored lights, it wasn't nearly as festive as Rockefeller Center where they set up a proper Christmas tree above the skating rink and played Christmas carols on loudspeakers and Fifth Avenue was filled with shoppers carrying bags that bulged with presents.

Just the thought of presents made Lucy groan. There weren't going to be presents this year, at least not the lavish presents of Christmases past. She and Bill had agreed to exchange one modest gift apiece, reserving the rest of their limited budget for toys for Toby. Limited being the operative word here, thought Lucy, who had a fifty-dollar bill folded in the back of her wallet and was keeping an eye on the assortment of trucks and stuffed animals at the IGA, anxiously hoping they held out until Christmas Eve when Dot, the friendly cashier, promised her prices would be cut by half.

Somehow she hadn't expected it would come to this when she agreed to Bill's plan to dramatically change direction, exchanging a well-paying job as a stockbroker and their comfortable life in the city to realize his long-time dream of living in the country and working with his hands. Back then he'd just gotten a fat bonus and it seemed that they could easily afford the fixer-upper farmhouse they'd found in Tinker's Cove. He'd learn by doing, he said, gaining the skills of a restoration carpenter by refurbishing the big nineteenth-century house room by room. But everything was more expensive than they anticipated and the fat bonus shrank rapidly, going to the hardware store and the lumber yard and the electric company and the grocery store and the oil company. Especially the oil company. When Bill tore out the old, rotted plaster and lath he discovered there was no insulation, and sometimes not even proper studs, in the walls. Which meant it was always cold even though the furnace ran constantly, burning oil at a ferocious rate.

Even worse, Bill's career change had alienated him from his parents. Bill Sr. and Edna had seemed so jolly, so easy-going when Lucy first met them but that had all changed when Bill announced his plan to give up corporate life. Bill Sr. had listened stony faced as Bill explained his reasons for quitting the brokerage firm he bitterly referred to as "Dewey, Cheatham and Howe."

"They don't care about the clients, Dad, all they care about is making a big profit. There's so much pressure to churn accounts to generate commissions, to sell limited partnerships and other products that aren't going to produce a dime until most of my clients are long gone. And there's the insider trading. I tell you, it's just a matter of time before the SEC gets on to these guys."

"You have a responsibility to your employer, son," said his father, looking grim. "They're paying you handsomely to make money for them. It's not some sort of welfare scheme, you know."

"You said it," snapped Bill. "They've got me taking from the poor and giving to the rich and I'm not going to do it. We're going to get out of this filthy town and go somewhere where the air is clean and people are honest."

"I'm warning you, son," said Bill Sr. "I can't approve of you putting your family and your livelihood at risk like this. Don't come whining to me looking for a handout when the wolf is at the door."

Lucy smiled grimly to herself. Despite Bill's high hopes they hadn't found either clean air or honest people. The local weather forecast announced frequent bad air days, thanks to prevailing winds that carried pollution from the entire country. And the big story last week in the town's little newspaper alleged that a sweet-faced church secretary, beloved by the entire congregation, had embezzled several thousand dollars for a trip to Las Vegas. Bill had succeeded, however, in bringing the wolf to the door, but there was no way he was going to give his father the satisfaction of asking for help. That would be admitting defeat and Bill wasn't about to do that. So they wouldn't be seeing the elder Stones this year, either.

So here she was, she thought, looking around the kitchen and not liking what she saw. There were no cabinets, no counters, just a stained old Kenmore gas range that was at least twenty years old that stood next to a nasty old porcelain sink with exposed plumbing beneath. The refrigerator stood across the room in lonely splendor, its white porcelain door speckled with rust and its rounded top a slippery slope for anything that she set on top of it. Which she did, having no other place to store things she didn't want Toby to get into. The wallpaper, a flamboyant pattern featuring black swirls punctuated with red and yellow teapots, was torn, and the patches of plaster that were revealed were painted in various colors of green and beige. Lucy regularly washed the green speckled linoleum that covered most of the worn wood floor but no matter how hard or how often she scrubbed, it still looked dirty and dingy. And this, she thought with a sigh, was just the kitchen. She didn't even want to think about the rest of the house, especially the breezy, rattle-trap room that served as a nursery where Toby was napping under a pile of quilts and blankets.

The cookie dough was ready, she realized, mixed to perfection as she fumed about her situation and she chuckled to herself. Anger and resentment were good when you needed muscle power, but not good for the soul. Or for relationships, she thought, hearing Bill banging nails in the living room. It was definitely time she adopted a more positive attitude. It was Christmas after all, and she wanted their first Christmas in their own home to be special.

Lucy was smiling as she stuffed the dough into the cookie press and screwed on the end cap. She heard the hiss of the burner as the oven heated and she switched on the radio, turning the dial until she found a station playing Christmas carols. She hummed along, turning the crank and squeezing out perfect little rosettes onto the cookie sheets. When she'd filled both sheets she placed a bit of glazed cherry in the center of each cookie and slipped the pans into the oven, which the thermometer she'd hung from the rack indicated was a perfect three hundred and fifty degrees.

Toby was stirring upstairs so she climbed the rickety back stairs that led to the second floor bedrooms. She pushed open the door and peeked inside, ignoring the walls that had been stripped down to the studs and the windows that rattled and went straight to the crib, where Toby was sitting in a nest of blankets and talking to himself.

"Did you have a nice nap?" she asked, lifting him out of the crib, nosing his tousled hair and sniffing his sweet baby scent, then took him by the hand and led him to the bathroom where he stood on a stool while she undid his overalls and then slid him on the blue plastic kiddie seat that sat on the toilet. The bathroom was another room that didn't bear close examination, she thought, refusing to look at the spotted mirror on the medicine cabinet and the cracked pink tiles. She checked the diaper he still wore for naps and found it dry; something to smile about. "You're getting to be such a big boy!" she exclaimed, and was rewarded with a tinkle. "You went in the toilet! Just like Mommy and Daddy!"

Finished, he raised his arms and bounced in the seat. Lucy slid him off and stood him on the floor where he squirmed and wiggled as she pulled on training pants and hooked his overall straps. At the second click he bolted shoeless for the door and she grabbed him by the back of his OshKosh's. "Shoes," she said, leading him back to the nursery where he protested loudly as she wrestled him into a pair of almost new Stride Rite oxfords that were already getting a bit tight. She was out of breath as she helped him down the back stairs to the kitchen.

Funny, she thought, helping Toby onto his booster seat. The cookies ought to be nearly done by now but there was no delicious buttery smell. She filled his sippy cup with milk and then reached for the oven door, intending to give him a warm cookie. But when she peered inside the oven she discovered it was no longer hot, it was barely warm and the cookies hadn't even browned.

She bit her lip and walked across the room to the refrigerator, where she reached for the box of graham crackers that was sitting on top. She opened it and pulled one out for Toby. She stood there, looking at the dry little brown square of cracker, and burst into tears.

"What's the matter?" Bill was at her side in a flash, his hammer still in his hand. "Are you okay?"

"No, I'm not okay," she said through clenched teeth. "I'm not okay at all. I can't live like this. Look at us! We're living in a wreck!" Her voice rose and she went on, unable to stop herself. "This is a big mistake. You're never going to be able to turn this dump into a house. You don't know what you're doing. It's been months and we don't have walls, or electric outlets or hot water. We're freezing and it's only December. I hate to tell you buddy but there're two, three more months of winter to get through." She marched over to the stove and pulled out the cookie sheets with her bare hands, slamming them onto the table and raising a little cloud of flour. "And the oven doesn't work!" she shrieked, shaking with sobs.

"That's simple," he said, taking the box of matches off the shelf and dropping to his knees, where he lit a match and reached into the broiler producing a satisfying whoosh. "See, all fixed," he said, leaning back on his heels and giving her a satisfied smile.

"It's not fixed," she said. "It'll go out again, next time the wind blows through these pathetic excuses for walls."

"Mo'," mumbled Toby, holding out his sippy cup for a refill.

Bill stayed in place, head bowed, while Lucy got the milk container out of the refrigerator. "I know it's tough, Lucy, but I'm really making progress."

"Great. That's terrific," she said, her voice dripping with sarcasm. "And what are Toby and I supposed to do in the meantime?"

Bill got to his feet and picked up Toby, hoisting him high above his head and making him shriek with delight. Then he settled him on his shoulders. "We're managing. We're doing okay. You're just feeling overwhelmed right now."

Lucy looked at him, at his sweet sincere face and his sparkling blue eyes. He needed a haircut and a hank of brown hair kept falling into one eye; he shook it back and grinned at her. She couldn't resist that cocky grin. "I'm sorry," she said. "I know you're working hard." The oven, which had been hissing, fell silent as the pilot light went out again. "I just wanted to make my mom's Christmas cookies."

"We'll get it fixed, I promise. I'll call Sears right away. Meanwhile, you need to get out of the house. You should take some time to yourself, go into town, do a little shopping. Toby and I will hold the fort, right Toby?"

Toby giggled. He loved sitting on his father's shoulders.

Lucy considered. It had been quite a while since she'd had any time to herself. "Okay," she said. "That's a good idea. Thanks."

"No problem," he said, swinging Toby down to the floor and taking his hand. "Come on, buddy. Let's find your tools. We've got some hammering to do."

When Lucy left the house, she could hear them both banging away. Bill was nailing up sheetrock and Toby was imitating him, pounding the pegs on his toy workbench. I wonder how long that will last, she thought, closing the door behind her.

She slid behind the wheel of Auntie Granada, the second-hand Ford they'd bought for her to drive. It was another expense they hadn't anticipated. Coming from the city they'd been shocked to discover there was no public transportation in rural Maine and that everyone had to provide for themselves. But Auntie Granada was one of the few things in their new life that actually worked and Lucy enjoyed cruising along the country roads with the radio blasting oldies. "I Saw Mommy Kissing Santa Claus" was playing as she turned out of the driveway onto Red Top Road and headed for town.

But where to go in town, she wondered, as she hummed along to the tune. There was no Bloomingdale's in Tinker's Cove, just a quaint little country store called Country Cousins that sold duck boots and rugged plaid shirts and corduroy pants. They had nothing at all for children, and only a few decidedly unstylish items for women. Definitely not the sort of place you went to spend your mad money.

Proceeding down Main Street she passed the newspaper office and the police and fire stations, eventually coming to Jake's Donut Shack. She considered stopping there and treating herself to a hot chocolate, but dismissed the idea. The few times she'd gone inside she'd felt uncomfortable, as if Jake's was some sort of exclusive club. Everybody seemed to know everybody else and regarded outsiders with suspicion. It was the same, Bill had told her, at the local fisherman's bar down at the harbor. The Bilge had a faithful clientele of regulars who were practically hostile to newcomers.

Reaching the end of Main Street, Lucy turned down Sea Street to the town pier, where she circled the parking lot. Nothing going on there, just a lot of boats sitting on shore and a lot of ice covering the harbor.

Well, so much for my afternoon out, thought Lucy, I might as well go home. So she headed back along Main Street where she noticed lights glimmering through the arched windows of the squat gray stone building that housed the Broadbrooks Free Library. Maybe they'll have some new magazines, she thought, turning into the parking lot. Or maybe even a new mystery.

The librarian looked up from the cards she was sorting at the main desk when Lucy entered. She was a white-haired crone but she greeted Lucy with a warm smile and a cheery hello. "Are you interested in anything particular?" she asked, eager to be helpful.

"Not really," said Lucy.

"Ah," said the old woman, looking at her shrewdly. "Just need a bit of a distraction?"

"That's it exactly," said Lucy.

"You're new in town, aren't you? You and your husband bought that old farmhouse on Red Top Road, right?"

Lucy was amazed. "How'd you know?"

The old woman flapped a veined and spotted hand. "It's a small town," she said, with a shrug. "You've taken on quite a challenge with that place. I understand the building inspector was just about to condemn it."

"I'm not surprised," said Lucy. "But my husband is determined to fix it up."

"Well, more power to him."

Lucy smiled ruefully. "He'll need it."

"It must be difficult for you," said the librarian, nodding at Lucy's tummy. "Especially with a toddler on your hands."

Lucy was taken by surprise at the woman's directness and was embarrassed to feel tears pricking at her eyes. She turned away, blinking furiously. "I'm managing," she finally said.

"Oh, dear," fretted the old woman, "I didn't mean to upset you."

"It's been a difficult day," admitted Lucy, wiping her eyes with a crumpled tissue she found in her coat pocket.

"Well, I have just the thing," said the librarian, coming round the desk and taking her by the elbow. "Come on into my office. I have a comfortable chair there and I can give you a cup of tea. Would you like that?"

"I'd love it," said Lucy.

It was warm and toasty in the office and the librarian, who introduced herself as Miss Tilley, brewed a bracing cup of tea. Lucy found herself downing several cups as she related the day's mishaps and actually found herself laughing as she described her struggles with the oven.

"I very much doubt that Sears will get to you before Christmas," said Miss Tilley, nodding sagely. "There's just the one repairman and I happen to know he's flat out."

"That's too bad," said Lucy, her face sinking. "I really wanted to make those cookies."

"Why not make them at my house?" suggested Miss Tilley. "My oven's working fine."

"Oh, I wouldn't want to put you to the trouble," demurred Lucy. "Besides, I can't really leave my little boy."

"Bring him along. I love children."

Lucy looked at the prim old lady, in her spotless white blouse with a cameo pin at the neck and her dark plaid skirt. "I don't think . . ."

"Nonsense. I'll expect you bright and early tomorrow. At eight. That will give us plenty of time because the library doesn't open until three on Thursdays." She peered at her through her wire-rimmed glasses. "You know where I live?"

Lucy suddenly felt inadequate. "I know I should but I'm afraid . . ."

"No reason you should know. You just moved here. I'm on Parallel Street, which is aptly named because it's parallel to Main Street, at the corner of Elm. Do you know it?"

"I do," said Lucy.

"And now, before you leave, perhaps I could suggest a few books. Do you enjoy mysteries?"

Lucy's spirits were much brighter as she drove home. She had a small stack of well-thumbed mystery novels on the seat beside her and she was taking a different route, following Miss Tilley's directions. It took her along Shore Road, past enormous summer cottages perched high above the bay. The view of rocky shore studded with tall pines, the dazzling expanse of blue ocean and the overarching blue sky was absolutely spectacular and Lucy began to feel once again that living in Maine wasn't so terrible after all.

New York City had nothing like this, in fact, the city could be pretty depressing sometimes. The subway smelled awful, the streets were full of litter, there was graffiti everywhere, and you couldn't walk down the street without having to step over at least one homeless person. And most important of all, Bill had truly been miserable at his job and that was something she couldn't tolerate. More than anything she wanted him to be happy.

Coming to the end of Shore Road, Lucy turned onto Packet Road which Miss Tilley assured her would eventually lead her to her own Red Top Road after she passed a cluster of houses. Lucy was exploring this new territory with interest and when she noticed a sign advertising a yard sale she impulsively pulled off the road and followed the hand-drawn arrow down a narrow dirt track of a driveway, eventually coming to a stop in front of a ramshackle log cabin. With a sagging porch and broken windows patched with cardboard and rags, it seemed to be in even worse shape than her house.

Undaunted, she turned off the ignition and got out of the car, eager to see what bargains she might find. Lucy had discovered soon after moving to Maine that yard sales offered the biggest bang for the buck, and a buck was just about all she had to spend. You never knew what might turn up, maybe she'd find a present for Bill, or a toy she could recycle for Toby. He wouldn't mind if it didn't come in a box, brand new.

But this yard sale didn't really deserve the name. There was only one small card table of household goods, with a carton beneath. And the items for sale verged on the pathetic: a stack of empty margarine tubs, a plastic ice cube tray, a few tattered copies of *Family Circle* magazine, and a plastic Christmas wreath that had faded from green to beige. Lucy was turning to go when the door opened and a young woman popped out.

"Hey!" she yelled. "I didn't hear your car."

"That's okay," Lucy yelled back. "I was just leaving."

The woman was zipping up her jacket, a dirty white parka that had long ago lost its puffy look and had gone flat. She tucked her dirty blond hair behind her ears and shuffled across the dirt yard in leopard-print fuzzy slippers. She wasn't wearing socks and her bird-thin ankles were blue from the cold.

"Did you see the box?" she asked, taking Lucy's arm. "There's some good stuff in there."

Lucy knew she was stuck. The woman, actually really only a girl, now that she had a good look at her, wasn't going to let her go unless she bought something and Lucy didn't blame her. For the first time in her life she was experiencing poverty and she recognized this woman as a longtime sufferer. The woman turned her head quickly, looking over her shoulder, and Lucy spotted two little children peering out of the broken window. She realized that this pathetic excuse for a yard sale was probably an effort to raise some money for Christmas.

"Well," said Lucy, reaching for her wallet. "I guess you can never have too many containers for leftovers."

The woman smiled, revealing a few missing teeth.

"These work great," she said, nodding enthusiastically and reaching for the pile of margarine containers. "Fifty cents?"

"Sure," said Lucy, plucking two quarters from her purse and reminding herself that she wasn't getting rooked, paying a ridiculous price for something she didn't need, but should consider it charity.

Encouraged by the sale, the woman pulled out the cardboard box from under the table. "Take a look," she said. "Some of this stuff is old." She paused. "Real old. Like antique."

Lucy planned to take a cursory look and then make a quick escape, but her eye was caught by a gleaming flash of red and white. She leaned closer, to investigate, and pulled out a giant candy cane made of . . . of what? She thought it was plastic but now that she was holding it she thought it was glass.

"What's this?" asked Lucy.

"A glass cane," said the woman, shrugging. "Go figure."

"There must be some story behind this," said Lucy, intrigued.

The woman didn't answer. She was looking down the drive where an aged blue pickup truck was lumbering towards the house. "Do you want it?" she asked, obviously nervous. "You can have it for a dollar."

"Okay." Lucy pulled out a dollar, the last of her week's grocery money.

"Thanks," said the woman, stuffing it in her pocket. She tilted her head toward the truck. "You better go now."

Lucy turned and saw a heavyset man with a bushy red beard getting out of the truck. Like nearly every man in Maine, he was wearing a plaid wool shirt-jacket, blue jeans, and work boots. "What's going on here?" he demanded, clumping across the yard and grabbing the woman by the wrist. "Didn't I tell you, didn't I say no way?"

"C'mon Kyle, you're hurting me," whined the woman, trying to twist away.

"I don't really . . . I mean, I'd be happy to give this back, if it's a problem," said Lucy, eager to defuse a situation that seemed to be getting out of control.

"You get out of here," snarled Kyle, spraying her with spittle. "This is between Dora and me."

Lucy looked questioningly at Dora, who nodded her head in quick little jerks.

"Are you sure?" she asked.

"GET OUT!" bellowed Kyle. "I got a shotgun, if you need convincing."

"No," said Lucy, backing away. "I'm convinced."

She was shaking when she got back behind the wheel of the car. She started the engine and backed around, catching sight of Kyle and Dora in the rearview mirror just as Dora broke free of his grip. Kyle raised his hand, and for a minute Lucy thought he was going to hit Dora, but instead he turned and waved at her, giving her a big gap-toothed smile.

Lucy stuck her hand out the window and waved back, signaling that she'd gotten the message. Everything was cool. He wasn't abusive, not at all. She'd just witnessed an unfortunate misunderstanding and the sooner she forgot all about it, the better. It was none of her business, was it?

Or was it? Lucy wasn't sure, as she bounced down the dirt track. She was certain Dora was a victim of domestic abuse but she hadn't seen enough to go to the police, and she doubted there was much they could do in any case. From what she'd read, most abused wives declined to press charges against their abusers for fear of even worse violence in retaliation.

But one thing was certain, she decided, trying to quell the queasy feeling in her stomach. She wasn't feeling sorry for herself any longer. There were people a lot worse off than she was, and it was time to count her blessings: a gentle husband who loved her, an adorable baby boy, a new friend. And if the glass cane was really an antique, it would make a great Christmas present for Miss Tilley.

Chapter Two

When she arrived at Miss Tilley's neat little antique house Lucy began to feel hopeful that their old farmhouse might someday look like something. Taking in the polished wide plank floors, the windows with their tiny panes of hand-blown wavy glass and the smoothly plastered walls and ceilings she found herself sighing in admiration. "What a lovely house," she said, setting Toby and her tote bag on the floor so she could take off her coat. She looked around eagerly taking in every detail as she pulled off his boots and mittens and unzipped his snowsuit: the gleaming antique pine furniture, the glowing colors of the Persian rug, the table top Christmas tree trimmed with tiny glass balls, the silvery sheen of the pewter plates displayed in a hutch, the portrait over the fireplace where a bright fire blazed merrily.

"My father," said Miss Tilley, indicating the rather stern gentleman pictured in the oil painting. "He was a judge."

"He does look judgmental," said Lucy, quickly biting her tongue. "No, I didn't mean that. Judicious. He looks quite judicious."

"He was named after General William Tecumseh Sherman, you know, the Civil War general, and I was named after Julia Ward Howe." She smiled, her eyes twinkling. "It's a family tradition, naming people after relics of the past."

Lucy scooped up Toby, who was heading for the fire, and perched him on her hip. "Toby was named after my great grandfather Tobias."

"It's a good old-fashioned name," said Miss Tilley, leading the way to the kitchen.

"We were trying to avoid the Js," said Lucy, using her free hand to grab the tote bag that was overflowing with toys, extra clothes and diapers, a bowl of cookie dough, a cookie press and baking tins. "Names like Jason, and Justin, and Jennifer are all the rage now."

"I have noticed quite a few of them at the library."

"Oh, my," said Lucy, startled to see an enormous black and chrome Glenwood coal stove taking pride of place in the middle of the Miss Tilley's kitchen. "That's a beautiful stove but I don't know how . . ."

"Never mind that old thing," said Miss Tilley, dismissing the gleaming monster. "I have a modern electric stove, too."

Indeed she did. A slim electric model was tucked into a bank of cabinets that was built against one wall and also included a double stainless steel sink set beneath a window with red and white gingham curtains. A porcelain-topped table sat in the middle of the room, on top of a cozy red and blue braided rug, and a hutch stood against the wall, filled with blue and white Canton china. Lucy felt as if she'd wandered into a Tasha Tudor book.

"I prefer the table for baking," said Miss Tilley, reaching for Toby. "Now, young man, we need to let your mother get on with her cookies."

Lucy expected Toby to resist but instead he smiled and reached out with his arms. The transfer was smoothly made and Miss Tilley carried him into the living room where she joined him on the rug and engaged him in building towers of blocks which they knocked down with a ball. Toby found this enormously entertaining and Lucy could hear him laughing as she set about the business of scooping dough into the press and squeezing out the shaped cookies onto the tins, then she decorated them with bits of candied fruit and colored sugar before popping them into the oven. Soon the whole house was filled with the buttery scent of baking cookies. Lucy was just sliding the last pan into the oven when Miss Tilley appeared, leading Toby by the hand.

"I think this young man is ready for a snack," she said, pulling an antique oak high chair out of the corner and setting it by the table. Lucy hoisted him into the chair and put a couple of warm cookies on the tray while Miss Tilley poured a small glass of milk. "Those cookies smell absolutely delicious," she said.

"Please, have some. I'm going to leave you some, too," said Lucy, with a nod to the overloaded wire cooling racks that were covered with dozens of perfect cookies, golden and brown around the edges. "I really appreciate . . ."

"Nonsense," said the old woman, with a wave of her hand. "We've enjoyed ourselves, haven't we, Toby?"

Toby took a bite of the cookie he was holding in his fat little hand. "Mmm," he said.

"I agree," said Miss Tilley, after taking a bite of cookie. "Mmmm."

Toby laughed and kicked his feet. "Mmmm."

Lucy was amazed at how Miss Tilley could turn the simplest thing into a game, making sounds that Toby imitated, playing peekaboo, reciting "This Little Piggy" while wiping his fingers with a washcloth. Soon the last cookies were out of the oven and Toby was rubbing his eyes.

"Why don't you put him down for a nap?" suggested

Miss Tilley. "Then you could get off your feet for a bit while I wash up these pans."

"Oh, I couldn't let you ..." protested Lucy, even though her feet and back were killing her.

"I insist," said Miss Tilley, using the voice that had maintained quiet in the library for thirty-odd years. She nodded toward a little downstairs room, the borning room she called it, and Lucy settled Toby on a daybed, removing his shoes and covering him with a handmade crocheted afghan. A copy of *The Night Before Christmas* was lying on the bedside table so she sat on the side of the bed and read him a few pages, closing the book when he was settled into a deep sleep and going out to the living room. There she found Miss Tilley waiting for her by the fire, along with two glasses of golden sherry and a plate of cheese twists.

"I think we both deserve a bit of a treat," said Miss Tilley, lifting her glass.

Lucy was about to protest that she rarely drank alcohol, and never in the morning, but the scene was so inviting that she changed her mind. "This looks lovely," she said, sinking into the down couch cushions.

"It is," said Miss Tilley, taking a sip and smacking her lips. "Dry Sack. Yummy."

The sherry was delicious and Lucy finished hers before she remembered the glass cane which she had left out in the car. She jumped to her feet. "I almost forgot," she exclaimed. "There's something in the car I need to get."

She hurried out and came back with the cane, awkwardly wrapped in white tissue with a big red bow. "I have a Christmas present for you."

"Oh, you shouldn't have," protested Miss Tilley, stretching out her hands to take the gift.

"I hope you like it," said Lucy. "When I saw it I thought of you."

"That is intriguing," said Miss Tilley, examining the oddly shaped package. "May I open it now?"

"Please do," said Lucy, eagerly anticipating the joyful reaction she was certain the cane would evoke.

But when Miss Tilley tore off the tissue there were no smiles, no raptures, no expressions of thanks. There was only shock and stunned silence as a single tear traced a path down the old woman's wrinkled face until it reached the corner of her mouth and she quickly licked it away with a flick of her tongue.

Lucy was dismayed at her reaction. "I didn't mean to distress you," she said.

"Forgive me," she said, as if coming out of a trance. "I was just overcome. This is wonderful. So thoughtful of you. An antique glass cane."

"I'll take it back. I'll get you something else," said Lucy. A bottle of Dry Sack came to mind. It would be expensive, but at least she could be sure Miss Tilley would enjoy it.

"Not at all." Miss Tilley got to her feet and laid the cane on the mantel. "This is remarkable, a wonderful find. And so festive." Her voice became soft and reflective. "I haven't seen one of these in years."

"So you know what it is. You've seen one before?"

"Oh, yes. There used to be a glass factory in town many years ago and canes like this turned up frequently. But of course they're fragile and I suppose a lot of them got broken and now they're quite rare. This one is a real find." She looked at Lucy. "Do you mind telling me where you got it?"

Lucy blushed, embarrassed. "Actually, well, it was at a yard sale."

"A yard sale," mused Miss Tilley, reaching for the sherry bottle. "Would you like a bit more?"

"None for me, I have to drive home," she said, watching the old woman refill her glass, setting the bottle on the table beside it.

"Where was this yard sale?" asked Miss Tilley, emptying the glass of sherry and refilling it.

"Out on Packet Road."

"Ah," she said, nodding. "Kyle and Dora. How interesting."

"That's right," said Lucy, who continued to be surprised at the way Miss Tilley seemed to know everyone in town.

Miss Tilley sighed. "I suppose I owe you an explanation."

"Not at all," said Lucy, wishing desperately that Toby would wake up and she could get out of there, away from her embarrassing gaffe and back home. But Miss Tilley was not about to be deterred.

"It was Christmas Eve," she began, taking another sip. Her eyes had lost their focus and she was looking inward, seeking the past. "I was just a girl. I'd been out skating on Blueberry Pond and when I got home the house was quiet. Very quiet, which was unusual, because my mother was an invalid and there were usually people around, a nurse, a cook, a maid. There was always someone in the kitchen, people going up and down the stairs. It was the stairs, you see. She'd fallen down the cellar stairs. Mama was there at the bottom, crumpled in a heap, and there was a glass cane, red and white like this one, on the floor beside her. Smashed to smithereens."

Horrified, Lucy's hand flew to her mouth. "I had no idea," she said.

"Of course not. How could you have known?" Miss Tilley's voice was thoughtful. "Nobody knew, really. It was all kept very quiet. Papa didn't want people to know the details, that Mama was wandering about the house as if nobody was taking proper care of her. He let people assume that she died a respectable death in bed, surrounded by her loving family."

Lucy's mind was full of questions but she wasn't at all comfortable asking them. She sat, trying to think of something appropriate to say, and watching as Miss Tilley refilled the glass yet again.

"It was horrible. He made me help, you see. He made me help carry Mama upstairs to her bed."

"Who did?" It popped out before Lucy could stop herself.

"Papa did. He took her by the shoulders and told me to lift her by the ankles. He said she wouldn't, she couldn't be very heavy, not after being sick for so long, but she was heavy. We kind of bumped her up the stairs, two long flights. And then he sent me back downstairs to sweep up the glass and tidy the basement while he put her in a fresh nightgown and tied her hair with a ribbon and tucked the covers around her, folding her hands around a Bible and laying them on her chest." Miss Tilley looked her straight in the eye. "Then he called the doctor."

Lucy found her eyes going to the portrait over the mantel. The stern, righteous man pictured there suddenly didn't look quite so respectable. That gleam in his eye, was it the light of truth and justice, or was it something more sinister?

Lucy thought of her own great-grandfather Tobias. He wore flannel shirts and khakis in the house, where he spent his days reading and watching baseball on TV from his armchair in the living room and making wooden furniture in his basement workshop, but he never went outside in such casual clothes. He put on a starched white shirt, a dark suit, shiny black shoes and a hat for the short walk down the street to buy the newspaper. "Times change," said Lucy. "When I was a little girl I wore white gloves to church. And my great-grandfather wouldn't go out of the house without a hat."

Miss Tilley nodded. "Straw between Memorial Day and Labor Day, felt for the rest of the year."

"Exactly," said Lucy, smiling. "So it's not surprising that your father would want to protect his family from gossip. Every funeral's the same: everybody wants to know all the details. Did she smoke? Was it expected or was it sudden? Did she suffer? I can see why he wanted to keep some things private. He wanted to preserve your mother's dignity, even in death."

"Oh, I don't know about that," said Miss Tilley. "Mama rarely got out of the house except to go to church on Sunday even before she got sick. She may have looked like a fine lady then, in her silk dress and her flowery hat, but at home she worked like a slave. Everything had to be just so for Papa. She even ironed his morning paper before he read it."

Lucy had never heard of such a thing and her eyebrows shot up.

"Oh, yes," continued Miss Tilley. "He had to have fresh linens on his bed every night, fresh towels every day, starched napkins and those shirts of his." She rolled her eyes. "The slightest little wrinkle, even a pucker from the iron and he'd have a fit. My goodness, the hours my poor mother spent at the ironing board. There was no permanent press then and if there had been Papa certainly wouldn't have allowed it. When I think of her, before she got sick, I think of her standing at that ironing board, her sleeves rolled up and her hair falling down, her face shiny with sweat."

"She didn't have any household help?"

"Not until she got sick."

"I wouldn't be surprised if she got sick on purpose," said Lucy, attempting a joke.

Miss Tilley's eyes widened. "Oh, no, she would never do that. It was the doctor who insisted that she needed bed rest and even then she would try to get up and make sure everything was just as Papa liked it."

"Perhaps that's what she was doing the day she fell," said Lucy. "She was probably weak and collapsed."

"An accident?" Miss Tilley looked at her empty glass and reached for the bottle, sighing when she realized it was empty. "I don't think it was an accident."

Lucy glanced at the portrait. "You don't?"

"There was a tense atmosphere in the house that morning. That's why I went skating. I wanted to get out."

"Did they have an argument of some sort?" asked Lucy.

"No. I never heard them fight, but I'd know that something was wrong. Papa would be very abrupt, his tone would be very sharp, and Mama would watch him anxiously, as if she were afraid of him."

"Oh dear," said Lucy, remembering the scene she'd witnessed the day before, with Kyle and Dora.

"I've always suspected that Papa pushed her down the stairs."

Lucy gasped. "That's a terrible thing to think about your father," she finally said.

"Yes, it is," agreed Miss Tilley, looking up at the portrait. "I loved him, I still do, but every time I look at that picture I have the same dark suspicion. If only I could know for sure what happened that day."

Lucy thought of the book she was reading, Josephine Tey's *Daughter of Time* about a British police inspector who attempts to solve the fifteenth-century murder of the Little Princes in the Tower of London. "Maybe we can try to solve the mystery," she said. "Just like Inspector Grant."

"I thought you'd like that book," said Miss Tilley. "But it's fiction. This is real life."

"But that mystery was hundreds of years old. Your mystery is much more recent."

"But the princes and Richard III were historical figures, things were written about them, there were documents and books."

"A lot of which was propaganda put out by Richard's enemies."

"And a lot of it was written quite a bit later, long after anyone who might have known the truth was dead," agreed Miss Tilley.

"Which is not the case here," said Lucy. "You were on the scene."

"But it's been so long," said Miss Tilley.

"Why don't we give it a try," coaxed Lucy. "You might be surprised what you remember."

Chapter Three

Miss Tilley sat primly on the little Victorian sofa with her ankles neatly crossed and gazed out the window, collecting her memories. "Papa was a terribly difficult man to live with," she began, rubbing the knobby knuckles of one age-spotted hand with the other. "He was always conscious of his position as a judge and believed his own behavior—and that of his family—had to be above reproach."

"That's understandable," said Lucy, with a little smile. "If a judge is going to enforce the law he has to obey it, right? Otherwise he'd be a hypocrite."

"This went beyond obeying the law," said Miss Tilley, speaking slowly, her gaze turned inward. "It was as if he believed he had received the rules for acceptable behavior from a Higher Power, rather like Moses receiving the Ten Commandments." She gave a small, rueful smile. "Only there were a lot more than ten, and Mama and I, and my sister Harriet—she was named for Harriet Tubman—had to follow them to the letter. We all rose at six, except for Mama who got up earlier, and we had to be washed, and combed and dressed, with our beds made and our rooms tidied before breakfast, which was served in the dining room at six-thirty sharp." She looked at

Lucy. "From time to time Papa would conduct a surprise inspection and, oh dear, there was such a fuss if a slipper was left lying on the carpet or the windowsills were dusty."

"What sort of fuss?" asked Lucy. "My mother says her father used to spank her with a hairbrush."

"Nothing like that. No hairbrushes. It was worse, really. We'd have to listen to a long lecture on irresponsibility and wickedness and ungratefulness and by the end I would feel absolutely worthless. And, of course, there'd be no breakfast for the sinner who would have to remain in her room to reflect on her crime until Papa decided—or remembered—to let her out."

"He locked you in your room?"

"He didn't have to. We simply didn't dare leave until we'd received permission."

Lucy, an only child who had always been able to convince her father to grant her every wish, found this hard to understand. "And what about your mother? Did he treat her like that, too?"

"Oh, yes. If Mama failed to live up to his expectations he would scold her, too." She shook her head. "Looking back it all seems ridiculous. A piece of burnt toast was treated as if you'd burned down the house. It was all out of proportion, but we were so cowed we didn't realize it. Except for Harriet. She was always more rebellious than I and refused to give up her friends from school—Papa considered them unsuitable companions—even when he threatened to send her away to boarding school. She was convinced that he was too miserly to pay tuition and she was right. Papa predicted she would come to a bad end and I guess she did, at least in his book. She ran away with a young man Papa did not approve of. He was a labor organizer and a big supporter of Franklin Delano Roosevelt, and of course Papa believed Franklin

Delano Roosevelt and his wife, Eleanor, were earthly embodiments of Satan himself." She paused and licked her lips. "Especially Eleanor."

"My great-grandfather Tobias thought that, too," said Lucy. "What happened to Harriet?"

"I'm ashamed to say that I don't know."

Lucy was shocked. "You don't know?"

"No. Papa disowned her and we never heard from her again." She sighed. "It was a great sadness to my mother. In fact, it was right after Harriet eloped that Mama's health began to fail and she became bedridden.

"I suspected she had tuberculosis and I knew she was terrified of being sent to a sanatorium. That's what they did back in those days. They packed people off to the mountains and hoped the good clean air and lots of hearty food would cure them. Mama didn't want to leave home so she insisted she had woman troubles because all you had to do was say that in those days and everyone changed the subject fast."

Lucy couldn't resist chuckling. "It's not so different now, at least in my house."

Miss Tilley shook her head. "No. I don't imagine your home is anything like that. My parents' house was a house of secrets. When you're afraid the truth will get you in trouble, you lie. You hide things. Everything becomes dangerous, even ideas, so you keep them to yourself. That's what happened to us. Mama, Papa, and I became strangers to each other, strangers living in the same house."

The baby inside her kicked and Lucy placed her hands on her tummy. "A house of secrets and strangers," she said.

"Exactly," said Miss Tilley, with a little nod. "But it all changed when Papa hired a nurse to take care of Mama.

He resisted for a long time, but when I fell ill, too, the doctor insisted. Papa didn't like the idea, of course, especially when the doctor recommended a nurse who was obviously Italian. As you'd expect, Papa did not approve of anyone whose name ended with a vowel—and he wasn't too keen on the Irish either. Angela DeRosa was her name and I'll never forget it because she was just like an angel to me, and to Mama, too. She was like a breath of fresh air, so efficient, so caring. You felt better the moment she entered your room, you just did. She was young and pretty and sang to herself as she made the beds and spooned out the medicine. But Papa always grumbled about having to pay a nurse as well as a cook and a maid."

Now we're getting somewhere, thought Lucy, mentally adding the nurse, the maid, and the cook to the judge as possible suspects. "What was the cook like?"

"Her name was Mrs. Sprout, if you can believe it." Miss Tilley snorted. "Helen Sprout. She was no angel, that's for sure. She was big and fat, and grouchy and she slammed around the kitchen, banging pots, and chopping up chickens with a cleaver, and punching the bread dough, and pounding potatoes with a big wooden masher. I stayed clear of her, that's for sure."

"Were you afraid of her?"

Miss Tilley reflected. "I guess I was, now that I think about it. There was something out of control about her. She was unpredictable, like a human whirlwind. Plates would break, smoke would billow from the stove, the sink would overflow, things like that were always happening."

"How was the food?"

"Fine. Really good. It was the oddest thing. You'd think everything would be awful, burned to cinders, but it wasn't. And after Papa had a taste of her apple pie, why there was no question about letting her go. He loved all her cooking, but especially her pies. That woman certainly had a knack—even Mama's pie crust wasn't as flaky as Mrs. Sprout's."

"My mother makes good pies," said Lucy, "and she's tried to teach me but mine are never as good as hers." She thought of her father, drifting in and out of consciousness in the hospital, and her mother who was spending every free minute with him and suddenly wanted desperately to talk with them. Later, she promised herself, maybe after dinner when Bill gave Toby his bath. "What about the maid?" she asked.

"Which one?" chuckled Miss Tilley. "We went through quite a few of them, if I remember correctly. There was a Brigid, and several Marys, and a Margaret. They never lasted very long."

"Your father?"

"Oh, no. He never took any notice of them. It was Mrs. Sprout. She made them work awfully hard. And I think some of them were afraid of Mr. Boott," said Miss Tilley, giving an involuntary little shudder.

Lucy's interest perked up. "Boott? Was he related to the Bootts on Packet Road?"

"I wouldn't be surprised. Kyle is probably his grand-nephew. Mr. Boott never married. He was a sort of handyman. He cut the grass and painted the trim and tended the coal furnace and sometimes he drove Mama when she went to see the doctor."

"Did he have a first name?"

"Oh, yes. Emil." Miss Tilley paused. "You know, I think that's why I didn't like him. I didn't like his name."

"Maybe there was some other reason?" prompted Lucy.

"Well, he was a convict, a trusty, from the county jail."

Lucy's eyebrows shot up. "A prisoner?"

"Yes. Papa had some arrangement with the sheriff

and men from the prison often worked for him. They painted the house, I remember. Things like that."

"No wonder you were afraid. They must have been in jail for a reason, right?"

"I don't think Mr. Boott did anything very terrible, or Papa wouldn't have had him around the house."

"But he was in jail for a long time, right? So it must have been a fairly serious crime."

"You're right, Lucy. I never thought of it that way before. He must have worked for us for at least twenty years and he was a prisoner the whole time."

"Twenty years is a long sentence," said Lucy.

"Even for Papa," said Miss Tilley. "He was tough but he rarely sentenced anyone for more than a year or two at most." She paused. "Only the very worst criminals, like murderers and embezzlers got long terms. He believed in getting them back to work as fast as possible so the taxpayers wouldn't have to support them, or their families."

"Your father sounds like a peach," said Lucy, sarcastically.

"Speaking of peaches, I almost forgot Miss Peach."

"Miss Peach?"

"Oh, that wasn't her real name. That's what Mama called her, because she was from Georgia. She was my father's secretary. Miss Katherine Kaiser."

"It sounds as if your mother was a bit jealous."

"I think she was and who could blame her? Miss Peach was everything she wasn't. She had a career as a trained secretary, she was independent, she could spend her salary any way she wanted. And what she wanted was to buy clothes. She always looked lovely, in beautiful suits and hats and high-heeled shoes with peep toes. And she went to the beauty salon every morning just to have her hair combed! Harriet and I were pretty impressed, you can be sure of that. Imagine! Going to the salon just to have your hair combed."

"That is pretty impressive," said Lucy. She heard Toby stirring in the borning room and struggled awkwardly to her feet, belly first, and cracked the door to take a peek. He was sitting up in bed, sucking his thumb. She quickly changed his diaper, then he scrambled off the bed and ran out to the living room, stopping short when he saw Miss Tilley.

"I think he forgot me," she said.

But Toby hadn't forgotten. "Mmmm," he said, remembering the game they'd played earlier.

"Mmmm," she went, right back at him, and he laughed.

"I guess I better get this little fellow home for lunch," said Lucy. "Come on Toby, let's pick up your toys."

It was a slow process but eventually everything was packed up, including the cookies, and Toby and Lucy were zipped in their winter jackets, and muffled in hats, scarves, and mittens, ready to go.

"Thanks for everything," said Lucy. "It wouldn't be Christmas without the cookies. And I haven't forgotten about your mother. We've got a list of suspects and I'm going to see what I can dig up."

"Suspects?"

"Your father, Emil Boott, Mrs. Sprout, Angela DeRosa, Katharine Kaiser, even the maids—any one of them could have given your mother a fatal push down the stairs."

"I never thought of it that way but I suppose you're right. They're all suspects."

But when Lucy had finally strapped Toby into the car seat and stowed everything in Auntie Granada's enormous trunk, and was starting the car, she realized she had to add another suspect to her list: tuberculosis. As Miss Tilley had told her, the disease had ravaged families right up until World War II when lifesaving treatments were developed. It seemed a lot more probable that poor, ill Mrs. Tilley had fallen down the stairs as a result of a coughing fit or a fainting spell than at the hands of a household intimate.

Chapter Four

When Lucy got home she found Bill had heated up the pot of split pea soup they had been having for lunch for the past week. The soup never seemed to end, it just got thicker with each reheating even though they kept thinning it down with the vegetable cooking water Lucy always saved. The chunks of ham and carrot which had been plentiful in the beginning had become scarcer with each reheating, however.

"'Pease porridge hot, pease porridge cold,'" chanted Lucy, as she unzipped Toby. "'Pease porridge in the pot nine days old,' and that's no lie. It's lovely pea soup for lunch again."

Toby didn't seem to mind. He kicked his feet in the high chair and spooned the stuff up eagerly, chasing down the little oyster crackers that Lucy sprinkled on top. She wasn't quite as enthusiastic but reminded herself that homemade pea soup was nourishing and tasty and certainly helped stretch the food budget. She was trying to think of something new to do with a pound of hamburger for supper when Bill came in the kitchen to heat some water for tea.

"Daddy! Daddy!" chortled Toby, flinging a spoonful of soup over his shoulder.

"So how did the cookie baking go? I'd be happy to

conduct a taste test," he asked, automatically reaching for the sponge and wiping the soup spatter off the wall, where it had landed.

Watching him, Lucy wondered why he bothered. Another stain on the wall would hardly matter. "Sorry," she said, rousing herself. "Toby already did that. He said they were fine."

Hearing his name Toby laughed, then picked a cracker out of his soup with his fingers and stuck it on his nose.

"I don't know if he's entirely reliable in matters of taste," said Bill. "I've had a lot more experience when it comes to cookies."

"You mean you don't wear them?" asked Lucy.

"Exactly," said Bill, plucking the cracker off Toby's nose and popping it in his son's little mouth. "I know that food goes in the mouth."

"Down!" ordered Toby, who had lost interest in lunch and was raring to go.

The kettle shrieked as Lucy wiped his hands and face with a washcloth and set him on the floor, where he made a beeline for the wooden crate that served as a pot cupboard. She put tea bags in two mugs, filled them with hot water and arranged a half-dozen cookies on a plate and, stepping nimbly over the pots that Toby was scattering on the floor, carried it all back to the table.

"Mmm," said Bill, savoring a bite of cookie.

"Mmm," said Toby.

Bill raised his eyebrows curiously. "Mmm?" he said

"MMM," hummed Toby, louder than before.

"It's a game Miss Tilley taught him. He loves it."

Bill's next mmm was very soft, but Toby didn't take the hint. His MMMM was louder and longer than ever.

"Is there a way to stop it?" asked Bill, reaching for another cookie.

"Don't go mmm anymore," said Lucy.

"MMMMM!"

"I will if you will," said Bill. "So did you have an interesting morning?"

"A lot more interesting than I bargained for. You know that cane I bought for Miss Tilley?" When Bill nodded she continued. "Well, she started to cry when I gave it to her. It seems her mother actually died on Christmas Eve many years ago, this must have been back in the thirties, and a red and white glass cane was found smashed beside her body."

"That's quite a coincidence," said Bill, taking a slurp of tea.

"I know. And it gets weirder. She told me she's always suspected her mother was killed by her father. He was a mean old character if ever there was one."

"She told you all this while you were baking cookies?"

"Uh, well, Toby fell asleep and we drank some sherry," admitted Lucy. "I only had a very small glass but Miss Tilley pretty much drained the bottle. I think it may have loosened her lips."

"I guess so," said Bill. "It doesn't seem the sort of conversation you have with a new friend."

"Not at all, but that's the funny thing. It didn't feel as if we were getting to know each other, it seemed as if we'd known each other forever. Like we were old friends, maybe in some earlier reincarnation or something."

Bill looked at her skeptically. "I think you need to get out more, Lucy."

"Well, I was thinking I might do a little investigating and see if I can't find out how her mother really died. There were a lot of people in and out of the house and one of them might have been a murderer."

"How are you going to do that? They've probably all been dead for years."

Lucy looked down at her empty mug. "I don't exactly know myself," she admitted. "But people don't live in a vacuum. There are bound to be records, newspaper accounts. After all, old cases do get solved from time to time. That's what the mystery I'm reading is about."

"That's a book, this is real life," he said. "And besides, you're already overlooking an obvious clue."

"I am?"

"Sure, the cane."

"You're right!" exclaimed Lucy, hopping up and running around the table to kiss him. "In fact, it just so happens that I bought the cane from some people named Boott, and the Tilley family had a handyman named Boott. And, get this, he was a trusty from the jail."

"Sounds like a prime suspect to me," said Bill, scratching his chin. "I'm thinking of growing a beard. What do you think?"

"I think you'd look like a real Mainer."

He pulled her into his lap. "It will be scratchy at first," he said, giving her a long, lovely kiss.

"Mmmm," said Lucy. "I won't mind."

"MMMM!" hummed Toby, banging a pot with a wooden spoon.

Surprised, they jumped apart, laughing. "I guess I better get back to work," said Bill. "That sheetrock isn't going to hang itself."

Lucy took the dirty dishes over to the sink and began washing them, looking out the window as she worked. She had a clear view of the rutted dirt driveway, the fence with its missing and broken pickets, and the road that nobody except the mailman ever seemed to use. And here he was now, in his little Jeep.

Checking to see that Toby was busy with his pots she threw her coat over her shoulders and ran down the driveway, hoping the day's mail included something good. A big fat check would be best, maybe they'd overpaid their income tax and the IRS was sending them a refund. But she'd settle for a card from a friend, or a Christmas gift.

Opening the flap on the front of the box, she smiled to see a small package wrapped in brown paper and string along with the usual bills and junk mail. The return address indicated it came from her mother, which surprised her because she knew her mother was spending all her time at the hospital with her father.

Back inside the kitchen, she found Toby was still busy arranging the pots so she threw the coat over a chair and sat down at the table to open the package. She slipped off the string and paper and found a slim little book, an old and worn copy of O. Henry's famous story, "The Gift of the Magi." It wasn't wrapped and there was no card but she didn't need one, she knew it came from her father. It was his tradition to read the story every Christmas.

Now, she realized, he was sending it to her so she could carry on the tradition. It was his way of saying good-bye. She pressed the musty, brown volume to her chest and tears filled her eyes.

"Book!" said Toby, attempting to climb into her lap.

She wiped her eyes and hoisted him up onto her lap. Then she began reading aloud, expecting Toby to lose interest. But he didn't. He was content to sit in her lap and listen as she read the familiar story of Della, who sold her beautiful hair to buy a gold chain for her husband's pocket watch, and Jim, who sold his pocket watch to buy combs for Della's hair. In the end, he had a watch chain and no watch and she had combs for her hair but no hair to hold them, but they had their love for each other which was the best gift of all.

Finishing the story, she set Toby in his high chair with a sippy cup of juice and a handful of Cheerios and reached for the phone, dialing the number she had learned as a child. Her mother answered.

"I got the book. Thank you so much."

"He insisted. I told him I didn't have time, it's a long

bus ride to Montefiore you know, but he kept after me and kept after me. 'You're wasting your strength' I told him, 'you should be thinking about getting well instead of worrying about a Christmas present for Lucy,' but he wouldn't listen."

"Well I really appreciate it. I know how much Dad needs you." She paused. "How is he?"

"The same."

Lucy reached over and stroked Toby's silky head. He popped a Cheerio in his mouth and smiled at her. "The same? What does that mean?"

"It means he's not getting better and he's not getting worse."

"Can't they try something different? Some new medication?"

"He won't let them."

"What do you mean?"

"He's refusing treatment." Lucy heard the anger in her mother's voice. "He's giving up."

Lucy found herself slumping, as if a heavy blanket of sadness had dropped on her. "Do you want me to come?" she asked.

"There's no need." Her mother's voice was sharp.

"But if he's dying . . . ," Lucy paused, realizing it was the first time since her father became ill that she'd said the word, "if he's dying I want to say good-bye."

"He isn't going to die. I'm not letting him. I'm seeing a lawyer and I'm going to court and I'll become his guardian and then I'll tell the doctors to do whatever they can to keep him alive."

Lucy bit her lip. "Are you sure that's the right . . ."

"Of course it's the right thing to do. I have to go now." Then there was a click and the line went dead.

Lucy wanted to tear her clothes and pull her hair, she wanted to yell at her mother, she wanted to feel her father's strong arms around her one more time, but she couldn't do those things so she lifted Toby onto his feet, standing him in the high chair, and gave him a big hug. Inside her, the baby seemed to do a somersault.

Toby wasn't interested in hugs and after his long morning nap he wasn't interested in his usual after-lunch nap. He was interested in banging pots but Lucy was developing a headache, so she decided to take him outside for a walk around the yard. It wasn't Central Park, with its zoo and merry-go-round, but it did offer fresh air and occasional sunshine.

Toby needed a hand getting down the porch steps, but then he was off and running, heading down the driveway. Lucy ran after him, scooped him up and swung him around, pointing him in the opposite direction. He tried to dodge past her, determined to flirt with death in the road, but she blocked him and scooped him up again. "Let's find a ball," she said, and this time he ran for the safer territory of the backyard. As she followed she thought about her conversation with her mother and tried to sort out her feelings.

It seemed to her that through the years she had played out this same scenario many times. She had always felt closer to her father than her mother, but whenever any real intimacy began to develop her mother would somehow intervene. It started when she was quite small. If Pop invited her to go for a walk down the street to the candy store, her mother would come up with some chore he had to do first and the little walk would be forgotten. Even when she was in college she could remember several instances when he called to say he would be in the area on a business trip and would take her out to dinner, just the two of them, but it never happened. A sudden crisis always seemed to arise—Mom suddenly developed a mysterious ailment or her car was making a suspicious noise—and he'd have to cut the trip short and return home.

Toby had found the ball, a big playground ball, and was running with it. When he got about ten feet from her he threw it to her, making a great effort, and she laughed at the sight. He was so cute. She couldn't imagine shutting him out or turning away from him, but that's what her mother had done to her. She'd always felt like a third wheel, like an intruder in her parents' life together, and she'd assumed that was the natural order of things. Now she knew differently. She caught the ball and threw it back, gently, so Toby could catch it.

Back in the house she put a Care Bears tape in the VCR for Toby and set a pot of water to boil, planning to cook macaroni for American chop suey. It wasn't fine cuisine, but it sure stretched a pound of hamburger. While she waited for it to boil she called Miss Tilley at the library. After thanking her for letting her bake the cookies and minding Toby and giving her sherry, Lucy got to the point of her call. "Do you know anything about the glass cane your mother had?" she asked. "Was it a family treasure?"

"I'd never seen it before, nobody had," replied Miss Tilley.

"Perhaps it was a gift she was intending to give someone?"

"I don't know where she would have gotten it. She hadn't been out of the house for months."

"Maybe someone gave it to her," suggested Lucy.

"She was too sick for visitors by then."

"I see," said Lucy.

"I'm afraid I'm not being very helpful," said Miss Tilley.

"On the contrary," said Lucy, who was beginning to think she was on to something. She might not be Sherlock Holmes, but she could use his method. It was simple logic that if the glass cane wasn't in the house before the murder, and if Mrs. Tilley had no way of obtaining it herself, then the killer must have brought it.

Find the owner of the cane and she would find the murderer.

She was explaining this to Miss Tilley when the pot began to steam and the lid rattled. "Oops, got to go," she said, "before the pot boils over."

Next morning it was the diaper pail that was demanding attention. Now that Toby was becoming more interested in using the toilet, the pail filled more slowly and had plenty of time to ripen. She sniffed the familiar odor and decided something had to be done. Fortunately, the septic system hadn't been giving much trouble lately, the sink and bathtub drained nicely, the toilet flushed properly without even a hiccup, so Lucy decided to risk running the washer. She filled it with hot water, added detergent and bleach, and dumped in the diapers. The machine chugged and swished and Lucy enjoyed the sense of virtue that came from knowing she wasn't polluting the planet with disposable diapers. Not that she wouldn't, of course, if she could have afforded them. But that didn't lessen the fact that she had made the ecological choice.

The cycle had almost finished and she was considering running a second load when she heard an ominous bubbling sound in the kitchen sink. She went into the bathroom and discovered the toilet was burping, a sure sign that the cesspool was nearing capacity and needed time to drain. That second load would have to be done at the Laundromat.

Lucy put the diapers in the dryer and got it going, then she packed up the dirty laundry, zipped Toby into his snowsuit, and advised Bill not to flush unless absolutely necessary. She didn't mind having to go to the Laundromat. It got her out of the house, and she planned to make a second stop at the Winchester College museum to inquire about the glass factory.

A light snow was falling as she steered Auntie Granada toward Main Street, passing the large old sea captains' houses that had been built in the town's nineteenth-century heyday. Back then there were huge fortunes to be made at sea, taking ginseng to China, and bringing back tea, and porcelain, and furniture. Those days were gone but the substantial houses had endured and were decked in holiday greenery, with wreaths and swags and garlands. A few even had decorative arrangements of fruit—pineapples, and oranges, and apples—fixed above their doors. Continuing on past the Community Church she spotted the traditional creche on the lawn and decided to show it to Toby.

She parked right in front of the church and climbed the hill to the creche, holding Toby by the hand. Another woman was already there, with a little girl a few years older than Toby.

"Hi!" said Lucy. "What a charming creche."

She wasn't exaggerating. The creche featured a collection of large plaster figures depicting Mary and Joseph, the shepherds, and the animals. In a wooden manger filled with straw a plaster baby Jesus lay with his plump arms and legs in the air.

"If that's a newborn baby, Mary is a better woman than I," said the woman.

Lucy looked at her, taking in her smartly tailored black coat with padded shoulders, her Farrah Fawcett hairdo, her red lipstick and her high-heeled platform boots. The little girl was also beautifully dressed, in a red wool coat with leggings, and a matching hat that screamed Saks Fifth Avenue's children's department. "Pardon me for saying so, but you don't look as if you're from around here," she said. "I'm Lucy Stone and this is

Toby. We just moved here a few months ago from New York." Then she added, "City," just to be clear.

"Sue Finch, and this is my daughter, Sidra. We've been here about a year." She sighed meaningfully "We used to live in Bronxville but my husband, Sid, didn't get tenure so he decided to become a carpenter."

"That's too bad," said Lucy, expressing heartfelt sympathy. "My husband wanted to get back to the land and work with his hands. He used to be a stockbroker."

"Why Maine?" asked Sue.

"Bill read an article years ago in *Mother Earth News*. . . ."

"I think Sid read the same one! So here we are." Sue held out her hands. "Strangers in a strange land."

Lucy laughed. "Look, I have to get going, but would you like to exchange phone numbers? Maybe we could get together for tea and sympathy?"

"You've got a deal," said Sue, scribbling on a piece of paper and giving it to Lucy.

Lucy tore off the bottom half and wrote her number on it. "Call anytime," said Lucy, visualizing the calendar full of empty white squares that hung on the kitchen wall.

"I will," said Sue. "By the way, do you think you could give us a lift to the IGA? My car got a flat and Mike at the garage said it won't be ready before noon."

"No problem," said Lucy, as they walked down the hill together. Sidra, she noticed, was making faces at Toby and he was clearly fascinated.

But when they got to the car, she was embarrassed by the mess of toys and papers, not to mention the dirty laundry, and began to try to clear the passenger seat for Sue.

"Never mind," she said, seating herself on top of some crumpled junk mail.

But Lucy did mind. She figured her new friendship

was over before it began. Who would want to hang out with a slob like her?

Lucy had a laundry basket full of neatly folded clothes sitting beside her on the front seat and Toby was nodding off in his car seat in the back when she pulled into the museum parking lot at Winchester College. The college's venerable brick buildings and quad reminded her of her own college days and she felt a bit wistful as she maneuvered Toby out of the car seat and into the umbrella stroller. She decided to take Toby for a little walk around the quad before going to the museum, hoping that the motion would lull him to sleep and the little toddler dozed off before she was halfway around. She enjoyed the reaction of the students she passed: the boys generally ignored Toby but the girls all smiled at him, probably imagining themselves as mothers some day. *Good luck to them* thought Lucy, whose back was beginning to ache.

Back at the museum, Lucy wheeled Toby inside, pausing to examine an Egyptian mummy that was displayed in the front hall. Wondering how it ended up in this backwater corner of Maine, she studied a directory posted on the wall and discovered the curator's office was on the third floor. She took the elevator and when the doors slid open encountered a thirtyish man wearing the academic uniform of tweed jacket, oxford shirt and bow tie. "Can I help you?" he asked, raising his eyebrows.

Lucy assumed he didn't get too many visitors, especially not mothers with toddlers in tow. "I'm looking for the curator," she said.

"Well you found him," he said, extending a hand. "I'm Fred Rumford. What can I do for you?"

"I'm Lucy Stone," she said, taking his hand and finding it pleasantly warm and his shake firm. "I'm looking for information about a glass factory that used to be here in town."

"Come with me," he said, ushering her back into the elevator and pressing the number two. "We have a display."

The second floor of the museum was devoted to local industry such as fishing and farming, and a corner featured enlarged photos of the Brown and Williams Glass Company, as well as samples of the wares it produced such as bottles, oil lamps, and fancy dishes. There wasn't a glass cane in sight, but the photos of workers caught her eye. One picture of office workers had a list of names beneath the rather glum group and she leaned closer for a better look. Sure enough, she realized with mounting excitement, there was Emil Boott standing in the back row, dressed as the others were in a dark suit. His face was round and bland and gave no hint that he was a criminal, headed for prison.

She pointed him out. "See that fellow there, in the wire-rimmed glasses? He did something very bad and was sent to prison for twenty years."

"You don't say," said Fred. "He looks nice enough."

"You never can tell, just by looking at someone," said Lucy, thinking of the photos she'd occasionally seen in the newspaper of murderers and other criminals. She studied them, looking for a clue to what made them commit such evil acts, but they usually looked like anyone else.

"Back in the nineteenth century they used to think there was a criminal physiognomy, that you could identify criminals by the shape of their heads," said Fred.

"If only it were that simple," said Lucy, with a sigh. "I'm interested in a particular item, a glass cane," she said.

"A whimsy."

"A what?"

"Whimsy. They were items the workers made out of leftover glass at the end of the day to amuse themselves."

"Would there be a record of who made them, or who bought them?"

Fred shook his head. "No. In fact, since they had to be left out overnight to cool, they were often appropriated by whoever got to work first the next morning."

"So a fellow like this Emil Boott, an office worker, could have taken a cane or two if he got to work early, before the glassblowers."

"Well, sure," said Fred. "But I don't think he went to prison for twenty years for taking a whimsy."

Lucy bent closer and took another look at the man identified as Emil Boott and remembered Miss Tilley saying that her father only gave long sentences to the very worst criminals, like murderers. Had he misjudged Emil Boott when he put him to work around the house? Had Emil Boott killed Mrs. Tilley?

"You're right. He must have been more than a petty thief," agreed Lucy, wondering how she could find out exactly what crime Emil Boott had committed to earn such a long sentence.

Fred cleared his throat. "I really have to get back to work," he said, with a sigh. "Budget projections are due next week."

Lucy's face reddened. "Oh, don't let me keep you. I really appreciate your help. Is it okay if I look around a bit?"

"Be my guest," said Fred, pushing the elevator button. "We don't get too many visitors, except for school groups." The doors slid open and he stepped aboard. "Don't miss the mummy," he said.

Lucy started to ask how the museum came to possess a mummy, but before she could form the question the doors closed and Fred was gone. "Another mystery," she said to Toby. "This town is full of them."

Chapter Five

When they lived in the city Lucy had always looked forward to the weekend when Bill didn't have to go to work. That meant they could sleep a little later, and then enjoy a leisurely breakfast while deciding what to do with the rest of the day. Sometimes it would be a car trip out of the city, with a stop at a farm stand. Sometimes it would be an excursion to the zoo or the botanical gardens, or a museum. And other times they would simply go for a walk, perhaps stopping for a big doughy pretzel or a hot dog from a street vendor. It didn't matter what they did, really, because there was a special holiday feel to the weekend that made it special.

But now that Bill worked at home, weekends were just the same as every other day. He couldn't take the time, he said, because there was so much work to be done on the house. And anyway, there wasn't really anywhere interesting to go. Tinker's Cove didn't offer much in the way of culture apart from the library and the museum, and Lucy was already familiar with them. The movie theater was only open in summer; it closed up tight for the winter. There was nature, of course, lots of it. Acres and acres of woods, lakes and ponds, and the endless expanse of ocean. But, oddly enough, everybody seemed to take it for granted and there was very little public access. Hunters roamed the woods, to be sure, but there were few easy trails suitable for family hiking. And most of the shore was privately owned, and rocky to boot, except for the little town beach. There was no open expanse for walking, like the beaches she knew on Cape Cod.

So here it was, a bright and sunny Saturday morning, and Lucy was sitting at the kitchen table, drinking coffee and leafing through the Pennysaver newspaper, looking for something to do. Toby was by her side, in his high chair, supposedly eating scrambled eggs and toast for breakfast. Maybe he would be the next Jackson Pollack, thought Lucy, watching as he smeared the eggs on the tray.

"Ready to get down?" she asked, reaching for a washcloth to wipe his face and hands.

"No." He shook his head and began chewing on a toast triangle.

"Okay," she said, turning the page and studying the "Things to Do" column. That's what it was called, but there was precious little that interested her. Goodness knows she didn't need Weight Watchers, she wasn't interested in seeing the new holiday line of Tupperware products, she didn't have money to spend on Mary Kay cosmetics and, darn it all, they'd missed the pancake breakfast with Santa at the fire house. "Maybe next year," she promised Toby. "We'll keep an eye out for it."

Toby rewarded her with a big smile, revealing a mouth full of half-chewed chunks of toast. Not a pretty sight, even if he was her own child. She turned back to the paper, where an announcement for an open house at the historical society caught her eye. Maybe someone there would be able to give her some leads on her investigation, especially concerning her prime suspect, Emil Boott. "It says there will be refreshments," she promised Toby, ignoring his protests and removing a soggy wad of toast from his little fist and cleaning him up. "Better save some room for punch and cookies."

It was almost eleven when Lucy parked Auntie Granada in front of the Josiah Hopkins House and wrestled Toby out of the car seat. As they walked along the uneven blocks of sidewalk to the open house she examined the antique house that housed the historical society. Built circa 1700, according to a sign next to the front door, the little Cape-style house was supposed to be the oldest house in town. It was named for its builder, Josiah Hopkins, who was reputed to be the first European to settle in Tinker's Cove. The white clapboard house appeared to be quite small from the front, with a low roof set over two pairs of windows and a center door, but a series of ells had been tacked onto the back as the family grew and stretched in an uneven line that ended at a lopsided barn.

Unsure whether she should knock on the wreathed door or just walk in, Lucy paused on the grindstone that served as a stoop. "I thought there'd be more people," she told Toby, as she hoisted him up and perched him on her hip. She was just about to knock when the door flew open.

"We saw you coming," said a little old lady who bore an unnerving resemblance to an apple-head doll. Her hair, which was carefully curled and blued, was an odd contrast to her wrinkled and puckered face. Her eyes, however, were sharp as ever and didn't miss a thing. "Ellie, Ellie," she called. "Come and meet this adorable little tyke."

She was quickly joined by another little apple-head doll of a woman, right down to the matching hair. "Isn't he the little man!" she proclaimed. "Come in, come in."

Lucy set Toby on his feet and unzipped his jacket, then grasping him firmly by the hand, introduced herself.

"Oh, you're the young folks who bought the old farm-house on Red Top Road," said Ellie. "Emily, they're the folks who bought the place out by the Pratts."

"We're the Miller sisters," said Emily. "We're twins. I'm Emily and this is Ellie."

"You can tell us apart because I'm the pretty one," said Ellie, repeating what Lucy suspected was a well-worn joke. Lucy made a quick mental note, observing that Ellie was wearing the pink twin set and Emily was in blue.

"Never mind her," said Emily. "We're so glad to welcome you to our open house. Do enjoy the house and we'll be happy to answer any questions you have, and be sure to have some holiday punch and cookies in the dining room."

"Thank you," said Lucy, who was admiring the wide plank floors and the simple woodwork which had been painted a deep shade of red. A small fire blazed in the hearth, which was ringed with a simple wooden bench, a rocking chair and a tall settle. Cheery print curtains hung at the windows and a hutch displayed a collection of antique china.

"All the furnishings have been donated by our members," said Emily, noticing her interest.

"Did your members do the restoration work, too?" asked Lucy, keeping a watchful eye on Toby, who was fascinated by the fire.

"Most of it. We also hired some craftsmen. We got a lot of advice from the state historical commission."

"I see," said Lucy, eager to see the rest of the house. She took Toby by the hand and together they explored the kitchen, with its enormous hearth, the buttery where food was stored, the pantry where dishes were kept, and climbed the cramped little staircase to the tiny bedrooms tucked under the eaves. Pulling Toby away from a display of antique toys she went back downstairs to the dining room, where black-and-gold Hitchcock chairs surrounded a cherry drop-leaf table that held a crystal punch bowl with a silver ladle and enough cookies for an army.

"Would you care for some punch?" asked Emily, popping through the door. Or was it Ellie, wondered Lucy, afraid she'd mixed up pink and blue.

"Be sure to taste the mincemeat cookies," advised Ellie, or was it Emily?

"Thank you," said Lucy, holding the crystal cup so Toby could drink from it, then handing him a cookie. "It's a beautiful house," she said, taking a bite of a lemon bar. "It must have taken a lot of work."

"A labor of love," said Emily.

"That's right," said Ellie, nodding along.

"I wonder," said Lucy, excited by an idea that was taking shape in her mind, "does the society have information about the early residents of Tinker's Cove? I'm thinking of census records, genealogies, wills, things like that."

The two Miller sisters exchanged a glance.

"We used to," said one.

"Before the fire," said the other.

"It was all lost."

"We were lucky to save the house and the furniture."

"Oh, dear," said Lucy, feeling extremely disappointed.

The sisters exchanged another glance.

"Would you like to sit down, dear?" asked one.

"Is there something in particular that you want to know?" asked the other. "Because most people in town have deep roots. Their families have been here for a very long time."

"A long time, that's right."

Lucy sat down and the sisters refilled her cup and passed her a plate of cookies. She sipped and nibbled and thought. She was reluctant to admit that she was investigating Mrs. Tilley's death, which might or might not have been murder, but she didn't want to pass up this opportunity, either. So far, the Miller sisters were her only lead.

"Well," she began, "I'm doing some research on a household. Sort of a social history, if you know what I mean. A well-off family and their helpers."

The sisters nodded. "Like that TV show."

"*Upstairs, Downstairs.*"

"Right," agreed Lucy. "I have all the information I need about the upstairs family, but it's the downstairs folks I'm having trouble tracking down."

The sisters nodded.

"I need information about a man named Emil Boott."

They shook their heads. "There's a family named Boott out on Packet Road," said Emily.

"Oh I don't think she wants to visit *them*," said Ellie, with a sniff.

"Oh, I've met them," said Lucy. Seeing the sisters shocked expressions she quickly added, "At a yard sale."

"I'd steer clear of that lot, if I were you," said Emily.

"Oh, yes. Oh, dear yes," chimed in Ellie. She lowered her voice. "Kyle's a bit, um, unpredictable."

"So I gathered," replied Lucy, with a nod. "Is there a violent streak in the family?"

The ladies exchanged glances but didn't reply. Lucy sensed she'd gotten all she was going to get from them concerning the Boott's and pressed on. "Angela DeRosa?"

They shook their heads.

"Katherine Kaiser."

The sisters exchanged glances, again, and sighed in unison. Lucy had the distinct feeling they knew something but weren't going to share it with her. She continued down her list. "Helen Sprout."

The two broke into smiles and giggles. "There are lots of Sprouts around," said Emily.

"Old Hannah Sprout, she must be going on eighty herself, lives over in Gilead."

"I bet she'd love to talk to you."

"I bet she would, too."

Lucy was about to ask how she could contact Hannah Sprout when she suddenly remembered Toby. He'd been right there, eating cookies, and now he was gone. She jumped to her feet. "Where's Toby?"

"He can't have wandered far," said Ellie.

"No, no, no," agreed Emily.

But Lucy was imagining the worst as she searched frantically through the maze of little rooms. He might have fallen in the fire. He might have fallen down the stairs. He might have wandered out a back door. He might have been abducted.

Then she heard one of the sisters sing out, "I found him."

Lucy hauled herself up the crooked little staircase as fast as she could, considering her condition. She was out of breath when she found Toby sitting on the floor in the room that was decorated as a child's nursery, surrounded by that valuable collection of antique toys. The toys, and Toby, appeared to be unharmed.

"Isn't it sweet?" trilled a sister.

"He found the toys!"

"I hope nothing's broken," said Lucy, pulling him to his feet and leading him to the stairway. She took a deep breath. "We'll pay if there's any damage."

"Oh, no, no, no damage," chorused the sisters. "No harm done."

As Lucy zipped up Toby and buttoned her coat and headed straight for the door, she had the feeling that a tragedy had been barely averted. "Thanks for everything," she said, as the door closed behind her and she let out a big sigh of relief.

Toby didn't see it quite the same way, however. Once

outside he yanked himself free and threw himself on the brown grass, shrieking and kicking his heels in a full-blown temper tantrum. "Horsey! Horsey!" he repeated, over and over, at the top of his lungs.

Lucy had read about two-year-olds and their famous temper tantrums in the child care books, but so far she hadn't experienced one. She stood there, in the middle of town, trying to remember the recommended course of action. Nothing came to her except an acute sense of embarrassment. Thank heavens nobody seemed to be on the street, at the moment, but if Toby continued screaming that was sure to change. The last thing Lucy wanted was to attract a crowd.

"Toby, stop it!" she said, in her firmest, most authoritative voice.

He kicked his heels harder.

Maybe bribery? The experts discouraged it, but it had been remarkably successful on the few occasions she'd tried it. "Toby, stop fussing and be a good boy and I'll buy you some ice cream."

The screams grew louder.

It was time to bring out the big guns. "Toby, if you don't stop that this minute I'm going to get in the car and leave you here all by yourself."

Not a good idea. The shrieks were now punctuated with hysterical sobs. Lucy felt her cheeks reddening, she felt angry and incompetent and frustrated and embarrassed, all at once. And now, she saw, a group of women were advancing down the sidewalk. Mature, matronly women who had mastered the art of motherhood. She had to get out of there. Adrenaline surged, she grabbed Toby by the hood of his jacket and the seat of his pants, and, tucking the screaming and kicking boy under her arm, she hauled him to the car and wrestled him into the car seat. Once he was securely strapped in, she slid behind the steering wheel and caught her breath.

The group of women, she noticed, nodded approvingly. One even smiled sympathetically at her and she gave them a little wave. Then, resolutely closing her ears to the din coming from the backseat, she started the engine and pulled onto Main Street, right in the path of a battered blue pickup truck. The driver honked and swerved, missing a collision, but Lucy's heart was racing when the truck braked and the driver turned to glare at her. To her horror it was Kyle Boott, and he looked as if he was spoiling for a fight. Stomach churning, she rolled down the window and stuck her head out, stretching her lips into a smile. "I'm soo sorry," she yelled. "I didn't see you. No harm done, I hope."

He didn't answer and for a moment Lucy thought he was going to get out of the truck, but instead he slammed it into gear and took off, leaving rubber. Weak with relief she turned round to face Toby "It's all your fault!" she declared. "How can I drive with you making this racket?"

Confronted with his mother's anger, Toby ratcheted up his screaming, which was now punctuated with sobs and hiccups. By now Lucy was sobbing, too, and all she could think of was to get home. So once again she gripped the steering wheel with trembling hands and turned on her blinker and checked her mirrors and very slowly and carefully pulled out of her parking spot.

The drive home was nightmarish. Lucy drove slowly and extra carefully, concentrating on the road as if she were taking a driver's test, and trying not to worry about Toby. How long could he keep this up? Could he stop? Maybe she should go to the emergency room? But then they'd probably call in social services, maybe they'd decide she couldn't cope and would take Toby away from her. Maybe she was a bad mother, maybe she shouldn't have children.

She was following this train of thought when she turned onto Red Top Road and the house came into view and Toby fell asleep, all at once. By the time she'd turned into the driveway he'd sunk into a deep sleep, punctuated by hiccups. He didn't even stir when she lifted him out of the car seat and carried him into the house.

"Look at that sweet little guy," cooed Bill, who was fixing himself a cup of tea in the kitchen.

"Appearances can be deceiving," muttered Lucy, lugging the baby upstairs and settling him in his crib.

Bill had followed and watched as she slipped off Toby's jacket and shoes and covered him with a blanket. "He'll probably wet the bed," she observed, with a sniffle.

"So what's the big deal?" asked Bill, leaning against the door jamb and sipping his tea. "He's just a baby."

"This so-called baby of yours is a monster," snapped Lucy. "You should have seen the tantrum he had, right in the middle of town."

"What do you expect?" asked Bill. "He's almost two years old and they don't call it the 'terrible twos' for nothing."

Lucy suddenly felt very alone. He didn't understand and she didn't have the energy to make him. "I'm tired. I'm going to lie down for a bit," she said.

"I was hoping you'd go to the lumber yard for me," said Bill. "I don't ask for much but I could use a little help now and then, you know. I'm beginning to think I'm a one-man show."

Lucy's chin dropped and she turned to face him. "One-man show! Is that what you think?"

"Well, yeah," said Bill, rising to his full height. "I don't see you pitching in."

Lucy stared at him, speechless. "Pitch in yourself," she finally said and marched out of the nursery, across the hall and into the bedroom. She would have slammed the door but that would have wakened the baby.

She lay there, staring at the stained and cracked ceiling, and listened to Bill's footsteps as they retreated down the hall to the front stairs. By the time he'd reached the bottom, she was sound asleep.

Two hours later she woke with a start, awakened by Toby's cries. Just regular cries, she realized with relief, he wasn't having another tantrum. She threw off the covers and shoved her swollen feet into her slippers and shuffled into his room. He stopped crying when he saw her and she picked him up, nuzzling his damp head with her nose and getting a distinct whiff of ammonia. As she expected his overalls were soaked and all the bedding needed to be changed. She sighed and led him into the bathroom, where she set him on the potty.

"Are you up?" Bill's voice echoed up the stairwell.

"Up and at 'em," she yelled back.

"Someone named Sue called," he said.

Lucy suddenly felt better.

"I got her number and said you'd call back."

"Thanks," said Lucy, pulling off Toby's wet overalls, even his socks were soaked. She sighed. It would be a while before she could make that call.

Chapter Six

"I don't think this is such a good idea, Lucy," complained Bill. He was standing in front of the mirror in the bedroom and fiddling with a necktie. "I can't believe I wore a tie every day back in the city. This thing is an instrument of torture."

"You look very nice," said Lucy, adjusting the tie and giving him a little kiss.

"I can't really take the time," he continued. "Why don't you and Toby go and I'll finish insulating the nursery?"

Lucy held his jacket for him. "Don't be silly. It's the last Sunday before Christmas and we haven't been to church even once. It will give you some Christmas spirit."

"I've got plenty of Christmas spirit," said Bill, slipping his arms into the sleeves.

Lucy set her jaw in a stubborn expression. "Well, I want to hear the carols," she said, pulling the jacket up over his shoulders and smoothing it out. "Do it for me."

Bill rolled his eyes. "You are a stubborn woman, Lucy Stone."

Lucy's temper flared. "I don't think . . ."

"But I love you anyway," he said, silencing her with a kiss.

When they arrived at the little white Community Church with the tall steeple they found it was bursting at the seams but people cheerfully slid down the pews and squeezed together to make room for everyone. Lucy assumed the crowd was made of folks her mother called "Christmas and Easter Christians," people who only came to church on holidays, a group which Lucy had to acknowledge she and Bill had joined. But a quick perusal of the bulletin revealed that the usual sermon would be replaced by the Sunday School's annual pageant, a local tradition which brought entire families out in force. She nudged Bill, who was holding Toby in his lap, and pointed out the notation.

"It ought to be really cute," she whispered.

"Hmph," said Bill.

But even he was smiling when the children, dressed as shepherds, advanced down the aisle, some holding stuffed lambs and other animals, including a few neon colored Care Bears, and arranged themselves in a tableau vivant around the teenagers playing Mary and Joseph. Mary was keeping a nervous eye on baby Jesus, who was a real baby, and Joseph seemed ready to flee; Lucy wondered if they were presenting a more accurate version of the actual events than they knew. The arrival of the youngest children, dressed as angels in white robes and homemade wings, with tinsel haloes, was greeted with coos from the congregation, and everyone joined in singing "Away in a Manger." Then came the Three Wise Men, a trio of high school girls with fake beards, robes, and turbans made out of upholstery material (Lucy recognized the pattern as one her mother had chosen years ago for a slip cover) accompanied by the singing of "We Three Kings," which was followed by Lucy's favorite, "Silent Night." When it was over the entire congregation burst into applause. This was new to Lucy, and an indication that it had indeed been some time since she had been to church and things had changed while she'd been away.

When the service was over most people trooped down the aisle to the front of the church where there was a door leading to the parish hall where coffee was served. Bill started to go in the opposite direction, but Lucy stopped him.

"Let's get a cup of coffee," she pleaded. "Maybe we'll meet some people."

Bill was less than enthusiastic. "Aw, Lucy. . . ."

She cut him off. "It won't kill you to be sociable, you know," she said, taking Toby by the hand and marching down the aisle. Bill followed, a glum expression on his face.

The parish room was crowded and there was a happy buzz as adults greeted each other and children, still dressed in their shepherd and angel costumes, dashed around and helped themselves to more cookies than was wise before lunch. Appetites would certainly be spoiled, thought Lucy, accepting a Styrofoam cup of rather weak looking coffee. She chose a plain sugar cookie for Toby and looked around for a familiar face. Bill, she noticed, was already deep in conversation with a man she recognized from the lumber yard. She was sipping her coffee and feeling rather hurt that he hadn't thought to include her in the conversation when she saw the Miller twins approaching her.

"So nice to see you, Lucy," said Emily.

"And Toby, too," said Ellie. "Maybe he can be in the pageant next year. He'll be old enough to be an angel."

"He will have to be quite an actor to pull that off," said Lucy, remembering the previous day's tantrum.

The two ladies' eyebrows shot up in surprise, then Ellie smiled. "It's a joke, dear," she told her sister. "Just look at that angelic little face."

Lucy looked at Toby, trying to see him through another's eyes. He was angelic looking, she realized, with his blond curls and pink cheeks. "Thank you," she said. "It was a lovely pageant. I really enjoyed it."

"They do it every year," said Emily. "It's always the same."

"And it's always wonderful," said Ellie. "We were in it, years ago."

"Ellie got to be Mary," complained Emily. "It wasn't fair."

"Emily was supposed to be Joseph," said Ellie. "She wasn't happy about it."

"No, I wasn't. I got Hannah Sprout to take my place. Oh, my goodness, here she comes."

Lucy watched as a tall, gray-haired woman in a bright red suit with a Christmas brooch pinned on the shoulder crossed the room. "Good morning, ladies," she said, looking curiously at Lucy. "Wonderful pageant, wasn't it?"

"We were just telling Lucy here, oh, this is Lucy Stone and her little boy Toby. They moved into the old farmhouse on Red Top Road."

"Nice to meet you, Lucy. I'm Hannah Sprout."

"We were telling Lucy about the time you had to play Joseph in the pageant because Emily wouldn't wear that beard."

"I don't blame her one bit," said Hannah. "That thing was scratchy. But, my word, that was a long time ago. We were just kids."

"Actually, Lucy's interested in the old days," said Emily. "She was asking about your mother."

Hannah turned to face Lucy. "Mother? What do you want to know about her?"

Toby was pulling on Lucy's hand so she picked him up and balanced him on her hip. She was beginning to put one and one together. Hannah Sprout, she realized, must be Helen Sprout's daughter.

"Was your mother a cook? Did she work for Judge Tilley?" asked Lucy.

"She sure did. But why do you want to know about that? That was ages ago. Before the World War."

"I'm doing a bit of research. I'm trying to write a sort of *Upstairs, Downstairs* sort of thing."

"For TV?" Hannah's eyes were big.

"Possibly," said Lucy, relieved to see Bill coming toward her. Toby was squirming in her arms and her back was beginning to hurt. She greeted him with a big smile, handing over Toby as she introduced him to the ladies.

"Are you ready to go?" he asked, perching Toby on his shoulders.

"Actually, I'd like to chat a bit more. Would you mind taking Toby outside to play?"

"Take him to the general store," suggested Emily.

"They have penny candy," said Ellie.

"You have to go to Country Cousins after church," added Hannah. "It's the Eleventh Commandment."

Bill knew when he was beat. "Okay," he said, nodding at Lucy. "I'll meet you at the car in ten minutes."

"Every mother deserves a break now and then," said Hannah, nudging Lucy.

"A break, that's right, a break," chorused Ellie and Emily.

"So tell me about your mother," said Lucy. "Did she ever talk to you about Judge Tilley and his wife?"

"All the time," said Hannah. "It was so sad, you see. 'That poor woman,' she used to say. 'How she suffers!' She was talking about Mrs. Tilley, of course. She was very ill and nobody, really, was taking care of her. The judge was occupied with important matters and the two daughters, well, Mother always said she thought Mrs. Tilley kept her true condition from them, didn't want them to worry or fuss. Not that it did her a lot of good, considering how that wicked Harriet ran off with that labor union fellow, eloped she did, and I don't think she was ever heard of again. But it wasn't until the judge finally hired that nurse that things began to improve. A blessing that was, at least that's what Mother used to say."

"Did your mother ever talk about Mrs. Tilley's accident?"

"Did she? She talked about nothing else for the longest time. She was devastated, you see, because she wasn't there. The cellar stairs were right off the kitchen, you see, and if she'd been there she could have stopped her from going down. She never would have let her attempt those stairs, not if she was there, but it was Christmas Eve and the judge told her to go home to her own family."

"Was the judge usually that considerate of the staff?" asked Lucy.

"Now that you mention it, he certainly was not. He made sure he got every cent's worth he could out of them, and more." Hannah leaned closer. "Mother didn't think much of him," she whispered. "Not that she actually came out and said it in so many words but I got the idea that the judge was having an affair with that secretary of his."

Emily and Ellie nodded and chimed in, encouraged by Hannah's frankness. "She was a fast one," said Ellie.

"Put on airs," sniffed Emily.

"I heard she went to the beauty salon every morning to get her hair combed," said Lucy.

"She did worse than that," crowed Hannah.

"She did?" Emily and Ellie were all ears.

"Now, remember, this was a long time ago, when people felt differently about what we call single mothers nowadays. They used to be called unwed mothers and that was most certainly not a term of approval." Hannah nodded knowingly. "But a week or so before poor

Mrs. Tilley finally got her blessed release and went to her heavenly reward, that secretary left town for six months or more *to care for a sick relative.*"

"Ooh," said Emily, her mouth round with shock.

"I never," added Ellie, with a sharp intake of breath.

"So you think she was pregnant, with Judge Tilley's child?" asked Lucy.

Hannah winked. "Oh, I never said that."

"Oh, no," said Emily, shaking her head.

"No, not at all," said Ellie, pursing her lips.

"I see," said Lucy, understanding that in this case no meant yes. Then she remembered Bill, who was waiting for her outside, in the cold. "I've got to get going, but thanks for all the information. It's been very interesting."

"Oh, yes, interesting," said Emily, nodding.

"Very interesting," said Ellie, licking her lips.

Lucy took her time walking around the church to the lot where Bill had parked the car. She rarely had a moment to herself and she was determined to make the most of it. A couple of inches of snow had fallen overnight and the reflected sunlight made everything bright. It wasn't too cold, though, and she was enjoying the fresh air and the quiet, as the snow muffled sounds.

She was thinking how strange it was that Judge Tilley's affair with his secretary was still a delicate subject, almost as if it had happened yesterday instead of fifty or more years ago. And even stranger, that their love child had remained a secret to many people for all those years. She was especially curious about the fact that even though Katherine Kaiser's child was born around the time of Mrs. Tilley's death, the lovers had not gotten married. Why not? They could have waited for a decent interval, tied the knot, and then added the child to their family claiming it was adopted. But the fact that hadn't happened seemed to indicate the need to continue keeping their relationship a secret. And that, Lucy thought, could have been because the judge didn't want people talking and speculating about his wife's death. It might have appeared a bit too convenient, and might have drawn attention to the judge and his mistress as possible murderers. And then there was the fact that he had dismissed Mrs. Sprout early on Christmas Eve. Did he want her out of the way?

Lost in thought, Lucy would have walked by the car if Bill hadn't honked. Startled, she jumped, then climbed in beside him. Toby was sitting in his car seat, contentedly nibbling on a long pretzel stick. "Two cents at the general store," said Bill, with an approving nod.

"Quite a bargain," said Lucy.

Bill shifted into reverse and backed out of the parking space. "So what were you thinking about? Christmas? The baby? You were miles away, you know."

"Both," said Lucy, smiling at Bill and rubbing her tummy. She hardly wanted to admit she was thinking about a scandal and murder. "Weren't those kids cute?" she asked.

Back home, Lucy decided to leave the pea soup in the fridge and splurged by making tuna-melt sandwiches for lunch. Toby could barely keep his eyes open to finish his and Lucy gratefully settled him down for what she hoped would be a long nap. Then, ignoring Bill's suggestion that she strip the ugly old wallpaper in the hall, she picked up the phone and called Sue.

"Sorry I missed your call yesterday, I was napping," said Lucy.

"Good for you. I was wondering if you'd like to grab some coffee tomorrow morning. At Jake's, maybe?"

"Sure," said Lucy. "Ten? Eleven?"

"Let's make it ten-thirty," said Sue. "The place quiets down around then."

"Great," said Lucy, who was already looking forward to their get-together. "Gee," she added, in a burst of candor, "this is pathetic. I can't tell you how excited I am about actually having some place to go and getting out of the house."

"I hear you," said Sue. "Sometimes I just pack my bag and head to my mother's for a night, just to get some time to myself."

Lucy felt a stab of jealousy. "Does she live nearby?"

"Boston. Close enough, but not too close, if you know what I mean. The drive's long enough that I have time to decompress, get rid of that 'I'd like to kill my husband' feeling."

Lucy was a bit shocked by Sue's frankness. "Doesn't your husband mind when you leave?"

"No. To tell the truth, I think he enjoys it. I mean, he probably wants to kill me sometimes, too, impossible as that seems."

"Not that impossible," said Lucy. "I think that if anybody was counting they'd discover that lots more wives are killed by their husbands than vice versa."

"I know," agreed Sue. "And I can never quite understand. Take that awful guy in Boston who shot his wife and killed her and then shot himself to make it seem like they were attacked by some entirely innocent black man—all that fuss when he could have just filed for divorce."

"Divorce is no picnic, either," said Lucy. "Imagine thinking you're in a perfectly happy marriage and then one fine day, your husband looks at you over the morning paper and says 'Honey, it's been great, but I've found this hot little chick and I like her much better than you, she never nags me about taking out the trash like you do, so what do you say we get a divorce?' "

Sue laughed. "I see your point. If he shoots you, well, he's a real bastard and all, but at least you can go to your death without feeling like a failure because he's having an affair."

"Yeah," agreed Lucy, thinking of Judge Tilley's insistence on maintaining appearances. "Like it was a perfect marriage right up to the moment he killed you." From the distance, she heard Bill calling her. "Gotta go save my marriage by stripping the wallpaper in the front hall."

"Honey, you'd do better to strip yourself."

"Point taken," said Lucy. "See you tomorrow."

Chapter Seven

Lucy knew she couldn't leave Toby with Bill when she met Sue for coffee so she didn't even ask. She was as big a believer in women's liberation as anyone, but it was unrealistic to expect anyone to keep an eye on an active preschooler while working with dangerous tools to perform tasks that required a great deal of concentration. Bill had explained this to her so many times that she'd come to believe it, though she did wonder why it didn't apply to her. After all, she managed to keep an eye on Toby while she chopped up chicken with a cleaver, or used pins and needles to mend a tear, or boiled up a kettle of water to cook pasta. Those were every bit as dangerous as his work with saws, and hammers and nails.

She explained it all to Sue when she joined her at a table in the back corner of Jake's Donut Shack. As Sue had predicted, the place was quiet, with only a scattering of retirees who had time to linger over their morning papers.

"Bill," she told Sue, "has a male brain. He can only concentrate on one thing at a time, which makes it impossible for him to mind a child at the same time he's cutting a board. I, on the other hand, have a female brain, which we know is larger and generally superior in that it can accommodate several thoughts at once."

"Right," said Sue. "Like how there's a designer handbag sale at Filene's Basement and a coat sale at Jordan Marsh."

"Exactly," said Lucy, smiling and nodding.

"I fundamentally agree with you," said Sue, tearing open a pink packet of low-calorie sweetener and stirring it into her coffee, "but what I can't quite figure out is how, if we're so smart and all, we always seem to get stuck with the kids."

"It's because," said Lucy, taking a sip of coffee, "we remember the fact that we actually have a child. Men's brains can't handle that information, which is why they tend to lose the children on the rare occasions that they take them anywhere."

"I think you're on to something," said Sue. "My husband, Sid, completely forgot he was supposed to pick up Sidra from nursery school the other day."

"Nursery school," said Lucy, wistfully, watching as Toby ripped open a sugar packet and poured the contents all over the table. "I wish we could afford nursery school."

"You know," said Sue, setting down her cup, "you're not alone. I bet there are a lot of people here in town who need child care but can't afford it. Maybe we could get some sort of cooperative going or something."

"I wouldn't know where to start," said Lucy, watching as Toby licked his finger and then dipped it into the sugar. For some reason the repeated licks and dips reminded her of a video she'd seen at the American Museum of Natural History. "If he used a spoon, he'd be as smart as a chimpanzee," she said.

Sue looked at her oddly. "I'm going to talk to some people, see if we can't get some start-up money from the Seaman's Bank. Maybe the church. Maybe the town, even. There's definitely a need here."

Toby was squirming, trying to get out of the high chair. "I guess it's time to go," said Lucy, reluctantly. "We ought to do this again. It's been great to have an adult conversation."

Sue smiled. "Men don't count, do they?"

"No," said Lucy, grinning. "But they are good for killing spiders, opening jars, and heavy lifting."

"I'll call you," promised Sue.

Toby seemed to have lots of energy so Lucy decided to take him for a little walk before putting him back in the car seat for the ride home. It was a typically gray December day, the temperature was around the freezing mark and the snow lingered on lawns and was piled alongside the cleared roads and sidewalks. She held Toby's little mittened hand tightly as they walked along Main Street, careful not to step on any cracks, just like in the A.A. Milne poem. They played the name game as they walked along, naming the colors of cars, the kinds of stores and the items displayed in their windows, the shapes of the signs. But all the while, Lucy's mind was busy mulling over the information she'd uncovered in her investigation. Everything she'd learned so far pointed to two suspects: Judge Tilley himself and Emil Boott. Mrs. Sprout, the cook, was out for the simple reason that Lucy liked her daughter, Hannah, and found her account of life in the Tilley household entirely believable. She was also inclined to cross the nurse, Angela DeRosa, off the list of suspects. Nobody seemed to have a bad word to say about her. And then there was Miss Peach, Katharine Kaiser. Nobody seemed to have a good word to say about her, but Lucy didn't have a sense that anybody suspected her of murdering Mrs. Tilley. Lucy was inclined to give her the benefit of the doubt, especially since she'd been pregnant at the time. She found it hard to believe that a woman could be both a creator and a destroyer of life, especially at the same time. But maybe that was a fallacious assumption, she told herself, especially considering Miss Kaiser's self-indulgent and independent lifestyle. But there was an even more compelling reason to cross her off the list: Miss Kaiser had been out of town, purportedly caring for a sick relative, when Mrs. Tilley died.

It wasn't long before they reached the library and Lucy decided to pay a visit to Miss Tilley. She wanted to update her on the progress of her investigation, but she wanted to do it as delicately as possible. After all, a father's infidelity would be a sensitive subject for anyone.

Miss Tilley was sitting in her usual spot at the circulation desk when Lucy and Toby entered and greeted them warmly. As far as Lucy could see there wasn't anybody else in the library, so she could talk frankly. She pulled off Toby's hat and mittens and unzipped his jacket and let him loose in the children's corner, where he made a beeline for the box of toys and began pulling them out and tossing them over his shoulder.

"Toby! That's no way to play," she reminded him.

"Never mind," said Miss Tilley. "We'll help him tidy up afterward." She leaned forward. "How's the investigation going? I'm eager to hear what you've learned."

Lucy looked at Miss Tilley, taking in her frail, birdlike shape and her wispy white hair, caught in a bun that barely held together despite an enormous quantity of hairpins. She seemed the very model of a typical old maid, right down to the cameo pin that caught both wings of her starched white lace collar. Suddenly Lucy wasn't sure she wanted to bring up such a sexually charged topic as Judge Tilley's infidelity.

"I understand you've been talking to Hannah Sprout," coaxed Miss Tilley.

"That's right," admitted Lucy, wondering if she was

doing the investigating or being investigated. "How did you know that?"

"I ran into Emily Miller at the IGA. This is a small town, you know, and all we really have to talk about is each other."

It was true. Lucy thought of the "Social Events" column in the weekly Pennysaver newspaper that included items such as "Mrs. William Mason and her daughter, Mrs. Henry Tubbs, entertained Mrs. Hildegarde Wilson and Miss Susan Wilson for tea on Wednesday afternoon," and "Mr. and Mrs. James Nesmith recently took a motor trip to Prince Edward Island in Canada where they visited with Mrs. Nesmith's cousin, Winifred MacDonald." She always read it, finding it oddly fascinating since she rarely recognized any of the names.

"Well, she's right. I did talk to Hannah Sprout at the coffee hour after church on Sunday. . . ."

"So you're a churchgoer?" inquired Miss Tilley.

"Occasionally," said Lucy. "It was the Christmas pageant. I think the whole town was there."

"Not me," said Miss Tilley. "I'm boycotting."

Lucy was surprised. "Why?"

"Oh, something that happened a long time ago. I'll tell you about it sometime."

"Okay." Now Lucy was truly flummoxed. She'd been encouraged by the fact that Miss Tilley probably knew all about her conversation with Hannah Sprout, but now it seemed the librarian was setting limits and she was afraid once again of offending her. "Well," she began, blurting it out all at once, "Hannah Sprout said her mother thought your father was having an affair with his secretary, and she left town for six months because she was pregnant with his child."

Lucy held her breath, waiting for Miss Tilley's reaction.

"Papa always was one for the ladies," said Miss Tilley, smacking her thigh with her hand. "He was an old devil."

Lucy exhaled. "So you're not upset."

"Not a bit. It just confirms what I always thought."

"You thought he had an affair with Katherine Kaiser?"

"I thought he was a mean, selfish hypocrite."

Lucy couldn't help it. She was shocked. Not knowing quite what to say, she looked across the library to the children's corner, where Toby was pushing a wooden truck across the floor.

"I suppose the affair could be a motive for killing your mother," she finally said. "But why didn't he marry Katherine Kaiser?"

"I expect he thought it would be an admission that he wasn't as pure as the driven snow."

The baby kicked and Lucy rubbed her stomach. "I can't quite imagine a man turning his back on his own flesh and blood like that and letting somebody adopt his child."

"I don't think men make the connection between the sex act and the arrival of a child nine months later. Not unless they're married, that is."

"Not even then," said Lucy, laughing.

"Well, you would know better than I. I can only draw on what I've observed. And my experience as a child, but it seems to me that men throughout history have had remarkably little interest in assuming responsibility for their offspring, especially female and illegitimate offspring. My father always behaved as if Harriet and I were my mother's hobby, like stamp collecting or knitting, and had nothing to do with him."

Just then there was a crash and Toby began to cry, so Lucy jumped up and hurried over to the children's corner, where she found Toby had knocked over a tower of blocks which came tumbling down on his head. She picked him up and kissed the boo-boo, a little bruise on his forehead, assuring him that he was all better. When she returned to the circulation desk, carrying him on her hip, Miss Tilley had a cookie waiting for him. She sat down with him in her lap.

Miss Tilley beamed at him, tickled his tummy and gave him another cookie. "So where do we go from here?" she asked.

"Well, I guess I better get Toby home for lunch before you spoil his appetite with any more cookies," said Lucy.

"I was referring to the investigation."

Toby leaned back against his mother, chewing on the cookie. "Well," said Lucy, "I think we can safely eliminate two suspects: Mrs. Sprout and Miss Kaiser. Your father sent Mrs. Sprout home on Christmas Eve, so she wasn't there when your mother fell. According to her daughter she always blamed herself for leaving, wishing she could have prevented the fall."

"And it appears that Miss Kaiser, vain and wicked vixen that she most certainly was, was also out of town and otherwise occupied at the time of my mother's death."

"But both those facts tend to point toward your father," said Lucy, smoothing Toby's hair with her hand. "But we also can't eliminate the handyman, Emil Boott, and the nurse."

Miss Tilley shook her head. "I knew Angela. I simply can't believe she would have hurt a hair on my mother's head. Or anyone else's, for that matter."

"Well, there is a link of sorts between Emil Boott and the glass cane. He worked in the office at the glassworks, but that's all I've been able to find out about him."

Miss Tilley leaned forward. "I never trusted him, you

know. There was something about him, the way he looked at me, that made me afraid."

Lucy tapped her chin thoughtfully. "The glassworks must have kept records about their employees. Do you have any idea what happened to them when it closed?"

"No, I don't," said Miss Tilley. "But I do know someone who may be able to give you some information about Emil Boott. His name is Sherman Cobb, he's a lawyer here in town and his father was the sheriff who ran the prison when my father was on the bench."

"I'll talk to him," promised Lucy, "but now I've got to get this little boy home for his nap."

Toby's eyes were drooping when Lucy buckled the car seat and she drove as fast as she could, hoping to get home before he fell asleep. She knew from experience that if he dropped off, even for a minute, she'd never get him to settle down for a nap.

But as she sped along the route that was already becoming so familiar to her, she found herself thinking about men and women. She and Sue had been joking when they made fun of their husband's short attention spans but she sensed that Miss Tilley had a deeper antipathy toward men. Lucy remembered reading somewhere that a woman's relationship with men depended on her relationship with her father. A woman like herself, who had a strong relationship with a caring father, generally had successful relationships with men. Daddy's girls, who had flirtatious relationships with their fathers, rarely found men who measured up. And girls who were abused or neglected by their fathers had destructive relationships with men, or avoided them altogether.

It was all pseudo psychology, she admitted, turning into the driveway, but she thought there was some truth to it, especially in Miss Tilley's case, but it did make her wonder if she could trust the librarian's assessments of

Judge Tilley and Emil Boott. She turned off the ignition and turned around to see if Toby was still awake and that's when she heard the boom and felt the car shake.

The noise, she realized, had come from the house. Something had blown up inside the house. Toby was shrieking in the backseat, strapped into his car seat. She was still sitting in the car, hanging on to the steering wheel for dear life. But Bill was inside the house. She didn't know what to do. She hopped out of the car and ran toward the house, then she ran back to the car, afraid the house might blow up with her inside, leaving Toby an orphan. She was standing, flapping her arms, torn between her husband and her son, when the door opened and a puff of smoke blew out, followed by Bill. She ran to him.

"Ohmigod, what happened?" she cried, taking in his soot-blackened face, singed eyebrows and hair. He was holding his hands out in front of him, the sleeves of his shirt and sweater were burned off and the skin was red and black and blistered.

"I tried to fix the stove," he said.

"Get in the car," she ordered.

"No, Lucy. Don't start the car. Get Toby and we'll go to the neighbors."

"Right, right," she said, yanking the door open and unsnapping the car seat straps with shaking hands. Bill was already halfway down the drive, walking like an automaton. He must be in shock, she thought, hurrying to catch up to him.

They could hear the sirens before they even reached the road; the neighbors they didn't even know must have called the fire department. So they stood there and waited as an engine and a ladder truck and, finally, an ambulance, screamed to a halt in front of their house. Forty minutes later it was all over. Bill's burns were treated and wrapped in gauze, the gas was turned off, the house was vented, and they were given permission to go inside.

"You got off lucky this time, believe me," said the fire chief. "The whole house coulda gone, you coulda been cooked. So if I were you I wouldn't attempt any more repairs. Leave the gas appliances to the professionals."

"Right," said Bill, thoroughly chagrined.

"Whew, that was a close one," said Lucy, surveying the damage. The stove had opened and collapsed like a cardboard box, and everything else in the room was covered with a greasy gray film. That included the ceiling, the walls, the sink and refrigerator, the table and chairs, even the floor, which also had big, muddy footprints.

"Like the man said, it could have been worse," said Bill.

Lucy remembered that awful moment after the boom, when she didn't know if Bill was alive or dead. "I was so afraid," she said, tears springing to her eyes.

"I know," said Bill, enfolding her and Toby in his bandaged arms. "I didn't see my whole life go before my eyes but I did see you, both of you," he said. "And at that moment, I loved you so, so much. It was really, really intense."

"How about now?" asked Lucy.

"Well, I still love you but I gotta admit I'd trade you both for a pain pill."

"I'll call Doc Ryder right away," said Lucy. "He can call a prescription in to the pharmacy."

When she finished talking to the doctor, Lucy carried Toby upstairs and settled him down in his crib for a belated nap. The tired little boy was asleep the moment his head hit the pillow. Returning to the kitchen she found Bill staring at the remains of the stove.

"Lucy, what do you say we give each other a new stove for Christmas?"

"My thoughts exactly, Santa," said Lucy, slipping into her jacket and reaching for the car keys. "But next time, try coming down the chimney, okay?"

"Very funny," he said. "And hurry back with those pills."

An icy drizzle was falling when Lucy left the house and had turned to snow by the time she got to town. She drove slowly and carefully down Main Street, which was slick with icy patches and, observing the signs that prohibited parking in front of the pharmacy, slid into a spot a few doors down. The sidewalk was icy, too, and she was relieved when she made it to the door without falling.

Inside, at the prescription counter, the pharmacist greeted her and told her the prescription would be ready in a few minutes. Lucy was tired, so she decided to sit in the waiting area. Turning the corner to the secluded nook that held a few chairs and tattered magazines, she found Dora Boott crouching there with a baby in her arms.

"Hi," she said. "Remember me? I bought the glass cane."

Dora raised one hand to cover her face as she turned toward Lucy. "Hi," she said, mumbling into her upturned collar.

Lucy wasn't fooled. It was clear that Dora had recently suffered a severe beating, probably at the hands of her husband. "Is everything all right?" she asked.

"Baby's sick," she said, avoiding meeting Lucy's eyes. "Doc said he's got to have some medicine."

Lucy's eyes fell on the baby, who was lying listlessly in his mother's arms. His face was quite flushed and his hair damp, he obviously had a high fever. "And what about you?" asked Lucy. "Did you have an accident?"

"Yeah," growled Kyle, suddenly coming around the corner. "She walked into a door."

"I don't think so," said Lucy, leveling her eyes at him. "It looks to me as if somebody hit her."

"C'mon," he said, grabbing Dora by the arm and yanking her to her feet. "Let's get out of here."

"But, Kyle," protested Dora, in a whisper. "We haven't gotten the medicine."

"I'll come back tomorrow and get it," he growled, pulling her toward the door.

"But the doctor said he needs it tonight," she whispered, even more softly.

"Shut up!" he growled, shoving her. "I've had just about enough of you. Now git!"

Bowing her head and curving her body protectively around the baby, Dora obeyed, shuffling down the aisle toward the door in her bedroom slippers. Kyle followed, turning to glare at Lucy before slamming the door open and leaving. The door had just closed behind them when the pharmacist called out "Boott" and plopped the little bag of medicine onto the counter.

Jumping to her feet, Lucy grabbed the bag and raced after them. Running toward the glass door, she could see them standing outside, face to face, on the sidewalk. Dora was apparently pleading with her husband, begging him not to leave without the prescription. Kyle was becoming increasingly frustrated and Lucy could see him raising his hand, ready to smack Dora on the head, as she pushed the door open and went flying across the icy sidewalk, right into Kyle.

Recovering her balance, she watched in horror as he slid in slow motion toward the curb just as a small, gray sedan driven by an elderly woman came skidding sideways across the street. The woman's mouth was an O and her eyes were wide with shock as Kyle stumbled, then momentarily regained his feet and finally fell beneath the car which rolled right over him before coming to a stop. Only Kyle's arm was visible; his hand twitched a few times and then was still.

Speechless, Lucy turned to Dora, who was still hugging the baby.

"Thank you," she said, looking Lucy straight in the eyes and taking the prescription. She glanced at the tag stapled to the bag and pulled herself up to her full height. "Three ninety-nine," she said, her voice clear as a bell. "I guess I'd better go inside and pay for this."

Chapter Eight

Lucy just couldn't get over it. She felt sick every time she thought of the accident, which she replayed over and over in nauseating slow motion in her mind. But as awful as Kyle's death was, she had to admit it had its upside. Now Dora and the children could begin a new life without the constant fear of his violent outbursts. And Dora's recovery had been amazingly quick, she didn't seem to have the least shred of grief for her late husband. In fact, the elderly driver of the car that hit him was far more shaken than Dora and had to be taken to the hospital for observation. Not Dora, though. She refused the sedatives offered by the doctor and when the EMTs expressed their condolences she only said, "Well, he had it coming. The wages of sin, I guess."

Lucy soon discovered there was also a positive side to Bill's accident with the stove, too. Since he couldn't work on the house with his bandaged hands he was free to mind Toby while she went on a fact-finding mission at the appliance store. She felt almost giddy the next morning as she hopped down the porch stairs and slid behind Auntie Granada's steering wheel, without having to break her back wrestling Toby into the car seat. Then she was off, flying down Red Top Road with the radio blaring Donna Summers and BeeGees tunes, mixed in with Christmas carols. She hummed along, tapping her foot to the beat, and before she knew it she was making the turn onto Main Street.

Proceeding at a more sedate pace she passed the library, the Community Church and the town hall. Slack's Hardware and the Appliance Mart were in the next block, but her eye fell on the sign for Sherman Cobb's law office. Funny, she thought as she braked and turned into the parking area beside the little white clapboard building, she'd never noticed it before. But now here it was, right in front of her, and there would never be a better time to ask him about Emil Boott.

When she entered the office's neat little waiting room she was greeted by the receptionist, a tall woman about her own age with long brown hair. The plaque on her desk gave her name: RACHEL GOODMAN.

"Hi," she said, "what can I do for you?"

"I'd like to talk to Mr. Cobb," said Lucy.

"I'm afraid he's not in," said Rachel. "His partner, my husband Bob, is available."

"I'm afraid I need to speak to Mr. Cobb," said Lucy.

"Bob is a very good lawyer," said Rachel, smiling. "And I'm not just saying that because he's my husband. He really is."

"I'm sure he is," said Lucy, laughing. "I'm not here about a legal matter. I'm doing some research on local history and Miss Tilley, the librarian, suggested I speak to Mr. Cobb."

"I see," said Rachel. "Well, he just went out for his morning cup of coffee. He should be back in a few minutes if you want to wait."

Lucy looked at the comfy plaid couch, the brass lamp and the stack of magazines on the pine coffee table and decided she could spare a few minutes. "Thanks," she said. "I think I will."

She tucked her gloves in her pockets and unbuttoned her coat, making herself comfortable on the sofa. Before she'd become a mother she never would have believed that the opportunity to spend a few minutes checking out the latest magazines would seem like such a luxury. She picked up a copy of *People* magazine and began flipping through the pages.

"I've seen you around town," said Rachel, breaking into her thoughts. "You have a little boy, don't you?"

"That's right. Toby's almost two."

"And you live out on Red Top Road?"

"I guess I'll have to get used to everybody knowing all about me," said Lucy. "It wasn't like this in the city."

"I suppose not," said Rachel. "Tinker's Cove is a pretty small town. Everybody knows everything about everybody."

"You said it," said a middle-aged gentleman, coming through the door. He had salt-and-pepper hair and was wearing a suit underneath his red-and-black plaid jacket.

"Mr. Cobb, this is Lucy Stone. She wants to ask you about some local history."

"Well, you've come to the right man," said Cobb, setting his paper cup of coffee on Rachel's desk, hanging his jacket on the coat tree and extending his hand toward Lucy. She grasped it in hers, then Cobb opened his office door with a flourish and she preceded him through it. Once inside he pulled out a chair for her and she sat down, facing his desk. He sat down facing her, carefully setting his coffee on the blotter.

"So it's local history you're interested in," he prompted.

Lucy looked around the office, which was decorated with Civil War memorabilia including Matthew Brady photographs, a small and tattered Confederate flag in a frame, and a shadow box containing two lead bullets and a minnie ball.

"Actually, I'm looking for information about a man

named Emil Boott. He was a trusty who worked for Judge Tilley."

"Emil Boott, Emil Boott, the name sounds familiar but I don't remember him. Kyle Boott, of course. Now that was quite an accident. Everybody's talking about it."

Lucy blushed. "I feel just terrible about that," she said.

He looked at her curiously. "Don't tell me you were the woman who . . . ?"

"I'm afraid I was. I slipped on the icy sidewalk at the same moment that poor woman lost control of her car. It was a freak accident."

"I'd say it was good work," said Rachel, appearing in the open doorway. "He was a brute and certainly won't be missed."

Sherman Cobb pursed his lips and furrowed his brow, and Rachel scurried back to her desk. "May I ask why you want to know about Emil Boott? Is it something to do with the accident?"

"Oh, no. It's just a coincidence. I'm interested in social history, sort of an American *Upstairs, Downstairs.* I'm studying the late Judge Tilley's household, in fact."

"For a television show? Do you write for TV?"

"Possibly," said Lucy, aware that she was prevaricating. "Right now I'm thinking more along the lines of a story for a women's magazine. How times have changed, that sort of thing."

"I expect you'll find they've improved quite a bit," said Sherman, prying the lid off his coffee. "I'm a Civil War reenactor and I can tell you life wasn't very comfortable back then. Clothes were itchy, shoes didn't fit very well, food was monotonous and a bath was a real luxury."

"And that's only the male side of things," said Lucy. "Think of all the work the poor women had to do."

"It killed a lot of them, you know. The old cemetery

behind the Community Church is full of old sea captains who have three or four wives buried beside them. You'd think going to sea would be dangerous but it was more dangerous for the women staying home."

"Childbirth was the big killer," said Lucy, patting her tummy. "I, for one, am thankful for modern obstetrics."

"And disease, well into this century. The judge always maintained that Mrs. Tilley died of exhaustion but most people thought it was TB."

"Did you know the family well?" asked Lucy.

"Not Mrs. Tilley. I came along after she was gone. But Judge Tilley took an interest in me. You could say he was my mentor."

"Really?" Lucy was surprised. "Everything I've heard seems to indicate he was rather stern and forbidding."

"There was that side to him, definitely. But he helped pay for my schooling, right up through law school. And he gave me plenty of encouragement and good advice when I started to practice." He took a swallow of coffee, then chuckled. "I often wonder what he'd think of the present day system."

"What do you mean?"

"The judge believed justice should be swift and sure. He actually tended to give rather short sentences, he wanted folks to learn their lesson and get back to work supporting their families. I've talked to some of people he sent to the county jail and they've told me jail was a picnic compared to the talking-to he gave them. Made them think, he did. He wouldn't approve of all these long trials and people sitting on death row for years and years of appeals."

"Did he ever sentence anyone to death?"

"No. He didn't believe in it. He said that should be left to God."

Lucy shook her head in amazement. "I had an entirely different impression of him."

"Don't get me wrong," said Cobb. "He was a tough taskmaster, believe me. I clerked for him when I graduated from law school and I have never worked so hard."

"You worked for him, but you don't remember Emil Boott?"

"I worked at the courthouse. I was never invited to the house."

"Isn't that odd?"

Cobb shrugged. "The judge was a private man. He drew a distinction between his work and his home."

Lucy nodded, remembering Miss Tilley's assertion that she had grown up in a house of secrets.

"Come to think of it," continued Cobb, "my father did the same thing. He was the county sheriff, he ran the jail, and you can be sure my mother and I had absolutely no contact with the inmates."

"There must be records at the jail, right?" asked Lucy.

"Well, this was some time ago, and I don't know if they kept all those old records or not. It's certainly worth checking out, though. I do know that my father would have kept meticulous accounts of the inmates' progress. He was a big believer in prison reform, you see, and thought it was important to rehabilitate the prisoners, not just punish them."

Cobb's phone gave off a little beep and he glanced at the clock. "I'm sorry, but that was Rachel, reminding me that I have an eleven o'clock appointment."

"I'd better get going, then," said Lucy, rising. "I can't thank you enough for your time and your knowledge."

Cobb blushed. "Nonsense. I enjoyed our little chat."

Back in the waiting room, Rachel helped Lucy into her coat. "Was Mr. Cobb able to help you?" she asked.

"He was very helpful," said Lucy, fastening the buttons.

"You know," said Rachel. "I have a little boy, too.

Richie. He was two last month. Maybe we could get together for a playdate? I only work mornings so I'm free in the afternoons."

"That's a great idea," said Lucy, jumping at the chance. "What about this afternoon?"

"Let's say two o'clock." Rachel scribbled down the address.

"Great," said Lucy, taking the slip of paper. "See you later. By the way, do you know where the county jail is?"

Lucy felt like kicking herself as she proceeded on foot down the street to the appliance store, leaving the car in the parking lot. The sun was actually peeking through the clouds and it seemed too good to waste. But what on earth must Rachel think of her, seizing on her invitation like that? She was probably already regretting getting involved with a woman who knocked people underneath cars and visited the jail. Respectable people stayed as far away from jail as they could, didn't they? She hoped Rachel didn't think she had some personal interest in the jail, like an incarcerated relative, something like that. Then again, she reminded herself, Rachel worked in a law office and her husband was a lawyer, and lawyers often had to go to the jail to interview their clients, at least they did on TV. Maybe she didn't think Lucy's interest in the penal system was at all unusual.

She hoped so, she decided, stepping inside the Appliance Mart and viewing the ranks of harvest-gold, avocado-green, and poppy-red refrigerators and washing machines. What happened to white? she wondered. And how soon could she get a stove delivered?

Not until after Christmas, she discovered.

"I'll take a floor model," begged Lucy.

"I'm sorry," said the salesman, writing up the order. "Three weeks is the soonest I can promise."

"But how am I going to cook?" wailed Lucy.

"My wife finds a Crock Pot quite handy," said the salesman. "And we have those in stock."

Reluctantly, Lucy reached for her wallet and unfolded the fifty dollar bill she'd been saving for Christmas presents. She felt badly about it, but as she headed home with an electric frying pan as well as the Crock Pot, she had to admit that life certainly seemed a bit brighter with the prospect of a hot meal.

Bill, however, wasn't quite as enthusiastic. "What do you mean we can't get a stove for three weeks?"

"That's what the man said," said Lucy, with a shrug.

"And where have you been all this time? Do you know what it's like to be stuck in the house for hours on end with a two-year-old when you don't feel all that well?"

Lucy folded her hands on her tummy and looked at him. Was he kidding? She was about to ask that very question in a rather sarcastic tone when she noticed the sheen of perspiration on his forehead. It certainly wasn't from the heat; the furnace could barely keep the house above sixty degrees.

"I'll get you one of those pain pills," she said. "Why don't you have a little rest while I make lunch?"

A beef stew, a bit light on the beef but with plenty of healthful vegetables, was simmering in the Crock Pot when Lucy and Toby left for the playdate at Rachel's house. Lucy was curious to see Rachel's place; until now Miss Tilley's house was the only house in Tinker's Cove that she'd been inside of.

She was a bit disappointed to discover the Goodmans lived in a modern ranch, part of a small development tucked behind the school complex. The houses were all variations on a single theme featuring a picture window with three rather stunted rhododendron bushes beneath. The Goodmans' house was gray with white trim.

When Rachel opened the door, however, Lucy was enchanted by the vibrant Persian rug on the living room floor and the curvaceous Victorian settee that sat beneath that picture window. "This is lovely," said Lucy, as Rachel took their coats and hung them in the hall closet.

A hall closet, she realized, was something you took for granted in a modern house but was definitely lacking in her own antique farmhouse. Modern houses certainly had their advantages. She was pretty sure Rachel had a working stove, too.

Following her into the kitchen, she noticed that Rachel not only had a stove and a side-by-side refrigerator, she also had a dishwasher. But the modern appliances were offset by cheery gingham curtains, a pot rack holding baskets and bunches of herbs, and a gorgeous golden oak table and chairs.

"I have to admit I'm dying with jealousy," said Lucy, stroking the table's gleaming surface. "What a find."

"It didn't look like that when we bought it, believe me," said Rachel. "It was painted pea green."

"Who refinished it?"

"Bob. It's a hobby of his."

"Make yourself comfortable," said Rachel, setting the kettle on the stove. "I'll get Richie. He's a little shy."

When she returned, Richie was clinging to her hand and holding a sad looking binky against his cheek. But when Rachel spilled a basket of Fisher-Price trucks and little people on the floor the two boys were soon absorbed in play.

"Have you lived here in Tinker's Cove for long?" asked Lucy, accepting a cup of tea.

"A couple of years," said Rachel, taking a pressed oak chair opposite Lucy's.

"What brought you here?"

"Bob answered Sherman Cobb's ad," said Rachel, stirring some milk into her tea. "He saw an article about Maine in the *Mother Earth News.*"

Lucy laughed. "So did my husband! And do you know Sue Finch? I met her the other day. Her husband read that article, too."

"That article has a lot to answer for," said Rachel, in a rather dark tone. She sipped her tea. "Sue Finch? She's that woman with the Farrah Fawcett hair and high heels?"

"That's her," said Lucy.

"Fashion's not really my thing," said Rachel, smoothing the sleeves of her orange sweater. "That's one of the things I like about Tinker's Cove. But I am glad to see more young people moving in. I mean, I went to a Women's Club meeting when we first moved here and there wasn't a single woman under fifty. And all they wanted to talk about was their most recent operations."

"Miss Tilley—the librarian—isn't like that at all," said Lucy. "In fact, I'm helping her solve a family mystery."

"She's a character," said Rachel, watching as the two little boys headed down the hall to Richie's room. "They seem to be getting along well."

"Yeah. I'm sure Toby really misses his playmates from the city. I used to take him to the park almost every day."

"So tell me about this article you're working on," coaxed Rachel.

She listened intently as Lucy recounted her investigation. "It's interesting that Miss Tilley never married, don't you think?" she said, when Lucy had finished.

"What do you mean?"

"Well, it seems she had an unresolved conflict about marriage and the role of women, probably because of her parents' troubled relationship."

"You sound like a psychiatrist," said Lucy.

"Actually, I was a psych major in college."

"So tell me, doctor," began Lucy. "Was it a psychosis or a neurosis?"

"I'm not sure," said Rachel, "but I think something was definitely not right in the Tilley household. So what's your next step?"

"Well, I want to get over to the county jail to look for information about Emil Boott."

Rachel glanced at the clock on the wall over the sink. "It's only three, why don't you go now? I'll keep an eye on the boys."

Lucy couldn't believe it. "Really? You'd do that?"

"Sure. They're happy as clams and if they get tired I'll let them watch *Sesame Street*."

"I'll be back before *Sesame Street* is over, I promise," said Lucy, grabbing her bag.

It only took Lucy about fifteen minutes to make the drive over to the neighboring town of Gilead, and before she knew it she had parked the car and was climbing the hill to the fortresslike county jail. Built of gray stone, it looked like a medieval castle with towers and turrets, but instead of a moat it had a tall chain-link fence topped with vicious looking coils of razor wire. Once inside, however, she was pleasantly greeted by a rather plump uniformed guard.

"I'm sorry but visiting hours are on Mondays, Thursdays, weekends and holidays," he said, folding his chubby pink hands on the counter. "I can take a message if you want."

"I'm not here to visit anyone," said Lucy, feeling slightly offended. "I'm looking for information about a former prisoner named Emil Boott."

"Never heard of him. Must've been before my time."

"Around 1930, I think."

"That was some time ago," he said, scratching his smooth chin. "Was he a relative of yours?"

Lucy was about to protest, then thought better of it. "Actually, yes. Emil was the black sheep of the family. I'm writing a family history, you see, and I want to include him. Do you have records going that far back?"

"Don't get much call for 'em but I s'pose we do, down cellar."

"Could I look?" asked Lucy.

"I don't think that's such a good idea," said the guard, shaking his head.

Lucy bit her lip in disappointment. "Is there some way . . . ?"

"I'll jes' run down and see what I can find. You keep an eye on things up here for me, okay? If anybody comes lookin' for me tell 'em I'll be right back."

"Okay," said Lucy. She'd never been in a jail before but she had the distinct impression they were generally somewhat stricter than this. If she were so inclined, she realized, spotting a big metal hoop filled with keys, she could let everyone out.

She wasn't so inclined, however, and was sitting on a convenient chair when the guard returned carrying a dusty cardboard box. "You're in luck," he said. "I found a big, thick file. Emil Boott must have been here for quite a while." He set the box on the counter and took out a fat manila folder, which he opened. "Yup. Twenty years for embezzlement," he said, closing the file and sliding it across the counter to her.

Lucy's heart was beating fast as she took the file. What secrets did it hold? But when she'd gone through every page she wasn't much wiser. As the careful notations documenting his days in the prison showed, Emil Boott was a model prisoner. His photo, a close-up much clearer and larger than the group shot in the museum, revealed a rather ugly, pock-marked face and Lucy could well imagine why Miss Tilley was afraid of him, but his records showed he was the mildest of men. He never denied embezzling several hundred thousand dollars from his employer, the Brown and Williams Glass Company, but he claimed he planned to give the money to workers who had been cheated out of overtime wages due them.

The jury hadn't been convinced, and even if they had been sympathetic, Judge Tilley's instructions made it clear that if they believed Boott had broken the law he must be found guilty. Embezzlement, he told them, was not a minor crime but an assault on the very foundations of civilized society. As for Boott, he accepted his punishment without bitterness, according to Sheriff Cobb's notes, and was soon assigned to the prison's woodworking shop. From there he moved on to a work-release program and was eventually assigned on a permanent basis to Judge Tilley's household. Upon his release, after serving his sentence of twenty years, he wrote a remarkable letter to the Sheriff.

Dear Sheriff Cobb, he wrote, *It is with great sadness that I will soon depart these walls that once appeared so forbidding but within which I found a true home. It is here that I learned the good Lord above forgives us all if only we ask for forgiveness. It is here that I learned the value of work and friendship. And it was through my work here that I met that most remarkable of women, Mrs. Leonora Tilley, whose kindness toward me, a vile criminal, I shall always remember. If anyone is certain of admission to Heaven it is certainly she and I hope that by following the pure path of virtue which she has showed me that I will someday join her there. Your most grateful and humble servant, Emil Boott.*

Lucy sat for a long time, reading and rereading the letter. Finally, the guard asked, "Lady, are you all right?"

"Yes I am," she said, folding the paper and returning it to the file. "I'm fine."

And so was Emil Boott, she decided, as she left the prison. He may or may not have been a Depression-era Robin Hood who stole from the rich and gave to the poor, but she was convinced he would never have harmed a hair on Mrs. Tilley's head.

"So how'd it go?" asked Rachel, opening the door for her. The two little boys were sitting side by side on the couch, apparently under Big Bird's spell.

"I found the information I was looking for," said Lucy, recounting her discovery of the letter, "but it only proved Emil Boott didn't kill Mrs. Tilley."

"I'm not so sure," said Rachel. "Maybe he had a guilty conscience and was trying to prove his innocence."

"Ah, Dr. Freud, thank you for that insight. I never would have thought of that."

Rachel smiled and shook her head. "You would assume, though, that with his criminal record he would have been a suspect if there was any indication of foul play."

"There was never an investigation," said Lucy. "After all, she'd been sick for a long time. Her death was not unexpected."

"I saw a lot of TB when I was in the Peace Corps," said Rachel. "I was in Haiti and it's practically epidemic there. People die of it all the time."

"So you think that's what killed her?"

"Probably," said Rachel, joining the boys on the couch as the familiar tune for *Mr. Rogers' Neighborhood* began to play. "Want to stay for Mr. Rogers? I love Mr. Rogers."

Chapter Nine

Lucy and Bill didn't need an alarm clock: Toby woke them up every morning around six o'clock. On Christmas Eve he was reliable as ever but Lucy ignored his cries, hoping Bill would go so she could catch a few more minutes of sleep. Then she remembered Bill's burned and bandaged hands and got up. Bill hadn't heard a thing, he was sleeping soundly.

Toby was standing up in his crib when Lucy went into the nursery. She shivered a bit in her in flannel nightgown but Toby was warm and toasty in a fleecy footed sleep suit. She picked him up and nuzzled his head with her chin, surprised to find that his hair was damp. He didn't seem to have a fever so she couldn't imagine where the dampness came from. She looked around the room for a leak and discovered a dusting of snow on his pillow. It had snowed during the night, she realized, and some of the snow must have blown through a crack in the wall. No wonder she was chilly, she realized, staring at the snow. The temperature in the unheated room must be below freezing, or the snow would have melted.

This was crazy, she thought, hugging Toby close and carrying him downstairs where it was somewhat, but not a whole lot warmer, and sat him in his potty seat. "We're going to have a white Christmas," she told him, listening for the tinkle. "It's Christmas Eve and tonight. . . ." She bit her tongue. There was no sense getting the little guy all excited about Santa Claus because the truth was that Santa didn't have much for him. Most of the fifty dollars she was going to spend on half-price toys at the IGA had gone for the electric frying pan and Crock Pot. That meant all Toby was going to find under the Christmas tree were the two packages Bill's folks had sent him, and the $50 savings bond her mother had sent.

The tinkle began and ended and Lucy didn't move. Really, all she wanted to do was go back to bed and sleep through Christmas.

"Up!" Toby, still perched on the potty seat atop the toilet was growing impatient. Lucy helped him down, zipped up his sleep suit and watched him run into the kitchen. Well, she thought, at least he didn't know what Christmas was supposed to be like. Maybe the tree would be exciting enough for him.

The tree, she thought, her emotions taking a nose dive. Bill had cut the tree a couple of days ago and set it outside in a bucket of water, intending to bring it inside on Christmas Eve. Now he wouldn't be able to do it, so she would have to cope with the bucket of ice and the eight-foot tree all by herself. Could she do it?

A clatter, alas not the "clatter and pawing of each little hoof," but a clatter of pots spilling onto the floor brought her into the kitchen. Toby had found his favorite toys. Goodness knows she had no use for them, without a stove. But the Crock Pot, she discovered when she lifted the lid, did a fantastic job cooking oatmeal overnight. Too bad she couldn't fit a turkey in there for Christmas dinner.

When Lucy and Toby finished their bowls of oatmeal there was still no sign of Bill so Lucy made a tray and took it upstairs to him. She found him sitting in bed, awkwardly holding a pencil and scratching away at a yellow legal pad.

"I thought you were asleep," she said.

"Just doing some figures," he said, putting the pad aside so she could set the tray on his lap. "Oatmeal, again," he said.

Lucy almost started to remind him that it was cheap and filling but caught herself. Christmas Eve was going to be hard enough this year and there was no sense dwelling on the negative. "It's oatmeal à la Crock Pot," she said, with a big smile. "Surprisingly good. I even put in some brown sugar and a few raisins."

"Ooh, goody," said Bill, rather sarcastically. "I hope you didn't blow the budget."

"Is that what you're doing?" asked Lucy, glancing at the legal pad. "Budgeting?"

Bill shrugged. "Since I can't work I thought I'd put together some financial projections, figure out what materials we need, see where we stand."

Lucy was collecting clothes for herself and Toby, intending to take them downstairs where it was warmer to get dressed. "Don't take too long," she said. "I'm going to bring in the Christmas tree so we can decorate it."

"Can you manage? It's pretty heavy."

"Sure I can," said Lucy, flexing her arms in a muscleman pose. "'I am woman. Hear me roar.'" She raised her chin and gave a wolf howl and Bill actually smiled for the first time since the explosion. Christmas presents didn't have to be wrapped, she reminded herself as she went downstairs. Sometimes a smile would do.

Lucy was singing "Deck the Halls" when she and Toby went out to get the tree, and Toby was chiming in on the fa la la la las. Some six inches of snow had fallen, but it was light, fluffy stuff, and Lucy had no trouble shoveling it off the porch and making a path to the car. Toby had a little shovel, too, but he preferred to roll around in the snow like a frisky little puppy. Lucy knew it wouldn't be long before he was wet and cold, so she immediately addressed the issue of the tree, which was now frozen solid in the bucket. She considered loosening it with boiling water, but without a stove she didn't have a way to boil water. The hair dryer might work, she decided, but she'd have to find an extension cord.

The really good thing about two-year-olds, Lucy decided as she stood outside in the snow attempting to defrost the tree with the hair dryer, was that they really didn't know how things were supposed to be so they didn't mind when things didn't go according to plan. So long as Toby got his three meals and two snacks, his *Sesame Street* and bedtime story, things were fine with him. She watched as he knocked the snow off the bushes, making snow showers, and gave the tree a budge. It moved, and she noticed that a small puddle was beginning to form in the bucket. She wiggled it a bit more and the puddle grew larger. Toby was now climbing onto the bottom porch step and jumping off into the snow, repeating the process again and again. Then he decided to go up two steps.

"Don't do that," she warned, as he launched himself, landing hard on the bottom step instead of the soft snow. He started to wail and she turned off the hair dryer.

Bill was still working on the figures when she took Toby inside. She stripped off his wet clothes, set him in the high chair next to Bill and gave him a cup of instant hot cocoa, made with lukewarm water from the kitchen tap. Then she was back outside and this time the tree came out of the bucket. She hugged it in a prickly embrace and dragged it across the lawn to the front door, then pulled it trunk first up the stoop and into the front hall. Then, because her heart was thumping, she sat on the stairs to rest and catch her breath. Now all she had to do was set it in the stand, string the lights, get the ornaments out of the attic, and trim it. Not bad, since she had all day. But first, she realized, hearing Bill yelling in the kitchen, Toby must have finished his cocoa and wanted down from the high chair.

"You smell like a pine tree," said Bill.

"It put up a heck of a fight, but I won. I've just got to get it in the stand, put the lights on and it will be ready for the ornaments."

"Don't forget that box your mom gave you at Thanksgiving," reminded Bill, as she lifted the tray so Toby could scramble down. "I think it's in the pantry."

Lucy had forgotten all about it, but when they visited at Thanksgiving her mother had insisted she take the ornaments, old family pieces she said she no longer used since she'd bought a small artificial tree. Lucy hadn't even looked inside the box, she'd been tired from the long drive and Bill had unloaded the car. Now, as she set the box on the table and peeked inside she saw shining and glittery reminders of her childhood. There was a red and silver plastic trumpet that made a horrible noise if you blew on it, a "Baby's First Christmas" card picturing a baby lamb that hung from a twisted red cord, several heavy glass kugels in the shape of grapes.

"I wasn't allowed to touch these," said Lucy, lifting out the red and green and silver ornaments. "They're very old."

"They're really beautiful," said Bill.

Lucy remembered her mother hanging them carefully, one by one, on sturdy bottom branches of the tree. Lucy always held her breath until the delicate operation was complete, and waited impatiently for the magic moment when her father would plug in the string of lights and the kugels would glow as if lit from within.

Suddenly nostalgic, Lucy decided to call home.

"Merry Christmas," she said, by way of greeting, when her mother answered the phone.

"It's not Christmas yet and it's not merry, either," said her mother.

"That's why I called," said Lucy. "To cheer you up. And to thank you for the ornaments. I'd forgotten how beautiful the kugels are."

"Don't let Toby play with them."

As if she would. Lucy sighed. "How's Dad?"

"They're giving him oxygen."

"Does it help?"

"He keeps pulling off the mask."

Lucy knew her father hated having anything on his face or head, not even hats or Halloween masks. "He hates . . ."

"I know, I know," replied her mother, sounding tired. "He could try to cooperate. It's only for his own good."

"I guess you'll be spending Christmas at the hospital."

"Of course."

Suddenly, Lucy felt quite bereft. She wanted—she needed—her parents' attention right now, but she couldn't have it. Her father was hovering near death and her mother was so consumed with caring for him that she hadn't even asked Lucy how she and Bill and Toby were doing. "Well, I'll be thinking of you," she said.

"I'll call if there's any change," said her mother, then hung up.

"And ho, ho, ho to you," said Bill, who had been listening. "I could call my parents and then we'd be so depressed we could commit suicide and end it all."

"You should call them," said Lucy. "They sent that nice box of presents. . . ."

"That was my mom," said Bill.

"And you'd feel better if you worked things out with your dad. I feel better, I do, just hearing my mother's voice."

"Liar," said Bill.

"Well, at least I have the satisfaction of knowing I tried."

"That's something I guess. You're a good daughter."

"And you're a bad son," said Lucy, perching on his lap and stroking his hair. Bits here and there felt stiff and brittle, singed from the explosion. "You should call them."

"You know that's why you fell for me," said Bill, changing the subject. "The good girls always go for the bad boys." And then he turned her face toward his with his bandaged hand and kissed her.

"Bad boys are the best kissers," said Lucy, coming back for seconds.

A couple of hours later it really was beginning to feel a lot like Christmas. Now that the tree was decorated the living room's half-finished sheetrock walls, stained ceiling and uneven floorboards weren't so noticeable. Swedish meatballs were cooking in the Crock Pot, giving off a spicy, beefy aroma. When Toby woke from his nap Lucy got the popcorn popper going for a snack and popped a Christmas video in the VCR.

"Light the tree for him," said Bill, settling beside them on the couch.

Lucy hopped up. "Good idea," she said, crouching on all fours and reaching behind the tree to retrieve the end of the cord. She plugged it into the socket—and everything went black.

"What the hell!" exclaimed Bill. "This shouldn't happen. The first thing I did was have the house rewired."

"Well I guess it wasn't done right," said Lucy.

"Maybe it's a blackout," said Bill. "Maybe everybody's lights are out."

"Maybe you ought to go down in the cellar and check the circuit breakers," said Lucy.

"Maybe you could light a candle, in the meantime," said Bill.

"We don't have any candles," said Lucy. "Get the flashlight."

"The flashlight's dead," said Bill.

"Don't we have any batteries?"

"I used 'em up."

"Well you should've bought more."

"You're right, I should have, but I didn't. They're expensive and I've been trying to economize."

Lucy's jaw dropped. She had no idea things were this bad. "I can't do this, Bill," she said, her voice steely. "We're going to have a baby in a few months and I am not bringing that baby home to this." She waved her arm. "Do you know there was snow in Toby's crib this morning? Snow! Inside the house, in his bed, on our child. That is unacceptable."

"I'll caulk the window. . . ."

"No." Lucy shook her head. "I'm not staying. I don't know where I'm going—maybe my mother's, maybe your folks', maybe a friend, I don't know—but I am taking Toby someplace where there are walls that keep out the weather and lights that work and a stove that cooks."

Bill looked at her for a long time. "You're right," he finally said. "I'm a failure. I tried, and I can't do it. I was kidding myself. I'll never be a restoration carpenter. It's time to go back to Wall Street."

Lucy had wanted to hear those words for months, but now that Bill had actually said them she didn't feel happy at all. Instead she felt guilty and terribly sad. "I didn't mean for you to give up your dream. You can finish up here and I'll stay at my Mom's and come back with the kids when the house is ready."

Bill shook his head. "We're broke." He shrugged. "And besides, being with you and Toby means more to me than any stupid, unrealistic dream."

"You worked so hard."

"It wasn't enough," he said. "But I'm okay with it." He looked out the window at the rapidly dimming sunlight. He opened his wallet and pulled out a twenty dollar bill. "This is it, the family fortune. I guess I'll get some batteries, so we can get the lights back on."

He left and Lucy sat in the darkening room, holding Toby in her lap and blinking back tears. This was not the way Christmas was supposed to be.

Chapter Ten

A sharp rap on the door roused Lucy and she stood up, perched Toby on her hip, and wiped her eyes with the back of her hand before opening the door. It was Wilf Lundgren, the postman, with a package.

"This came in the last delivery and I thought I'd bring it along since it was on my way," he said, looking for all the world like Santa with his red nose and cheeks. "Otherwise you wouldn't get it until Tuesday, Christmas being on Sunday and all."

"Thanks," said Lucy, her voice still thick from crying.

"Have you got some trouble here?" asked Wilf, looking past her into the dark kitchen. "I see the lights are out."

"I must've overloaded a circuit." Lucy shifted Toby to the other hip. "My husband went to get some flashlight batteries."

"Is that all? I've got a flashlight in the truck," he said, turning and hurrying down the walk to the driveway. In a moment he was back carrying the biggest flashlight Lucy had ever seen and marching straight to the pantry and lowering himself through the hatch to the cellar. "Better unplug a few things," he said, before ducking beneath the floor. "Ready?" he called.

Lucy dashed around the kitchen, unplugging appliances, and scurried into the living room to turn off the TV. "Ready," she called back and in a moment the lights were on and the Christmas tree was radiant with glowing colors.

"Well, isn't that a beautiful sight?" said Wilf, who had emerged from the cellar and was standing in the doorway.

Toby, excited by the sight of the tree, was bouncing in her arms. "Now it feels like Christmas," said Lucy, setting him down and keeping a watchful eye as he toddled toward the tree. "I don't know how to thank you."

"It was nothing," said Wilf. "Just being neighborly, that's all."

"Well, I really appreciate it," continued Lucy, who was terrified of the old-fashioned root cellar beneath the pantry and the spiders and mice and snakes she imagined lurked there. "I mean, you *went down into the cellar* . . . and you brought that package, too, when you didn't have to. It was really awfully nice of you . . . can I give you a cup of coffee or something before you go back out in the cold?"

"I wouldn't mind a cup," said Wilf, amused by Lucy's extreme expressions of gratitude.

"The pot's still hot," sang Lucy, pouring a cup for him and one for herself, too, and setting some of her precious Christmas cookies on a plate. Toby had followed them into the kitchen and she hoisted him into his high chair, pouring a glass of apple juice for him.

"Very good," said Wilf, approvingly, chewing on a cookie. "Looks like you've got company," he observed, glancing out the window.

"Probably Bill," said Lucy, going to the door. But it wasn't Bill, it was Miss Tilley she saw walking carefully along the path.

"Come in, come in," said Lucy, opening the door and shivering in the cold blast. "Come out of the cold."

"I was just making my rounds, oh, hi there, Wilf," began Miss Tilley. "And I thought you might like some of my eggnog. It's an old family recipe."

"That's so kind," said Lucy, accepting two old-fashioned glass milk bottles filled with creamy liquid.

"I wouldn't mind trying some of that," said Wilf.

"You know, I didn't get a chance to taste it myself," said Miss Tilley. "I wanted to make my deliveries and get home before the snow starts."

"Well, let's all have some," said Lucy, popping into the pantry to get the punch cups she received as a wedding present but had never used.

"If you're getting cups, you'll need some more," called Miss Tilley. "The Miller sisters have just pulled into the driveway."

"Really?" asked Lucy, staggering out with the heavy crystal punch bowl filled with a dozen cups. "What brings them here?"

"Merry Christmas! Merry Christmas!" chorused the sisters, entering the kitchen which was becoming a bit crowded.

"We brought you some cookies," announced Emily, or was it Ellie?

"That's right. We made them ourselves," added the other, holding out an enormous tin with a jolly Santa design. "Sand tarts."

"I haven't had those in years," said Wilf.

"My mother used to make them," said Miss Tilley.

"Well, let's all have some eggnog and cookies," invited Lucy. "Can I take your coats?"

She was just hanging the ladies' matching red coats on the hooks by the door when there was another knock on the door. Lucy was beginning to wonder if this was some sort of planned invasion, or perhaps it was just what people in small towns did at Christmas. Whatever was going on, the table was filling up with people and the house was filled with chatter and laughter. She opened the door, hoping whoever it was had brought food, and found Sherman Cobb holding a foil-covered pan that looked like it contained a turkey. A turkey! And behind him she recognized Rachel Goodman and Richie, along with a man she assumed was Bob, Rachel's husband. They were all holding foil-covered dishes, except Richie, who had a can of cranberry sauce.

"What is all this?" she asked.

"We heard your oven was broken," began Sherman, smiling in Miss Tilley's direction. "So we brought you Christmas dinner. Are you going to let us in?"

"Oh, please, please do come in," said Lucy.

"By the way, we haven't met, but I'm Rachel's husband," said Bob. "Do you have a stereo?"

"In the living room," said Lucy.

"Great. I brought some Christmas cassettes," he said, handing off a bowl of stuffing and heading down the hall with a shopping bag slung over his arm. Moments later the house was filled with Bing Crosby's mellow voice.

Lucy was standing there, holding a bowl of stuffing and trying to decide what to do with the turkey when there was yet another knock on the door and Fred Rumford stuck his head in.

"Hi, everybody," he called, marching in and setting a jug of wine and a case of beer on the table. "Merry Christmas!"

"Merry Christmas!" they all cried back.

"Now it's a party," said Wilf, reaching for a beer.

"Where's your dining room?" asked Rachel. "I think we better set the food up there."

"This way," said Lucy, feeling rather dazed as she lead the way. "I can't believe this."

"I hope it's all right," said Rachel. "You didn't have other plans, did you?"

"No, no. We were just going to have a quiet celebration," confessed Lucy, shaking out a cloth and spreading it on the table. From the kitchen she heard voices and laughter, there was music in the living room and Toby and Richie were chasing each other through the rooms. "This is much better."

"Good," said Rachel, setting down the turkey. "Now we'll need plates and silverware. . . ."

"In the pantry. I'll be right back."

Entering the kitchen she encountered Sue Finch, who had arrived with her daughter and a man dressed in a Santa suit. "This is Sid," she said.

"Not Sid, Santa," he replied, hoisting a bulging red bag. "And I brought presents."

The party was in full swing when Bill arrived. Plates were filled, glasses were emptied, music was playing, and the kids were dancing around the tree. Everybody was having a great time.

"What's all this?" he asked.

"The neighbors dropped by to wish us a Merry Christmas," said Lucy, giving him a peck on the cheek. "Eggnog?"

"Sure," he said, taking a cup and shaking his head in amazement.

Lucy and Bill were still amazed several hours later, when everyone had left and they were tidying up.

"I just can't believe it," said Bill. "They gave us an entire Christmas. Food. Drink. Even presents for Toby."

"I think Miss Tilley organized it," said Lucy, clearing off the kitchen table. She was gathering up paper napkins and wrapping paper when she found the package Wilf had delivered. "I forgot all about this," she said, taking a closer look. "It's from your parents."

Bill glanced over. "It's probably fruitcake," he said

with a marked lack of enthusiasm. "They send them every year."

"Oh," said Lucy, rather disappointed. "I suppose it's nourishing, with all that fruit and nuts."

"If you can digest it," said Bill.

"Don't you want to open it?" asked Lucy. "Maybe it's not fruitcake. Maybe it's a surprise."

"My parents don't do surprises," said Bill, cutting the tape with a knife. "It's fruitcake."

Lucy took the box and opened the top, hoping he was wrong. He wasn't. Inside was a gold and brown tin with MOTHER'S TRADITIONAL HOLIDAY FRUITCAKE printed on the top. "There's a note," she said, handing him a cream-colored envelope.

"You open it," said Bill, whose hands were still bandaged. "It's probably just a printed card. 'Holiday Greetings from the Stones.'"

"So it is," said Lucy, "but there's something else." She unfolded a piece of notepaper and a blue check fell out onto the table.

"Is that a check?" asked Bill, who had seen it out of the corner of his eye.

"It is," said Lucy, sitting down.

"The usual fifty bucks?"

"Not exactly," said Lucy, who was holding the little slip of paper in trembling hands. "More like fifteen thousand."

Bill's jaw dropped. "Say that again."

"It's for fifteen thousand dollars," repeated Lucy. "And there's a note."

Bill took the check. "I can't believe it. What possessed him?"

"Read the note," said Lucy, handing the folded piece of paper to him.

Bill's eyes quickly scanned his father's neatly printed, squarish letters.

"Out loud," prompted Lucy.

He cleared his voice. " 'Dear Son, Your mother and I figured this might come in handy about now. We've had some experience with home renovations and we know they always cost more than you expect.' " Bill snorted in agreement. " 'We also want to wish you well in your new endeavor which we're sure will be successful.' Mom must have twisted his arm," said Bill, pausing.

"Give your father some credit," said Lucy. "Is that all?"

"No. He goes on. 'I have to confess, now that I'm facing retirement and looking back on my career, I wish I'd had your courage and pursued my dreams instead of a paycheck. Love, Dad.' "

"Wow," said Lucy.

"Wow," echoed Bill. "I guess I'd better give him and Mom a call."

Later that night, while Bill snored gently beside her, Lucy was still too excited to sleep. She knew people always said Christmas was a time of miracles, but this was the first time she had actually experienced it. For the most part, truth be told, Christmas had always been a bit of a disappointment, never quite living up to the hype. But this, this was amazing. Now Bill would be able to finish the house and start his new career. And, even better, the ruptured relationship with his parents that had hung over them like a dark cloud had been cleared. Now they could look forward to family gatherings, and Toby would once again have grandparents to shower him with love and attention.

Lucy smiled and turned over, spooning her body against Bill's. She would never forget the way her new Maine friends and neighbors had given them such a wonderful Christmas. Living in Tinker's Cove certainly had its advantages; she couldn't imagine her neighbors in New York City behaving like this. There, people gave to charity, but they didn't concern themselves with their neighbors' misfortunes. In fact, she realized, she herself had never given a thought to little Miss Delaporte down the hall in 12G, who was at least eighty and never had a visitor. Maybe she could have dropped in with a plate of cookies, but she'd never bothered to take the time.

From now on, she resolved, she would be more like Miss Tilley. She would take an interest in her neighbors and if she saw someone in need, she would try to help. In a way, that's what she had tried to do when she attempted to solve the mystery of Mrs. Tilley's death. But it hadn't gone the way she'd hoped. Her eyes were heavy and her breathing was becoming regular, she was sinking into sleep, and her last thought was regret that she had failed to bring peace of mind to Miss Tilley.

Christmas dawned clear and bright, the sunlight magnified by the fresh snow that had fallen during the night. Outside was a glittering white wonderland and inside was the usual chaos as Toby opened his presents: new clothes and books and a go-cart from Bill's parents, and an impressive assortment of marked-down plastic trucks and balls and a super-sized teddy bear Bill had picked up when he bought the batteries. When they added the recycled toys that Sid Finch had brought, it added up to quite a pile and Toby was happily investigating his haul, playing first with one and then another. Lucy and Bill took advantage of the moment to exchange their gifts for each other.

"You go first," said Lucy, handing him a cheerfully wrapped present.

"I thought we'd agreed. . . ." protested Bill.

"It's little enough," said Lucy, smiling as he unwrapped a Walkman cassette player.

"This is great," he said. "How'd you know I wanted one?"

"I didn't. I just thought you might like to listen to music while you work."

"I do. This is perfect. Thanks. Now you go," he said, handing her a drugstore bag tied with a big red bow. "Sorry about the wrapping."

"I guess I'll forgive you this time, since your hands are burned."

"Right," he said. "Open it."

Lucy withdrew a paperback book, a compendium of New England crimes. "This is great," she said, delighted. "How'd you think of it?"

Bill blushed. "Well, I knew you were interested in what happened to Miss Tilley's mother, and you've been reading mysteries."

"That was very thoughtful. Thank you," she said, opening the book and scanning the table of contents. One listing immediately caught her eye: The Angel of Death. Settling back into the corner of the couch she turned the pages and began reading, fascinated by the story of a nurse who was thought to have killed more than twenty of her patients using a variety of hard-to-detect methods such as drug overdoses, poison and smothering. "Oh my God," she breathed, her eyes glued to the page.

"I didn't think you'd like it this much," complained Bill, who was feeling ignored.

"You won't believe this. This woman, this nurse, she's the one who killed Mrs. Tilley. It fits, exactly. It all fits."

"You're kidding."

"No. It's all here. Even her name. Well, her aliases. Anne DePasquale, Andrea Dale, Anita DeSouza. Always a first name beginning with A and a last name beginning with D. Angela DeRosa, that was the name she used when she was supposedly caring for Mrs. Tilley. Everybody thought she was an angel, but she was actually killing off her patients."

"How'd they figure it out?"

"People started getting suspicious when none of her patients ever seemed to recover," said Lucy. "One man who happened to be a chemist analyzed the medicine she was giving his wife and found it was arsenic and went to the police."

"Did they arrest her?"

"They tried," said Lucy, reaching the end of the chapter, "but she killed herself before they could take her into custody. A lethal dose of strychnine."

"She must have been nuts," said Bill, lifting Toby onto his lap and opening a picture book.

"I've got to call Miss Tilley," said Lucy, heading for the phone.

Miss Tilley answered the phone with a cheerful "Merry Christmas."

"Merry Christmas to you," replied Lucy. "And thank you for yesterday. It was a wonderful surprise."

"I think everyone enjoyed themselves," said Miss Tilley. "I put quite a bit of brandy in the eggnog, just to help things along."

"So that's your secret," said Lucy. She paused. "I think I've found your mother's murderer—and it wasn't your father."

"Who was it?"

"The nurse. Angela."

"No, no. She was so kind. . . ."

"It's in a book. She killed at least twenty of her patients, maybe more."

"She was convicted?"

"No. She killed herself before there could be a trial. There was an investigation, though, and some of her victims were exhumed and their bodies contained poison."

"I can hardly believe it."

"Nobody could. That's how she had so many victims."

"Papa never liked her."

"He had good instincts."

"He was innocent!" announced Miss Tilley, joyfully.

"Absolutely," said Lucy. "I just wanted you to know, but I've got to get back to my family. . . ."

"Thank you. This was a wonderful Christmas present. The best Christmas present I ever had."

"But I still don't know where the cane came from," said Lucy. "Maybe it was a gift from Emil Boott."

"Or maybe my mother planned to give it to my father as a Christmas gift."

"We'll never know," said Lucy.

"No, that will have to remain a mystery," said Miss Tilley. "Merry Christmas!"

CHRISTMAS SPRITZ COOKIES

Lucy's mother always made these cookies every Christmas. They require a cookie press, which is a gizmo rather like a caulking gun that is available in kitchen supply stores.

1¼ cups sugar

2 cups butter

2 eggs

5 cups flour

1 teaspoon baking powder

1 teaspoon almond extract (or vanilla)

Cream butter, adding sugar gradually. Add unbeaten eggs, then sift dry ingredients and extract. Dough will be stiff.

Fill cookie press and press cookies out onto cookie sheet and decorate. (Lucy sprinkles colored sugar on the long strip cookes and puts bits of candied cherry in the center of the flower shapes.)

Bake at 375 degrees for 10–12 minutes, remove to rack to cool. These cookies keep well in a tightly sealed tin, but you'll have to hide it well if you want to save them for Christmas.

SAND TARTS

These cookies are named for the dusting of cinnamon sugar that looks like sand. They're delicious and not very well known anymore. Lucy remembers them from her childhood, when her grandmother used to make them. This is her recipe, written in her style.

Cream ½ cup butter.

Add:

1 cup sugar
2 beaten egg yolks
1 tablespoon milk
½ teaspoon vanilla

Beat mixture until light.

Sift together:
1½ cups flour
1 teaspoon baking powder
½ teaspoon salt

Add to first mixture and blend well. Chill for several hours. Roll dough very thin and cut with a star or circle cookie cutter. Place on buttered baking sheet and put a split blanched almond on each cookie. Brush with unbeaten egg whites and sprinkle

with mixture of 1 tablespoon sugar and $\frac{1}{4}$ teaspoon cinnamon.

Bake at 375 degrees for 10 minutes. Cool on racks.